Norah

PAMELA HILL

Norah

St. Martin's Press   New York.

PART I

I

ON THE NIGHT of the child's birth there was a storm blowing. The wind and rain drove in mighty gusts up the valley to Curle Hall, whose rough stones, pewter colour by day, withstood the onslaught as they had done for four centuries. Upstairs the hushings and whisperings of the womenfolk in the lying-in chamber could not be heard, and below in the great hall, Sir Ludovic Curle, the coming child's grandfather, sat as he did increasingly now, removed both in body and mind from their anxious fuss. He held a cup of warmed wine between his hands, and stared meantime at the logs where they burned and fell in the hearth, spat upon every now and again by drips leaking down the wide chimney.

The old man was listening to the rain. Outside, he knew, the horses were warm in their stable; his first care was for them. He spared a thought for Emma Curle, his younger son John's wife, who had been taken in labour eighteen hours since, and a physician had had to be summoned to aid the women. "Unnatural nonsense!" grunted the old squire. He had maybe been mistaken in selecting Emma Wraye in marriage to his second heir, that matter of the first having already ended in disgrace and failure. His mind turned away from that and back to Emma. A fine-drawn, pallid thing, all airs and graces, no spirit to her, not what he'd have taken to bed for himself: but he had hoped that, with her blood, that of the heavy-boned, heavy-haired, fearless clan into which Emma had been married would sire a good boy on her. How she herself fared, at this moment, mattered little, but the boy, the heir . . . "The inheritance itself is at stake," muttered the old man. With young John Curle, Emma's husband, lying sick to death in his own chamber, never having recovered his wits, let alone walked again, since that hunting-accident five months since in which his spine had been smashed and they had carried him home: with that, and the remembrance of his brother's fate, hanged like a felon . . .

"No," said Sir Ludovic aloud, and kicked at the logs with a booted foot;

he was still dressed to ride abroad. After this birth was over . . . ay, this birth! John could never now father more children; the second son also might as well die soon. He himself, at past sixty, was spry enough to have wed again, and fathered heirs for himself from new stock. But his own wife Maud still wandered in her rooms upstairs, attended only by the servant who saw to her needs, and for the sake of what was past he would not hasten Maud out of her life, which he had made sorry enough. Maybe the parsons were right when they said a sin and a curse returned to the giver: if so it was too late to mend it. The future, not the past, was what must be in his own mind tonight; the future, and this coming heir. *He* must live, and be healthy enough to carry on a tradition which had continued unbroken in the male line since the first Curle, or carle—they said he had been of the household of great Earl Siward of Northumbria in his time, perhaps even Siward's bastard son—had come here, after William the Norman had conquered the tamer south at Hastings, and had built himself a dwelling below the remote, frowning fells.

The squire permitted his rambling thoughts to embrace the past again; not his own, but that further past beyond count of man, tales which had been handed down over the generations, truly enough after their fashion. "We Curles never submitted to the Norman yoke, but fought 'em for a half-century. In the end, after blood-letting 'em—and, by God, there would be a man dead for every one of ours—in the end, it was clerkly King Henry who came at last to treat with us, not we with him. He knew we'd be a running sore in his northern kingdom, and that it was better to make peace," Sir Ludovic told himself, with pride that the legend need never be written down, for it was told to every child here in the valley, father to son. He'd heard it from *his* father, before the latter rode off to die for the King in Ireland. The outside world knew little of Curle and the legend, and cared nothing; "nor do we for them," he thought, pondering on life lived in the valley and the way it had changed hardly at all, he could believe, from the Norman's day, even now in the eighteenth century. Its folk, closely thirled and alike in both feature and nature by long intermarrying, still lived in dour simplicity, alien to change; the men herding the hardy fell sheep, the women spinning the fleeces and making curd cheese from ewes' milk. A portion of all money made must be paid over to the squire; that was law, thought Sir Ludovic. His permission must also be asked for marriages: "and if they do not, then they knaw well enough 'tis out for them at quarter's end, withouten a roof to cover 'em," muttered the deep north-country drawl. The full-length portrait of the squire himself as a young man, painted in the year of Oudenarde, hung farther back in the shadows of the hall. It was the summer after, or maybe the one after that, that he'd ridden off with Maud Bellingham to take her for his bride: there seemed small outward change in him yet. He still wore his thick chestnut hair—despite his years it showed little grey—in the long, abundant fashion of that far-off time, so that many nowadays thought it a periwig; and his great height and heavy bones had neither bowed nor shrunken with the years. Maud feared him still, so that he never now visited her; letting her scrabble as she would at the locked door of that room of hers, then turn away and stare into vacancy with the grey eyes that had once been a part of her beauty. It wasn't that that he had taken her for, but her full coffers, wrested from the Romish Church; she'd been making her chaperoned way to a nunnery in France, but he, Ludovic Curle, waylaid her and the chaperones. They whispered still in the valley, he knew, that he'd crazed Maud before the birth of the second son. Well, let them whisper. There was no taint in the blood . . . not till his dead elder son, the fool, had got a gipsy wench with child and been forced by her clan to marry her. *He* knew that, but no other soul should know it. Tonight's child, not that other, should be the heir.

Damn young Ludovic! Damn his fool's soul and his unbridled lusts! To risk all, perjure all . . . then afterwards the gipsies had hanged him, ay, hanged him on a tree.

The old man's great body shifted, as if such feeling itself unmanned him; he forced his thoughts to return to Emma and the birth. There'd been small choice, when all was said, for John when he sought a bride; such a one must first meet the demanding standards of the old man's decree of ancient blood. Apart from Curle's own, the Wrayes were as good as might serve, though their politics displeased Sir Ludovic, with Wraye himself still riding south to present himself to the German king in London twice yearly. Anne Stuart had reigned at the time of Oudenarde; after that the Whigs had brought petty Guelph landowners over. Sir Ludovic spat into the fire. Let Wraye curry favour there if he chose! He might be Lord Lieutenant of the County now, but he had a poor seat on a horse. "And the title no more than two-three generations back, by reason of his grandsire's having been a pretty boy of Dutch William's." But they'd all of them bowed and scraped, excepting himself, Curle of the valley; he needed no titles and no favour.

So Emma Wraye had married John Curle, with his blessing; he grinned a trifle at the notion of his bestowing such a thing. John himself had fancied, his father wouldn't be surprised, one of the bookish young women from the mealy-mouthed parson's family who had come north;

what was the name? Stroyan; a good enough name in the south, living given to a younger son, all the rest of it; but he hadn't liked the fellow, and for a woman to have book-learning irked him. "A fine seat and good hands, they must have, and let them mind their needle if they will; as to the rest, that's chance or nature," he decided, dismissing the Stroyans and returning his thoughts to Wraye. That nobleman, now, had built himself a fine new Palladian house nearby the old castle where his forebears had lived for centuries. Let others do so; *he'd* conserve Curle and the farms as they were. A good enough landlord, he knew he was, though the men said he was hard even for a Curle: as for the women, they'd said other things in his heyday. That was in decline, no doubt; soon it would be time for the boy, the coming boy, to roll women in the hay in summer, his bed in winter, and otherwise make a fine marriage.

Wraye himself would send over, no doubt, before morning, to ask for news of his kinswoman and how she fared in her labour. By then, the child should be born.

Wraye! Why should that personage disturb himself over the news from Curle, blood or no blood? Wraye still had two grown sons of his own, who were a credit to him though George was said to be idle and Jonathan a young prig. Two grown sons . . . while his own . . .

An expression of almost animal cruelty and rage spread over the formidable slab of a face, thick brows close-drawn as by habit so that two deep curved lines were forever etched between them. Of other lines there were few; Sir Ludovic's eyes were small and red-brown, as if to emulate the bear that stood on his escutcheon. They gleamed close-set and angry now; Sir Ludovic bared his teeth. These were sparse and yellowed by time, almost the only sign of age in him; he clenched his great fist about the cup of wine, so that it would have broken had it not been made of heavy silver.

He was thinking of his half-gipsy grandson, Jody Curle.

Curle! To have called the boy that itself meant nothing; all of his own bastards used the name. A bastard that boy should be, if he had to brand it himself on the smooth young forehead. Gipsy's get, to aspire to the inheritance! "But I foiled the brat's mother, that day she came here; ay, I cast her marriage-lines in the fire."

He kicked the grate now, causing the slumbering logs to send out a shower of sparks and, briefly, burst into flame. Presently this died down again, leaving the squire's face in darkness.

"James Curle! Where the devil are ye? Bid 'em bring more logs; grate's empty."

One of his love-children, who combined the duties of bailiff and house-steward, hastened to the old man. The latter drained the contents of his wine-cup, and set it down; the refurbished fire gleamed soon on the cup's chased surface, showing the coat of arms engraved in the silver. That cup had been saved from the Civil Wars. The squire thought of it, unheeding of the scared and sleepy servants who scurried about with wood to mend the fire, and out again. If it was his bidding that the fire burn till dawn, then it should burn. He needed its light for his memories, this night of the new birth.

Ludovic. Young Ludo, the dead heir, Jody's father by a gipsy girl. Why could Ludo not have married as his father bade him? Even the Counts of Little Egypt, as that rabble had been used to call themselves, could not have forced a wedding on a man already wed. "He could ha' done his duty, then ta'en his pleasures as he would," muttered the father. But the lad had been wilful with the iron will of the Curles, and would take no telling. That was, no doubt, why Sir Ludovic had loved him by far the better of his two sons; John was a soft biddable thing, like his mother.

"He was flesh of my flesh, Ludo, despite all; and they hanged him. He'd ta'en the honour of the wench, they said, and must make amends; a Curle to make amends! But they value their women high. Afterwards I chased them across four counties without avail; I never did get the man who slung the rope to the tree; had I done so I'd ha' torn his guts out ere he died. But he did that in his flea-bitten bed in the end, they say; they travel like shadows, such folk."

But he had seen the woman. She'd come, years after, into Curle alone, leading her grown boy by the hand. She'd been married again, she said, to a man of their own; and the boy must claim his due.

"His due? Bite and sup in my hall, like the other bastards; that's all he'll get from me." But he had grown fond, despite himself, of the cozening black-haired boy. Jody was six now; asleep in his bed over the stables, like as not, unless the comings and goings over the birth disturbed him. When it was over, Jody must learn to yield place to the new heir, ay, the heir, the chosen future squire of Curle: and he'd take it hardly. "But when he's grown he must go out and earn his bread, not batten on me with the rest."

It had been the sight of the boy's grey eyes that had convinced him, that night, that he was a Curle and his grandson. They were Maud's eyes. Young Ludo had had them also.

Like a felon they'd hanged Ludo, from an oak tree, mocking the symbol of Siward.

Why think of it? It was over; the past was done, save for tradition, legend, heritage saved for the new heir. What the devil was the heir about in being so long in coming?

The wind howled. Sir Ludovic roared above it for news of the birth. They were cosseting his son's wife overmuch; time she did her duty! Even Maud had delivered her boys within five hours and seven.

No one answered. The echo of his own voice, slurred with the wine he had drunk, still sounded in his ears above the storm: by God, he'd go up to the lying-in chamber himself, and see! They should not answer him with silence. He rose to his erect huge height; then subsided again, muttering in sulky fashion. Best not to look like a fool, an old man awaiting the last of his race.

He stared in the fire again, his mind fidgeting and empty. Into it the memory he had sworn to cast out came again, bringing with it, among the dying flames, the gipsy woman's face. She had been comely, but that was to be expected; but also—and this Sir Ludovic would not own to himself— he had feared her. No doubt that was why he'd shown her out of Curle with courtesy, leaving the boy, and then done the thing he'd done afterwards. "This paper proves it," she'd said to him. Be that as it might, by now there was no paper; none had seen him burn it that night except the child, and he was over young to know what befell, standing alone on the staircase in his bizarre clothes, with his feet bare. He was shod now and fed, and had a roof for shelter. No more could be expected for Jody. The woman herself had never come back: she'd gone with her new man, her own people. Thinking of it and of the time since, he became aware that never once in all their talk together had the child asked for his mother. That was strange.

The blood of Siward, mingled with that of the Counts of Little Egypt . . . Jody, the baby-name the child had lisped for himself, and the effrontery the woman had had in calling her son Ludovic was softened, made familiar by that daily name . . . but a bastard, never in any event to inherit . . .

Sir Ludovic slept.

Upstairs above the stables, Jody Curle moved his small body beneath the covers of the bed he shared with Sam the groom. There was not space enough in Curle itself, where all the attic rooms were given to servants. Jody knew he was not one of them. He knew also, for he had heard the comings and goings tonight and had seen the physician arrive and his horse taken in to be rubbed dry and fed, what all of it portended; a birth. Jody had seen births before, among his mother's people; none had been attended with the fuss and drama of this. It was because the heir was being born, Sam the groom had told him. Jody already, as he had learned to do, kept silence.

He thought of his mother, as he still did sometimes when matters grew unfamiliar, at the same time sliding a thin hand inside his night-shift to feel for the talisman she had given him. It was a gold ring, slung about Jody's neck on a grimy bit of cord; Abigail, his mother, had made him swear never to part with it. He'd managed to hide it while they were stripping him of his gipsy's clothing after first coming to Curle. He had kept it in his mouth till they were done bathing him, and had then slipped it round his neck again under the clean gorgio shirt they put on him before sending him to bed. That had been a year ago. Since then Jody had not seen his mother nor, he knew, might he ever do so again, unless the tribe were perhaps passing by the valley and she left a sign for him. "But if I were ever in need, and sent her the ring, she said, she'd find me quickly," Jody told himself. He put the notion away in his mind to leave room for more pressing things. This birth tonight wasn't the heir's. *He* was the heir of Curle. His mother had said so.

"Y'father married me proper, before a parson. Aaron and Jim made 'un do't, and afterwards they killed him, for dishonouring me. But I was willing; he was a fine man." Her voice had been flat, unemotional in its acceptance of what had happened. For a Romany woman to be dishonoured by a gorgio meant death by Romany laws: Jody had always known this. There had even been a king once who essayed one of the women, and the tribe had flogged him through his own forests with a heavy pack laid on his back. "But I was made y'father's wife before he died, and ye were born in wedlock. I have the bit o'paper as says it, and the ring."

The bit of paper she had afterwards shown to the squire, that night last year when she had first brought Jody to his grandfather. He had already been told that he must leave the tribe and live at Curle beneath a roof; it was fitting, his mother said. She herself had taken a new man and there was less than room for Jody beside them in the caravan: besides, he must claim his due. To prove it she had given the squire the paper. Jody could recall clearly seeing, as soon as his mother had gone, the terrible old man tearing the paper in four, then casting it into the fire and watching it burn. Jody had stayed quiet, as he had been taught to do in danger; presently the old man had turned and fixed his red bear's eyes on him. "Well, little bastard, we had best find ye a bed," he had shouted, as if to proclaim to the whole world his triumph at having branded Jody bastard without delay. "But that I am not," the child thought proudly. In due time, he knew, he would claim Curle: perhaps when grandfather was dead. Yet, in ways, he had come to like grandfather: he was in no hurry for him to die. Besides being warm, fed and clothed at Curle there were other things; nobody beat or deprived him, and although on two occasions now the squire had roared that he must get the parson, for tutor to so thrawn a brat, nothing of that kind had yet happened. Twice now grandfather had let him, Jody, ride pillion, and once had promised him soon a pony of his own and every now and again, when he thought no one noticed, Jody would glance beneath his thick lashes to surprise a look of pride on the squire's face at some saying, look, or deed of his that showed he feared nobody, not even James Curle the steward, whose word was generally law below the squire's.

The parson for tutor! "He may teach me to cipher and sign my name, no more," Jody told himself, and the implacable young mouth set against any further thought of book-learning. He wanted to be a man like grandfather, a great landowning, swearing, hard-riding, wenching man, to whom everyone listened. And Curle must be his; grey Curle with the rain like a veil about her, and mist high over the fells. Because his father had been a gorgio Jody knew he himself had no discomfort under a roof; his colouring however was that of his mother, swarthy and black, except for the grey eyes. He was lithe as an eel, and tall for his age; he could make a pony obey him already, and row a boat on the tarn, and soon he would handle a gun. Ay, he'd come up from the ragged imp who arrived here last year, and on whom, once they'd scrubbed him clean, they put shirt, breeches, coat and shoes. The last he hadn't, he remembered, wanted to wear. But no squire went barefoot; so Jody had used himself to the feel of leather, and to the other things that must be worn and done. Wearing shoes no longer irked him half as much as the remark James Curle had made, which Jody heard often repeated and implied, that he'd been a beggar before he came to Curle. "Kin to squire, ye are, and no beggar now." Maybe so; but Jody knew, from his mother and his mother's kin, that long, long ago their ancient race had made its way here from somewhere far away, a place called Roum on the eastern plains, though many called the tribe Egyptians. A Romany man could hold his head up, kin as he was to kings: and some things gorgios allowed to happen would never be permitted in the tribe. Jody himself had seen the poor woman they kept in a locked room here at Curle, with her grey hair streaming unkempt, and her loose mouth trembling. She would appear so, sometimes, at a window; but she never went out. Jody had asked James Curle who she might be, and had been told he was his grandam, poor Lady Maud, who must never be mentioned to the squire.

He listened to the storm that blew about the rooftops now, and was aware of the bustle, stir and suddenly glimpsed light of the birth-chamber, spilling out in a yellow pattern on to the dark yard. He must have slept, for what awakened him at last was the lusty crying of a new-born child, and the yard was grey now, for dawn had come. Jody climbed over the groom's slumbering back and took himself to the casement, opening it and leaning out till his hair and skin and the secret talisman were all soaked with the rain. The baby was noisy, he thought; it must be a boy, and when it was grown they two would fight, and he, Jody, would win the inheritance. There was no question but that he would win, by whatever means. The right was his, and this boy should not take it from him.

He heard, later, that it was after all a girl. Perhaps the noise of the saddling of the squire's horse, as soon as the news came, primed Jody; certainly when James Curle came up later to tell him, mouth chumbling strangely for lack of his porcelain teeth, and wearing his night-cap still, that it was a girl, Jody was not surprised. "It be a little lass, a young lady, Jody," said James. "I brought ye a sup o' wine, lad, that we may drink the health of her, she being the last of the stock." The squire, James did not add, had drunk no health, only riding out alone into the dawn in a fury, his age notwithstanding.

Jody took the wine and solemnly drank it, at the same time holding his tongue. Within his cool mind there occurred a change of plan. There would be no need, he knew, to fight a girl for the inheritance. She would not oust him. Instead, he would marry her.

Sir Ludovic had heard the old midwife Hannah Thwaite coming downstairs at last heavily, almost as though it were she herself who had given birth to the child. The storm had abated somewhat and there was quietness upstairs. Hannah held the baby, wrapped in flannel. The old squire stared at them with a strange suspension of all feeling; whichever way the dice had been cast, the thing was done with now . . .

"Well?" he said hoarsely. She would take her time, old Hannah, he knew, about telling him; once long ago he'd taken his time over *her*, in a summer hayfield with tall daisies, yellow and white, in the grass before they'd cut it. She'd borne a child, later; he was a shoemaker now, in Carlisle, having left the valley. "Well? Is it an heir? Speak, woman; is it my grandson?"

Hannah Thwaite, grown hard as the rocks themselves by his cause, had never been afraid of the squire. Her red-rimmed eyes peered without expression from beneath her curch; how little he had changed outwardly, the big, brutal man who had once been her lover! A lifetime of cruelty and sin could scar a man's soul, Hannah knew well, as she knew what was truly said of him; that not one could be found in the valley who loved Sir Ludovic, or wished him well. Yet she could not find it in her heart now to do other than pity him somewhat, this man who had lost her good name, and now was about to see the end of his own. For a lass, when all was said, must marry another.

Hannah shook her head wordlessly, and the squire gave an oath.

"A puling girl? Is that what ye'd bring me?" He raised his arm, as if to strike both the woman and the bundle she held; then it dropped to his side again, on its way disturbing the silver cup; this crashed to the floor, rolling sideways. "No weakling, this one," said Hannah. "She has a likeness to yourself, I believe, squire; I saw't at the instant of birth."

She stared down calmly into the baby's face, scarlet still with its late exertions; it opened its mouth, and gave a strong yell that drowned the noise of both wind and rain. Hannah laughed, her toothless mouth for moments taking the shape it had had when she was a young girl, free of cares. "See her, how strong and mettlesome she be," she said. "She'll be a handful, a lusty sweetheart like her grandfer; to be sure, 'twas as though I'd heard ye swear." It was the first time she had jested with him since their long-ago coupling; but Sir Ludovic did not smile.

"No woman's talk, or woman child, could pleasure me at such a moment," he said. "Take her and drown her in the tarn, for all of me." He turned on his heel, and strode out of the hall into the still gusty night, now beginning to pale with coming dawn: presently, the flicker of a lanthorn and the sound of hooves told them he was going on a journey. Shortly afterwards James Curle came in, rubbing the sleep from his eyes.

"Old devil's gone," he said, "gone off to his harlot in Carlisle."

Hannah had made her way upstairs again with the baby; no one heard him, and the echoes of his voice sounded through the empty hall. He warmed himself before the half-dead ashes of the hearth for instants, then took himself back to his bed. No one else enquired for Sir Ludovic; nor was surprise shown that the squire had failed to ask concerning the welfare of the baby's mother, or how the news of the birth had been received by his dying son.

Mrs. Emma in fact was in parlous state, but by morning the women told one another that, setting aside any child-bed fever, she would live;

though, poor soul, not as she had been, for the forceful child's battle into life had half torn its mother's narrow body apart. As for John Curle, he hardly heeded the news that he had a daughter; the bed he lay on was not sufficient for his comfort now that he was covered in sores, incontinent, paralysed, and fevered, with but little nursing-care. He died four days after Norah made her entry into the world. The first strong influence in her life would, therefore, be that of her grandfather; but while she was still yelling for the wet-nurse's breast, which she needed sooner and oftener than other infants, Sir Ludovic had already ridden far enough to knock on a certain door. He did not return till news came that his second son was dead. That information, coming when it did, would mean little to the squire; he took heed to nothing any more except an hour or two's pleasure in a woman's flesh. Perhaps it was true to say that his heart, if he had one, had died with young Jody's dead father, and by now was set hard as a stone.

There was also Jody himself, taken by the hand the following morning and made to lean over the cradle at Curle. He stared down at the child's sleeping face, and said nothing.

2

THE FIRST THING anyone noticed, from babyhood, about Norah Curle was her lack of fear. While she lay in her cradle the wind might howl in the chimney, but Norah never whimpered nor had evil dreams. By day she was docile enough, though stubborn when crossed and shrewdly noticing of everything; from before the time when the large, scowling child learnt to crawl, she was in company with dogs, horses, grooms, Jody and her grandfather; and feared none of them.

Almost before she could walk she was put on a fell pony, and from the first delighted Sam, who taught her, with the way she made the easy-going, short-legged beast do her bidding. Sam had never heard of centaurs, but Norah Curle in the saddle was soon to be as much a part of the mount she rode as one of those fabled creatures: as time passed she grew too heavy for the small fell ponies, and pestered her grandfather for a larger mount.

"I want to hunt," she said when she was five. She had heard the belling hounds in cry to the far south often, and was already like an animal sniffing the wind to be after them. Sir Ludovic shrugged it off, remembering her father's limp broken body carried home. "This an't hunting country, lass; content you with riding the farm-tracks for a while." But she would not leave the matter, till he forbade her to speak of it; then she said one day almost two years later, eyeing him below her thick fringe of hair, "I want to go with you when you ride out beyond the valley."

He guffawed, at the same time wondering if Jody had put her up to it. "Better bide where y'are, miss, and learn manners and stitchery."

"Stitchery be damned," said Norah, using a word she had heard in the stables. During the years that followed her opinion did not alter. "Why should I spend my time on't? I hate it, leave it to mama." For the afflicted Mrs. Emma spent a great part of her days in embroidery, if no company should have ridden over: lying on her sofa, which she would seldom nowadays quit, holding a tambour-frame between her languid fingers. The squire looked down as so often on Norah's wide square grin that resembled his own, and grinned back. "It's time we got ye a fancy-mannered governess," he said again, "to teach ye what words to use in fine company, and to cipher ye, Norah, when I'm gone." The child took his reference to his own passing placidly; she was used to hear him mention it, and knew moreover that when the squire went, she was to be the lady of Curle. She ignored all mention of the governess. Two were found in due course, and at the end of three months and four respectively, professed themselves unable to stay. Norah returned afterwards to the matter in hand.

"I can ride Barley, grandfather, if you'll say the word to Sam. I can ride as well as Jody." She was uncertain in her own mind why it was often necessary to compare herself with Jody, who was, she knew, a mere half-gipsy bastard; Norah was unsure whether to admire or despise him. This indecision was, perhaps, instilled by Sir Ludovic himself, who somehow failed to treat Jody in the off-hand way he used with the other bastard Curles: at times he would roar at the lad to come and pull his boots off for him, then the next moment would cast a great arm round Jody's shoulders, so that they went off together, the two of them, smiling together at some bawdy jest. At such times Norah was aware of jealousy; today, however, the squire turned on her at mention of Jody's name. "I'd not have ye bear company with that gipsy," he swore, and Norah got out of his way quickly before her twelve-year-old calves suffered a cut of his riding-crop. She would not, she knew, have cried out with the pain, for she had never done that in all her life. Curles didn't cry. For good measure, she called back down into the hall where the squire stood, brooding as usual by the hearth, "Jody can help me into the saddle, if I choose; and I *can* ride Barley." Then she escaped, as she did on occasion, upstairs to mama's room till the old man should have forgotten his temper; though to be sure it was dull with mama and there was better sport, and company, downstairs or else in the stables.

She tossed her thick, unmanageable chestnut curls. Their colour, and Norah's resemblance in build and feature to the squire, had early enough caused heads to be shaken through the valley. As time passed they did not still their shaking. If it were not that Mrs. Emma, poor widowed creature, were a virtuous lady, one might think the old devil himself had sired this brat, not poor Mr. John. But whether or not such a thing were possible, there were—the gossips foresaw it—high times coming when such a young madam of Curle temper ruled the valley. The squire himself, they said, held his peace often nowadays, as though he were at last growing old or—it was just possible—had after all accepted, even grown fond of, his granddaughter and the ending of the direct Curle line. But others said he was as ill to deal with as ever, and that he and Miss Norah used few except hard words to one another. It was true; neither understood soft language.

Mrs. Emma, who long ago had withdrawn her timid affections like a snail its horns, was lying in her widow's gear on her day-bed. Since Norah's birth she had partly in fact, partly in fancy become an invalid, and this state was in itself interesting enough to procure her the occasional caller as the years passed. One of them was with her now, and as by custom had been made mildly welcome with a dish of tea: Emma's own stepmother, the Dowager Duchess of Wraye, who had arrived hours since in her antique coach, and was herself like a walking historical mammet, for she still wore a fontange and plumpers, the latter held inside her wrinkled mouth against her cheeks. Norah stared at her and thought how like she was to an ancient monkey, clad in a scarlet coat, they'd had on a chain at Hob's Fair in the valley one summer at the horse-sales. Folk came from as far as the south parts, and from Scotland, for the sturdy ponies bred hereabouts. Norah screwed up her nose, still savouring in imagination the beloved smell of horses' sweat and fresh dung. Her mother's voice, so plaintive as to be almost a moan, broke in upon her.

"Make your curtsy to grandmama, and recall your manners," she wailed, at the same time manipulating her widow's lappets to fall more becomingly on her bosom. Norah bobbed in hostile fashion, and the two ladies exchanged a glance with one another. Norah scowled, suddenly at a loss and inadequate, she knew, in face of that determined gentle insistence that she was clumsy, ill-mannered, and in some way strange. And it was the second time lately that manners had been mentioned; grandpapa had become as bad. Resentment flared up in the child, as it often did, at sight of her mother in weeds. Had she been able to interpret the feeling to herself, it would have been clear that what she found false was the wearing, by her mother, of mourning for her father, whom Emma could doubtfully have loved for the squire boasted often, sometimes in his daughter-in-law's presence, that he'd arranged the marriage, as though Emma had had no say in it for herself. But as Norah was unable to formulate all this to her own mind she merely stood glaring, after making her bob, so that Mrs. Emma raised her pale eyes and pale hands again to heaven. Her Grace's tongue intervened.

"Do not despise everyday manners, miss; you must learn those before Court ones, or how can you ever be taken to London to make your curtsy to the Queen? The time is not far off now your twelfth birthday is past: sixteen is the age when young ladies are presented."

"The Queen's damned ugly," Norah muttered. "Grandfather said it," but although the Dowager gave her loud sudden laugh, almost seeming in danger of displacing the plumpers, Mrs. Emma stirred and sighed aloud, "Alas, who will take her? I declare I cannot undertake such a journey at any time, and by then—"

"Have no fear; there's time yet," said the Dowager. "I'll do't myself, if I'm still in the land of the living; otherwise, maybe Shawhope will—will have a wife." The hesitation was, as both ladies knew, by reason of the fact that a discreet hope was nourished that George Wraye, present Marquis of Shawhope, might perhaps have settled in his ways enough to propose for Norah herself, with her lands and fortune, when she was older, and himself take her to London for presentation on the marriage, with the aid of some noble lady not yet named. A pity the anticipated bride were not prettier, for George was already known to be a connoisseur of pretty ladies. But there was still time to make a stylish young personage out of Norah Curle, for even if she would never be a beauty she could cultivate a grand style. "Provided she be not lacking in wit, there is hope for it all, but how can one tell? The child is dumb, except to utter stable-words, or quote her grandfather." The Dowager opened her fan, and over its edge assessed the Curle heiress, not for the first time; so clumsy a creature, still with too-large hands and feet, and her grandfather's scowl! "Her hair is her best feature, my dear Emma; when it is dressed it will be an advantage." She murmured the words, but Norah heard her and her scowl deepened; they were at it again, speaking of her as if she were not present, or were a deaf-mute. Rage surged in her and, to her mother's mortification, she spoke out. "The paint on both your faces is running with the heat," she growled. As if she didn't know they laughed at her, seated here drinking China tea out of cups like eggshells, and making fools' chatter!

Genuine colour appeared in patches on Mrs. Emma's neck. "I beg your pardon, step-mama; the child is too much in the company of stable-hands and rough folk, and her grandfather will not have anyone say her nay; what am I to do? Norah, leave the room instantly."

"Sound beating is what I'd give her," announced the Dowager. "Go and look at your own grimed face in the mirror, miss; a handful for you, my poor Emma! If any of *my* daughters had ever shown me anything but respect I'd have 'em thrashed, ay, and sons too. Norah will never find a husband until her manners mend, unless it's some fortune-hunter."

Husbands! Manners! Was there nothing else in anyone's head? Norah slouched along the stone passage, hands behind her back. Let them talk and titter as they would, now she'd gone. Mama never did want her in the elegant room, and she herself would by far rather be down there among the stable-lads, only it meant passing by grandfather again and no doubt he was still enraged. It didn't matter, but she—she didn't want to have to look in a mirror; she knew well enough what she'd see. The voice of the squire, heard often in his cups, sounded in her ears above the noise of her own feet on the flagstones. "Here's to my big filly! Here's to the lady of Curle!" And they would, he promised, find her a stallion when she was grown.

A big filly. She *was* big, making Madge Beck, who came nowadays to share lessons although her father was only a smallholder in the valley, seem like a fairy, so tiny and dark-eyed and dainty, even her hands small enough to get lost in Norah's clasp. And Madge could mock her; small people could always mock at big ones, in ways no one else would understand; but she liked Madge. There was no one else to talk to, apart from the superior Wraye cousins, and Jody; nearly seven years older as he was, Norah could already tussle with him and give him a fight for his money, almost winning by sheer weight, pinning him down beneath her, only he'd get above her again with a twist like an adder, till the next time; but she still wasn't afraid of him. There was no man she couldn't fight. Here was the mirror. "Go on, look and see yourself," muttered Norah, staring at last at her own face confronting her behind a layer of dust; everything not in Mrs. Emma's rooms was dusty at Curle, for no one troubled to clean and polish greatly except for what was under the eye of the squire, who never came upstairs.

The face met her, the same face she'd always seen, changing from a baby's to a child's, and from that to whatever she was now. Some things didn't change; her eyes didn't. They were small, of a colour between brown and green, set deeply, like an animal's, beneath thick brows. Her teeth were square and good, set well apart. She bared them, fingering the eye-teeth with one hand. Madge's teeth were beginning to go, even those that had newly grown in. Good teeth were something to have, even if everyone said one was no beauty. "Maybe they can bite," Norah said aloud. As she did so, Jody's lithe tall shape came into view in the mirror. He was smiling his closed smile. Norah spun round. What was it someone had said about those one saw in a mirror? Had Jody heard her speak?

He had; and teased her for it. "Folk who talk to themselves end by talking to the moon," he said. "What ails the lady of Curle that she has no one to listen to her?" He smiled on with his closed lips; he was, she saw, in one of his arrogant moods, but it was of no importance. She thrust past him, and would have gone on her way, but Jody held her back by a grip on her arm. "You'll not have heard," he told her, "what our grandfather has in store, as you said you disliked stitchery. He has decided that you're to come with me in the schoolroom to the Reverend Railsby–" he sneered –"to learn Latin and history. That old toad will keep you in order, Norah."

"Does he keep you so?" she said, and downed her feeling of dismay. Learn Latin? They might laugh at her for a dunderhead; she was apt enough with figures, and less idle than Jody, who, she knew already, did no work. What good was Latin to a fine lady? "I know some history," she said defensively.

"Ay, that that poor mim underpaid thing Maria Baynes stuffed into your head before she left, with her nerves in tatters, like the one before, and the one before that. Never fret, you can beat all of them on a pony's back, centaur that y'are, if Railsby hasn't grazed your fists with that ferrule of his; he uses it as others use snuff. Creeping hypocrite! He'll bow and scrape to grandfather, but when we are alone upstairs he's God Almighty, to himself if not to me. One day I'll beat *him*. I'm too old now for them to educate me." He laughed again, and strode off.

Norah found herself looking down at her hands, which were grimy; not a lady's hands, mama would say. Too late, grandfather had taken the notion of book-learning for Jody: but why include herself? Why should she have to learn Latin and mouth French phrases, which the governesses had tried to teach her already? Except for curtsying to the Queen, which must be done, she'd never, never leave Curle, even when she married. No one spoke French here in the valley. And she'd remembered what it was about seeing someone in a mirror; it meant you were going to marry them.

But she would never, of course, marry Jody; the idea was absurd. He was a bastard, almost a servant, even if grandfather did have him tutored in Latin by the parson on a sudden whim.

The sessions with the Reverend Railsby taught Norah one thing, even if it were not much Latin; Jody was even more idle than anyone had thought, and had been so all his boyhood. It took a very short time for Norah herself to catch up with him; far from showing a properly defensive spirit over this, he only smiled at it, and lounged while she left him behind over declensions and verbs. She found, a thing unnoticed in the days of the governesses, that it was necessary for her to see something only once before she remembered it; this was already so for known faces, for Norah forgot nobody she had ever met. But the printed word, as well as figures, now came readily to mind. Railsby began to preen himself on Norah's progress while at the same time continuing to rap Jody's knuckles with his ferrule as though he were a child. At first Norah had been surprised that the dour, agile young man submitted to this series of insults to his adult dignity: then one day, without any warning at all, Jody took the ferrule, which was made of yew wood, and broke it across the Reverend Railsby's head, thereafter falling on him with his fists.

Norah stood back from the schoolroom table, where they had all three been working, and watched, as if in disbelief, the toppling of the quills and ink. When Jody rubbed the reverend gentleman's face in the latter she began to laugh: and went on laughing while Railsby struggled to his feet, and with notable alacrity went hastening out of the room and downstairs, leaving his hat. Jody by now had joined her in her laughter. They stood and rocked together for a matter of moments; then Norah said, as if she were talking to a much younger child, "Grandfather will be very angry; he'll beat you himself, as like as not."

"Then, I'll hide myself, till he's got over it. Do you suppose I've never been in trouble all the years you were growing? I have places to go, that you don't know of." He stared down at her, grey eyes half-shut beneath their thick long lashes, a smear of ink, left over from the struggle, on one swarthy cheek. Norah was aware of a sudden feeling of strangeness, an awareness of difference between herself and him, between Jody and the rest of humankind; ordinary folk, that was. Now she came to think of it, there had been times when no one had seen him for long . . .

"Tell me where it is you go," she said; it had suddenly become important to know, and she would tell no one; she seldom talked much even to Madge; Jody must surely know that. But he shrugged, unsmiling.

"When you're grown I'll tell you—maybe. Now I'd best be off, before the squire sends for me. Don't let him put fear in you, Norah; not that he ever will. Tell him what happened; Railsby's a liar, and will say anything to save his reputation and his silver that he thinks he can earn here. But I'll not learn more Latin; tell grandfather so." He went away, and Norah did not follow him far; let him think she didn't care where he went, if he wouldn't tell her of it till she was grown. It would be diverting, maybe, to go downstairs and see the abject sight Railsby made in front of the squire, and what he was saying. Perhaps, if she could make grandfather laugh with a recital of what had really happened, she could cozen him later into buying a bigger pony for her to ride below the fells.

It might have been that same day, or the next, that Norah heard the pipes. It was not the first time; she knew what they were, and that Jody played them, an old set that he had somehow acquired, and somehow taught himself, or been taught, to play. Why did she know so little of it? They were remote and gentle, these small pipes made of leather, less bitter and sharp than northern bagpipes, less sad than tender, yet they mocked her. She knew this and did not know how; in the same way as she understood that, having refused to let her know where he had hidden himself, Jody tormented her by playing them where she could still hear. What was the use of it all, this hurting of her? Why was she, Norah Curle, hurt by Jody at all? She did not answer her own questioning, knowing it was purposeless; only went on listening, half absently, to his distant playing, noting how the tune faltered here and there as though the player were not yet sure of himself. A new Jody, this, from the sly yet cocksure creature that was about her daily; but not today or yesterday. He had gone, as he said he would: and even the squire had ceased to roar for him. "Jody'll go his own gait," he had grumbled, at the last: and it was true.

Jody's gait. "He hates me because he knows I shall inherit Curle," thought Norah suddenly, and to draw her own mind away from that reasoning wondered, in a kind of discipline already put upon her by herself, where it could be that Jody sat playing. It was too far away to be the stable-loft, where last year there had been apples stored, after a good harvest; she and he had climbed the ladder together and eaten some, biting into the sweet white flesh in companionable silence. At such times Jody perhaps forgot to hate her; but now . . . "If I climbed up to where he is, and came upon him with his pipes, he'd swear at me, and we'd fight to make an end of it," she thought. But something was missing from the ending that would have been there a week ago; she wouldn't, even if she did know where he was hiding, follow him now. Last week, yesterday, when she was still a child, she wouldn't have known enough to stop herself going after Jody if she wished it. The time at the mirror today had altered things: now, she was still.

"Grandfather, what's a centaur?"

Sir Ludovic stirred, wine-cup in hand, from his troubled thoughts of Jody; where the devil was the boy? "Eh? What is't? Who has put fancies in y'head? If it's that damned parson with his face stained with ink—" Good for the boy, if one thought of it, to have downed parson; same as he'd have done himself, damn the fool! He glared at Norah, resentful of the fact that she should have been the one to be there, and see it happen; a rare jest, would have warmed the blood. What was she saying?

"Parson and I don't trouble each other, save over Latin verbs. Tell me what the thing is I asked, if y'know it." She crinkled up her eyes; it always paid to taunt the squire with ignorance, if one did it carefully. He fenced a while.

"Where did ye hear of't, in all the world? Such things don't exist and never did; 'tis all a fancy."

"*What* is a fancy, grandfather? You still haven't told me; I doubt if y'know."

"Stubborn filly, ain't ye? They were monsters, if ye will; part horse and part man, or woman, doubtless, if they mated. Who in the devil's name told ye of't? Answer me; was it Jody?"

"No," she lied. She wasn't going to look a fool. Let the squire think she'd read it in some book; let him think what he liked. The wound stabbed deep, while Norah schooled her features to a mask, to show nothing. A monster, a monster . . . how Jody hated her! She must make herself hate him in return; despise him, the half-gipsy bastard. A gipsy was worse than a monster; there, she could say that next time Jody came near. He was holed up somewhere, gipsy that he was; should she tell the squire?

But Sir Ludovic quaffed his wine, eyes on her now with a look that made her uneasy. In fact, as he was thinking, it was as well if Jody ran off; mustn't let him and young Norah run wild together too long. Parson was all very well, and Latin declensions; procure the boy a place as clerk, maybe, soon. But gipsy's get was no fit mate for his Norah, and the years went on and her breasts were growing; best start looking about him soon, to Wraye and elsewhere. Devil take a London season! A Curle should stay here in the valley to breed heirs, not go gallivanting south. He'd not lose Norah, last of his race. Things being as they were, it'd need to be a

Wraye match, if he could bring himself to pay young Shawhope's debts; Jonathan, the younger boy, he couldn't stomach, mim as a maiden with his eyes forever on the ground. There was another of them thereabouts, a young fellow, young Stroyan . . . David Stroyan. He was nephew, was it? —or half-brother, some such thing, of the filly he himself had refused long ago for John, but times were changing and young men scarce. Stroyans were scholars, parson's get instead of gipsy's; they might furnish a stallion quiet to the hand. The old man grinned, and saw his grandchild wondering what diverted him; he wouldn't tell her at her age, put notions in her head. Human flesh was like horseflesh, when all was said; nothing paid better than plenty of far-sighted preparation for a mating, and the coffers were full enough; he could buy the best for Norah. But he'd keep young Jody out of the way on one ploy and another from now on; when the boy returned, this time, to Curle there'd be no welcome. He'd remember that, tomorrow. He drained the wine, and presently slept. Norah rose, lifting her skirts aside and moving carefully, and left him.

3

WITH HER OWN COMPANY, on a pony, Norah did not miss Jody or anyone: it was different when other young people were present. Divided into two kinds as the latter were, the tenants of the valley and her own social equals, Norah knew she could do without either. The first-named had supplied Madge Beck, who still bore her company at lessons now the Reverend Railsby had departed; the third or fourth governess proved less meek than lazy, and left the two girls often alone. Madge's wit, allowed exercise in these absences, was earthy, and gave Norah the more pleasure as she herself was never made the butt of it. Madge had been well drilled at home to wait till Miss Norah spoke before speaking, and bob a curtsy before answering, and always use the full title of the young lady from Curle Hall. Madge took it all as it came; she had already taken the size of the big, often clumsy young mistress, and would dip her hodden skirts briefly and point a clog as if about to dance, then come out with some such devastating statement as, "Ah, it was a strange unchancy thing m'granfer saw the night he'd drunken overmuch wine. 'Tis not for you to hear what he said, Miss Norah, for the words he used were bad ones, and m'father 'ud have the hide off me for telling you o't."

"Tell me the words," said Norah, whose list from Sir Ludovic was already longer than most. But the tiny dark girl clapped her hands to her mouth, and shook her head, all curls and dimples. Norah knew an instant's useless longing; if only she herself could ever look so! But she knew she never would, and that was that. "Do as you're bid, now," she told little Madge, mindful of Sir Ludovic's fiat that the tenants had best learn who was master: *she* would one day be so. She scowled at Madge, who still pretended to be unwilling.

"My dad 'ud thrash me, I tell ye, Miss Norah, if 'twere known—"

"Well, *I'll* thrash you if you don't." The imp stood swinging her foot, then told Norah the words, poker-faced. The young lady from the Hall tossed her head; she knew them already.

"If that's the best your grandfather can do when he's drunk, mine can beat him at it sober. I know words that'd take the skin off you, Madge Beck, without a stick." She turned away, and again mounted her patient pony; how dull the world was lately! Jody was otherwhere, had come and gone all last winter and last summer, and she had no one against whom to pit her wits. It'd be different, no doubt, if more folk of one's own kind were nearer. But there were only the two Wraye boys, who rarely left their new Palladian house nearby the castle, except that Shawhope lately had taken up with tavern-wenches, leaving the younger Jonathan with his books and harpsichord. There were the Stroyans . . .

Afterwards Norah found that she could not recall her own first meeting with David Stroyan: he always seemed to have been there. It might have been that Sir Ludovic, now Jody was removed from frequent contact with Norah, had arranged matters so that they might, the pair of them, feel as if they had known one another all their lives: or it might have been chance. It had happened, at any rate, by the time Norah was sixteen: about that time two young girl-cousins came north, to find themselves husbands if it could be done. Norah could trace the relationship when she troubled to; everyone was kin to everyone else, through Mrs. Emma and the first wife of the old Duke.

The cousins were unpleasant young women, at least to Norah's ear and eye. They were small-boned, colourless—neither Caro nor Amelia was either fair or dark, both having a kind of dun overall colour of skin and hair, like two mice—and excessively well-bred in their own estimation: they were in fact perfectly pleased with themselves. They were also conventional, and had been sent to a genteel provincial school in the south;

almost every act or word of Norah's sent both young ladies into an access of giggling behind carefully gloved hands. One day they were all of them, with the party from Wraye, out together on the moor, and the young ladies' mama, left behind in the Palladian mansion, had particularly enjoined them not to ride bare-handed, as Norah herself knew every horsewoman born preferred to do. But the cousins, so similar in every way, had likewise one ambition in their conjoint lives, which was to attact for themselves the entire notice of any male whether or not worth marrying. Granted their mama, a provident lady, would spare no effort meantime on their own behalf, and what a triumph if they could snare a Wraye or Stroyan offer! As time passed—the minutes, in such company, seemed to drag themselves out into hours, and Norah already found the visit wearisome—the demands of gentility were dwelt on and, in her case, found to be sadly lacking: this was made evident by more sidelong glances and whispering behind gloved hands. The stay-boned bodices of the pair pricked up in the saddles like slate-pencils, for both rode side-saddle with more or less grace. Norah, who when alone rode astride, like a man, but who for the sake of today's company had been persuaded into a riding-skirt and to hook one thigh over the pommel, felt nevertheless at ease till she rode alongside the cousins. There, no effort was spared, she found, to make her feel clumsy even in the saddle. The pair smirked and signalled to one another, at the same time making much of timid young Jonathan Wraye; his brother Shawhope rode to one side, diverting himself by making a fool of Amelia, though no one else knew it. Norah herself, on Barley at last, balanced her generous young body rhythmically to the trot, and rode alongside. Caro turned her unremarkable head.

"You ride in front; 'Melia and I have a matter to discuss." Her eyes roved over the Marquis, very handsome today in top-boots.

Norah felt a flush rising in her own cheeks, and said, "I'll ride where I choose." She drew rein, and Amelia gave a titter.

"You're so big and clumsy, how can there be room for all of us abreast? Why, David! I didn't see you come, for Norah sat in the way," and with one accord the sisters enveloped David Stroyan, on his grey, as well as young Shawhope on his chestnut. Norah dug her heel into Barley's side and brushed past the party; to hell with them! They'd laugh, no doubt, together at the sight of her backside, cantering; let them laugh till they fell in a rabbit-hole, and cracked their paltry bones. She felt the wind ride behind her already, and once free of the constricting company was herself again, and a law unto no other. That was the way it must always be, and she couldn't accustom herself to their ways. Why ape such chicken-arsed folk? "I'll tell mama so, and the squire as well, next time they try to make a lady out of me," Norah promised grimly.

It must have been later that same afternoon that David came upon her. She was sitting among the heather by herself, with Barley cropping a little way off. It was a late summer day when the fells, as the sun wore on, were clad in heat-mist, and the stems of the heather were still almost black, though small butterflies and insects moved there. She'd been staring at these without seeing them, aware of the hurt inflicted by Caro and Amelia and their kind. When David sought her out and came and dropped down by her she didn't turn her head, or think it singular. She didn't know, or care, what had happened to the riding-party, or the Wrayes, or that Shawhope had by now ridden off, deserting Amelia for better sport at the tavern. There was only David's grey pony and hers, cropping turf, and the pair of them here on the heather, and a small powder-blue butterfly uncertainly hovering between them, among the stems.

"How beautiful that is," said David Stroyan, and Norah heard him as though he spoke in a foreign tongue. The men she knew, the squire and Jody and even the Reverend Railsby, were not in the way of praising or even noticing beauty, unless it belonged to a woman or a fine house, or horseflesh maybe if one had paid enough for it. Yet David was different. He had, she recalled hearing, much knowledge of birds and insects, shells, flowers, the like; folk laughed at him for it, saying that if he were a woman he would be called a bluestocking, like the learned ladies who aped Paris salons in London. For a man to have a liking for such things, unless he was set to be a parson, seemed odd. Yet David looked ordinary enough, if looking like nothing and no one would suit such a term; it was almost as if he denied any strong identity, even in his colouring, which was pallid, and he was of slim build: although he must be four or five years older than herself he was, or soon would be, less tall. Norah slewed her eyes round, for the first time in her life assessing a man as a new species, somewhat like the butterfly. The latter preened its wings between them for instants, then flew away.

"It is wonderful to meet with so rare a variety here, in the north," said David, using the faintly pedantic language of the scholar and bookworm. He was the only boy in a family of unmarried sisters, all of whom either doted on him or ignored him: his eyes were short-sighted and he peered into the heather in search of more butterflies. "They are beginning to be rare in the south also," he said. "Soon there will be none left as the city grows, for they like lonely places."

He sat up, hands clasped about his knees; he seemed to have forgotten her. "How wild it is!" he said. "At home, in Surrey, we have only tame downs, or ordered gardens with an artificial lake and a folly. There isn't the natural beauty you have here, so near the hills." He turned and smiled at Norah, who did not point out, for it would have shown a lack of manners, that they called them fells in these parts. David was a southerner, and as such could not be expected to know such things. Norah's sullen, guarded gaze lifted slightly, but she said nothing: she'd been made, she was thinking, enough of a fool already today. Let him talk. She wasn't going to fawn, like Caro and Amelia, round any male with presentable manners. At the same time the thought came to her, surveying David's delicate appearance, how much better he would fit a background such as he was now lamenting, of the tame south; an ordered garden suited him far better than the wild moor. He wore a coat of buff cloth, unremarkable but well enough cut, and his stock and linen were fastidiously clean. So were his nails, although he wore no gloves; a point in his favour. Yet the fact that he was like a fragile plant, that the first rough wind might blow away, made her despise him till she remembered the harebells, and the way in which their hair-fine stalks bent before the wildest gales here, then straightened afterwards with their own resilience. She stifled her laughter; to have to compare a young man with harebells!

"Why are you smiling?" David said, gently. "You don't smile often; when you do, it's pleasant." He flushed, as if unaccustomed to offering compliments. He blundered on. "You like it here best when—when there are no visitors, do you not?" he said. "You like your own company? So do I."

The colour in his face deepened further, and Norah guessed that the whole speech had been a great effort for him; yet why, in that event, make it? She decided to humour Stroyan, as he was civil. "I'm used to it," she said. "This is my place; it'll be all mine when grandfather dies." The statement sounded boastful in the clear air. David Stroyan stared down at the grass and heather and traced a little pattern with his finger along the stems. He was smiling, and the sun, struggling through the heat-haze, picked out an arc of pale gold across his eyelashes. "Then it is as well that you can be content here," he said, "and—and not solitary."

"I shall marry." Having said it, Norah felt unwonted colour creep into her own face. Such things as he made one say! She had never, she knew, hitherto been made to talk of any matter in particular, in the way David Stroyan drew it out of one. Mama's tenets of polite conversation included nothing they had discussed here in this half-hour. But she preferred it, at any rate to the company of Caro and Amelia and Shawhope, swollen with his own importance to all young women till he was like a mating toad. David Stroyan at least was not like that; and had after all done his best to make her feel one with the company, wherever it had dispersed to.

She rose. "I don't often speak of such things," she said truthfully. She stared down at David for some instants, then mounted Barley again. David scrambled up at once to help her, but he was too late; Norah was quickly in the saddle. "No one ever has to help me up," she said proudly, adding "I'd best be getting back; dark falls early."

She turned Barley's head, feeling him respond as always to her lightest pull on the reins. Why was it that all things connected with horseflesh she did delicately, easily, and yet when it came to other folk was dumb as a heifer? But if Caro and Amelia mocked her riding, that was spite; she could ride them, she knew, out of the saddle. She tossed her head to the unspoken thought as Barley and she made off, knowing the riding-party was somewhere on the moor: but whether to impress the rest, or David Stroyan only, she could not have told herself. Yet she knew David stood there watching her as she rode off back towards Curle, and that despite all the rest he wasn't laughing at her. That knowledge in itself brought unexpected comfort.

When she reached home the squire was in the hall, and greeted her with "Well? Well? Had ye a good day?"

"Well enough. There was some sun, and Barley carried me."

"Damn the sun and the pony; what company had ye? Was Shawhope by?"

"Shawhope doesn't heed me; he likes witless women he can look down on."

"Ay, maybe, Norah. What of Jonathan? Was he out? Did he ride by ye?"

Norah told him briefly of the ride, and the two impolite young women. She did not mention Stroyan till the end, and surprised a look of cunning on the squire's face. "Stroyan's boy spoke with ye, eh? How was he? They say he's a bookworm, but the blood's good enough; his grandsire was a younger son in a parson's living in the south, and gave it up and came here, then died, like the fool he was; some scandal or other, and he left a wife and a quiverful o' daughters she couldn't marry off, for they'd no money. *You* won't be in that case, Norah; can take y'pick; but have an eye to young Stroyan. It came to me lately that he might make ye a match, without ever leaving Curle to find one."

"Sounds as if I were a mare in season." She kept silence concerning any talk of butterflies, or gardens. "Eh? What talk's that?" the squire would have said: he had never thought to talk of butterflies in his life. Norah realised that he had encouraged young Stroyan to come, perhaps even to talk to her and win her over; but she wasn't sure that she was to be won. It was too soon; the squire was forever hinting at marriages, whether with Shawhope or another. But Shawhope, Norah knew well enough, disdained to heed her existence, and she did not admire him: too puffed up and handsome for his own good, and flying at every woman.

4

LESS THAN A MONTH after that riding-party word came to Curle that George Wraye, Marquis of Shawhope, was sick of a fever: soon further word came that he was dead. Sir Ludovic, who would ride over for the funeral, sent for Jody, who had meantime returned, to help ease on the tight, high boots over his legs, which were somewhat swollen. He was less concerned with this than with the young man's death. "Can't be the gout, never had it in m'life," he said, grimacing as Jody pulled on the leather. "Never tell me there ain't a curse on the entire Wraye brood! The pox, as like as not, that boy had; forever womanising. Now young Jonathan, who never looked a man straight between the eyes in all of his days, 'll be Marquis, and Duke when the old one dies. The old one!" He grinned. "He's younger than I by a twelvemonth. Hand me my hat, boy. I may return tonight, but maybe not: dine when you're hungry, within waitin'."

Norah watched the scene from where she half sat, half sprawled on the far side of the hearth; her hand caressed a dog's head absently. It was not the custom for women to attend funerals, and she must bide here without viewing handsome George Wraye laid out in his coffin surrounded by candles, and weeping tenantry. It was hard to imagine Shawhope dead; though he had lived his life as if each moment were the last. Perhaps that was the way to live.

She heard the squire ride off to the accompaniment of the usual friendly curses, barking of dogs and whinnying of horses left behind in the stable. Norah doubted if Sir Ludovic would find as merry a reception when he reached Wraye. Apart from the sadness of the occasion, there was, she knew, some matter for ill feeling between her grandsire and the Duke, and they seldom met; and Jonathan, while remaining civil enough, made it evident that he found the squire's loose ways and foul tongue distasteful. However no doubt even the latter would be stilled while they buried George, and after that Sir Ludovic, as he had said, might or might not ride home. Norah knew well enough where else he might go; he had always kept mistresses in the house in Carlisle, and had gone there more often of late as if to defy the onset of age. After the grimness of the burial, no doubt, he would ride there to recover his spirits.

She was thinking of it all, and staring at the fire, when she became aware that Jody had sidled in, and had dropped down into the ingle-nook opposite. Norah raised her head to survey him, brows drawn together. "I thought ye'd ridden off with the squire," she said, in the dialect. It was more homely to speak so with Jody.

"Why so? I'm not his keeper, and he'd sooner be rid of my company on the return journey." Jody smiled his catlike smile. "He's got himself a yellow-haired doxy, a new one; not a day more than eighteen, I'll swear. The burying? I did not like Shawhope, nor he me; why should I help bury him?"

Norah shrugged, and did not answer; she felt disinclined to talk, as if the slight rise of discomfort Jody's presence brought nowadays could be downed by silence. As if to prevent this cure, he talked on.

"There was another reason why I did not go, and that is—Norah, do you not see how they keep us apart nowadays? If I want a privy word with you, it is the devil's business to arrange, between your mother and our grandsire. And now that Jonathan is Marquis, and looking to inherit, I swear they'll try to make a match between you and him: with George, they had no hope of't."

She frowned: no use asking why they'd had no hope of George, for she knew. He had liked pretty dolls of women, like—like the squire's yellow-haired doxy. But Jonathan! At the thought of him as a husband, she put up her hand across her mouth to hide her laughter. It would be like marrying a mouse to a lion, she thought; but would not say so to Jody. But his own smile broadened; damn him, he had always been able to fathom her thoughts! But when she would almost have smiled back, his face had grown grave again, part hidden by the lock of black hair which had fallen over his eyes. Beneath it, the thin nose and brooding mouth looked grim. There was a part of Jody she would never know. It was like the day, not so long ago, when she had heard pipes and knew he played them: and hadn't disturbed him of purpose.

Suddenly he reached a hand down into his shirt-neck and drew out the talisman. It gleamed dully in the firelight; Jody turned it in his hand.

"This is my mother's wedding ring," he said, "that my father put on her finger before they hanged him."

Norah turned away. "Why show it to me?" She had not previously known of the existence of the ring, or the marriage, if that last was true, but everyone knew Jody was a liar. If it *were* true, then—her mind grasped it quickly—he would think to be heir of Curle, for his father had been the elder brother. "It is not true," Norah's mind dictated to her. She repeated the words aloud, and Jody flushed beneath his dark skin.

"Ay, 'tis true, though they have reared you to believe otherwise. *You* have never thought of me but as a bastard servant, have you, Norah my fine lady? How would it be if the boot were on the other foot, and I claimed my own—yes, it is my own by right—and left *you* landless? But I've a better plan, if ye will listen."

A plan? What did he speak of now? She let him talk, while her fingers tightened spasmodically meantime in the dog's thick coat. The animal raised its head, and gazed at her with shining eyes. He knew who owned Curle, she was thinking; let her but say a word, and Bran would fall on the gipsy and grapple him. Jody still talked of his plan. When Norah made herself heed, she was astonished at the effrontery of it; and yet, in some way, not so. She should have foreseen it; as the squire surely had, to forbid Jody her company lately, except with others present.

"If ye were married to me, it would right the wrong, and keep Curle in the family. With Jonathan as a husband, ye'd be thirled instead to Wraye; the Lady Marchioness, eating your heart out. For ye'll always long for these bleak acres, Norah; nowhere else could ever be your home."

"And nowhere else shall be," she swore, "for I've a right to it."

"That I say ye have not, for I have shown ye the ring."

"A ring? What's a gaudy piece of counterfeit? I'll swear you bought it from a pedlar, and that it is not gold at heart; you have never the money for't."

His face darkened. "I have all that's in Curle coffers and more, if I had what's my right. When I was a child, younger than you ever knew me, I saw the squire cast my mother's marriage-lines in the fire. I know her now; I see her, Norah, often, the times I vanish from here, when she leaves a word or a sign for me, and I go up on to the fells and stay awhile with her, and her people."

"Go and stay for the rest of your life, for all of me. When Curle's mine there will be no place for such as you to set foot in't, lying bastard that ye are, Jody Curle; I know well enough there was no marriage. D'ye think the squire would have given all to me, a woman, if he had a due male heir?" She rose, and shook out her skirts as if to shake his dust from them. "My mother is calling me; I must go." She turned towards the stairs.

"Who's the liar now? No one is calling, nor cares a jot what ye do; nor are ye a woman yet. Come here, and I'll make one of ye." But she had begun to ascend the staircase, heartbeats coming a trifle faster. She told herself it was the climb; the long spiral climb, up to the rooms where Emma was, and farther up, if one would go, to where Maud Curle wandered, secure in her madness from the incursion of the world. Time passed too slowly for some folk, and too fast for others. They would have buried Shawhope by now, Norah was thinking; her grandfather, whether or not he turned aside to Carlisle, would ride home in a day or two. She'd not tell him of Jody's insolence today; it was of no importance, and she herself would forget the more readily if no one else was told.

At Wraye, the funeral was over, and mourners had gone their ways after the wake-feast of spiced meats and wine. Upstairs in the room where he preferred to sit, for he had privacy among his books, the Duke of Wraye faced his new heir, Jonathan. The latter's unremarkable features were half-seen, for he stood with his back to the light; but there was even, the father thought, a sheen of greyness in the colour of his hair and skin. Such a one to live, while George, the hope of his own old age, lay cold in a tomb, his laughter stifled for ever! Jonathan never laughed; he liked books and music; had, no doubt, never fancied a woman or got himself too drunk to stand. Yet these were the faults the old man had loved in his elder son, and almost wished for in his younger. But nothing would change Jonathan now.

The Duke's face, which was that of a tired old eagle, lifted to catch the last of the sunlight coming in at the narrow-paned casement. Soon he, too, would be in the grave. It was imperative, now death had struck his beloved heir so swiftly, to ensure continuance of the line; ay, even to the making of a marriage with Ludovic Curle's black blood, though he had once sworn to have that, and had never obtained it. The old squire, his own old enemy, had ridden off boisterously enough after eating and drinking with the rest. Why, he himself should have killed Curle, if he'd intended it, long years since when the latter had ravished Maud Bellingham and made her marry him against her will. She'd already refused his,

Wraye's, proposal: he'd respected her wish that she should become—her family were Papists—the bride of Christ, no other; and, by God, to think of her instead as the bride of Ludovic Curle, forced to the altar and into bed!

He'd sworn to revenge Maud, as soon as he heard; then hadn't done it; she was already with child to the devil who'd carried her off, and he himself considered all of it, and left it as it was. Considering, planning; too much of that, in cold blood; maybe that was where Jonathan got his clerk's ways. That young man must, now he was the heir, play the man, and wed such as Norah Curle for the sake of speed, for the girl was near at hand, rich, and fit to bear children. "That is all that matters," said the Duke aloud. "You may pursue your separate interests thereafter as you will."

"I—I have an affection for Norah; but it is sooner that of a brother than—" The young man stammered uncertainly; he was not yet, having always lived in the shadow of his splendid brother, used to making decisions of his own. It had not mattered until now, and now . . . he found it difficult to say it, but he knew that he must have some time to reflect, that to enter into a hasty marriage would be inadvisable for the reasons his sire offered. "Sir, I have no wish to disobey you, but—"

"But what? You are the heir now, boy. If aught befalls you there is no one left; title'll die out as it'll do at Curle. Have to see to it; no use delaying such matters. If you're willing, I'll speak to the squire this coming week." Better to speak than write; writing committed one. A civil bargain, sealed over a cup of wine at Curle, while Maud wandered mindless in her rooms abovestairs, knowing neither of his visit nor of anything. "She was beautiful when young," the Duke thought. Was it conceivable that Jonathan—Shawhope he must remember to call him now—and such as Norah Curle could rekindle that beauty out of the blood she bore? Such things happened. If he could see his grandchild with Maud's face and eyes, before death took him, it wouldn't have been in vain, any of it; but Jon—Shawhope—loitered still.

"Do not, I pray you, speak to Sir Ludovic yet, father. Let me have a little space to—to think awhile. I—I would go away, to the south, I believe. One can see more clearly from elsewhere. It—it is not a matter to be settled lightly, and I—"

"Tush, boy, one lass is much as another to you; you're not as y'brother was. But if you wish it, well, then, go; will you ride alone?" Have a care, he was thinking; accidents, as much as fevers, befell young men. He was relieved when the new Shawhope answered, smiling a little.

"I'll ride south with Stroyan. He has—since my brother's death—already bidden me to stay with them all in Surrey. I had intended asking your permission, but—"

"You have it," grunted the old man. He dismissed his son with a brief gesture. If only Jonathan were such a young man as would bring back a bride with riches and breeding from the south, setting aside the need for Norah Curle! Yet the thing would in the end have to be done as he had planned it, he was sure: there was little choice in the north.

5

"I MUST BE carved out of fell rock," thought Norah. "I feel nothing." The mirror was before her again and in its depths she saw, as always, her own broad steady features, the hazel eyes showing no hint of tears. Yet the news which had come today should have sent any marriageable young female sobbing to her room, as Mrs. Emma had herself done on Norah's behalf as a jilted bride. For gossip had it—and when was gossip ever wrong?—that Jon Wraye had met, and promptly betrothed himself to, a penniless young beauty in the south. She was some relative of the Protestant branch of grandmother's family. No one knew anything else about her except that Jon had written to his father of the betrothal and asked his blessing on the marriage, which would take place, it was evident, whether the Duke gave his blessing or his curse. Who would have thought prim Jonathan had it in him so to flout the conventions? "Not I, I swear," Norah told her reflection, and scrubbed at a damp-spot on the glass with one of her square fingers. They didn't keep anything clean abovestairs at Curle. She was beginning to notice it, as well as a great many other things.

She looked at herself again, and found she was frowning. Curle was the only thing she really cared for. Nothing, not Jon's wedding nor George Shawhope's death, nor anything else that had happened, had changed her at all. Even the adult changes that came to women's bodies had happened, naturally and painlessly; she never had trouble with her courses and generally forgot about them till they were upon her. She had large breasts now, bigger than those of most girls of her age; little Madge Beck, who had the miller for sweetheart these days, had stared at them one day and for once said nothing. They didn't meet, she and Madge, so often as formerly. "Our ways have diverged, as mama would put it," said Norah wryly. She herself had no sweetheart, not even Jon if the news were true. How her grandfather would roar when he knew! The squire was less often at Curle of late; no doubt the yellow-haired doxy detained him in town.

As it chanced he rode home that evening, thick brows knitted in wrath as Norah had foreseen; he had called in at Wraye in passing, and was acquainted with the latest tidings, which were of course of Jon's marriage. The bride's name was Amy Bellingham.

"Poor as a church mouse, they say; and dumb as a faggot *you* be," to Norah, who awaited him silently. "Had ye contrived to get y'self some ladylike manners and winning ways, I don't doubt ye might ha' snared Shawhope"—Sir Ludovic still thought of the dead elder brother by this title—"or at worst young Jon. The coffers they say are empty at Wraye, for all the grand title and their new buildin' on; any silver Wraye's sire won, and that was precious little, has gone on't. Well, naught's to be done now, with the knot tied; but guard y'fortin, Norah, lest some hunter wi' pockets to let come here, when I'm gone. I'd fain see ye wed, and look on my great-grandson, ere I go."

"How did the Dowager take it?" said Norah, to divert his mind. He had grown, not infrequently of late, into the habit of wishing for a sight of his great-grandson, and although Norah had become used to hearing him she could still not let the talk flow over her head, as if it were no concern of hers. "It's I myself shall have a say in't," she muttered defiantly. She'd marry, like as not; but it would be for Curle. She didn't grudge Jon Wraye his bride; they could live in their Palladian house and play the spinet. But the squire might hold his tongue. "He'd have me yoked to any man of breeding that crosses our threshold, and they all take fright, and run," she thought, without rancour for she had cared so far for none of them. The one the squire overlooked, David Stroyan, who had no fortune and less name, for everyone knew his folk were only parsons, had visited Curle now several times when the squire's frank talk of matings flowed on unhindered. David had merely smiled quietly, as he had done that day on the moor. He had—how had she ascertained it?—a small portion of his own now, inherited from an uncle in Wiltshire. His blood was good enough, if not distinguished. Norah was the more positive as to this because she knew David in some manner had a feeling for her; it was not— God knew!—love; men didn't feel so for her. Perhaps it was pity. Stroyan was always courteous; his manners had been learnt in the south, and he would offer her his arm as they went in to supper as though it mattered nothing that he was a good head shorter than she. The courtesy was evident in other ways; although David listened to the squire's lewd stories patiently, he related none of his own, and Norah guessed that he was used to less earthy talk, and preferred the other. Although she felt no particular wish to move in his chosen kind of company, Norah knew that it was now quite on the cards that she might marry David Stroyan, lacking anyone else. It was she herself—she herself, with whom the choice in the end must lie—who put off the decision. It was possible there were other folk to be met with than David, others with whom her mind would be more in tune. But this in itself was as far as Norah could see; her mind could not yet embrace the fact of a larger world beyond the valley.

In any event, Jon Wraye as a suitor now was out of the running—or she herself was. The notion of herself married to Jonathan, now that she could dwell on the prospect with ease as it would never occur, made her laugh; they would scarcely have contented one another. She looked down at her own large hands. They could deliver a calf, she knew, though they couldn't stitch aptly; last week on the farms there had been a tricky twin-birth she'd handled for the farmer in a hillside shed. The smell of the new-born beasts mingled with that of fresh hay in Norah's remembrance. That was what she liked best, to be with animals and at peace and do her best for Curle. Later, later, she'd give it an heir.

"Where's Jody?" said the squire suddenly.

"How should I know? You said we were not to keep company. If you want y'boots off, I'll do't." Her voice, as she was beginning to be aware, was pleasant enough; low and a trifle lazy, as though the world amused her. Mama, forever lying on her sofa planning for the future, would frown if she saw her now, pulling off the old man's boots; and at any other time the squire himself would have been angry, saying it was no fit task for the lady of Curle. "They can't make up their minds, either of them," thought Norah suddenly, adding for no reason, "the present is enough for me."

She straightened, still with the boots in her hand, as Jody came through the doorway. He came straight over and took them from her, saying he would lay them by. A shiver went through Norah; what was it about Jody that made her feel nowadays that a cat had walked over her grave? He and she would meet by chance in the stables, saddling their mounts or watering them, if the groom were elsewhere; and that was all. Why, then, should it seem tonight as though his presence—not her own or Sir Ludovic's, seated there in his hose—were the chief one in the hall?

．　　．　　．　　．　　．

Jody set the boots down and advanced slowly. All at once the other things, to which she had been accustomed all her life, grew less important, and withdrew into the shadows; the great portrait of her grandfather as a young man; the oaken dresser that had sword-cuts on it from the Civil Wars when Cromwell's men had ridden into Curle to seek the squire's grandfather, who by then was well hidden from their sight; and the long refectory-table, which had belonged to the nearby Abbey before King Harry's men sacked it and gave the lands and revenues to a Curle; all these receded. She was left looking at Jody, or rather at a figure like him that had suddenly grown taller. He no longer wore even the mask of humility. The firelight played over his features, showing them to be those of a Curle. He might, tonight, have been a younger, darker, more lissome version of the gross old squire himself, staring over now as he was from his familiar place by the hearth. As if to give voice to the things which made up Curle, which belonged to the Curle of everyday, a log fell, scattering its soft ash along the stones. Jody did not bend, as he would in the ordinary way have done, to mend the fire. Instead, he spoke. His voice came clearly in the silence. He faced both the girl and her grandfather, so that his words could be heard equally by both.

"I heard the news from Wraye. It makes no odds; why don't you listen to me? I can give Norah a son, if you'll let me marry her."

Silence: in her own heart, with its beats coming slowly now and carefully. Silence; then Sir Ludovic's loud laugh. Jody's mouth grew hard; he thrust his hands in his pockets, as though not to be seen clenching them.

"It would atone, would it not, for what you did to my mother? I'm your true heir. If I marry Norah—"

Why had he spoken so wild a thing? With the squire's laughter, all things were back again in their places they had by day. Sir Ludovic was still laughing, as though he were full of wine. He heaved his great body round to face his grandson.

"Do ye think to make mock of me," he said, "for all I've given ye and done? Get out of my sight, nor come back again till all's as it should be in y'mind, ye fool. A servant bastard, and to speak of wedding Norah Curle? A toss i' the hay wi' the maids is what ye should be at; go after it."

Jody still stayed. "It'd be a favour to her," he said, choosing his words carefully. "She's not for most men; and she'd as soon not leave Curle."

The squire's face was contorted. "By God, man grown as ye are, I'll take my stick to your sides, ye gipsy's get, ye." He reached for his cane; it swathed through the air. Jody ducked to avoid it. He still spoke quietly. "It is time we talked as between men, not as a child and a man. I am the true heir of Curle. My mother was married to my father, as you know well." He reached in his bosom and drew out the gold ring. "This she left me; it was hers, and he put it on her finger. Did ye suppose, squire, that even a child such as I was the night I came has no eyes in his head, to have seen the burning of her marriage-paper? She had told me already what it was; and who I was. Ay, all these years, when at times I've been your boon companion, set with tutors and the like too late, and at other times your servant to pull off your boots—all the time, I've remembered. I am no servant, but your heir; and can prove it if I must. Let me wed Norah, and no more shall be said of proof. Will not our son be a Curle, and doubly so? Whey-faced Stroyan will never make the boy on her that I will."

"Be silent, ye havering cantrip!" yelled the squire. "Must I break the nose on y'face before I have silence on't? It shall not be, I say; it shall never be. No gipsy beds with a Curle in any house of mine."

He half rose; in the resulting moment of quiet, it was Norah herself who spoke.

"Am I nothing in this matter but a cow or a mare, to be mated with?" she said. "I am the true heir; Curle's mine, or will be, and I'll wed no low-born person. Hear that, Jody Curle, for what y'are; whether it's tent or house for ye, it will never be Curle. For I'll not do as ye say; I'll never do't."

Afterwards she wondered what had made her say all of it. It was not courage, for this she knew she always had; the sound of two men quarrel-ing wouldn't turn her blood to whey. She'd never cried when beaten, as a child, or when the pony stood on her hand once, as she'd stopped to pick up a fallen bit of harness; the hand had been swollen for a month, but she never complained or had it dressed, or feared horses thereafter. Nothing made her afraid; then why was she so against marrying Jody? It was the cool, cautious voice of Mrs. Emma in her, speaking like a lady. Already she regretted it. If the chance came again—

"Get out o'here," said Sir Ludovic thickly, "pests that ye both are, I'll—"

Quite suddenly he toppled sideways, falling back on to his hearth-bench. His face had grown black with suffused blood; his mouth was agape. Sounds began to come from him which were like snoring. Norah ran to him and lifted his head.

"Fetch wine," she said curtly to Jody, as though the servant he had lately denied being stood there. He turned on his heel and went out. Norah was left with the weight of her grandfather in her arms, waiting till someone should come. She cursed Jody, and mingled with her curses were difficult tears for the old squire. Would he die, and if so—it didn't matter about Curle—who would be left to take her part in a thousand ways, pamper her, swear at her, laugh at the things she'd done which shocked her mother? His big filly, he'd always called her. That, and his heir. He hadn't denied her tonight and sold her to Jody to seal the black bargain. He—

The servants came running. Jody must have summoned them. Between them they carried Sir Ludovic to his bed. Later she was able to go up and see him, alive still, lying in the shadow of the great tester with its escutcheon of a bear in faded gilt, the bear of Siward. He was grey-faced now, for the physician had come and had bled him. He seemed weak, but himself again. He knew her.

"That's you, Norah, is it, my lass? Bend closer here, so that all may not hear what I'd say."

She went to him, and bent so close across the pillows that her young, smooth face almost touched him; their thick hair mingled. A stranger couldn't tell which was his hair and which mine, Norah was thinking. We are alike in many things, the squire and I. If only I'd been a man—

"Hear this, Norah, I'd have ye wed, and soon: but not to Jody. Get David Stroyan in your bed as soon as may be; he'll serve well enough, and ye'll always be a woman of your own will, your own way; few men could ever rule ye."

"*You* can, grandfather." She felt tender and gentle towards him, the old devil, now he was ill. Even as she thought of it she heard Sir Ludovic chuckle.

"Not I, and none knew it better than I or you: ye have the devil's own will, Norah. Power I've left ye; much power, much land, much gold will be yours, for a woman. Don't squander it on some good-for-nowt who'll gamble all away on cards and wenching, in London; marry Stroyan, as I bade ye. He's not to your misliking, hey? He'll do no harm."

"How can I tell?" She hadn't thought of David Stroyan more than half a dozen times, and never with either liking or hate. He was a whey-faced thing, no doubt, as Jody had said, but Jody . . .

She got up meantime from beside the bed. "Give me a week or two to think on't, grandfather. I'd sooner wait till you're well."

"I'll never be better, maybe. I would not leave this world knowing that that rapscallion was lying in wait for ye, and for Curle. Give me an heir such as I hoped for when ye were born, Norah, do't before I die." He struggled upwards on his pillows, and she knew fear at the ghastly colour of his face by candlelight, with the tiny broken veins seeming livid against the pallid skin. If he died—if grandfather died before she'd given him what he wished—

"Do you live another week," she told him gruffly, in the manner they used to one another. "I—I would be alone a while to think of it; I'll ride out, maybe, tomorrow on the moors, and later bring word." She laughed suddenly. "Has David asked for me?" she said. "Such an offer will maybe surprise him. I'd not be made a fool of in the matter, y'hear?"

"I hear well enough," grunted Sir Ludovic. "The devil was never as obstinate as a woman. Leave me now, and I'll sleep; douse the candle, there's a good lass; and tell me when you may. Stroyan won't baulk at it, I warrant; he's got a widowed mother in the south, and little means, but the name's sound; d'ye reckon I'd have had him twice over the doorstep here, had it been other? I've watched for ye, child, as though . . . as though ye were the lad ye are not. Give me what I ask, and soon."

Norah felt the candle's flame singe her fingers as she put it out, not quickly enough. She was not adept at such finicking things, she knew. She went away sucking her burnt finger, and trying to think of David Stroyan; but try as she might the only features that came to her were Jody's, as he had looked tonight beside the fire. Tomorrow, how would he seem to her? What would the pair of them say, when they met, maybe, in the stable, between Barley and the Cleveland bay?

But by the morrow Jody was gone, on one of his absences. He must have gone out into the night soon after Sir Ludovic had had his seizure, by the fire. No one knew or cared which way he might have journeyed; in the bustle that had followed, none took heed of Jody.

He had climbed up to the high places among the fells, where his mother's people were for a season. He took his lithe body slowly across the turf which separated him from the painted caravans. His mother's, where she lived with Jacob Smith her husband, was wine-dark with yellow wheels. A pony cropped the turf, with some of the men guarding it. They eyed Jody and nodded to him in silence; he was not an enemy, yet, they knew, still not one of themselves. They would, in necessity, shelter him; this he was aware of, for at sundry times, when he and the squire disagreed, he had taken advantage of their shelter till the squire's anger spent itself. He knew he could count on their loyalty, if not their friendship. He shrugged, and went on. He did not need friends.

His mother was in her place, making pegs. He went and sat by her and watched her long brown fingers intent on their task. Jacob was nowhere to be seen at this time; he would be out poaching, to bring home hares or chickens for the night meal. An aroma of cooked meat and herbs still hung about the stopping-place, where ashes littered the ground. The gipsies lived well and seldom went hungry.

Abigail turned her bright eyes upon him; they were the brighter for the loss of her teeth, which nowadays made her face leap out at the high cheek-bones and compress the mouth by contrast to nothing. But she smiled a little, and nodded. This was the son of the man she had loved in such a way as no Romany woman should do; the man's death had been just but she had wept when it had happened. She hugged the knowledge to herself that Jody was the most precious thing she would ever have; she was glad that she had borne no children to her second husband. She knew instinctively that something was amiss with Jody, and waited till he should tell her of it. Meantime she appraised him, this tall son of her love. He was not like his father, except for the eyes, and he did not easily wear the clothing of his father's people. "He is as much one of us as one of them," Abigail told herself, "although it will anger both him and them to tell him of it." So she said nothing. Presently Jody turned to her and spoke, looking down at the pegs and fingering one of them.

"I may need help."

Abigail nodded. If she asked it for him, aid would be forthcoming from the tribe; they could send word swiftly across the fells, more swiftly than the gorgios' horses brought news. And they knew the country like a hand's palm. It did not matter when or where Jody needed the help; it would come.

"It will be given," she said.

Jody laughed suddenly. "You are like the powers of God," he said, "you never question, never pause, and are—certain." Had they, so certainly, closed in for the hanging of his father, and gone their ways again afterwards in silence and so swift the squire's men could never catch them?

Abigail crossed herself; inside the caravan was an icon they had always carried, and at Easter candles were lit and there was a festival. "If you tempt God, the evil will recoil on you," she told him. "You think too much of your own power."

He thought of Norah Curle, and how she denied power to him; and the squire also. An ugly smile curled his lips. "I must keep a high opinion of myself," he said, "since no one else will." He did not tell her that they had again called him bastard at Curle; he knew that would trouble her. But she guessed at the cause of his own trouble and spoke of it.

"They will not have you for bridegroom, then." There was no surprise in her voice, not even indignation. She was unable to understand his longing to possess Curle, or any house or land. But he was as he was, her son.

"They will not have me tied to Norah by the church, so I must do without it."

Her calm eyes surveyed him. "Do you mean to ravish her?"

"Maybe."

"That will bring trouble to you and to us. Need it be so? There are other women."

"But only one Curle. That I desire above all else in life or death. If I should need help, after—"

"I have said that you shall have it. Will you stay here tonight?"

"Tonight, and maybe tomorrow and the day after that."

She nodded; one day more or less made no difference, and the months confused themselves with years as in the old stories and a visit could be any length. It did not matter. Her son knew what it was that he would do, and when to do it. The rest would be decided in time.

6

TO PLEASE THE SQUIRE, Norah agreed to allow her betrothal to David Stroyan to be made known when he should return from the south. He had written her one letter from his home in Surrey, and although it contained no loverlike phrases, merely describing the weather and the country and mentioning, in passing, that Jonathan and his bride were making a honeymoon journey into Italy, Norah knew no qualms. The thing would be settled, she knew, less by herself and David than by their families; on David's side, a widowed mother who would be only too delighted to accept the overtures of the squire and Mrs. Emma.

It was, therefore, as her betrothed that David at last came north by coach, bringing his mother with him. This lady's appearance took Norah by surprise a little. Mrs. Stroyan was of medium height, and unremarkable features; but her clothes were in the last extreme of fashion and her hair powdered even by day, and she lost no time in boasting that she had met the Queen herself, and had attended bluestocking receptions in Portman Square, held on one auspicious occasion in a room which was lined with feathers. Feathers, thought Norah, seemed to stuff the good lady's head, for all of her speech was made up of affected utterances and she considered herself very learned. However she expressed due satisfaction over her prospective daughter-in-law, and told Mrs. Emma that she was certain dear Norah had parts which might be turned to her advantage, for it was no longer the place of a woman to be only a housekeeper and mother. Mrs. Emma, too indolent to express any opinion, smiled vaguely; Norah herself, after initial indignation, was diverted. What else might she do that was not connected with the daily care of Curle and the bearing of its heirs?

"You must come to London," said her future mother-in-law, but would not commit herself to the extent of promising to present Norah at Court; in fact, she had not the status to do so. Norah shelved the subject, which did not interest her greatly, and gave her immediate attention to a matter which concerned her far more; Madge Beck's marriage, in a white satin bonnet and veil, to her handsome miller, George Yonge, who despite being the finest man in the village was rumored to have a weak chest. But nothing could mar Madge's happiness nor the delight the newly wed couple took in one another. "I shall bake the new flour George has milled, and sell it to the folk who are too idle to make their own bread," said Madge pertly, and Norah made a mental note to send her a tithe-note if she did. Any money made in the valley must return a portion of it to Curle; such had been the case since early times, and because Madge and she were old friends would be no reason for allowing the latter to ease out of payment. At the same time Norah was aware of a wistful certainty that bliss such as had come to the young pair, and still rested on them like a halo, would never be her own. She was not in love with David Stroyan, nor he with her. At least they could be honest with one another regarding it; but her own difference from the everyday lovers of this world came to her strongly and with a bitterness it had not held since the days of Caro and Amelia and the riding-party on the moor. She was different from other young women, that was all; different. Best accept it.

Norah did not admit to herself that this troubled her also: there had been no further sign nor word, since he departed that night weeks since, from Jody. He had vanished as if he had never been at Curle. None of his earlier absences had lasted as long.

Often she would look over, from the window which gave on to them from her own chamber, at the fells. By night they would loom dark and forbidding, with here and there a yellow light shining out, like a star, as folk kindled their lamps on the lonely farms. Already Norah knew each farm and how many acres it held, and what the tenant did with his days, and how many children he had and who his wife had been before her marriage. It was, would be her duty to know such things. But the fells, she was certain, also held Jody. It was impossible to picture his being otherwhere than in or above the valley. He was a creature of it, in the same way as she herself was. So now that he had gone, she could remember a thousand things, deeds, sayings they had had together since her babyhood, his childhood. She had been nearer him and her grandfather than ever her father or mother, the former of course having died too soon for Norah to have known him. But her mother never spoke of John Curle, and when Sir Ludovic did so, it was sparingly, without curses upon the name of the dead, true enough, but with no blessing either. Her sire must have been, when all was said, a shadow of the old squire himself, perhaps less. What soul at Curle, or in the valley either, but fell within that same shadow?

While he had been ill, she'd had foreknowledge of the immense change there would be, in all things, when the old man was dead; but within days he had rallied, and by now was journeying almost weekly over to see his mistress again in Carlisle, but in his coach, no longer astride the Cleveland bay. Norah grinned. It was like them both, she and her grandfather, that the kind of horse most folk used for carriage-work suited them best for riding. She recalled the high words there had been, between herself and Sir Ludovic, the day she first asked him to break up a coach-pair, well matched, so that she herself might ride one.

"Break a matched pair? Ye are wood-mad, woman; ride Barley, that ye plagued me for long since, and got."

"Barley's too short in the leg for me now. I need a tall mount, like yourself. Do you take one, and give me t'other; that will cut out the need for any coach." That had been before the old man took ill.

He had given her the Cleveland bay in the end, of course, with much cursing, and the cut from his cane that she'd long ago learnt to avoid; it meant, Norah knew by now, no more than a raised arm pretending a blow that never came. She'd got to know his ways, the old squire, and he hers; they'd grumbled along comfortably enough together, neither Mrs. Emma upstairs nor, in these past weeks, David Stroyan coming between them. David had brought himself, correctly enough, to signify his pleasure and his mama's at the betrothal; the wedding date was still to be arranged. It was left to Norah to select a date for it, but so far she had not done so, putting off from day to day as Sir Ludovic rallied. The fact was, she herself admitted, that this prospect of childbearing irked her; nor did she want to lose her freedom to go where she would, nor ever have a moment when she might be alone.

"She is very beautiful," said David Stroyan regarding Jonathan's bride: but he said it as if he were describing a flower he had noted and described in one of the botany-lists he kept, and Norah was not jealous. The bride must be, she had already decided, a designing minx; for tongue-tied Jon, marquis or no, could be ready prey for such. Norah suggested as much to Stroyan; and was surprised to see him flush like a girl, as though he were almost—and for one of his gentle nature this was rare—angry at her implication.

"Amy Bellingham is the sweetest creature who ever lived. She would never act to her own advantage; rather against it, for she has done countless good deeds for others, although her family have no money."

"If you would be rid of me for having it, and for doing no good with it, you have only to say so."

He submitted at once. "You do a great deal of good, Norah, for you do your duty. I have heard of the way you ride about the farms and help there, and—and you are kind to your grandfather."

"Kind to the squire!" She suppressed a yelp of laughter; would David ever get to know them? "He takes no reck of kindness, of that you may be sure." She heard her own voice, with surprise, grow less broad in the vowels when she talked to Stroyan; with the squire it was still as it had been with Jody, in the accents of the valley.

"Everyone on earth needs kindness at some time," he replied.

Norah swerved away from the subject. "Tell me more of this Bellingham relative who has wed Jon Shawhope. How did the Duke take it, eh? I'll wager he was not pleased with a bride with empty coffers, for they need money at Wraye. The old Dowager will have had something to say of that."

"At first he—the Duke—was angry, but when he knew the bride was Amy Bellingham he professed himself glad, and wished them much joy. What the Dowager said I have no notion."

Bellingham, Norah was thinking. Why should a kinship to her grandmother please the Duke? She asked David Stroyan, but he knew nothing of any reason, and merely repeated what he had said before about the goodness and beauty of the new Marchioness. "I swear I shall dislike the creature when she comes here, if she is such a sugar doll," thought Norah, and yawned behind her hand. David, seeing nothing, added unforgivably that the new Lady Shawhope was also extremely accomplished. "She can play the harpsichord very well, and sing, and is a graceful dancer."

"So much for me. I can do none of those things."

"But you can listen," said David, and of his own accord kissed her. Norah was not displeased, although the contact of his lips against her cheek affected her little enough. She turned away and forbore to ask when Jon Shawhope and his bride were returning north.

It was bad enough coming from Stroyan, but worse when Mrs. Emma repeated everything Norah had already heard about the new bride. Norah held her tongue, however, and contented herself with shrugging her shoulders; should one more small, exquisite and accomplished creature in the countryside alter her own set ways, alarm her, or else cause her to shed, at this date, jealous tears at not having captured either Shawhope brother on her own account? "I need not trouble with titles, with the name I bear," Norah boasted to herself in a way she had not done, nor had to do, since she was a child. It was the kind of thing the squire had used to tell her when she was small enough to sit at his feet, and listen to tales of the Curles and how they were better than anyone, as even the Norman conquerors had had to admit, by the end, long ago.

It must have been thoughts of the Norman submission that caused Norah to think, now, after many years, again of Churl's Leap. This was a rock-face of such incredible steepness and inaccessibility that it was said even now to be only possible to be climbed by a Curle: and that it was none other than the Churl, or Carle, who had first made his escape over it from the armies of William Rufus, who had blinded and castrated the other fighting men of the valley who fell into their hands. But Norah's ancestor had scaled the steep climb, and had leaped the wide gully between it and the neighbouring rock, and had survived to build Curle Hall and beget heirs. Sir Ludovic in his hot youth had himself achieved the climb; her own tame father, John, had never done it; and the blood raced in Norah's veins now, daring her, a woman to essay the climb, if not the leap.

"It will be my last act of freedom," she told herself fiercely. "Who will deny it to me? After this I'll be a married woman, trammelled with duties, pregnant as a cow." She would go tomorrow, she told herself often: and then the day would dawn and with it other reasons why she should not go. For the best reason of all, that she knew he would forbid it her, Norah did not mention Churl's Leap to her grandfather. But the notion gained credence in her mind, and by now—she would be David's wife soon—it seemed to Norah that it must be done, and should be; she would do it, taking Barley for he knew the fells; and none should stop her in the carrying out of her will.

Sir Ludovic sent for his granddaughter next day. He was half stretched on his settle, and pouches of debauchery had begun to appear beneath his eyes and about his mouth, in the light of day. He roared at Norah "Well? When's the wedding-date to be? Ye can't make a fool of the man now, and of me also; by God, if ye do not name the day I will do't, and devil take the hindmost! Do ye think to make mock of me, girl? I swear—"

"Damn you and your swearing, I'll name it when I choose," blazed Norah suddenly. "D'you take me for a brood-mare? That's all I am to you, or have ever been. Never fear, I'll name you a day, and you can invite all the gentry, and Shawhope and his new bride, and the Duke, and get some pipers. A fine fool's sight I'll make in a white gown and veil." Her eyes grew sullen.

He brushed that aside. "When, then? When?" he said impatiently. "When will ye name the day, Norah? I feel a sinking in me that I will not live to see my heir-male; would ye let me die forsaken, child? There was never a wish ye had I denied ye; when I ask for this one thing, ye toss your head and put off, and have the vapours, like any fool female."

"I've never had the vapours in m'life, as you'll know well. I will tell the date tomorrow. Today I want to be left alone."

"Where? In your chamber?"

"No, I'll ride Barley out on to the moors: tell them to fetch me a bite to eat in a saddle-bag." She was, for no man knew what reason, ettling to be gone. It would be a fine day, with long cloud-shadows driven over the fells, but no rain; not unlike the day long ago when David Stroyan had sat by her peering at a butterfly. Why the devil think of Stroyan now? He'd be here by night and day soon enough.

She rode out an hour later, clad in her oldest habit, bare-headed, with her thick curls blown back by the wind from her face. Seen thus, she had perhaps for the first time a kind of beauty, massive and unchanging as the carven beauty of the hills. She cantered out on Barley until the fell path was reached, then walked him evenly up to the farther heights, with Curle already out of sight.

Churl's Leap was seven miles on, well into the trackless places made by the jagged scarps of bare rock. There was no life to be met with here, except the unnatural butterwort that fed on flies. Norah ignored its beckoning purple flower, drooped head and sickly yellow leaves. She was staring ahead of her at the Leap, seen from this height like a jutting pillar. The gully across which the Saxon had long ago leapt was sharp from here, like a giant's knifecut, before the rock-faces began to appear in formation again. A haze of heat, from the afternoon sun, turned the shadows blue among them, behind one another, making phantom shapes where no shapes were.

Norah came to the place, and left Barley. There were no trees to which to tie him here, or turf for him to crop. "Wait," said Norah, to him, and knew he would be there when she returned. Barley and she understood one another; that was one reason why she hadn't brought the big Cleveland bay, used as it was to coachroads. There were thing here that had been, and would be, long after roads had come and gone. She was alone with the primal creation of the world, the rocks themselves.

She ascended the path. It wound at first steeply, starred with light gravel-grains, then gave way to pits and hollows in the mother rock. Soon she was grasping outcrops, setting her foot in crevices, helped only by one hand; the other had to hold aside her skirts. Damn skirts! Why had a woman to be thus trammelled? The sweat started to run into Norah's eyes, with the sun hot upon her; her own heavy hair and the thick stuff of the habit she wore made the ascent worse than for a man. The challenge itself stirred her. If she could say, even to herself, that she'd climbed the Leap unaided, clad as she was, then she was a Curle indeed, and as good as any man of them! She smiled against the sun; if the squire saw her now, or knew where she was, he'd curse till the roof-beams shook. "But I care nothing," Norah told herself. She climbed on; and by now had to stop, every few moments, to regain her breath; the heat and height made her dizzy.

The old Saxon had in his time climbed to a place where the jutting of the scarp above was beyond the lower, like jostling narrow houses in a town's streets. Norah reached upwards, and set her mind firmly on the goal she had sworn to attain; it had been done before, she wouldn't falter now! Yet the act of bearing backwards, setting her body's balance against the devices of the devil's pillar, jarred her; what if she should fall, having tripped over her own fool's clothing? They would take a month to find her here, by which time the crows would have made a fine meal. Fear? No, she, Norah Curle, was not afraid . . . yet now she'd reached a place where she could neither venture upward, nor go back.

A hand reached out above her then; and grasped her wrist. In the instant's incredulous terror she felt Norah hung, with all the weight of her body, an instant from the gripping hand, and had it let go her wrist, she would have fallen. Then she returned the grasp, and allowed herself to be levered upwards, while still the sun grilled down from a sky that had become much nearer . . .

"Set your foot in the crevice to the right," said Jody. "That's it; and don't look down."

Gasping, sobbing now for breath, she had to let him aid her up to the topmost place on the pillar, a flat space, hollowed out a little as though by some monstrous hand. Norah saw it open before her eyes as if it were made of the strange substance of a dream; she sank down upon it as if uncertain whether it would give way and swallow her up, like lava, or retain its form.

But it was hard, and hot; she felt the heat through her clothes. Then another thing changed from unreality to fact, as her exhausted body told her. Suddenly, in the instant she had lain down upon the rock, the sky changed to contain only Jody. There was nothing in earth or heaven but Jody, bearing down upon her like a great bird, with wings outspread. Then there was the weight of Jody, a hard determined force, unyielding as the rock on which she lay, and purposeful, which the rock was not. Jody thrust; soon he was all about her, within her; soon there was nothing in the world or in her body which was not Jody, and she could hear her own sobbing cry as he entered the core of her, the place none yet knew of, which she had not herself known to exist, while his weight did not diminish.

There had been instants when space and time and every other dimension and all worlds had been herself and Jody, only their two selves become one, strangely, inevitably. It was as though—even afterwards she admitted that it had been so—for that time he was herself, and she him. They had no words then. Later, words came. She heard him speaking, answering a question she must herself have asked though she could not remember it. Her eyes were closed; the sun still grilled down on the rock.

"How did I know you would come? I knew: and I watched from the fells. I waited, Norah, patiently. Now that you are mine they cannot give you to any other."

They must have separated by then, for Norah was again aware of herself, and of resentment; what did he mean about waiting? His tribe must have spied on her. Deep anger grew in her, and the thirst for revenge, even before he himself had finally left her body. He should pay, the gipsy: pay for having ravished her, a Curle. To force her when she was weary after climbing up a rock . . . "I would have fought him off, otherwise," Norah told herself. To him, she was silent. If she waited, some plan would form. It was necessary to be patient, lest Jody become aware of her planning.

He took her again. This time it was more as a lover of everyday, certain of possession. He called her love-names; his queen, his goddess, Ceres. "How could you think to wed that little southron man?" he said to her. Norah's mind remained aloof and cool. I shall wed whom I choose, she was thinking; I shall not wed *you*. She would kill him, if she could, she was thinking, when he'd finally rolled, sated, off her. This high rock . . .

She had to wait; and when at last the chance came he was on his feet again, standing with his back turned, looking out over the hills which cradled Curle. He is thinking, she told herself, that he has it now, all of it; the house, and myself, the heir. So sure of her, a Curle, and she the only heir, not he, ever . . .

She did not subsequently remember the doing of the thing. She must have made herself twist about and upwards, suddenly, still with disarranged clothing; and grasped him below the calves; then with one great thrust she sent him hurtling over the slope, down the rock-face. For some moments after he had vanished from sight she stayed where she was, sick and faint; then she staggered to her knees. There was, she found, blood on the rock, and on her skirt. It was her own. She staunched the bleeding as best she could with her linen and later crawled, cautiously, to the place where Jody had gone over, and when she still could see nothing lay down again flat on the rock, head craned over the gully. There he lay, far below; his body was tumbled in an awkward way, and his face turned from her. Norah did not know whether or not he was dead. She found a stone, of the size of a great loaf; some lay about, but one should be enough, and would crush him. She made herself get to her feet, and lifted the stone with both hands and hurled it down. It struck Jody where he lay, causing a spurt of blood to gush up from his head, then this subsided and trickled, growing thick and slow in the sun's heat. Presently, she thought, the flies would come. The thought itself brought horror.

Norah fled then. Afterwards she did not know how she had contrived it, unsteady as she was, or what had helped her down: down the jutting rock-formations, each one like a phallus which had lately entered to her hurt, so that it seemed now as if she must have been deflowered by ancient gods, not any man, and her body began to throb with pain at last, like an awakened wound. When she had reached the flat level again, with shaking knees, she found a place to clean herself, and rubbed and rubbed again with her linen, now drenched with blood and dirt. She'd wash it herself, in case the servants gossiped. No one must see, or know; no one.

Barley was waiting. They'd ride downward, the two of them, till they found a beck and she'd wash herself meantime in that, as much as she might; and give the pony a drink, he'd waited well and patiently. Ordinary things began to crowd in again; there were the Hall chimneys jutting above the rise, as though it were . . . how long? since she'd left, surely only a matter of hours . . .

No one should know of what had happened. Norah left Barley in the field, for he was grazing out for the summer; she couldn't remember taking the saddle off him, or hanging it in his stall. Then she crept upstairs to her own chamber, and took off her garments and cleansed what she could in the ewer, and what she couldn't would have to be burnt somehow in the fire.

No one should know. Norah stared at herself in the mirror, saw her unchanged face flushed a little with the sun and the climb, and smoothed her hair. She'd put on another gown, and presently would go down and face her grandfather. Unhurried, that was it; the warm lazy voice that mama had told her was a worldly asset should drawl, now, the news the old squire had wanted to hear; that she'd marry David Stroyan, for as he had often said they'd better get it over and done with; within the month, it must be. She would insist on that.

They brought Jody home.

They had found him in the place where he had not lain many hours, for little can happen on the fells but such folk know of it soon. They drove off the flies that feasted on the drying blood and, later, cleansed and bound up the wound with herbal unguent. It was not easy to know what bones were broken; they would leave it till he was conscious, and could tell them. Later they found that he was bruised only. The bruises, gigantic and already black, covered almost his whole body; but they would heal. The eye would not. It was put out, and the socket about it so suffused with blood and bruising that there might have been splinters of bone there, but none knew yet and it was better not to ferret after them. Time would better Jody, for he had been young and strong and his mother would nurse him well.

She was waiting for them when they carried him back, four of them making slings of their arms, purveying the dead weight evenly between them though there were not often such tasks to do. It was their pride that they were too quick for the gorgio, but the gorgio had done this to Jody;

and at that a woman, for they knew of her as they know all such things. For once, in any case, Abigail betrayed herself when she fell upon Jody's hurt body, crying in a high keening wail as she had not done for his father.

"*She* did this! Norah Curle did, and has killed my son!"

"He is not dead." It was George Smith's voice, the brother of Jacob himself who had been too old to go. His tone was contemptuous and dry. "He will be better. Give it time, woman. You must nurse him and give him broth and wine." They had brandy ready in flasks, brought from France; that might be better, but Abigail stood up and flashed at them "Will ye tell me what to do? Can I not aid my own son? He shall not die, I say. *She* shall not take him, living or dead, again, save in her soul." And she bade them bring Jody into her sleeping-place and set him down on Jacob's pallet, where he lay still. All that night she sat by him, and when his lips opened and he moaned fed spirit into them, and later broth when he could eat. It all took a long time; Abigail could not tell how long, and he took a fever, and shivered with cold when it was summer's heat beyond the door, and then in the cold of the night woke in a sweat. He asked for nothing; but once when she called to him to find out if he had everything he might want, she saw the ravaged face twist in a smile.

"I took her, mother. She may bear a son who is mine."

His voice was no more than a whisper, but she heard it clearly. Tears shone in her eyes and she drew her sleeve across them. "Never heed that," she said, "get yourself better, Jody." She had accustomed herself to look at the seamed cavern which had been his eye; the place was healing. Soon he could wear a patch. What would he do then? Where would he go? "Wherever he goes," she thought, "folk'll know him by it, a patch."

She lifted her fists to the sky to curse Norah Stroyan, who would have killed her son and had maimed him.

7

PREPARATIONS FOR THE WEDDING moved apace, but as the small army of sempstresses who had been called to Curle were fitting and making Norah's wedding gown, word came from Wraye that the Duke had died in his sleep. Mrs. Emma, who had had a fondness of her half-brother, was moved to come downstairs feebly wailing and wringing her hands. The marriage could not take place, she declared; it would not yet be seemly.

"It will go on," said the bride. "What's it to us that Wraye's dead? Women don't attend funerals, you always tell me." She stared towards her mother with the mixture of apparent insolence and contempt that had increased, Emma decided, since the announcement that Norah would marry Stroyan. The match was not, in anyone's view, good enough for the Curle heiress, but who ever consulted the heiress's mother? "The squire and she do all their own way, and it has been thus almost since the day I gave her birth," thought Emma resentfully. Aloud she said "It will be proper, at least, for you to accompany me to pay a visit of condolence to the Dowager at Wraye."

Norah had no objections; she was weary of standing still for the sewing-women with their mouths full of pins.

At Wraye, the Duke lay in state almost in solitude, guarded by retainers but few kin. It would not be possible for the new Duke and Duchess to return from Italy in time for the funeral, although it would be expected that they hurry home with all haste once word should have come. The Dowager Duchess herself, stricken by a palsy which angered her the more in that it was now barely possible for her to enter her ancient, lumbering coach in search of gossip, lay painted and raddled as ever on her day-sofa, in purple mourning. She surveyed Norah briefly as that young woman made her curtsy after her mother. "Be seated, both; ay, I knew I'd see Wraye out. He waited but to hear tell of the Bellingham marriage, then made ready to die happy: which is more than I'll do myself, with not a ha'porth of dowry alongside the bride. However 'tis like enough you yourselves prefer to talk of bridals now than funerals."

Her eyes, the left lid drooping with the palsy, surveyed the Curle bride and her shy, slight betrothed, who had come with them in the coach. Stroyan would never serve that great wench, the Dowager was thinking; yet there was some change in Norah Curle since she'd last set eyes on her, some malign thing; the hazel eyes stared unfathomably, the features were more than ever strong, as though carved out of rock. Certain it was that the girl was not in love with Stroyan, or perhaps with anyone except herself. Love was difficult to picture as occurring to such as Norah Curle. "For the guineas she'd have brought, I'd as lief either George or Jon had taken her, but as for her nature, it would never have been tamed; there would have been a daily battle of tongues among us," the old woman thought, half regretting its absence now; she relished few things more than a good set-to with words, and maybe a stick. But those days were done now, and all she herself was fit to do amounted only to this, lying forever on a sofa and having a chamber-pot brought, and the servants not heeding her as they'd been used while she was active and her stepson Wraye alive. But one thing the Dowager was certain of; Norah Curle, say what they liked, was no maiden. Would it be that Stroyan was to blame, and was that the reason for such haste about the marriage? The Dowager doubted it; but for once held her tongue in presence of Emma. They exchanged the usual courtesies, with young Norah yawning mean-time behind her hand; then they departed in their coach. Perhaps Jon and his bride would be home in time for the wedding, if not the funeral. That a Bellingham should reign at Wraye presented the old woman, if not her dead stepson, with certain misgivings. Maud Bellingham in her day had been a sweet creature, certainly, but now she was crazed. The cause of it met with no sympathy in the Dowager's musings. A woman of spirit put up with whatever life might send, and didn't try to escape to a convent or, when that was prevented, to the retreat of madness. Life was good, and she herself had, when all was said, savoured it to the full. In such ways she was perhaps akin to Norah Curle herself who was, incredibly, Maud's granddaughter . . . "Well, the matter will play itself to a finish once she's wed. I wonder how they will fare?" There was some word of a pipe-band, Emma had said today, and that they might as well dance to it at the wed-ding. Such things became speedily available when there was word of a marriage; the gipsies would have carried the news over the hills.

The guests for the wedding had meantime begun to travel north. Caro and Amelia, still both single although the latter considered herself virtu-ally betrothed to a clergyman in Wiltshire, accompanied David Stroyan's mother north in the coach; the talk was suitably elevating, enabling both young women to forget their chagrin that clumsy, speechless, provincial Norah should be the first of all to marry. "It is the money, of course; poor David!" was in the thoughts of the company, but no one spoke of it; curi-osity was the more excited by the identity of a nearby couple in a swifter-travelling coach. "It had a coat of arms on the door, but went by us so fast I had not time to decipher it," said David's mother, who was short-sighted. Caro shrugged inside her travelling-cloak and, as usual, wondered if the wedding would mean the appearance of any presentable unmarried men; the groomsman, one had heard, was Corder Bellingham, but of course *he* —But there would doubtless be others.

Curle came in sight on the afternoon of the following day; all three ladies, their crisp bonnet-ribbons wilting a trifle after the night's faring at an inn, alighted smoothing gowns into which they had changed: Amelia's was lilac, Caro's water-green. They were met by Norah, still clad in her rough grey hodden. Looks were exchanged; the two nudged elbows together.

"Where is your fine array, Norah dearest? Nobody would take you for a bride."

"Wedding's tomorrow, not today. You'll be sharing a bed together in the west tower." As usual she had over-seen all the arrangements, leaving Mrs. Emma limp as a stranded water-weed in her own room. An exquisite young personage came into view behind the bride; and kissed hands punctiliously. This was Corder Bellingham, the groomsman, whose sister had married Jon Wraye. Corder had the profile of a Bernini sculpture and the curls of a St. James's belle; his clothes were perfect, a little too effeminate, as was his habit of perfuming himself, even to his kerchiefs. He was also a clever mimic, and would, Norah already knew, give an amusing imitation of the two over-eager damsels as soon as they were out of earshot. He also, Norah shrewdly guessed, imitated herself in her absence. She did not mind; she had never had exalted notions about her personal inviolability, and Corder diverted her. He had been sent for by David Stroyan from the south, and would stay for some weeks after the wedding.

She edged away from the falsely ecstatic greeting of the cousins. Since her betrothal she had felt oddly free; her future was settled, and she was moreover at liberty to make interesting friends. Stroyan was adept at finding these for her, and this compensated, she now thought, for his habit of mooning by himself over ivy and beetles. She knew Corder liked her despite his concealed mockery; not in the way men admire women, for Corder, she suspected, was hardly to be classed a man. It was rather as a worshipper may admire a goddess; Ceres or—

Why had she thought of that?

She brought herself quickly to recall the evening of Corder's arrival. "You are above all other creatures," he had assured Norah rapturously, with Stroyan, amused, looking on. If it gratified David that his friends admired her, Norah was pleased. That a *double entendre* had been sandwiched delicately into the compliment disturbed her not at all. She had always been taller than most men; all except the squire and Jody.

Up on the fells, the gipsies were moving silently in on Curle. They had come north by night from Lancashire, where they had sojourned some weeks, while Jody grew healed of his wounds the swifter by means of his will. With them was Abigail, a woman no longer young, twice widowed, with rings in her ears of plain worn gold, and two rings on her finger. One had been given back by her son for safe keeping. "I am going to far places soon," he had said. He had told them nothing more of his plans: they did not concern them.

Abigail herself had shown no emotion over the ring, any more than over the fact that Jacob himself had now fallen ill of a tumour which nothing could cure. It was as if all her feeling had burned away over Jody's sick body, and there was now none left. In her caravan, which Jody continued to share with Jacob and herself, were rich things; the icon, a silver teapot, somehow acquired, and bits of china that had belonged to great folk. It was no longer held against her that she had borne a child to a gorgio, and it was at her request that the tribe had aided Jody and brought him home. That her son had a plan, worked out in progress of his illness, she now knew; the fierce determination he had to carry it out had helped to cure him faster than most men. He was not yet fully well; he must take the tribesmen with him in pursuit of his purpose, but now he trusted them. Had they not carried him back from below Churl's Leap? He was recovered now and swore that he must play the pipes at this wedding.

They cared little; if it pleased him, they thought, he could do it; he played well enough. He had said in any case that he would soon go abroad, and it accordingly mattered less what they did with him. Of mixed blood as he was, had he attempted to order the tribe or take a foremost place among them, it would have been different. Meantime, and as a guest, they welcomed him and would even do his bidding in the matter of the pipes.

8

NORAH'S WEDDING DAY dawned dark and sullen. A bitter wind swept down from the fells as they walked on foot to the church, the bride on her grandfather's arm, with Mrs. Emma conveyed in a light carriage behind. By her was the Dowager, despite mourning and the palsy, resplendent in a purple turban and Venice cape, and her paint. David's mother had chosen to accompany the cousins and the rest, who with the bridegroom and the groomsman already waited at the church-porch, shivering somewhat in the cold wind. A rumour had sprung up that the new Duke and Duchess of Wraye would come over, as they had lately arrived home. The prospect of catching sight of the Duchess eclipsed the likelihood of seeing the bride.

The wind whipped irreverently at Norah's veil, which had belonged to her mother. She jerked it into place with one hand and set her jaw, to control her shivering. "It's the cold that makes me do't, not the prospect of bedding with David, damn him!" she muttered as the squire conveyed a jest. He laughed the louder at her answer. He himself felt neither heat nor cold, she knew, and wasn't in any event clad in a fool's thin gown. How glad she would have been of the familiar hodden on such a day! As it was, though, the valley folk looked forward, she knew, to the spectacle of a dressed-up bride. Little Madge, herself so newly married, had thrust forward as small folk will, to wish the bride good luck and a son in the first year. Her imp's face and dark eyes stayed in Norah's mind after the porch was reached, and then the candlelit interior where the grand folk sat. The very candles guttered in the wind, and as Norah and the squire strode to meet David by the altar two went out. It was to be hoped it wasn't an omen, everyone thought.

Outside, the wind was blowing still; Norah could hear it. Upon it was borne, very faintly, the sound of the tuning pipers, who would play later on at the marriage-feast in Curle Hall. The noise of the tuning was ghostly, an echo of the wind itself; something like the sound it must be making now high up there among the rocky fells, about Churl's Leap and what still lay below it. She'd have heard, they would all have heard, if anyone had passed by and found him lying there, where she'd left him; lying still, in his congealed blood.

Be damned to that, in any case; the foxes and crows would have picked him clean by now, leaving little except bones. "Nature has no scruples, any more than I," thought Norah, to the sound of her marriage-vows.

She stared beyond the uneven candles to where Sir Ludovic stood in plum-coloured brocade, his great feathered hat in his hand; and wondered how often he thought of Jody and wondered when he might come home. Perhaps the thought had come to him that the young man had found his mother's folk again, and stayed with them this time in pique at being refused the hand of the heiress of Curle. "He has never been gone as long before," Norah told herself, then realised the folly of her own thoughts; with Jody dead, how could he ever return? She focussed her gaze on her own familiar hand, with the new ring on it, lying on a man's sleeve; Stroyan's. That he did not enter her reckoning in any way she already knew. He had freed her to take her rightful place in the world, given her the status of a married woman, and a father for whatever child she might bear. That he was inoffensive and kind, and would not trouble her, were assets Norah Curle had already counted coldly. So many things had had to be counted . . . and now she, Norah Stroyan, had said her marriage vows without knowing of it, and had been made a wife.

On the way back, she walked with Stroyan on one side and the squire on the other. The valley folk cheered. Norah inclined her head graciously; it was easier now the damned veil was put back, and she could see clearly. A threat of rain was coming; she turned to say as much to the squire, but before she could utter he had forestalled her with the very thing she had been thinking, earlier.

"I'll wager Jody'll be sour as turned milk when he hears of this wedding," he said. "Hear of't he will, at that, before morning. They have ways o' passing news from hill to hill, so that what's new on Skiddaw may be stale in Appleby, next day. Never heed that."

"I do not."

"That's my good lass." He patted her hand; he was pleased with her, and with the marriage; maybe now they would get on with the making of an heir. "D'ye mind how *he* had the impudence to ask for ye, Norah, and I sent him to the rightabout?"

She lied, and said she had forgotten. Sir Ludovic talked on. "He'll sulk for a while, like enough, among his gipsy kin; he may find a wife there, if—" His face turned grey, and she knew that he was remembering Jody's father and how they had hanged him for dishonouring a Romany woman. "Never heed," she said, in her turn. "He'll come sidling home in the end." She did not know, even now, how she could say it without any kind of feeling. It was like acting a part on the boards, if she'd ever known how to do such things. This marriage, all of it, was mummery, to please the tenants; always that. She, Norah, was an image set up before them, such as the Papists had used to have in their churches. The thought of that would make her laugh aloud later, when the wine was passed round and she felt warm again.

They had not reached Curle yet, however. Stroyan walked by her side in silence; he had said little on the journey, smiling narrowly at the folk lining the way. He wore a coat of pale-blue velvet braided in silver, with matching buckles on his shoes.

The squire raised his harsh old profile beneath its feathered hat to the sky. Norah knew that, more than anything in this world, more even than her marriage, he was wishing at this moment that Jody would come home. He'd curse him, if so, and get him to drink deep alongside him so that they could end up drunk together, on this day. How was she or anyone to tell him "Jody's dead, and will not come again; he's no more than a heap of picked bones under a hill"? The lines of an old Scots ballad she had heard came to her now, as she walked decorously back to Curle beside her bridegroom.

> O'er his white banes, when they are bare,
> The wind sall blaw for evermair.

How was it then that Jody was even yet real to her, whereas the man at whose side she walked remained a shadow?

There had been other reality within the dark church; she remembered it afterwards. Beyond the guttering candles in the aisle, where the guests were, she had seen, on returning, a strange face. That it should be strange was in itself singular; surely she had always known, had hoped for, such a meeting? At that same moment Stroyan had given a small, friendly pressure to her wrist, as if to reassure her of his fondness and care. "But he'd not have married me without the money, and Curle," she recalled thinking. Yet all the time she was obsessed by the girl's sweet face, with great blue eyes beneath a mourning-hat and blonde hair curling under: of course, this must be Jon Wraye's bride, come in time to the wedding after all . . .

"I should like to know her better," Norah was aware of saying to herself, almost shyly. Some, she knew, had expected her to be jealous of Jonathan's bride, but it was Jon himself she envied. When had she felt so about any other woman? Never before, she was certain. This was no sugar-doll, as she'd expected. Impatience took her to get the marriage-feast over, and what followed, and to be free thereafter to cultivate Amy Wraye.

The pipers had been bidden to assemble in the former minstrels' gallery, often used in old time when there had been, as now, weddings or wakes at Curle. Minstrelsy there had been none at Sir Ludovic's own wedding; as if to make up for the lack of it he sat now in his great chair, beating a finger against the arm to the rhythm of the piping. Norah, borne out before them all on her new husband's arm, led the dance to the skirl of it. Was it her fancy that it held a sinister note, akin to the cold wind that sang always beyond? The smoke and haze of heat in the hall had risen up to where the players sat and she could not, for managing her flimsy gown and veil, see them clearly except for one man, who wore a black patch over one eye and blew mockingly and loud on the pipes at the head of his fellows. He it was, Norah knew well, who was making so weird a noise as to turn her wedding-feast into a travesty, the very wedding itself to ghosts and moaning. At any other time she would have gone to the squire to have so insolent a fellow put out of doors, with a parting kick to his back-side. But she led the dance, and Sir Ludovic was drunk; drunk with the good wine after feasting, and the pleasure of seeing his heiress creditably wed. So, and it might have been to please him, Norah danced on, circling the length of the hall again and again with Stroyan, during which time a deadly sickness and certainty came to her about who the piper must be, for the tune he played was one she had heard years ago in the apple-loft, but she must dance on, and on.

The pipes grew wilder. Jody was playing a tune now of life and death, of revenge and undying hate and sorrow; never love, for Jody himself had never loved her. He had wanted the great possessions that she would have, and had taken her body, but he should never have Curle. Never, never, never . . . she was Stroyan's wife now, let Jody play all he would, and the marriage had come within the month and no one would ever know, she herself would never be sure . . .

"I can deny I was ever up there with him," she heard her mind saying, "so he can prove nothing, it is my word against his, a Curle's against a gipsy's. I will deny everything that has happened between us, and he knows it and that it is his own dirge he plays, for he will never now gain Curle." And she danced on, and laughed, and presently stopped for lack of breath and called for a cup of wine. Stroyan held it to her lips and they shared the cup, and there was the saying that two who had drunk from the same cup would have fates forever intermingled, but her own fate would never be Stroyan's, for he was no part of her and never would be so.

"Another tune," called the squire, and damned everyone if he wouldn't get up out of his chair and lead a round himself, but Mrs. Emma dissuaded him. "You are not well yet," she said, and he roared, so that it could be heard above the sound of the pipes, "Not well? This is the best day of m'life! Get a son on her this night, Stroyan, and I'll live to call ye a fine man yet." And the curse in the pipes faded as another player took the tune and tamed it, making it fit for deaf ears and fools' tongues. The talk and boisterousness doubled now the guests had dined and wined well. Suddenly Norah looked about her for Amy Wraye, as if the sight of that exquisite face could heal her soul. But the Wrayes had gone, quietly, back to their own house straight from the church: they were still in mourning.

The night ended, as all nights do; it was time to bed the couple, and everyone filed past later and kissed the bride, seated ready in her four-poster bed twined with lavender and rosemary for a fertile marriage. There were herbs on the floor also, as there had used to be in the times before carpets; that had been Mrs. Emma's notion, so that the servants could sweep cleanly tomorrow once everyone had gone. They were beyond the farther door now; there was only herself and Stroyan. Not for the first time Norah thought of him as a stranger: but it did not matter, behind the drawn curtains. They said all cats were grey in the dark, and it was best to get the matter done with. As for the pipers, they had taken their silver and gone.

PART II

I

FOUR MONTHS AFTERWARDS, a homeward coach from London plodded through the mud, carrying five passengers as well as their baggage, making less speed now that the roads had grown rougher towards the north. Norah Stroyan stared out of the window and felt glad to be coming home; glad, again, of the sight of treeless hills and grey villages and tarns, unlike the tamed, stuccoed south. This wild hard land was hers, and had her heart as it should have her bones. She preferred rather to look out in silence, savouring her private pleasure, even to regarding Amy who sat opposite, a little tired by the journey but looking delightful as was her custom, in a travelling-gown of dove-colour and a fashionable Leghorn hat, with her dark-gold hair dressed high on a frame beneath. Jon Wraye, who out of courtesy sat by Norah while her own husband occupied the facing seat with Corder and his sister, could not, now or ever, take his adoring eyes from his wife. Norah knew this and smiled to herself; Amy and she were both pregnant. Amy had informed her of her own state before they left London. The joy on the other bride's face was something Norah could not understand. Women must bear children; it was an unpleasant business, but in her own position and Amy's was especially necessary for the sake of the inheritance, and that was all there was to it. She herself was glad enough of her condition in that the matter would the sooner be over and done with. But Amy Wraye's happiness made it seem as though such a proceeding were by especial favour of the gods—or God, no doubt, as Amy was deeply religious—a gift beyond all gifts. Norah stared on at the passing hills and wondered for the hundredth time how an upbringing which had been straitened and in a country rectory, had produced, housed in Amy's slender body, a great lady. For such the new Duchess was, and not only by reason of her marriage. The latter she would grace, but her ways were her own. "She showed no hesitation in presenting me before the Queen," Norah reflected, unaware of the fact—

how should she think of it?—that she herself had been unaffected also. The wait had been long and the carriage stuffy, and her own tight corsage and Court plumes taxed the endurance, but otherwise it had ended by seeming a very ordinary occasion. The ugly swarthy little Queen, though elegantly dressed and smiling valiantly, would have passed unnoticed in the great hall at Curle. "The King was civil," decided Norah. It would divert the squire to tell him of all of it, and assure him that the third George of the Hanoverian line could not only speak his subjects' tongue in odd staccato fashion, but seemed, as he claimed to be, all Briton, with his abrupt manners and straining prominent blue gaze. The Court, everyone said, had grown dull nowadays, with the King and Queen mostly at Kew with their children.

Children. One had to live for them and, no doubt, with them, and when her own child was born there would of necessity be some curtailment of the freedom of her life at Curle. However she'd employ a wet-nurse, and later a governess and tutor; she would see that her son should be educated to resemble these gentle-spoken folk in the coach here, instead of swilling wine and fondling women like the squire, who knew no better.

"The squire! He will be glad to hear tell of't," she thought, reverting in her mind to the broad accents of her childhood, and shedding any late contempt for her grandfather in affection, the glad desire to see him again and tell him the news, the news! She had not written to him of the coming child, preferring to wait to inform him herself and watch the pleasure dawning on his face. She smiled at the prospect, and turned again to the occupants of the carriage. Handsome Corder, who had joined them in the south and who knew everybody, had made their sojourn there the gayer for his presence. Norah joined in the pleasant talk, exchanging remarks with Jon and Amy; nothing was ever said between those two that jarred or was harsh. Stroyan sat quiet, but that was his wont; always his kindly self-effacing, dutiful self, her husband. Norah was pleased with him; he knew his place, and was useful to her in small ways, and had escorted her creditably in London. She had not thought to ask if he were glad of the return to the north; in any case it had been time for them to go home.

Ah, the north! There was Hindscarth now, rearing up behind the fantastic assembly of many-named hills. She had never before left her own country, and now doubted if she ever would any more, seeing it again. There was a sharpness in the very air here that could be felt even in the crowded, perfumed warmth of the coach; Norah breathed it happily. How far away, in fact and in truth, the London town-houses seemed now, with their dressed-up flunkeys and elegant tea-drinking and cards! And the country estates to which Corder had procured them invitations were, as Stroyan had long ago told her, each one no more than a house, a park, a flat lake scooped out by a landscape-gardener, a folly, and affected company. No brown stagnant water pricked with reeds, with mallards nesting annually beneath the ancient fells . . . soon, now, she'd go out with the guns again. She'd not heed this pregnancy to the extent of givng up her old pursuits yet, till the time of the birth. The new heir of Curle must learn early that his place was on a horse's back. But they wouldn't ride as far as Churl's Leap . . .

Where was Jody now? What had happened to him after that eerie pipe-playing for her wedding night? Sir Ludovic had written twice in his ill hand, but there hadn't been word of the half-gipsy returning. "He'd better not be in Curle when I set foot in it," thought Norah. "I'll have him whipped out." All power would be hers, she knew, once it was known she was carrying the new heir. Sir Ludovic would deny her nothing.

She switched her thoughts from Jody to Amy. The new Duchess seemed languid now, and somewhat white about the mouth. Compassion took Norah; it was a long way, and she herself hadn't had the patience to wait overnight at an inn, so they had journeyed on . . . No doubt Amy was different, less robust than she. How delightful their friendship was, and how many tastes they proved to have in common, though she hadn't known, till she heard it in the south, how much she enjoyed harpsichord recitals. Johann Christian Bach, that was the name of the Queen's music-master. Amy had said his father was a famous composer and organist in Germany, and all of the family were gifted in their different ways. She must remember that; and the names of the rival fashionable London painters who were so envious of one another they never spoke. Reynolds and Gainsborough. How diverting the world was in the south! She and Amy must bring it north; invite musicians, artists, all such people, to Wraye and Curle, and have the county to meet and listen . . .

"Are you feeling unwell, my love?" said Wraye to his wife.

Amy shook her head gently. "It is only a little farther, is it not? I think Norah will be pleased to be home."

Wraye began to fuss ineffectively. There was nowhere to stop, he knew; it was all of it bog and inhospitable moor now, till they reached Wraye. When she was there, his new Duchess should go straight to bed, with a hot brick to her feet. How Corder and the Stroyans were chattering together! The voices seemed suddenly loud to Wraye, as if they would never arrive.

Norah Stroyan was talking to Corder of some Dresden shepherdesses which they had seen. "Such things are never encountered here; we must buy some. No one here but is so ignorant as to know of nothing except the belling of hounds and filling their own stomachs," she was saying. "Now that you are here . . . you will stay for a while, Corder?"

"I will stay for ever if you should want it, dear goddess; and if I have a place in which to stay." Corder was, if it had been known, in extensive debt; it was convenient to him to leave his southern haunts for the time. His blue eyes looked laughingly at Norah. It would be diverting, she was thinking, to have so elegant a person as Amy's brother about her; he could arrange the pastimes she had been dreaming of. There was no subject under the sun but Corder knew a little of it, be it concerning shepherdesses in china lace or who was married to whom in Staffordshire. He had been everywhere and had never ceased to acquire information on his travels. There was an empty house, Windyett, of her own a little way above Curle; she would have fires lit in it, hoping perhaps to lease it later to Corder at a low rent fit for his pocket, to persuade him to stay. Until then, of course, he could visit them at Wraye, or even Curle, though he'd not deal well with Sir Ludovic. And, again he was Amy's brother. How pleasant to have a messenger between herself and Amy, frequent visits and exchanges of the notions she already had for bringing talents to the north! But all that must wait, no doubt, at least in great part, till after the birth. How long a time it seemed till that would be over! It had its inconveniences already; sick as a dog, she'd been, most mornings in London, but nobody got up till late; and damned if she or anyone knew whether the child was Stroyan's or . . .

There must be no question of doubt bandied round. As for Stroyan, if he had suspicions he'd kept them to himself.

There was no closeness between them. If she hadn't thought of it before, the fact was brought home here, now, in the carriage, witnessing the unspoken constant love which showed itself in every look, every touch, between Their Graces of Wraye. After the brief anxiety he had shown, Wraye had relapsed into his usual state of watchfulness of Amy, as if intent on some miracle, some angel; not a young woman to whom he had after all been married now for some months. Norah stifled a yawn to hide her envy. It was unfashionable, she knew, for married couples to be in this state. But nobody could condemn the Wrayes for their intentness one with the other; only it was strange that Amy, the gentler partner, who appeared to yield to her husband in everything, was in fact the one who always had her way in the end. "But nobody ever heeded Jonathan in his life," Norah reminded herself, looking sideways under her lashes at the man who had all his youth been nothing but a plain, pale, wordless shadow of his brilliant elder brother. If George Shawhope had lived, would this marriage have turned out so? Perhaps; at any rate Amy had made Jon fulfil himself and be born again. "I could wish it were so with us," Norah thought suddenly. She knew that it would not be; David Stroyan could never satisfy her physically, as Jody had done on that brief, unspeakable encounter on the hill. That she had known passion then she had found, later, in her lack of it with Stroyan, and the knowledge was bitter. Sometimes, especially at the beginning of the marriage, she had tried to rouse Stroyan to the state necessary to excite her body, clinging to him after their coupling was done with, forcing him to try again. But it was useless, and of late, with the pregnancy a declared fact, she'd let David be. His mind was of a different mettle from her own, and contained much that, were she prepared to admit it, would be of benefit in her new search for the things gentlefolk understood and cherished. "But I must never let Stroyan feel he's instructing me; that would be intolerable," Norah told herself. The thought that he was in many ways unknown to her had already occurred, but did not trouble her. Such things as she wanted of him she could get, and the rest could go to the devil.

Stroyan, as if he had known she must be thinking of him, made a remark, his first in an hour; it concerned highwaymen. "We have been fortunate to meet none on the way, but one understands there are fewer as one nears the border," he said.

"You are armed, both of you, and the coachman as well," Norah replied drily.

Amy had made a little *moue* of terror, and Wraye leaned forward and patted her hand. "There, my dear, did you not hear Stroyan say there would be none?" he assured her, and Norah felt brief irritation with Stroyan for having, even briefly, alarmed Amy. Perhaps he lacked his full five senses, and this was why he could tolerate herself. He had never, she already knew, been in love with her; and the brief, bright-cheeked handsomeness she had once had was beginning to grow shoddy as she paled with the unborn child, and soon now she'd thicken. How well the squire would understand, and how he'd rejoice! "Grand lass, grand lass," he'd roar, and pour wine for them all, and drink a rousing toast to Curle and its heir. It would be pleasant to have a taste of heartiness again after all these months of gentility, when all was said.

2

ONE MATTER disappointed Norah in the midst of her joy at again seeing Curle: when they reached there, the squire was absent. A servant, taking her cloak as she shrugged it off, said his master was in Carlisle. "He'd not know, madam, that ye'd be here before tomorrow, for we were none of us expecting it," said the man, using the freedom of one who had been in service at Curle for years.

Norah frowned, stretching her hands out to the fire. The old man must have ridden off to his whore. He had been used, in former days, to finish with such matters briefly, returning the same night or maybe the next. But even before her own departure for London he had been growing into the habit of staying away longer; either he was growing old or the whore was demanding. She grimaced, and forgot it. "Bring us food and wine, for we're weary," she said. But when the food and wine came Norah toyed with the meat in a way which was unlike her. It was time the squire had done with whores.

"We'll wait till tomorrow, and then send word I've come home," she told Stroyan. Suddenly hearing her own voice loud and strident in the silence, she rounded on him. "Can ye not care aught for the squire, sitting there ox-dumb as ye are? Ye have dined well enough on his provender." Then she felt ashamed of herself; he was so unresistant it was like striking a child. "Come, drink more wine," she said, and herself went to fill Stroyan's glass; but he shook his head.

"You are tired with the journey," he told her gently, and Norah knew a sudden overriding need for a loud-voiced man; a man who could beat her and bully her, not cozen her with gentle words when she behaved like a shrew. Tired! "No Curle ever wearied at a journey in a cushioned coach," she told Stroyan, who did not answer. He has milk in his veins, not blood, she told herself; and turned and went to the window, looking out past the darkening fells for a moving lanthorn-light, some sign perhaps that Sir Ludovic was returning home. Damn the woman in Carlisle!

Word came next day. They had feared to bring it to her; it was Stroyan who heard it first. When she saw his considering, gentle gaze Norah swore suddenly, and shouted at him to get it off his tongue. "It's ill news, I know."

"Ill news indeed, Norah. It will make you grieve."

"Is he dead, the old man?" That was the worst that could befall; any other thing would be less grievous. "Tell me."

Stroyan hung his head; if she had known, he was searching for words. She did not wait for them. "As ye have not denied it, then, it's true. He is dead. What killed him?" and she was aware of a stabbing sense of loss. Never now would he know about the heir, the old man: never now. And she herself, lacking him, was, she realised, quite alone.

"Was it on the road? He'd have liked to die like that, quickly."

"No—it was—"

"In his harlot's bed? Tell me all; may as well rid yourself of't." And so he told her; and it was as she'd thought, and the old lecher had died in a young girl's bed, thinking himself, no doubt, young again and spry. If he'd had to choose a good end, maybe, that would have been what he'd choose; that, or on a horse, or over a bottle of good red wine. She became aware that Stroyan was looking at her with deep pity, and she was about to turn on him again when a sound came from somewhere in the house that neither of them had ever heard; a woman's laughter, harsh and strange. It rang through the upper corridors and then was stilled. "My grandmother knows, then," said Norah. It was the first time she had ever thought of Maud Curle as knowing anything. "She's . . . glad."

She turned away from Stroyan towards the stairs. Action was a crying need with her, now as never before; she must get out of Curle and away from that unseen woman's mad laughter. "I ride to Carlisle," she told Stroyan, eyes cavern-dark in her face. He tried to plead with her. Her state . . . the child . . . "Wait for a little, my love, and they'll bring him home."

"*I* will bring him home, and I'll see for myself how he died. You may stay here or come, as you will."

She shouted for the grooms to saddle the horses; no, she'd go in no coach! Stroyan, bewildered but aware of his duty, made ready to ride by her. He said no more. He put on his drab cloak and wide hat, accordingly, went out after his wife into the drizzling rain, and let himself be put up docilely on Barley. Four servants followed, ready to bring home the body of their master. The drizzle thickened as they rode, clustering on the riders' eyelashes and making the road ahead hard to see; but they went on. It would be evening before the city was reached; did young Mrs. Stroyan mean to stay overnight in the whore's house, or at an inn?

But nobody asked Norah, riding ahead; there might have been not a soul present on the road but herself. If she shed tears for her grandfather, they were washed from her cheeks by the rain, and no one saw them. She spoke no word to anyone, merely digging her heels in the bay's sides to make him ride on. The rest followed in silence also, as they must.

When they reached the house the quiet was broken. Norah Stroyan slid from the saddle, tossed the reins to the nearest man and hammered on the panelled door. There were glances between the men; he was lying dead in there, the old squire; there should be silence, for decorum's sake, not that *he—*

The door opened timidly; a servant stood there. She stared at sight of Mrs. Stroyan; everyone in the city knew who she must be, she was so bigly made and finely clad: and like the dead squire, even to his very scowl.

"Take me to my grandfather," said Norah, and went in. A quick jerk of the head beckoned Stroyan and two of the men to follow; the rest would see the horses to stable. Norah mounted the stairs; she might have known the house from birth. There was a paved courtyard inside the door, such as one finds in Italian houses. The stairs were straight and steep, leading to an upper floor where two rooms were. Norah entered one, without knocking.

3

THE FIRST THING to meet her gaze was a dazzle of candles; they had been placed about the dead man's head and feet, and made the bed whereupon he lay the room's centre; beyond, and out of the ring of yellow light, a young woman sat; she rose as Norah entered. Norah ignored her in the first instance, and went to stare down at the face of her grandfather as he had been when a young man. She had heard often enough that this was an early trick of death, to iron out wrinkles so that the old look young. He lay there silent and sardonic, the young man of the year of Oudenarde, his thick curling hair disposed about him, his linen seemly. The candles flared, pointing their spears of light upwards: Norah came out of the instant's sharp regret the sight of the dead man brought her, and turned to face his mistress, the cause of his death.

It surprised Norah that the woman should be so young; hardly more than a girl, when all was said. She wore a gown of grey moiré silk, its bodice laced with ribbons of rose-colour, and her braided hair gleamed smoothly in the light of the candles; it was gold, the colour of Amy Wraye's, and the superficial resemblance this gave the girl to Amy herself roused anger in Norah. A whore, to resemble Amy!—and one who, it must be remembered again, had killed the old squire; of that there was no doubt; had he remained by his hearth as suited his years, he'd be alive yet. Norah let her mind dwell on this as she spoke to the young woman, and kept her anger high and without pity. The whore's eyes, she saw, were red-rimmed; had she been weeping for her protector? "More likely for the doubt of her present state, for she knows well enough I'll turn her out of doors," thought Norah. To this end she spoke, noting as she did so that the whore's hands and features were somewhat clumsier than Amy's, not so fine-drawn; a servant, she'd no doubt been. She had grey eyes.

"Where do you come from?" she said coldly. "Where are your parents, or other kin? You must return to them, as you may not stay here."

"I have no parents, madam." The voice was low and, Norah noted, courteous; the fact roused further anger in her, as if insolence would have been less unwelcome. In such a calling as the girl professed, niceties were out of place.

She made herself speak levelly. "You are an orphan, then? How came you to the notice of my grandfather? On the streets, were you? A profitable calling; you may return to it."

"Madam, I was apprenticed to a milliner, and one of her customers, a woman, saw me and bought my indentures; then she made me sit at her window high up above the street, dressed in a low-cut gown; and it was there Sir Ludovic saw me, and bought me of her. He was a kind gentleman to me, madam—"

"No doubt," said Norah drily; but the other did not seem to hear, and went on speaking as to herself, looking constantly at the dead squire's face. She must have combed him and laid him out, Norah found herself thinking; she and the servant together, maybe. He's all as he should be; and looks as though he smiled. A seemly way to die, in bed with one's whore!

"—and bought me gowns, and shifts and shoes. I never had pretty clothes afore, saving only the dress my mistress put me in, which shamed me. I was reared godly enough; but *he* was kind, and I didn't mind any of it; his wife was mad long ago and his two sons dead, he said; now that *he's* dead too, I'm sorry for't. Will you not let me bide here, madam, till—"

"That I shall not, indeed; out on the streets with you this night; you've hidden away enough to keep yourself, no doubt, till you find another protector. With your fine silk gown that should not be difficult." Norah's voice had grown loud and bitter; she herself, she knew well enough, had never looked half as well in any gown. The girl was comely enough; but so were a dozen others, and what was it about this one that the squire should have lost his wits over her? For it appeared that he had done no less than that, if he had spoken of his wife and sons; now that she looked closely, it seemed that the young woman might well be with child herself. Angry denial rose in Norah; the old man could never have sired more children at his age!

"Sir Ludovic said he'd see me right, madam, and that he had put in his will that I was to be well treated, and have money given me." The statement was made placidly, as though the girl had no doubt of her rights; Norah gave vent to a burst of her harsh laughter.

"Do you suppose that you are the only young woman my grandfather favoured? There are a round dozen of 'em; and how am I to know that he's your child's father? Many a day and night you had to yourself, my fine girl, to ask customers here; and I don't doubt you did. To say my grandsire is to blame for't! A fine bold lie!" Norah swung round. "What is your name, my wench?" she said. "I ask only that you may receive your deserts; for I'll wager there is no mention made of you in anything my grandsire set his name to. Nevertheless if I know, I'll make enquiry concerning that." And, if found, she added mentally, it should be overturned through the lawyers; the squire must have been in his dotage before he left a bequest to—"Your name?" she said again, haughty and frowning; a glass on the wall showed her her face, and the dead man's lying below. There's nobody can say I'm not the spitten image of the squire, she reminded herself; no one in the county, or beyond.

The girl meantime had begun to cry. "My name is Mary Deas, madam, but he—they call me Molly. If you will let me stay until I have found a place to go, madam, even before my child is born, though that won't be easy—"

"You should have given thought to that when you let some man get you with child; never blame my grandfather. Out of doors with you, now; you may take a cloak with you, and such money as you have."

Tears streamed down Molly Deas' face. "Let me bide till the morning, madam, for where am I to go on such a night? It's raining, madam, and dark, and—"

"Yes, and will shortly put your hair out of curl and wash the paint from your face; make haste, then, before the customers leave the streets. It is likely one of them will take pity on you, and take you home with him till morning: but that's no concern of mine."

The girl stood to her full height, and her eyes met Norah's. "You're hard, Mrs. Stroyan. You would not use one of your own servants so."

"Indeed I would, if my servants had killed my grandfather. You killed him, did you not? He died in your bed? You were not in a silk gown then, I'll wager; sell that, if you will. Now get from my sight; I'll order my men to thrust you from the house if you will not go of your own free will. Get your cloak about you, and be gone."

She turned away and did not watch the now hopelessly sobbing young woman go; she was staring down at the squire again. Soon there would be nothing of him left, she knew, but bones; of his mortal flesh, this was the last remembered sight, perhaps the finest, that she'd ever had of him, that old man who for this hour seemed young. The door closed on Molly Deas' going and opened again now so that the candles swayed their flames; Stroyan faced her across them. Norah stared almost without recognition at her husband. He should have left me alone with my dead, she was thinking; his place is outside this room.

She became aware that he was speaking to her. "Norah, there is a young woman who they say is—is—" and his voice faltered over the indelicacy of the situation. Norah sneered.

"Who is, or was, my grandsire's harlot, and professes herself with child by him; who will believe such a tale, or that she has nowhere to go? Such women have places for themselves."

"She cannot go out into the night, where no inn will receive her. You cannot be as heartless; it may be your own state that causes you to act so, my—"

His voice sank uncertainly again. Had he been about to call her his wife, his love? "I was scarcely either; he is nothing to me or I to him, nor ever will be," Norah thought without feeling. She turned back to the corpse again and said over her shoulder, "My servants know my orders; the woman is to go. See that you do not cross me, Stroyan, or you will rue it; I mean what I say."

"Then you are indeed a woman without a heart," he told her, and went out. She remained staring down at the squire's dead face, and a faint glint beneath the shut lids mocked her by its uncertainty; had she done well, or ill?

"It is as you would have counselled me, had it been any other," she said aloud, as though Sir Ludovic could hear. She would not yet admit even to herself that what she had indeed felt was passionate envy of the young woman who had been his beloved, whom he had loved enough in the end to lose his life, and what would her own be now without him? They had always been as one mind, she and her grandfather, however keen his disappointment that she had not been a boy. And she bore that in her womb that would have cheered him had he known of it; and he would never know now. This Norah knew was the final bitterness; and now that he and she were alone in the death-chamber she could feel her own hot heavy tears flood her cheeks, splashing down on the dead man's face and linen. "There were only two left of our like in the world, and now there is only myself."

She turned away, feeling all at once heavy with her pregnancy, and weary as she had not been all through the journey tonight. Had Stroyan been by her even then he might perhaps have essayed to comfort her. But Stroyan had gone. She found the room silent and hot with the candles' heat, and quenched all but one of them; then went away, leaving Sir Ludovic Curle alone in his darkness.

The whore, Molly Deas, put her hooded cloak about her and went out alone into the darkness and rain. It blew about her, soaking Molly so that she huddled the warm everyday hodden round her with small ungloved hands. The hood she wore had no strings, and soon the rain blew it back and leaked past the cloak's fastening and trickled down against Molly's soft skin, taking as it went the curl out of her hair and darkening it to the hue of clay. The tears on her cheeks mingled with the rain. She had at first no idea in which direction to walk and for a while struggled aimlessly about the town; few were abroad, and she was not once accosted. But young Mrs. Stroyan's taunt had in any case repelled Molly; she could not yet sell herself to every stranger. She lifted her head against the rain, a trifle proudly. No, she was no common harlot, whatever they said; her folk had been honest countrymen, down in the Yorkshire dales, and had it not been that her father had died, and her mother was ailing, there would never have been any question of sending Molly to the city to work for the milliner; it had been while she was newly there word had come that her mother was dead, and there had been no one to whom to turn, no one

. . . But if she were to go back to those parts now, and perhaps take work on a farm, if not as a housekeeper?

Molly clenched her smooth palms against the rough stuff of the cloak; she was shivering with cold. In her state it'd not be easy, and she'd never been used to hard manual work, being an only child and spoilt a bit, though of course she'd helped mother about the tied cottage they had all lived in, and now and again mixed meal for cakes and baked them on a griddle. The pleasant remembered smell of the baking came to her now, in the storm and cold. Yes, she'd go back; but no sense in starting out on the unlit roads till day, or one would end in a bog as like as not.

She huddled in an entry till dawn came, then, stiff with cold and damp, made her way out of the city gate as a farm-cart came in with vegetables to sell. The rain had stopped. Perhaps when the man returned, if he were travelling in her direction, he'd let her sit up on the empty cart. She trudged on meantime, her thin satin shoes, made for a kept woman's wear, ragged about the soles already and with one of the rosettes loose: soon she would have to take them off, for they were useless, and her silk hose and garters, to save those should she ever need them again. But the time of silks and satins, of caresses in an old man's bed, and a life of ease were over, Molly knew; all of that had been stripped from her, in a single hour, by Norah Stroyan. Tears sprang to Molly's eyes as she thought of that rich uncaring woman, and how she'd had no pity, and hadn't even given a sixpence for the journey, let alone wish Molly luck. "A better whore 'ud have saved summat against hard times," she told herself without rancour. She'd never been able to see a yard in front of her nose, that was her trouble; someone long ago, her father perhaps, or the milliner, had told her that. But already memory and recollections were blurred in the oncoming of exhaustion, and as she walked on Molly began to stumble, and her face and hands lost their chill and grew hot, as if the wind dried them, then cold again. Soon she was staggering like a drunken thing, as the time went by towards noon; it was only the clear way of the rutted road that showed her her course to the south. The dales . . . they were many and many a mile away from here still, but she remembered the rolling slopes and the boggy colours of the rough fields and heather and grey dykes. If she found a dyke, she'd lie up perhaps in the shelter of the low wall, away from the wind, for a while till she felt better. How hungry she was, or had been some time since! It wasn't good for the unborn baby not to eat; if she passed by a farm, she'd beg a drink of milk, and offer to work for that, if they'd let her.

The miles followed one another; it was a long time now since Molly had left Carlisle. As evening fell she saw a lone stone building rear, and went out of her way to go up its uneven path and knock on the door; no one answered, and in the end Molly found a haystack growing green with age and lay down there overnight, her hunger gnawing at her through broken sleep. Next morning she pulled up grass with her fists, and ate it. There had been no sign of the returning farm-cart, and she was no longer even certain of being on the right road, with having had to turn off, and having no great sense of direction except for the sun. It rose in the east, and provided she kept it to her left, that was the way she should go . . . the way she should go . . .

It was two days later that Matthew Scarsgill, the dalesman who lived alone at the north of the valley, went out to see to his ewes and found a soaked flimsy shape lying inert against the dyke wall; on bending over it it proved to be a young woman, with tousled gold hair and flushed cheeks. She moaned when he stirred her, and made no sense with anything she said; and Matt, who was a kindly man although dour, picked her up and set her across his shoulder, like a stray lamb, and carried her back to the warm cot-house and laid her on the bed. Her clothing was soaked, and had it been a man Matt would have stripped it off without thinking, to dry it by the fire; as it was, he grew bashful, especially as he could see that the sodden useless silks had belonged to a fine lady. Still, there was no help for it if the lass were not to die of chill and exposure, and in the end Matt wrapped her naked in a warmed blanket, and set about making a posset of gruel for when she should wake. She was feverish, and seemed to know nothing of where she was or who she might be, and he forbore to question her, glad only that she ate some of the food in the end and kept it down: when she turned her head away he let her sleep again. He mended the fire, set water on to boil, and went out meantime to finish the task of seeing to the ewes; when he came back it was growing dark, and he made supper for both of them. Later on there was nowhere for him to lie down but his own bed or else on the earth floor; gently, he slid between the blankets which also housed the young woman. Her hair was scattered about her like liquid gold, dried now and with its own slight curl. A tress of it touched Matt's bare flesh and made him aware of pleasure, of a kind he knew little of for he had had small ado with women. He would not touch the lass yet, for she was ill; maybe later, when she was better . . . Eh, she was pretty, with her hair and daisy-white skin, and the long bright-tipped lashes sunk on her flushed cheeks! He'd found her, like a stray lamb or bird, and maybe one day she'd tell him where she came from, but meantime one made do with what God might send. Matt had his own stern notion of God, for they walked together daily over the hills and dales and on Sundays he would go to the meetings of his sect. He asked now that he might be permitted to keep the golden-haired young lady and that she might grow content with him, for he would see that she should want for nothing. Before Matt slept he felt that his prayer had been answered, although she had said nothing more and he only felt her even breathing against him, as though she knew she had come home.

4

A T Curle, Sir Ludovic's coffin, lit by candles head and foot, lay in the great hall. The coffin had been closed early, and Maud Curle, the widow, who had been brought down from her place of restraint to keep watch as was proper, had caused a diversion by behaving most improperly. Not having looked on her lord's dead face, she laughed, and tapped on the closed coffin. "Is he in there, indeed?" she said in a clear voice which penetrated the silence. "Is he in there? If it is said by all, it must be true."

None answered, and she gave a laugh that was not like the harsh sounds she had made on hearing of the death, but young and uncaring. She addressed the oak lid and said "Are ye there, then, bones and dust before myself? I would ha' looked on your face at a time when ye might not answer me, but it's late, it's too late; ye are rotting," and then she gave another crow of laughter like a mischievous child, and Emma Curle, arrayed in deep mourning like the rest of them here today, edged nearer and gently took the crazed woman by the hand. "Now, madam, be at peace, and sit over here by me; it is John's wife Emma, ye will mind?" Then they sat down side by side nearby the great coffin, two no longer young women in heavy black veils; behind them, Mrs. Emma's eyes kept decorously downcast, while Maud's grey gaze wandered forever about the hall. It was so long since she had been let come down here that the place was not like her home; had never been, she was thinking. That was, should have been, with God, and now Ludovic had gone to God before her. Would such a man's soul receive pardon in the end? "No one can tell," Maud murmured, and looked down and fingered her black sleeve, and wondered

who John was? The woman called Emma she had been used to see sometimes, when the packman had come; *that* had had to be done while the
squire was away. Emma, the packman, John. John and Ludovic. The pain
of childbirth. Maud Curle remembered it all now, and how she had been
permitted no word in the rearing of her children. She would see them
sometimes from her window riding their ponies, ever bigger and stronger
as time passed, and then one day one of them had brought home a bride.
But she was never permitted to come down to weddings, only funerals.
Only the dead played host, never the living.

The bride. Emma. Emma now had grey hair and red-rimmed eyes.
Time must have passed. Where was Ludo, and whom had he married?
They hadn't told her of that, and she hadn't, come to think of it, set eyes
on Ludo, even from the high casement, this many a long year. "Where is
my son?" she called out, and Emma hushed her fearfully. "John is dead,
mother-in-law; that is John's daughter Norah, and her husband, that you
see." But Maud would not be comforted. "It is my son Ludovic I mean,"
she said. "Why did they not permit him to marry? The blood's as good as
any in the county, for that was why his sire wed me against my will, as
soon for that as the money. Where is Ludo my son?" But no one answered; Emma was in tears.

Lady Curle grew querulous. "None heeds me nor ever have, for all ye
sit there in a mourning row, but ye cared nothing for him; nor did I. Why
should I love a man who forced me? The bridegroom I wanted was God's
Son, not a lust-sodden squire, but he—"

But Emma, white-faced, summoned the servants to take her away, for
she had said a thing that should not be said. Some days she would be
lucid and others wild, and one never knew . . . "But the packman can
calm her," thought Emma, like one reciting a bidding-prayer to keep away
evil things. "He can bring her what gives her solace. I'll have them fetch
him again when this is done with," and then she looked timidly over at
her daughter Norah, so large and handsome in her mourning and so like
the dead squire. Perhaps dear Norah would be heedless of such a matter,
which need not concern her directly, and would let the packman continue
to come to the poor old woman in her room . . . "It is no wonder she is
crazed," she thought, "even if it were only by reason of such a marriage;
but after she'd done bearing they say *he* shut her up in her room whether
she would or no, lest she taint the children with her Papist notions. And for
many a year now she has been spoken of as mad." Yet Maud had flashes
of sanity in the things she spoke of, and Emma felt more at home with the
old woman than ever with her own daughter Norah. Now the squire was

gone perhaps she could see Maud oftener, and lighten her days a little. "When I was brought here as a bride I would hear her crying aloud in the night, and it affrighted me; but she has not done it now for years, except that time the news came of the death, and that caused her laughter."

They were leading Maud out of the hall and on the way she had to pass by her granddaughter. Emma thought that Norah looked as she had always done; she had wept not at all for her grandfather's death, and seemed in some manner to have hardened and thickened, as if she were fashioned of rock.

Maud Curle's grey eyes surveyed the hazel ones. "You are like *him*," they said. No word was exchanged between the two women, the old and the young, as the former went out. Norah had made her curtsy, formally, to her grandmother; now she turned from watching the thin, wispy figure led upstairs and encountered the gaze of Amy Wraye, who with her husband had come over for the funeral. They had already spoken, and Norah scolded Jonathan for permitting his wife to come; Amy's face looked drawn and her eyes shadowed. But she had insisted on being present. "How could I leave you to grieve alone, dearest Norah? I know how greatly attached you were to your grandfather, and how sad you must be. Will you not come back with us to Wraye after the funeral?"

No, she wouldn't leave Curle; not the moment the squire had been carried out of it to his burial. It would be like abandoning his trust in her. Stroyan could go. Stroyan had been behaving oddly since they returned from Carlisle; he had slept in his dressing-room, saying it was out of consideration for her state. My state's as usual, thought Norah; he is piqued that I dismissed that whore. Perhaps he had a fancy for her.

She returned to her place by the coffin's side and, standing by it, saw Jody.

He had entered the hall quietly, none gainsaying him; everyone came and went, leaving their daily pursuits to come and pay last respects to the squire. Jody stood now with one long hand resting lightly on the coffin. It was uncertain whether he had heard Maud's outburst or not. He had the air of owning the hall, the dead, the past and the future. He wore his old caped cloak worn and faded with use in all weathers, and over his left eye was the black patch Norah had seen him wear at her wedding. A puckered scar coursed beneath it down his pale cheek, drawing the mouth awry. They had marked one another for life, he and she, thought Norah.

They did not shrink from one another. She had a full awareness of the slim powerful body beneath the cloak, supple as an animal's and as ruthless. She knew, too, that of all the assembly gathered here today only two persons mattered one to the other as did herself and Jody Curle. In that hour Norah admitted his power over her, a power no other being had or ever would hold. Jody was the man for her, and it was too late; as Maud had lately said, late, too late!

She knew also an overriding desire that the child in her womb should be this man's, and not Stroyan's. She recalled the name of Stroyan vaguely, as if it belonged to someone met briefly long ago, perhaps in the south.

At the same time anger came, thrusting up through her other feelings; it was the anger of custom. How dared the gipsy's bastard stand here, show himself in the midst of them all as if he were indeed heir to Curle? She heard her own strong and bitter words trying to force him back, out into the uncaring darkness. Where he had come from and where he might now go were not her concern, were no one's here, at Curle. "You cannot stay here," she said aloud, and in a lower voice "You must return to your own kind."

He did not answer at once. Was he, she wondered, a leader among them already? Ordinary folk knew little of the gipsies. Certainly it was they who must have carried him away that day and tended him, perhaps watched how it had all befallen . . . She thrust that thought down: since then, at any rate, they had let Jody live among them, given him one of their own women perhaps. She let herself believe this and that he was evil, evil . . . She saw the teeth gleam between his parted lips, in the light of the candles which shone down on the squire's coffin. Jody looked down, as if the dead man and not herself were uppermost in his thoughts.

"We two were the only ones who cared for him," he said. "His blood runs hot in both of us, Norah. That was why it happened as it did, that day on the hill."

"Be silent," she told him. She was fearful lest he say more, and render her unborn child a bastard in the hearing of them all. "Leave here, now that you have seen his coffin closed. He died a good death."

"Ay," he said in a low voice, "and the cause of it you drove out into the night and the rain, caring nothing for her, as you cared little for me. But you shall have your reward, Norah Stroyan; such things do not remain unavenged, nor are folk as heedless as you believe of other affairs than your own. I swear you have not heard the last of either of us, myself or our grandsire's doxy."

"Is she yours now?" Norah sneered. His single eye regarded her gravely.

"No, but we have common cause in that you injured us both. I made it my concern as soon as I heard, for our news travels fast, to find what had become of her. If she had needed shelter we would have given it. By then, she needed none. She is well enough cared for, and her child when it is born will live."

"So you see into the future in a gipsy's crystal, do you? Get out of Curle; now is no time for such things."

"I will go indeed, and farther than you in your narrow dreams have ever reckoned, for the world's wider than north or south. A ship waits to carry me to far shores."

"To make your fortune, naturally." She still spoke with sarcasm, but could not avoid, for all her banter, a pang of envy; to have been free to sail with Jody wherever he chose to go! The Antipodes, America perhaps; yet here was Curle, and she its owner.

"That, or else leave my bones whitening in some foreign land. But if my plans succeed—I have made them with another, and one cannot be sure of others, eh, Norah?—if so, I shall return to the valley a rich man, who will live to plague you."

"You've done that from the start. Do I have to tell you a third time to go, or must the servants throw you out?"

"Few of your servants would lay a hand on me, for I'm a Curle as they are. Permit, though, that I say farewell to *him*, then I'll trouble you now no longer."

She turned, her eyes pricking by reason of the feeling she dared not name. She did not watch Jody as he stayed for some time by the coffin. Suddenly she had wanted to cry out to Jody to leave his plans, stay here, never leave her or Curle. She'd give him what he wanted, anything at all except the inheritance, anything, money, her body; she'd let him have a place of his own to live, rather than giving Windyett to Corder Bellingham for pin-money rent. Jody might come and go as he wished, and nobody would ask him of it; he might do as he chose, except be squire of Curle. And they would both of them remember the old man and when her son was born he—

Jody had gone.

He had gone, and when she turned to look beyond the dazzle of candles there was only darkness. She did not even know which way Jody had taken. She felt rather than saw Stroyan again at her elbow, face creased with anxiety for her.

"Norah, the Wrayes have called for their carriage. The Duchess felt unwell. They asked me to make their excuses to you and send their love, and to say they hope to see us soon at Wraye."

To see us? she was thinking; why us? Who are we, together, this man I married and myself? What reason brought us together? It had been to please the squire, she recalled; that old man who lay now for the last time among them all, and who would never know of the heir to follow him. It does not matter now, Norah thought. I and none other am the heir to Curle, I and what lies in my womb. And then she thought again of Amy.

"I will send," she said aloud, "as soon as may be, to find out how she fares." And she stared down for the last time at Sir Ludovic's oak coffin. Amy and her child, she herself and her heir, were the future; she must live for that and for Curle, and what she might make it. The half-forgotten ferment revived in her mind about the bringing of southern culture to the valley, with Amy and herself in their separate seats as patronesses of such a culture. They would rival the great hostesses of the south in their salons, aping in their turn those of France where wit vied with wit, talent almost extinguishing talent. But here they would be friends and not rivals, she and Amy.

"How the old man would have mocked at all of it!" she thought. But new times were coming to Curle, the sound of a harpsichord, the timbre of a famous voice, the brush of a painter, informed gossip, melody cozened below the rafters that hitherto had listened only to roystering.

All this Amy had done for her, by taking her south to be presented to the Queen. Through the long night that followed the funeral Norah lay awake, and made her plans, wondering from time to time how Amy was faring. There was no one now on the pillow by her; she was glad Stroyan continued to sleep elsewhere. It meant renewed privacy, and her thoughts shaped themselves best when alone. Only at times in all that night did they dwell on the settling dust above the vault which held her grandfather's coffin.

Next day sad news came. Amy Wraye had miscarried of her child, and it was the old Dowager herself who had held her in her arms and comforted her.

5

THE DAYS THAT FOLLOWED were dry and the sun showed itself weakly among grey clouds. One afternoon Norah took herself up to a high part of the house from which it was possible to step out on to a part of the lichened roof, looking out over the fells and valley. She stayed there for some time, reciting the ancient shape-names she knew so well, trying, by the very repetition, to forget the sight of Amy's wan little face as she had last seen it at Wraye. Jonathan and Amy both had worn a look of stricken grief which was, Norah thought, needless for the loss of a part-made child; there would be others. She had not been allowed any speech alone with Amy; Wraye himself had hovered over them like a watchful parent, or someone in possession of—Norah thought of the analogy again—a delicate Dresden shepherdess, which a rough touch would break. Amy was surely not made of such fragile stuff. Later, when the weather was better, she herself would go over in the light carriage and persuade her to come out for drives. The scenery would divert her mind and—Norah did not add this to herself—they would be alone, without Jon Wraye to fuss. That he looked greyer and older Norah had also noted.

She jerked her mind away from the tragedy at Wraye and let it dwell instead on little Madge and her miller. Yesterday she'd gone down on foot to the mill, to see how matters there were progressing after the squire's death. Madge's tall husband George had been at work, with the sweat making runnels in his face which was grey with a fine mist of flour. No doubt it was the flour which made George cough. Madge herself, her tiny body distended with the miller's child, had been up to her elbows in yeast dough, making her bread. "Taste if for y'self, Mrs. Norah," she had called out pertly, and had handed her mistress a fragrant, new-baked crust from the ovens. That hadn't stopped Norah from taking the tithe-money; the couple must be doing well enough, and even with the baby expected they would have been able to set something aside. She'd seen Madge's mouth tighten after her request, but the money had been brought, and Norah had put it in her reticule and said goodbye graciously. She must have an eye to that cough of the miller's; it might be the flour and it might not.

She stayed in her high place, aware of the everlasting bustle of Curle below her, with its thousand noises which had been familiar since she had ears to hear; the sound of the servants shaking out their brooms from the morning's cleaning and sweeping, and the chatter of two maids who were plucking fowls for tonight's dinner and stowing the feathers in a sack, to be made later into pillows. In the yard the other hens still pecked and crooned contentedly, and among them, armed with buckets and stable-brushes, the grooms came and went. It was all of it soothing. Norah leaned, for her greater ease as she had begun to grow heavy with the child, against the chimney-stack behind her, and surveyed the jumbled houses of the village with their plots of cabbage-rows. Between here and there was the small house called the Moat, left from the days when there had been such an item at Curle; it bridged the space across what had once been water. Old James Curle, long retired from his tasks as groom, lived there, but would surely die any day now; his sister, who was married to a farmer on the hill, came daily to see to his needs. There would be the Moat to let and . . . Windyett. She saw it, rising from the slope of the op-posite hill, and recalled that it was still empty. The squire in his old age had grown lax about the lettings, and a good deal more than firing would be needed before she could suggest that Corder Bellingham move in. At the moment he stayed on at Curle, being good company for Stroyan; oddly, the frivolous young man and her anxious husband agreed well to-gether. Perhaps it was impossible to disagree with Corder; at any rate, she herself would rather he remained in the north, and nearby. He contributed to the diversion of the long evenings, for she could not yet make arrange-ments for visiting musicians and guests at Curle: he taught amusing card-games, and had even more amusing stories built round them. She herself now enjoyed a good evening's play, almost nightly, with Corder. Stroyan sometimes took a hand and sometimes wandered off to his books, or letter-writing; whatever he did. Norah became aware that she could no longer ac-count for Stroyan's every hour, but the fact did not trouble her. No doubt it was to acquaintances among his mother's bluestocking friends, or to his mother herself, that he wrote. Apart from Corder, Stroyan seemed to have few friends of his own. She must try to devote more leisure to him. Where he might be at this moment she did not know.

She continued to gaze idly down, watching and noting, despite herself, the activity of everyone else in the place. It was already a feature of hers to annotate, stow away details in the depths of her mind, for future use. The grooms in the yard she had already decided were sleazy and unkempt. Before long she'd make it a rule that they must wear livery coats, and powder in their hair, as was done in the south. The maids like-wise—her fancy roved and expanded—should wear, every one, gowns of the same blue cloth, with ribbons threaded in their linen caps according to station, laundry-maid, cookmaid, housemaid, all. If she herself put on an appearance of prosperity—and the money for it was not lacking—it would be the first step towards being known as a hostess who was worth visiting for her well-ordered house. Later the candlelit assemblies at Curle would be talked of as far south as Surrey. She was determined on that.

A visitor was approaching now. Norah espied the swaying, jolting coach as the horses rounded the road-turn, a half-mile off. She took her skirts in one hand and negotiated the step back to the house-top floor, and twisting stairs; and hurried down the latter. The thought came to her again that her pregnancy hadn't deterred her yet from doing any single thing she wished; she still lived her life as she was used, ate heartily—but that was to be expected—moved easily, and rode out on the bay whenever she would. That was as it should be, and sickly fancies were for folk like Stroyan, who at the beginning had tried to stop her. "I'll do as I choose in my own place," she had told him, and thereafter he said nothing more of the matter.

"Madam, Mrs. Stroyan, 'tis the Duke's coach from Wraye; and I swear 'tis the old lady herself inside, though they say she's nigh dead."

The excited little maid, broom still in hand, received a cold glance from her mistress; such announcements must be made properly and formally in future, and not bandied as if from one equal to another on the stairs. Norah made this clear, then let the flushed girl go. "I will receive the Dowager Duchess myself, but in future remember what I have said." It was probably, she thought, Mrs. Emma the Dowager had come to see. It was certainly an occasion; the old woman had not been to Curle itself for a matter of years except for Norah's wedding day; she had not even bestirred herself to attend Sir Ludovic's funeral.

The coach lurched to a standstill; seeing Norah on the Hall steps the footman jumped down, and would have opened the coach-door, but the Dowager wound down the window. "I'm not getting out, you fool; tell Mrs. Stroyan to come in here to me," she commanded. Norah went, obediently; how that harsh authoritative voice brought back the lumpish awkward child she herself had been, not so long ago!

She shook out her skirts and seated herself beside the Dowager, whose feet were propped up on cushions. The old face turned to her, innocent now of paint. The Dowager, as Norah realised, looked very ill, and old; as old as the fells, and wiser, perhaps. Norah tried to smile her welcome, all the time wondering if there were further bad news of Amy.

"Ye are beginning to show," said the Dowager, her yellowed eyes on Norah's middle. "When's the birth?"

"Truth to tell we are not certain." Norah disliked prying, and answered coldly. Trust that old woman to ask awkward questions of her!

"Ought to be. Can't your physician tell you?"

"I have not consulted a physician."

"Wraye's wife had to have one. But ye know of that. Expect ye're wondering why I've come, without asking for y'mother. I didn't want to see Emma today, but y'self; that surprises you, eh? But Amy is not well."

"She will recover, given the summer and plenty of rest."

"Won't rest, even now; works in her garden. She guesses at the truth, y'see, and it grieves her as well as Wraye. But it's worse for Wraye, although the title's young; small matter, maybe, if it ceases. But he thinks on't all the same, and that if Shawhope had lived, and married, all would have been different. No sense brooding over the past, I say; ay, even at the age I am. Do ye know my age, Norah Stroyan? I'm ninety-one; we're a long-lived family. But *she* won't make old bones. The Bellinghams, mind ye, are unstable; haven't I always said so, ever since y'grandfather would take Maud? True, Maud had enough to drive her out of her wits; but there's another sister, Edith, down in Somerset, where she married, that no one ever sees. Amy mustn't get like that. We must all see to it, you also, Norah. Ye don't feel love for many folk, but I believe y'love Amy. Do what y'can to divert her mind, will ye? Wraye says ye have some notion, after this birth, of invitin' fiddle-players and the like; do that, and ask Amy."

"Do you suppose that I would not?" exclaimed Norah. "But surely all hope is not lost of their having other children." It had been an early miscarriage, she thought; nothing so out of the ordinary as everyone made it seem. "Amy will conceive again within the year," she said, smiling.

"That she will not. Physician says it'd kill her; her heart's weak. Wraye won't have her told."

"Wraye won't—" Poor Jonathan, courageous at the last, with a kind of courage his brother perhaps would not have had. He would take the blame, no doubt, for Amy's barrenness. For that exquisite creature to be barren, like a useless mare . . .

Norah realised that tears were scalding her eyes and she could no longer see the Dowager except as a blur. Later it struck her as singular that the bitter old woman should have taken the trouble to come over herself in the coach to tell her, Norah, of the situation. Perhaps it was because the old woman too loved Amy. No one could look on that charm and beauty without feeling love; and she herself, who had neither, was not even envious. That itself was singular; so was the fact that she found herself, while they still sat together in the carriage, telling the Dowager of her own plans for bringing talents to the north. Spoken aloud the plan sounded stilted, but the old woman nodded her bewigged head.

"I never did like you, Norah, as a child," she said candidly. "Ye were spoilt rotten, and had y'grandfather on a string, and knew it; and I wouldn't give twopence for that man y'married, if he *is* a man," and she glanced again at Norah's thickened waistline. "There are others, maybe . . . but ye have the power. Power's not a good thing, always, for a woman; it wasn't good for *me*. But I wish that good fortune may attend ye, not at the birth—that'll happen easy—but after, with these grand ploys o'yours. They'll divert Amy and, maybe, console Wraye, if anything can. He was always second to that brother of his, and now—"

Her sagging face fell, and she closed her eyes. Norah offered her wine, which she refused, and likewise would not alight and come into Curle. Presently the coach departed again, precariously as it had come.

6

THE WINTER PASSED. While there was snow on the fells the roads were blocked, and no coach could get through. One of those stranded by the weather was Corder Bellingham, who had intended returning to Curle briefly after a round of southern visits to shoot wild duck with Stroyan before the weather broke. Unable to leave, he made an agreeable fireside companion, for Norah was by now too indolent to play cards. She would sit, idly amused, forgetting her bulk in watching Corder's animated face and expressive hands, with their curiously stubby fingers and short thumbs. He was as she already knew an accomplished mimic, and spared nobody, neither the oddities they had all of them met with in the south or, nearer home, the aged Dowager of Wraye. Corder pilloried the latter mercilessly, his features, so like Amy's in their blue-eyed innocence, somehow taking on the stiffness of plumpers and larded paint. That news of the old woman's last illness would come with the thaw mattered nothing; Norah, hands shielding her belly, laughed boisterously at the resurrection of the face that had mocked her as a child; the encounter in the coach seemed to belong to another life. They were walled in by the snow; it began to seem as if there had never been a time when she was free to walk and ride about Curle. Norah knew well that Corder would in due course go away from here, and imitate herself as aptly in the next house he visited. She had few illusions about Corder, but still hoped to persuade him to rent Windyett when, if ever, he decided to settle down. Meantime it was pleasant to sit, waiting and laughing, over a high-piled fire of logs, and drink mulled ale.

"Dearest Norah, queen of women—" so he was used to address her, kissing her hand with as much ceremony as if she had been Queen Charlotte at Kew—"I am frail blossom, not strong, ready to perish with the first cold wind. But you yourself are an ice-goddess, seated here by your fire with the icicles without the window; brrr! As soon as may be, you know, you'll be out in all of it, with your rich bonny hair blown back by the wind."

"Stop your nonsense, and tell me what you were doing in Liverpool. Amy said"—she had seen Amy before the snows—"that you had been there three weeks. Did you plan to emigrate, Corder?"

"What a witch you are; I had, indeed, a mind to travel abroad, but decided against it. The sight of the grey heaving river was enough." He cast an apprehensive glance at Norah, as though recalling that she was a woman in late pregnancy, and added "There is a tale I would tell, but would not upset you, my goddess."

"You know well enough nothing upsets me. Tell on." She sensed rather than saw Stroyan listening, from the other side of the fire.

"Well . . . I saw your odd relative, Jody Curle."

Norah's expression did not change; within herself, she felt nothing. Jody must be somewhere; she should perhaps express polite interest in what he did. "Well?" she said, smiling, and Corder talked on, his blue glance rolling warily with one eye closed momentarily in a wink, as much as to say he knew the rumours of Jody's status at Curle, and who his father was.

"He was engaged in—a very lucrative occupation. No doubt if he goes further with it he'll do very well, but it'd turn *my* stomach."

"Is he a moneylender?" said Norah flippantly, and stared down into the dregs of her wine. Stroyan still sat unmoving at the other side of the hearth, his features pinched with cold although the fire burned high. His eyes watched the pair of them. Does he certainly suspect, wondered Norah, that he may not be the father of my child? Does he suspect Jody?

She downed her thoughts to take in what Corder was saying. For some reason she felt unwilling to hear all of it. Jody had been at the wharves, testing the muscles of a blackfellow who waited there among others, chained to an iron ring, brought across from Africa as they had all of them been. "I daresay they will find a good market for him, as he has lived," said Corder. "They tell me the scoundrels—my apologies, Norah—who take ship and go and hunt out these poor souls, tearing them away from their native places and their families and bringing them here, earn much gold. They lose a great part of the merchandise, to be sure, with sickness, on the way over, herded down into ships' holds like cattle as these blacka-moors are. The men are sold for hard labour and the young women into brothels." The light voice ceased, and Norah was reminded of another, deeper voice saying, here at Curle, above a coffin, "A ship waits, and will carry me to far shores." So that was the trade Jody had decided to engage in; no doubt he was seeing service as a slave-master before making enough money to buy a share in a ship. Corder's disgust was understandable, but . . .

A wanton notion came then to Norah, able as she was to assess both men, the present and the absent, objectively. How much of Corder's ex-pressed disgust was for the mere thought of living by one's hands at all? He had never done a day's work or earned a penny. They said his inherit-ance from his clergyman father, which in the nature of things had been slight, had all of it been dissipated in debt before Corder came of age. "He lives finely, if mostly on his friends," Norah thought. A rich wife would perhaps be the answer for Corder; if he could not, with his win-ning ways, persuade one to wed him, she herself, after the child was born, must see what was to be done for him among the minor heiresses of the north.

But Jody, perhaps at this moment busied in a torrid swamp or alien forest, trapping black slaves? How could she cavil at him for making his way with no man's help, nor woman's either?

If she had had pity, even that day on the fells . . .

A sound brought her back to the hall; Stroyan had risen and was stir-ring the logs with his foot. Corder had begun another tale. "I will go up to my room for a while, I believe," said Norah. Both men rose, and she moved her unwieldy body across the hall and up the staircase, slowly. Halfway up she turned again to look down on the hall, the fire and the men, and smiled. This was her home, as she loved it; intimate, warm, and a shield from the snow without, which still lay thickly, darkening win-dow-panes. She'd go upstairs and lie down for an hour, and then come downstairs again, and they'd play cards after supper. The child within her was beginning to stir, and she was bigger than she'd expected with the birth not due till spring. Well, it lived in her, and once born she'd have done her duty to Curle, and that should be an end of it. There were things which diverted her more than the notion of many brats clinging to one's skirts; to ride out, free and lithe again, on the bay, and hear the wind singing; to guess at the aces held in a rival's hand by firelight; to gather talent and friends under one roof, and listen and preside, and by day guide the fortunes of the valley folk and see to the properties and farms . . . ay, all that waited, once this ordeal was over for her. She had no great fear of it; she had never in her life known a day's illness, even that time when Jody—

Jody would be on the high seas now, with his harvest of souls. She had best forget him.

7

NORAH HAD DELIBERATELY confused her dates, and by now was uncertain even in her own mind when the birth might take place. The lethargy she had felt during the long winter passed, and after the ice melted she was aware of a new upsurge of energy, of the will to act, order and partake. That day she had followed the guns on foot, a heavy cloak wrapped about her body, and had gone with them all up into the lower fells where the mallard were clustered in the reeds about the tarns. She raised her head as the chill wind caught her hair, sensing with renewed keenness and joy the young year; she heard the familiar sounds of all her life, the splash of water and whirring of wings as the shots cracked out, and the almost noiseless, purposeful rustle of dogs nearby in the heather-stems and furze. They made a good tally, and Norah and the men, Stroyan among them, returned home at the day's end tired, but triumphant, the dead mallards lolling from the gunmen's wrists, the bright sheen of their plumage picked out by the fading sun. They would hang four days from the high beams in Curle's hall, and then there would be a feasting. Tonight there was to be roast pork to eat, and Norah already sniffed the cold air hungrily, her cheeks bright. When Stroyan came over to ask if she felt tired she answered him absently that she did not. They came back to Curle and she went straight to the great hearth with the men for wine, not pausing to wash or tidy her hair. This was a day such as her grandfather would have loved; the high water just ruffled by a light wind, and the birds rising well to the challenge. Often despite her knowledge that his day was past, she still sometimes thought of herself as in Sir Ludovic's company, so strong was his remembered presence at Curle. One might almost imagine his great shape tonight in the firelit shadows, toasting the day's bag. "And he himself would have brought down more than any," Norah thought.

There was not further leisure to recall Sir Ludovic that evening: after the supper of roast pork, when Norah had eaten well, she felt the first onset of labour pains; they were so intense as to make her dizzy. She said nothing, and dug her fingers hard into the table's edge to still and subdue the pain; but it would not be stilled. Again and again the knife-sharp sensations came within her, until at length she knew that it would be necessary to withdraw before the meal's end; this angered her. A force that wrested its way out of her, that would neither wait nor obey; this was what women were subject to, and did it not prove that despite all worldly power she was still only a woman, and prey to all they must endure? She grimaced, and with difficulty rose and left the hall, holding her skirts high against her body and keeping her head erect. When Stroyan tried to come to her to escort her to her room she turned on him savagely.

"Get back to your own affairs, and leave me to mine. Keep them drinking down here a while; there may be—" the pain came, and she twisted her lips against it—"an heir to toast before morning. I'll be quick at the business, I promise you." And she went through the door to the great chamber; not looking back or thinking of Stroyan at this moment.

Once lying unlaced among the pillows Norah bore down, and sped the business as she had sworn she would do; a son was born before midnight. The candles still bore a haze in strange rings before her eyes; she felt no cessation of effort, no abating of the force in her; only this now was an echo of that first fierce pain, as though she'd grown used to it. An animal's business, all this was, with the pain and indignity, and the smell of blood! No one could share it with her; but it must soon be done, for the last time: the last time, she swore.

They brought her the boy, and she could see in the queerly hazed light that his hair was dark-red, and clustered about the tiny skull in curls like shells. Norah smiled faintly; the thing was mostly done with now, and she had the heir. "He is to be called Ludovic," she said clearly. Then another pain tore her, and precipitately, for they had not expected it, the second child was born; a girl, small and puny, with light hair and skin that at first seemed bluish, though with the coming of day the colour cleared. Norah

cared nothing for naming her daughter, and it had been left to Mrs.
Emma, ailing as usual up in her chamber and unable to partake in events,
to choose a girl's name. She had chosen Elizabeth, for no reason. After the
babies were clean they sent for Stroyan, to see his children; he came, bent
dutifully over the cradle and then came to Norah, kissed her on the forehead and asked how she did. She answered at random, as she had done
earlier; now that the births were over she had the intense desire to sleep.
Before drifting over the thought came again to her, as if for the first time,
regarding Stroyan, "He is nothing to me nor I to him, nor is my son any
part of him." Had she been fully awake the last part would not have been
said, perhaps even thought; but always she was to comfort herself with the
certainty that young Ludovic had the true Curle colouring, and the girl
might resemble Mrs. Emma as much as Stroyan himself. "No one can
know now," Norah told herself, lips curved grimly in the shadow of the
great tester above the bed. It was true enough; no one, not even herself,
with the twin-birth and according confusion, would ever know with certainty who had been the children's father. But she was aware of a strange
wish that not Stroyan, but Jody should have bent over her lately, to give
her his kiss; then the notion on waking became so strange that she
laughed at it. Jody, busy with his trafficking of wretched slaves between
the high seas and the ports that looked towards Africa! "He need never return for all of me. That farewell by the coffin might be our last."

Why had she this certainty that it would not be? Jody might never, at
least as long as he were doing well for himself, return. It would be better
if he stayed away from all of them at Curle . . . Curle, wherein even
since the squire's death she herself had begun to reshape its ways and
manners; and from her son.

Upstairs—Norah had given birth in the dais-chamber where all Curles
were born—farther up, Mrs. Emma had permitted, as she sometimes did
nowadays, that old Maud should sit with her. The older woman had been
less strange in her ways since the squire's death, less beset by fear and
foreboding, and was accordingly allowed a measure of liberty. Emma had
the babies brought to her, exclaiming with propriety over her grandchildren, no more, for she had never been a devotee of infants, being too
much taken up with herself and her own ills. She gave them back to the
nurse, and did not so much as look towards them again until, some way
off, she heard a woman's low voice murmur, out of the shadows.

"I baptise thee in the name of the Father, and of the Son, and of the
Holy Ghost."

Mrs. Emma gave a gasp, and looked quickly about her; she was chiefly aware of the luminous stare of her mother-in-law's grey eyes. She really is quite lacking in her wits, the younger widow thought; I should not have allowed the children near her. She bridled in her cap and stays, and began to upbraid poor Maud for what she had done; instantly the madwoman thrust away the second baby, the girl whom she had not yet christened, and began to cry. "I did nothing," she protested, "and I'll not do't again, no, I will not, no matter should it die and salvation be lacking. Do not berate me, good sir, I beg, and I'll not do so again," and her sobbing, together with the certainty she still had at times that her dread spouse was there to be accounted to, made her uncontrolled, and Emma had them take her back to her room and the key then turned, so that she was safe. Thereafter for a long time she herself listened to Maud sobbing and praying, and in the end unlaced, turned her own face into the pillow and went to sleep. She had sat up all night, as she reminded herself, for dear Norah's confinement; it had been a great exertion to do so, and tomorrow she would surely be unwell. Too unwell, assuredly, to say, now or later, what the presence of a jug of water beside her bed had done, or been done to, by Maud. The babies would be christened properly and with pomp in the chapel in presence of the tenants and servants of Curle, and the relations, such as would come. There was no need whatever to mention Maud's lapse to the youngest Ludovic's mother; dear Norah at best would only be very angry.

8

ON Ludovic Stroyan's ninth birthday his mother sent for him to be brought down, with his sister, to the hall after dinner. There she handed him a cup of red wine, as if he were a man. Ludovic was proud of the attention and pleased with the cup, which he had seen often by custom standing in its place on the great oak sideboard. All important healths and toasts were drunk in it, for it had belonged to his great-grandfather, and it was made of worn chased silver with figures of a stag running before hunters about its rim; one turned it and perceived hunters and hunted, then a shield. But tonight he was himself of much importance, and must not spend time toying with the figures. "Before I was born your great-grandsire toasted his heir in this cup, and now I bid you drink to your manhood in it," his mother told him. Ludovic, uncertain whether she was jesting or not—one could not always tell with mother, and her husky lazy amused voice—grasped the cup steadily, although it weighed a great deal, and looked down at the dark wine and his own darkened reflection. Then he looked up at the tall figure of his mother herself, clad today in a velvet gown the colour of the wine, and diamond earrings that swung and sparkled as she moved: and he drank, still watching her. The wine tasted heady. Grown men, he knew well enough, like Cousin Corder, often grew drunk on wine. Shyness took Ludovic; he did not think that he would like to be drunk, and lose his balance and his wits. But one must not say such things to mother.

Norah laughed, helped her son steady the goblet, and led him, still carrying it, to where the portrait of his great-grandfather as a young man hung, in the shadowy place it had occupied from the beginning. "Now that you will soon be a man, drink a bumper to the squire's memory, and try in all things to become such a one as he was," she said, as though she mocked his late thoughts. Ludovic looked up, with his gentle and considering grey gaze, at the terrible eyes of that other after whom he had been named. One must not hurt mother by saying one did not care greatly for the squire, who continued to stare grimly out of the canvas as if oneself and everyone else were not there. However it was only a painting. Ludovic drank politely, then turned his head to look for Elizabeth, who had hung back, shy and awkward, and was left as usual standing by herself at the farther end of the hall. Ludovic felt a quick rush of sympathy for his sister. Nobody except papa and himself had remembered that it was, when all was said, Elizabeth's birthday as well. Ludovic had given her a lace-edged handkerchief and papa a box of paints. "Can Eliza taste the wine, mother?" he said timidly. He had always been aware, from the time he could crawl, of the needs of others; every tenant, servant, cat and dog about the place was beloved of him and loved him, and he feared no one, not even his mother. It was advisable, as he already knew, to pretend to be a little afraid. Norah frowned now, as he had foreseen she might do. "You, not your sister, are the heir of Curle," she told him shortly. "Do as you're bid, boy; drink up the wine."

Ludovic raised the heavy vessel obediently, and with difficulty managed to quaff the contents, which made him queasy. Norah laughed again, and cast an arm about her son's shoulders. "Now you have drained your draught, and henceforth you shall take your place at the table at dinner, not upstairs in the schoolroom: 'tis time you were among men." She led

Ludovic back to the company at the hearth, talking all the time in the way she had, as though there were no one except herself to answer or ask questions. The boy might have been a shadow. He was uncertain when it had become manifest to him that what he himself felt for his mother was a kind of pity, which was strange. Mother was so large and powerful, and had only to give an order to have it obeyed: everyone here tonight hung on her words: she had the grandest gowns in the county and the broadest acres, and yet . . . What was it mother lacked, and the new governess, Miss Pryde, possessed in abundance, though she was small and plain? "She has only the one gown," Ludovic remembered Elizabeth's telling him, as if it were Miss Pryde's fault she were poor. But Miss Pryde had other things. Ludovic remembered her pleasantly. Perhaps after all mother wouldn't keep him altogether from the schoolroom, and he could then ask . . . could ask what? What it was mother lacked? That would be like discussing her with servants; Miss Pryde was, in her way, a servant, and when she arrived mother had made her unpick the bands of braid that embellished her one gown. It didn't matter, except that that left nobody whom he could ask. Papa would only turn away his head and start to talk, very gently, about shells or flowers. Eliza would be frightened and would start to gnaw at her thumb; she bit her nails badly. To ask mother herself would in the nature of things be impossible. So that left nobody. Perhaps when he was older the matter would become clear to him, like so many of the things which were to happen then. Meantime, he had better concern himself with other things; the things Miss Pryde could readily talk about.

"She knows a great deal," the boy told himself. She had already made lucid, without pain, in Ludovic's mind the position of the planets about the sun, and that God had put them there. This was fully clear to the listener, for God figured in all things concerned with Ludovic's waking day; the buds on the trees, the grace of a cat as it walked across the yard, the limitless nature of the sky, all were God's work and God was somehow in all of them. Only one couldn't say so to mother. God for her was strictly in church on Sundays, and should then be dispensed with. Oddly enough, and this apart, it was strange how little about anything mother knew; excepting of course the judging of a mount or a gun, and the correct keeping of account-books to be gone over with the bailiff twice monthly: all the things she said he, Ludovic, must know in due course, but as to the rest . . . "She cares nothing," a voice in his mind said, in adult fashion. The same voice told him what he knew already, that both papa and Miss Pryde, who knew so much in their separate ways, must none the less take their orders from his mother. Perhaps this was not so extraordinary after all: perhaps his head was muddled with the wine. Mother was certainly a judge of wine, and food—she was said to give the finest dinners in the county—and sometimes, as would happen tonight, singers or musicians came, and the great folk of three shires would assemble at her invitation to hear them. "They are as famous as the concerts at Wraye," thought Ludovic, who had not attended the latter but had been told of them by Cousin Corder Bellingham. Cousin Corder told one a great many things, but one could not trust him enough to tell him things in return: they would be repeated and made fun of, as soon as there was other company.

Ludovic sighed. The things he had always known were changing a little. Cousin Corder, who though untrustworthy was so amiable and amusing when he was not drunk, had come home to Windyett lately from the south with a new wife. Mother had been angry: Ludovic recalled her pacing the floor. "I'd have found him a bride with a dowry, and a name besides, in the end: if only he'd heeded me! Now his debts are as bad as ever, and who will redeem them? Not I, I swear." But she had allowed Corder and his new bride, who some said had been a milliner and others a lady's maid, to live on at Windyett, where Madeleine, which was the bride's name, aped finer airs than anybody. She seemed, Ludovic privately thought, too stupid to have made hats and bonnets; certainly she made none now, but sat like a dressed-up doll all day, while Corder chose new gowns for her. Perhaps she had been a lady's maid after all.

"Will they be here tonight, mother?" he asked suddenly, forgetting that she could not have known he was thinking of Corder. He became aware of the other company, assembled about the fire, dressed in finery because of the concert later; even papa wore powder. Stroyan however kept himself somewhat withdrawn, merely conversing with the bailiff who dined fortnightly at Curle, on the days the books were due. The boy moved a little nearer; it was comforting to be beside papa. He and the factor, whose name was Thwaite and who was blood-kin to old Hannah in the days of the squire, were speaking together of the miller George Yonge and his wife Madge, down in the valley. Tragedy had overtaken them and their small son, Wil. The cough Norah had long ago noted in the miller had worsened, and by now he had begun to spit blood and Norah had ordered that they all of them remove to a farm-cottage high on the slope, to tend pigs and chickens. It was a step down in the world for Madge, and she resented it bitterly, and the loss of her income from baking. But Norah had been adamant. "They are taking it hard," Ludovic heard the bailiff say, and the man added that a new miller would be difficult to find and that perhaps it would be necessary to go as far as Westmorland. "It'll not please Mrs. Stroyan if we bring in foreigners," said Thwaite in low tones. Mrs. Stroyan's husband did not reply. As everyone knew, it was not expected of him.

Norah meantime had sought to answer her son's query and had found him gone. She beckoned him from where he stood by Stroyan. She was smiling, with the imperious, placid smile Ludovic knew so well. When he reached her, she put a broad finger under his chin.

"Are you flown with the wine you have drunk that you ask me a question and then go away?" she said amiably. "Will who be here tonight, child? A hundred folk are coming, to hear the Italian singer; and as it is your birthday you and Eliza shall come downstairs with your preceptress, and watch."

By this time—how soon she would forget what she had said, and that she had already told him that he was free of the schoolroom!—Ludovic knew that all he had to do was bide his time to see whether Corder and Madeleine came or not. If they came—and it was like enough the bride would want to show off some new toilette—he himself would be able, as he often did, to watch Cousin Corder bow over his mother's hand, and speak to her as if she were a queen. And yet, behind her back—"I have heard him imitating mother," the boy thought shamefacedly. It was true that Corder imitated everyone, and that he had not known Ludovic was listening; but, even so, to have watched the miming of that goddess-stride, the scowl and fine bosom, and the giving of orders in the lazy complacent voice, had been . . . unpleasant. That was when he'd decided Corder was not to be told things, things of his own. The boy closed his finely curved mouth over the knowledge. No doubt as one grew older it was necessary to keep a great many things to oneself, like papa.

He was suddenly aware of being intolerably lonely in the hall among men; he wanted Eliza and Miss Pryde. Presently he crept away and found them, knowing his mother would have forgotten she had ordered him to stay downstairs. Mother was like that, and had found a new interest already to discuss with one of the guests; it concerned the singer, and someone said, "But where will my lord be put to sleep?" and all the company laughed, and to the sound of their laughter Ludovic made his silent way upstairs, Elizabeth following like a shadow. She had not said a single word since descending to the hall, having received any birthday congratulations there had been in silence.

·   ·   ·   ·   ·   ·

Tina Pryde the governess had not accompanied her charges downstairs. She had not been bidden to do so, and in the course of only a very short time at Curle she had learned that to make assumptions as to Mrs. Stroyan's unexpressed commands might very well be considered a fault. "Had I wanted you to show yourself I'd have sent for you," that lady might state, unequivocally, glancing down from her superior height and grandeur on poor Tina shorn of her harmless braided bands. The governess, therefore, whose professional timidity was not assumed—she was naturally very shy—did not question the matter. In the series of households wherein she had hitherto served she had been browbeaten, frozen, ignored, and tacitly insulted in almost every manner excepting seduction. Curle was no worse than most, and she was fond of her charges. She was knitting a wool wrist, now, on four needles. As the children entered she laid down the work and smiled. How handsome Ludovic looked, in his blue coat and with the sun on his copper-bright hair! He would make a fine man, if—

"What are you making?" enquired Elizabeth, using the tone of mild condescension she might have done to the grooms, or the kitchen-maids. Norah's daughter was subdued only in presence of her mother, whom she greatly feared, and otherwise regarded all humanity, with the exception of her twin, as inferiors. Stroyan she tolerated. She was an unattractive child with pinched features in which the blood ran too thin, and her eyes seemed always red-rimmed; she had chilblains, and her straight lank hair hung limply on either side her cheeks half-an-hour after emergence from curling-rags. Had she shown hope of beauty her mother might have exploited her; as it was, she ignored her, a state of affairs to which Elizabeth submitted with relief.

"It is a surprise," replied the small governess placidly. She had taken up her knitting-needles again, and seated there in the late sunlight looked what she was, a no longer very young woman who had never been other than plain. She had no single remarkable feature and it was this fact, and her undoubted quiet talents, that had procured her a steady succession of posts in her precarious calling. The needles clicked steadily. Elizabeth opened her mouth to say that she didn't think there ought to be a surprise they didn't know about; but she was forestalled by a knowing, merry expression on Ludovic's face, and before she could speak he pointed to the knitting and said, "It's for Eliza, eh?"

The little governess nodded, and said she was afraid that it might not be completed in time for the birthday. "But perhaps for tomorrow, and if it is a cold day, you shall wear them. I have the other complete already;

see!" And she produced an object from her reticule which proved to be a brown woollen mitten. Elizabeth stretched it over her small chilblained hand, wordless but pleased. In all of her life nobody had thought of supplying such humble comfort for her; certainly not her mother.

That night, when the singer Isabella Vianti came to Curle, was the zenith of Norah Stroyan's fame as a hostess and patroness of culture there. Over the years she and Amy Wraye, half in partnership and half in friendly rivalry, had attempted many such ventures. They had been tentative at first and with a few invited guests only. Few hereabouts at the beginning cared for music, or would summon the patience to listen and learn. To make it the fashionable, the desirable thing to do to come to concerts and recitals at Curle had been part of Norah's self-imposed task: even now, if she were honest with herself, she was uncertain whether it were not the glory of playing hostess rather than a true love of the arts which sustained her. With Amy it was otherwise; but Amy was restricted by lack of money, and her purse would not summon the finest singers and players, although she never lacked for guests. Every now and then, it was she who would hear of a needy harpsichord player, or harpist or 'cellist, who might be persuaded to come north and play at Wraye or Curle for a fee. Gradually Norah had assimilated knowledge from Amy, and added her own shrewd ability to assess which was talent and which was fraud. She would never be a connoisseur, but she put a good face on it; and the county knew no difference.

The singer tonight was another matter, celebrated enough to have been heard of even in the north. This time Norah had not obtained her knowledge from Amy, but from Corder, who had heard the singer in London and knew her tale: a young girl, trained by the nobleman who was her protector, and who had herself once—as Norah had ascertained—been no more than Isa Smith from Clerkenwell, although by now one of the most renowned sopranos in Europe. She had already sung before the Court, and in the bluestocking circles patronised by Stroyan's mother, who was lately dead. That Norah should have been indebted to her mother-in-law for an introduction would have been barely tolerable; towards the end they had parted on bad terms. It was all on a par with the death of Mrs. Emma, who after many assumed attacks had suddenly taken one of a morning which left her grey in the face, and fallen dead of it. "Grandmother Maud still wanders upstairs, however," thought Norah, letting her mind drift for instants. It was incredible that of all those who peopled her own clumsy, foolish past only that cobweb remained. Maud had her sane hours at times; she had heard of them from Ludovic, who showed no fear of his great-grandmother and visited her often. But she herself had no wish to see any such reminder of her own ungracious youth. Now—as Corder would assuredly tell her—she queened it over them all; all of the invited county seated on gilt chairs specially brought to Curle by the York carrier. Among the powdered bewigged heads La Vianti's middle-aged protector, who had fathered her four children, nodded his. He took snuff and scratched his shaven pate beneath the wig, and Norah watched him indulgently. It was both useful and pleasant to have another titled guest at Curle.

In moments, when she herself gave the signal, the concert would begin. She scanned the invited heads and consoled herself that there was one member absent, for he had not been sent a card: her present tenant at the Moat House, Walter Shillingthorne.

Norah shrugged beneath her velvet. Later there would be a time to think of Walter; later. She had hoped to curb his arrogance by not inviting him tonight; tomorrow, she'd call and find out how he fared. It could not but wound his pride to lack an invitation, which was as well: by degrees, she'd tame it.

Where was her son? Ah, there he sat, with his sister and the governess. She'd sent instructions to the creature to bring them down; afterwards, Miss Pryde could go back to her attic room. Many in her position, as Norah had pointed out to her on arrival, were not given private quarters and must sleep in the same room as their charges, but there was room and to spare at Curle. Tonight, though, they were cramped enough, with La Vianti and her viscount staying with a maid and a valet . . .

The accompanist had come in now, bowed to Norah and the assembly and seated himself at the harpsichord. A buzz of talk continued throughout the hall.

This is where I once danced to Jody's piping, thought Norah suddenly. What has become of him? I have heard nothing, nothing, since that time at the squire's funeral, but I know he must be in foreign parts if he is alive; and if he were dead I would assuredly know.

Why was she so certain that she would know? What had been between them was buried, and the feeling she now had for Shillingthorne a mere echo, a fantasy on the theme. How knowledgeable she was becoming about words! It was all due to Amy, seated there in the crowd by Jonathan Wraye; dear Amy, a trifle *distraite* now that her barrenness continued and, in despair of children, she must squander her energies on such things as these. Yet they were not worthless in themselves.

There was an instant's hush; La Vianti had appeared above in the gallery. When they had viewed her the talk renewed itself, but Norah retained an impression of childish beauty. "She might be sixteen, and her dress that of a vicar's daughter," she thought. She leaned forward in her place to catch Amy's glance; the other smiled expressively. La Vianti nodded to the accompanist, arranged her skirts, then began to sing.

Her voice was pure as a boy's; the liquid notes dropped through sudden stillness. I have never, Norah thought, known the folk here to be so still, listening; perhaps the air is familiar to them, or perhaps at last they are beginning to understand and appreciate. The singer had chosen a simple north-country tune, and at the end everyone clapped, and demanded that she sing it again, and again; but La Vianti made her customary modest curtsy and the harpsichord, below, played the opening bars of a melody by Lulli. The notes thereafter fell lightly as a thrush's song, dropping through the thick air of the hall. That everyone was still silent was a tribute to La Vianti's greatness. Often enough an ignorant squire would prose aloud through a concert, as through a sermon. But tonight everyone listened, and Norah was content.

Amy Wraye and her husband sat nearby the centre of the great horse-shoe of seated guests, suitably placed for a full view of the harpsichord and its manipulated notes and pedals. Amy had felt warm satisfaction at being so favourably placed by Norah's unobtrusive, well-trained house-steward. Dear Norah never forgot her comfort, and would go out of her way to see that she and Wraye were made to feel at home. Amy glanced along, without appearing to turn her head, to where her brother Corder and his new wife sat; she herself would have made the darkly beautiful Madeleine welcome, but Wraye said she must keep a suitable distance, a *froideur* between the households; and Amy always obeyed her husband, to whom she was devoted. If only she could have given Wraye an heir! But time passed, and it had begun to seem as if she would never bear a living child; best not to think of that tonight, with all the company here . . . Norah's children were so healthy; how straight Ludovic sat, beside his sister and his preceptress, for all the world as if he were still in the saddle, to which his mother had of course early accustomed him! Dear Norah. Everything in her house was as it should be, all the servants in their prescribed livery, with the men in powder. "Curle is a great house, and is becoming as famous as Chatsworth or Hardwick in the south," thought Amy, who had seen both. Ludovic would be a fitting squire for it. How like the Curles his colouring was, with the fair Saxon skin and chestnut hair! His chin—she could see from here—was cleft a trifle, and the line of his cheek was already high-boned and proud; of whom did he remind her? Amy could just recall his great-grandfather, the old squire on whom Norah so doted, and the portrait in the hall was like him in feature and expression, so grim and forbidding . . . The girl also was different. Amy had tried to feel affection for Elizabeth, for she could hardly deny it to any creature; she observed that the child was correctly dressed tonight, in grey watered satin with matching French slippers. Perhaps one could cultivate her when she should be a little older, and Norah had—as Norah of course would—contrived to have her taught dancing, and to use a fan and curtsy . . . The women here seemed more apt to follow the pursuits of men, however; riding hard through the night, trampling after shot birds, climbing the high fells. Wraye would never permit his wife to do such things, nor did she desire to.

La Vianti sang on. Soon tears began to roll down Amy's cheeks, making channels in the rouge. Jon Wraye, himself with an ear inclined to the divine music, kept his eyes on his wife; he still watched constantly, in love and fear for her. Since the loss of their child—and Jonathan knew well enough there could be no more—Amy's state had bordered increasingly on the unstable. He had the unvarying remembrance of Maud Bellingham, Norah's grandmother and Amy's own kinswoman, in his mind, and for this reason he would seldom let Amy drive or walk alone. By day, as he knew, she worked in her garden, or played wild airs of her own on her harpsichord, and apart from the concerts saw little company except for Norah and Norah's children, and her own brother Corder . . . who by now had saddled himself with an unsuitable wife.

Wraye saw a teardrop spill down on his wife's gown, and knew relief when the aria came to an end. Poor Amy was affected so passionately by all music that sometimes he asked himself if she should be permitted to listen to it. But it gave her pleasure to look forward to such things. "It is anticipation that is the greater joy," Wraye told himself. "The reality can be sorrowful. It is to be compared with life." He contemplated his own without expression.

La Vianti finished her songs. Afterwards she retired and was not presented to the company. The viscount himself drank Norah's wine, and ate supper with the rest of the assembly. Everyone would go to bed late and rise early, when the men and Norah would shoot. The viscount expressed interest, and subsequent satisfaction; it was many a year since he had seen such a handsome rise of birds, or spent as profitable a visit.

.   .   .   .   .   .

"Papa, Eliza had three birthday presents yesterday; what do you suppose was the third?"

"It was mittens," said Elizabeth downrightly, displaying her warmed hands. "Miss Pryde made them for me."

"That was indeed kind."

The four, the children, the preceptress, and David Stroyan, stood by the wall, having encountered one another on return from a walk. Stroyan had not gone out with the guns. He shed his bitter mood and made himself agreeable now, feeling as he did so the constant, subtle awareness of insult leave him. Here was kindness, from an unexpected quarter; the small plain woman whom he had for some time seen in charge of Elizabeth and Ludovic curtseyed and flushed, evidently unused to notice or thanks. That was pleasant. Stroyan looked down at this other, lesser being than himself; even her height was less than his, and she seemed almost shapeless in the enveloping shawl she wore against the cold. He was weary of grandeur in which he had no part, weary of mouthings concerning this and that; how pleasant it would be to sit for an hour by the fire beside this quiet creature, and the children!

"Come in to the hall fire," he said, "it is being kept high against the shooters' return."

"But Mrs. Stroyan will not expect—"

"I have invited you to join me," he said with sudden dignity, and smiled. "My son tells me you have much knowledge of the planets and the stars. That is a field in which I am ignorant."

"But you have knowledge of—of botany, sir; I have it from the children."

It was a pleasant hour. When Tina Pryde—he was only to find, after long and close acquaintance, that her full name was Clementine, and she had been advised to suppress it because of its Jacobite affinities—took a child by each hand, and led them upstairs for their bread-and-milk, Stroyan saw her go with regret. He would not have described himself as anxious to pursue a relationship with Tina in any other sense than that they were both lonely; perhaps even that notion had not yet formed itself in his mind. But he would see her again; it would become a habit with him to join her and the children in their walks, and talk to them of wayside flowers and the flints of slate one could find hereabouts which sometimes, rarely, contained shining garnets in their heart. Such things filled his mind until, soon enough, he was to become aware that the soothing influence of Tina on him was necessary to him and he would not be quit of it, or of her, willingly: for more than any other thing she made him forget that, in all these years since the children's birth and before, he had not in any physical sense been Norah's husband. It was in fact incredible to Stroyan even now that he should ever have possessed Norah. To couple with a goddess was no part of common man. And he was such, if no more, and in need of kindness.

9

"I HAVE TWICE sent word by my factor that that chimney must come down; the smoke from it enters my windows, and stinks abominably."

"I have no control over the wind. You should keep your casements shut. Without a tall chimney the fire does not draw."

"You take small thought for anyone but yourself, Walter Shillingthorne." She looked round the room at the Moat in some anger, tempered by curiosity; the children had been in here often during Walter's tenancy, for he whittled them toys. He could make or mend anything with his long, habitually grimy fingers and a worn sharp knife he carried. Other than that, his baggage was small. The room, she saw, was in an incredible state of filth, with egg-shells and other rubbish lying about the unswept floor. Norah wrinkled her nose in disgust. "You might at least keep the place clean." And yourself, she failed to add; his person stank somewhat when one drew nearer. She was, as always in Walter's presence, half ashamed of her interest in him, which she knew, without prevarication, to be sexual. Despite the dirt and odour she would give much to have this man in her bed. It was doubtful however if he had been in any woman's. There was a strangeness about him, which from the beginning had both attracted and repelled Norah. He had come to the door of Curle one day, asking if there were instruments to mend; and she had given him a broken harpsichord peg to turn, and had been pleased with the way he had carried out the task. Thereafter she had let him stay on at the Moat for a low rent. In speech he was a gentleman, but any questioning as to how he came to be travelling the roads on foot, like a pedlar or horse-dealer, met with short answers. She knew nothing more about Walter Shillingthorne than the day he had come, except that he made a pittance by mending rakes and reaping-hooks about the farms.

In appearance he was very tall, and if cleansed and dressed in fine attire would have looked like a prince. His greying hair had once been fair, and he had the faraway blue eyes, with a cleft between them, that belonged by descent to the Angles, that strange folk who had come north long ago, and settled in Cumberland, leaving the warlike Saxons and Jutes, and even their own Anglia, to fare as best they might. No Angle was warlike; they described themselves as men of peace, having a vision somewhat like the second-sight of the north, so that they could foretell events and sense matters which passed other men by. But Walter was such a liar he would have claimed to be an Angle whether he were one or not. Norah returned to the immediate question of the chimney, which he had himself extended, out of local stone, without her permission. It was not that she could not live with the smoke, she thought; it was the fact that a tenant had made alterations to a house of hers without consulting her. In the end, no doubt, she would have let Walter have his taller chimney. But now—

"Are you going to demolish that smoke-hole, or must I send in my men to do so for myself? Answer me, if you please; I've had enough of your silences."

"I will speak when I choose, and keep silent when I choose. I have no desire to talk with you. I pay my rent, and that is all the concern you need have with me, Mrs. Stroyan."

The blue eyes scanned her coldly. An arid he-virgin, that's what he is, she was thinking. At first she had tried to tempt him to her society by invitations to wine-drinking, a concert at Wraye, the like; but he continued self-sufficient and uncommunicative, though Norah had seen him talk with her daughter Elizabeth and at that time his face had been quite different; lit up with interest, even affection. Why should he prefer the company of an unattractive child to her own?

But company did not matter greatly to Walter Shillingthorne; he was, she guessed, in love with himself, and she would only make a fool of her position by cozening him further. She had long ago stopped sending him invitations to social events, hoping that perhaps enforced solitude and scorn would sting him to come to her, even to seek her out on some unimportant matter. But it had not happened.

What was wrong with her that she should feel attraction to such a man —if he *was* a man? To counter it, to rid her mind of him for a while, she had yesterday ridden up with the children on their ponies to visit Madge and her sick husband at the hill cottage, and ask how they fared. "I might have saved myself the trouble," thought Norah grimly. Madge was no longer a friend. She resented, far more than did the stricken miller, the cavalier way they had been put out of their mill; being made to care for pigs and chickens was a come-down, even though they must agree that she couldn't have blood in the flour. The sight of Madge's bitter, changed face, mouth indrawn now that she had lost her teeth, troubled Norah. As some recompense, she had arranged that Wil, the boy, should come down to the great house to take daily lessons with Ludovic. Madge should be grateful that her son would not grow up an illiterate boor; but all she had said was "Is he to be page or groom, madam? One or the other it will surely be," and had turned indoors before Norah was out of sight, back to her fleshless skeleton of a husband whom she loved. The whole episode had left Norah with a feeling of inadequacy, though she had only done as she ought; and now here was Shillingthorne, troubling her still.

She studied him in exasperation. "So you would prefer to leave the Moat sooner than comply with my wish? I'll have no hesitation, I assure you, in turning you out. What I order here is done. You may have your last few weeks' rent returned if you wish." She said this to anger him, for he was proud; he raised his head.

"You may keep the money, for money is your god. It is time I went in any case; I have stayed here too long."

"Where will you go?" She would not have him know she regretted his going.

"Where I choose. I am free, which you are not, Mrs. Stroyan. I would never shackle myself with possessions, and the continuing of a name."

"You are impertinent," she said angrily, and turned to go out. At the door she paused. "The children will miss you," she told him. "Have you no message for them?"

"They have their father." The ghost of a smile flitted over his face, and Norah felt the colour rise in her own. She had best be gone, she knew; it was like enough he had read what was in her mind from the beginning.

She went out, and did not look back. Early next morning she saw from her window the tall laden figure, its bony shoulders hunched below a dilapidated pack, make its way out of the valley. Later they brought her word that Shillingthorne had been seen making towards Wensleydale. In the meantime, to be rid of reminders of him, Norah had her men go down at once and demolish the new chimney. "You had better clean the place while you are at it," she told them. It was hard enough to find tenants for the Moat, and no one would come while it was in such a state. After it was all done Norah fell into a depression of the spirits that lasted for several days, till she made herself find tasks to set, which lifted her mind from its despondency.

. . . . . .

One night as usual she lay in bed with the curtains undrawn, for the weather had grown stifling hot: and watched the moon sail in the sky, casting brightness across the covers and the wall. The hour was late, but Norah could not sleep, and knew that this was a night when sleep would not have come by dawn. What ailed her? She had always slept healthily as an animal hitherto, not troubled by her lonely bed. In fact she had been glad of it, but now—

Shillingthorne was after all nothing to her. He had gone out of her life, and would never return to it. Why did the memory afflict her with anger and shame? She was not, had never been since Stroyan left her bed, avid for any man to share it. Stroyan himself she had found inept, and did not miss his lovemaking. Even now, when she felt herself solitary, her pride would not allow her to go to him. They had grown further apart with the years, "and," she thought, "we were never close." It occurred to her for the first time that Stroyan shared her table many nights without a word passing between them, although they both talked with others. He was more of a stranger than Corder Bellingham, who called her his queen and would, she knew well, have served her in any way she wished before he married that paltry Madeleine. Madeleine! Milly, more like! What blindness had possessed Corder? And he was still in love; there would be no solace there, though he continued courteous, even affectionate. Corder Bellingham was not what she wanted. But if such as Walter Shillingthorne could disturb her peace, what was amiss with her life?

If Jody should ever come home . . .

Norah threw back the covers and found a wrapper. Using the moonlight—there was no need to take a candle, it was so bright—she made her way along the corridor towards the stairs which led down to the bailiff's office. If she could not sleep, she would at least pass the hours looking over the accounts, for she could not trust Thwaite or any man not to cheat her. They all thought, all of them, that a woman was fair game, but she'd already shown them otherwise; and woe betide Thwaite and his like if there were sixpence unaccounted for to help the lining of other pockets. She'd never caught the bailiff out yet; he knew, doubtless, that she kept an eye on him, and there was no time like the remaining still hours of the night for being undisturbed.

She stopped, and drew a breath.

Some way from where she stood, up a half-stair, was the governess's room. She had not even remembered Tina Pryde, so retiring and, to all appearance, so adequate at her duties, was that creature. But now, a figure emerged from the room, and not seeing her where she stood made its way back again to its own place; Stroyan, in his night-shirt, creeping back like a rat into a wall. So *that* was where he spent his nights! Norah knew a rising of deep anger. Tina Pryde, indeed! Tina, with her plain only gown and preceptress's cap, to deceive *her*, and trifle with her husband!

"If it had been one of the maidservants it'd have mattered less," Norah thought, and at the same time the notion occurred to her that never, in all these years, for she'd have been aware of it, had Stroyan been unfaithful with a servant. But now—

"She shall go tonight," a voice in Norah's mind said. No sooner was it sworn than the thing must be done. Norah went and lit a candle, surprised that her fingers were steady. Then, shielding the flame, she went back to the governess's door. She did not knock. The latch gave at a touch.

Miss Pryde had not yet returned to her narrow bed. She stood, vulnerable and small, in her night-shift, her short-sighted eyes blinking in the combined dazzle of moonbeam and candle-flame, and Mrs. Stroyan standing like an avenging fury at the door. It was to have been expected; she had known they couldn't go on as they had been doing, ever since the day a lonely and despised man had first laid his head on her breast, and the shame afterwards lest the servants guess that he often came at night to her room. It wasn't as if Mr. Stroyan himself could do anything for her now; an employer's husband needn't. Tina made a motion with one hand as if to draw together the shift over her flat bosom, then let the hand drop. There was nothing to be done. She said nothing. It was Norah who spoke. She looked the governess up and down contemptuously, holding the candle in firm steady fingers so that the tallow did not drip. The flame reached the corners of the small, shabby room.

"You had best pack your gear now," said Norah, "and leave before morning. I will order the coach."

"Madam, I—"

"You must hurry; the horses will be put to within moments, and I would advise you to leave quietly. The carriage will set you down at an inn on your way, wherever that is. You will receive a purse of money with a month's salary. That, I believe, is as much as you can expect. Few would have given it to you."

"Mrs. Stroyan, may I—"

"I fear I cannot supply you with references; was that what you were going to ask?"

"Madam, I have nowhere to go; there will be no situation for me without . . . your reference." The prim voice trembled. Norah laughed.

"Need we assume that that will deter you from finding a profession? I am going now to wake the grooms. It is perhaps needless to explain why I must lock your door. Kindly be ready and dressed when I send; there will be no loitering, and you must go as you are."

"What shall I do? Where shall I go? Have you no pity?"

"You should have thought of that earlier, should you not? What am I to say about so scheming a young woman as you have proved yourself to be?" God knows, Norah's mind was telling her, the sight of Stroyan and this creature together on a bed would be . . . comical; a pity I didn't surprise them sooner. Through her mockery remembrance came, half-veiled; somewhere, a long time ago, there had been this scene before, with a distraught young woman pleading with her, Norah Stroyan, not to send her defenceless into the night. But then it had been raining.

She heard herself speak coolly. "It is clear moonlight, and should be a fine day tomorrow," she told the other. "Even if you have to trudge a few miles in the end, the going will be pleasant enough. It is nothing to me where you go."

As she opened the door she turned. "By God, woman, many in my place would have flogged you from the house in your shift, and without a penny." She looked at the weeping woman again. What in the world had Stroyan seen to attract him? No doubt, when Miss Pryde had gone her ways, he would be glad enough to forget the matter.

Tina suddenly straightened and spoke with red-eyed dignity. "I asked you if you had pity, madam, but I know that you have none. You have had little all these years for—*him*." The tears started to flow again. "He was so lonely, and so much kept out of all your concerns; you ignored and overrode him in all ways, and I—"

"Pack your gear as you're bid, and not another word." Norah left the small room, turning the key in the lock behind her. She felt the sudden warmth of the doused wick as her fingers snuffed the candle. It was point-less to waste good tallow when the moon was shining. She was glad that the little *mise-en-scène* had been accomplished without noise: she would prefer to be rid of Tina Pryde without waking the household.

By the time the smaller carriage, with two horses put to it, had clattered discreetly out of the yard it was near morning, though not late enough for anyone except the grooms to see the wan, bonneted figure in the interior. Miss Pryde had received an urgent summons, they had been told. They were to drive her a distance of thirty miles, to her direction, then set her down at an inn. Norah, wrapped in a dark cloak, herself stood in the doorway to watch the carriage start; she would not demean herself by appearing openly to bid farewell to Stroyan's mistress, but neither would she lend, by her absenting herself, substance to rumour that there had been other reasons for the governess's going. How much did the servants suspect in any case, Norah thought, and were they laughing already behind their hands, at *her*? The thought filled her with fury. How dare Stroyan make a fool of her with Mistress Pryde!

Stroyan came into breakfast, clad in riding-clothes; he often took a horse across the moors, especially in early morning. He greeted Norah with his usual courtesy. "I see one of the carriages is out of the stables already," he remarked equably. "Was there some untoward matter? I did not hear it go so early."

It was of some satisfaction, after all, to continue eating her food with head lowered, taking her time to give him the answer he must, sooner or later, receive; though she might have hoped to keep the woman's departure from him for a few hours longer, if only to speed Mistress Pryde on her way. Norah suddenly laid down her knife and flung up her head, looking her husband full in the face. "Yes, the governess was compelled to depart unexpectedly. I am glad that her going did not disturb your sleep; the cobbles are noisy. I think, however, that Miss Pryde will have an uneventful journey; the ways are dry and clear." She smiled a little, wiping the gravy from her mouth with a napkin. "Will you take coffee, Stroyan? I fear this may not be hot by now; I'll have them send for fresh, if you should prefer it."

He had turned white about the mouth, in a manner she had never seen in him before; with a small awareness of excitation, almost of fear, she realised that he was deeply angry. David Stroyan angry! "In the whole of our married life I have not seen, still less imagined such a thing," Norah thought. A sudden almost amused sympathy with, perhaps for the first time, understanding of him, came to her. I must not laugh at his affair, she told herself; it's natural enough, after all, for a man to need someone. The memory of her own sleepless night accosted her vaguely, as if the cause were by far removed from Stroyan's late need for anger.

"Where is she?"

He had not answered, not even aided her to keep up the pretence there was, should be, between them. Norah motioned the single servant out of the room. "You will fetch fresh coffee from the kitchens," she said clearly, and waited until the man had gone before turning again to Stroyan, still with that grim white mouth and expression that made of him a stranger.

Strangers, though, they had been in truth these many years to one another, perhaps almost always . . . "Contain yourself before the servants, I pray you," Norah said coldly. "Admittedly your tastes must run to such a class of folk if you can reveal concern over—pah! What was she but a missish pedant? What in God's name, Stroyan, overcame you to couple with such a one? Her teeth needed attention: was her breath foul? I wonder at you, but need do so no more; she's gone, and you need never ask me where; I do not know, and made certain that I should not." She reached for a piece of bread, and crumbled at it; despite her resolve to maintain coolness, her hands were shaking.

"Nothing is more foul than your mind, and your tongue," he told her. "She had what you will never have; kindness."

"Kindness? Would you be coddled, then, like a child in his crib? I've never had the leisure, nor the inclination; you must continue to look elsewhere. But not in my house, David Stroyan; not within the walls of Curle. *That* I will never endure."

"You might well be forced to endure it," he said. "Has it occurred to you, as my wife, that as your husband—and I know well you were not virgin when you married me, God knows whether the children I call mine are so indeed—"

"Damn your fool's tongue, will you talk less loudly? You'll have the household listening at the door by this, with the stir you have made, both now and last night—"

"—that *as your husband* Curle is mine, all of it, despite your boasted pretensions; and that many a man would have flaunted his mistress here openly long ago and have insisted, had he wished it, on his rights to yourself also, though I do not desire that and have never done after the first? Instead, perhaps as reward, I've been the least among your pensioners here, hardly so much to you as your lap-dog or your paid singers, never included in the great designs you have to make Curle the centre of a provincial kind of culture, for you are too ignorant in yourself to know the true from the false; I, the fool, undertaken by you at the first only because you feared you were with child and wanted a father for it who would say naught, as I've done till now!"

"Then say no more, fool as you have said you are; *I* ignorant? I know more than you credit, Stroyan, you with your scholarly pokings among wildflowers and governesses; such ploys for a man! Get out of my sight now, for I cannot endure you this morning; we'll say no more of this; she has gone, and that ends it."

"That may end it, but not in the way you think; for I am going also."

"Are you mad?" she sneered. "You haven't a penny of your own to keep even Tina Pryde in the way she's used, granted you can find her."

"I shall find her, if it takes me the rest of my life."

"Did you purpose to do so on one of my horses? I'll not have it taken out of the stable; you can go on foot."

"I shall go on *my* mount, which shall be returned to you, never fear, Norah; it is time this fable concerning my possessions, or lack of them, and yours, was put to an end for all time. The very horseflesh at Curle is mine to dispose of, as I wish; I shall use it for my journey, and then of courtesy return it to you. The carriage I may take, for a time, when I have found it returning; it also will be sent back."

"You'll ruin the horses; they've already been one way. Go up to your study, Stroyan, and for God's sake cool your head, and think over all of it; tomorrow you'll curse yourself, if you should go."

"I shall curse myself for all my life if I stay, and you also. Long years ago I saw the brutal manner in which you cast a young girl out unprotected into the storm; now you have done the like with the woman I would have wished to marry, and shall do, if I am ever free of you—"

"*Marry* Tina Pryde? You must be out of your senses. I'll not free you, Stroyan; direct your thoughts otherwise." She was sullen now; her fingers gripped the table in the way they had when she was enraged, and her face was suffused; dared Stroyan leave her? The fact that he might indeed do so, and within the hour, raised in Norah, despite herself, remembrances of what he had been, this slight man whom she had despised; might have been to her in greater degree; a gentle companion, a faithful lover, a husband in more than name. But now he would go his way to a flat-chested woman with brown teeth. "To the devil with you, then," said Norah suddenly. "Follow the carriage-tracks, and you'll find the way the bitch has gone; I wish you joy of her season."

She had turned away, and presently heard the door close quietly. She did not watch from the window later as Stroyan went. Still later she learned that he had taken leisure to say goodbye to the children, and had said no word to them against herself. She knew that she would be indifferent to his going after the first sting of insult to her pride had lessened. She still had Curle, and her son.

10

LUDOVIC COULD NOT remember when he had first noticed the packman. It might have been after papa left, when he was often lonely. The packman had not been a part of his life for always, as other things were at Curle; lessons and pony-rides, the company of his mother and Elizabeth and, at times, of his great-grandmother. Since Emma Curle's death old Maud had been less constantly supervised, largely because no one took time to remember about her; and she was often to be met with nowadays about the corridors and stairs, mumbling to herself and clutching her stomach, which she said pained her. Sometimes she whimpered like a child with the pain, and often Ludovic himself was the only one who troubled to comfort her, for the servants feared the tales they had heard of Lady Curle's mad fits and she was all but forgotten by the family downstairs, for she ate alone. Ludovic became familiar with the upper part of the house, where Maud rambled; and it was in this way that he met the packman, whose visits with his wares gave the old lady pleasure; she never failed to ask if he had coloured ribbons, or buckles, and such things. Ludovic noticed that though she asked much, she bought little, for she never had any money. Nevertheless the packman, in his plain dark clothes and shouldering his leather pack, climbed uncomplainingly to see her whenever he came to Curle, and, as such things will his visits to her had long ago become customary, so that no one now remarked them. When her great-grandson was with Maud, he also met the packman; and strange things followed the meeting.

The pack itself was well filled, with thick straps and a buckle to hold it fast; it sagged a trifle with age and use. The packman's own age was itself difficult to determine; he might have been anything between thirty-five and fifty, and had a gentle blunt-featured face tanned by the weather to the colour of wood. Out of this brown lined face his eyes looked, level and blue as the sea. It was the eyes, and their expression, that first attracted the boy; not, as would have been the case with other children, the glories hidden in the pack, the marchpane and oranges; the rag-mammets from France and the leather shoes with red laces and other lace by the yard for trimming shifts. Elizabeth might have busied herself about such things, but not Ludovic after the first. Once when the packman came downstairs from Maud's room the child was waiting, and said to him civilly, "Good day, sir; how did you find my great-grandmother? She was not well yesterday, but perhaps today she is better?" For he knew, without being told, that the packman had befriended Maud, as Ludovic himself had long ago befriended her; she was one more of the helpless things, like Elizabeth and the servants and cats, that could not fend for themselves and needed a protector. Ludovic saw nothing comical or unreasonable in his offering himself in such a way; one understood how people felt if one took time to think about them. Even papa needed understanding; perhaps especially papa.

"She is a little better in her body," replied the packman, "and greatly solaced in her mind and soul." The direct gaze dwelt cautiously on the heir of Curle. If it had been a child like the other, who blabbed, and ran to its elders, there would have been nothing more said except trivialities, the offer of an orange perhaps, and then parting. But now the packman said, in his voice which was not rough, like a countryman's, or with the long broad a's of the north, but cultured, like Corder Bellingham's and papa's, "Do you know what brings her comfort, Ludovic? It is something I carry in my pack; a secret from most folk, and the most wonderful thing in all the world."

"May I know what it is, sir?" It was natural to say "sir" to the packman, as one would not have done to Yonge the consumptive miller, or to Thwaite the bailiff, or the house-steward or grooms. The other's face grew grave; it wore an expression Ludovic would never forget for the rest of his life, so reverent was it, and yet so loving; the packman's worn hands caressed his bundle.

"If you will speak of it to no one, except perhaps to your great-grandmother when she is well, I will tell you, and perhaps one day I will show it you, and let you share in it. But on that day you must kneel, Ludovic, and sign yourself thus." The priest crossed himself. "What I carry, not only to one great house and the next, but also to simple folk, is none other than the Body and Blood of Our Lord, Who died to save us. And many have since died, and I myself may die, for His sake. But as long as I may live I must serve Him as I can. Will you kneel, Ludovic? Will you kneel now before Our Blessed Lord?"

The boy knelt then on the bare stones, and the packman's hand reached out and blessed the bright hair.

After he had left Curle the packman walked with long loping strides out past the valley to the lower slopes, and then the higher. Midway between the two places was a small hidden field by a beck, and here, for the past weeks, the gipsy tribe had stayed, and he with them. A swarm of half-naked children ran towards him, eager for oranges. He dispensed them, smiling, and then turned away towards the Smiths with whom he slept by night. The brothers, George and taciturn Abel, nodded to the priest from where they sat over their fire, where a pot steamed, but did not rise or show him any servility. The folk here had their own forms of Christian religion and rite, brought by them long ago from eastern Asia; they would not trouble him with the differences nor he them. It was another matter from the fell-farms, where he made many converts or, as in the case of Maud Curle, ministered to those who had never forsaken the old faith. Here, with the gipsies, he was any man among other men; they asked no questions of him.

When he had talked with the Smith brothers for a while he went to see Abigail. He knew her of old, and also her one-eyed son who was as a rule elsewhere, but rejoined the tribe sometimes between voyages. He was spoken of as a rich man now, and sent Abigail many presents. She wore one this evening, fingering her ears with pride and smiling quietly, bedecked as she was with earrings of bright gold, worked with graining and zigzag patterns, and very heavy.

"You are grand this evening, Abigail." He sat down by her and drew at a pipe. It was pleasant to relax amongst these unquestioning folk; they, like he, had known persecution. Abigail preened herself and the earrings swung against her neck.

"My son sent me them. He says he will come one day and buy a fine house and take me with him, for a part of the year. I would not want to stay for all of it. These are gold, he says, and belonged to a king's daughter. They are worth much money."

Ay, and no doubt were torn from the ears of some poor soul condemned to a lifetime's slavery after being taken by force from her native forests, thought Father Talbot. He knew that it would only anger Abigail to condemn Jody's trade, so he said nothing. The woman had, he already knew, small knowledge of good or evil; she did as she was bid, by certain folk only. Her husband, old Jacob, was dead. His widow held aloof from the tribe but was still one of them.

"I saw Jody's people today," the priest ventured, thinking that she would like to talk of her son. The bright eyes snapped at him, and he withdrew into silence.

"There is a curse on them. I have cursed everyone at Curle, for what Norah Stroyan did."

"Not the boy, surely," he said gently. "He may make a man of God."

He was already certain of a separate quality about young Ludovic Stroyan; but time would tell. She said nothing more, and soon he left her. In the morning he rose and breakfasted with the tribe, then went his ways down into Lancashire as he had already arranged.

Corder Bellingham and his wife sat in Norah's withdrawing-room with her, nibbling sweetmeats. Corder's blue eyes, slightly bloodshot nowadays, narrowed mischievously. He had news to impart to dearest Norah, and tingled to impart it, though he knew it would not be very well received. Perhaps it would be better, as half his mind had suggested, to let a third person do the telling, as if by accident and without saying where he had learned it. Corder was certain that he did not want to lose Norah's patronage. Had she not done infinitely more for him than his own sister at Wraye? Windyett was let to him at a low rent, and he had brought cartloads of beautiful furnishings and china there, and pictures, none of them paid for; "and the fairest one of all is my wife," he murmured, while his eyes slewed round again to Madeleine in, today, a rose-coloured gown with silver ribbons. Corder delighted in choosing her gowns for her; he took more pleasure in this than lovemaking, in which he seldom indulged, firstly because he had no great liking for it and, secondly, because he did not want to spoil Madeleine's slender beauty with childbearing. It was more of a pleasure merely to look at her, especially here against the elegant background of Curle. He flattered himself that Norah had improved Curle greatly under his own discreet guidance, altering things agreeably from the discomfort of the old squire's day, to which she had at one time tended to cling. But it had only been a matter—and Corder was adept at such matters—of persuading Norah that she had in fact thought of the changes herself. The striped satin curtains, woven in France, outlined Madeleine's exquisite profile and her rich dark curls beneath the hat. How well she responded to dressing! And she was not intellectual enough to question his taste or his sayings: that in a woman with whom one actually lived would have been unbearable.

He passed Norah another of her own comfits, arrayed in a small silver repoussé dish. "Bad for the teeth and the figure," said Norah. "You and Madeleine can afford it; I can't."

"Dearest, you know that you set off that velvet very well; it would not show on a scraggy figure."

Norah smiled, and nibbled her comfit. It was pleasant, and not demanding, sitting here with Corder and his wife, who had at least the advantage of not intruding her presence; indeed, Norah wondered if Madeleine were not a trifle bored. "But that is her affair," she thought. Visits from Corder were a solace only second to visits from Amy, who had ridden over oftener since Stroyan's leaving, with her kiss the warmer for it. She had pressed Norah again to come to them at Wraye for a few weeks. "The flower garden is so beautiful, and it would be a rest for you, dearest, away from your many responsibilities; leave them to the bailiff and the steward for once." But Norah had stayed on here at Curle, and damn the gossip; at first she'd given out that Stroyan had ridden south on his dead mother's affairs, in case he were to come skulking back. By now, there was the less likelihood of that, nor any word from him.

She became aware of Corder's blue gaze focussed on her. "Norah, I heard lately that . . . a certain person, with his company . . . has set out for Australia. That is far enough away, in all conscience, for them to live as man and wife."

"Not if I can help it," said Norah. She'd write a letter, she thought instantly, to an acquaintance she had on the Lieutenant-Governor's staff: there should be no queening it at Port Jackson by Tina Pryde as her husband's wife. "Leave it to me," she said.

Corder made a resigned, helpless play with his squat hands, and smiled. "I knew that I could safely do so," he said limpidly. "Society will not receive her there, when you're done."

"Why should it? I detest deceit, Corder, you know well. Come, tell me of your visit to York; I see you have bought Madeleine another confection, extravagant boy."

Madeleine said nothing. She sat looking ravishing in the new hat, eating comfits. When she married Corder Bellingham it had been already made evident to her that she was to be a peg on which to hang clothes, a model to sit for portraits, and a foil for her husband's passion for connoisseurship: never a woman. Privately, she agreed that Mrs. Stroyan was growing too stout. But it would never do to say so.

After they had gone Norah sat down and penned her letter. Its safe arrival would put paid, as she knew, to any hope of secure and happy tenure for Tina Pryde in Australia. Such places were even more conscious of caste and social position than the provinces here; a woman living with a man to whom she was not married would receive no invitations or callers.

After the letter was sealed and sent off Norah felt weariness descend, as it often did when she was alone. When society was present, it was as if she had grown an outer armour, which nothing could penetrate. It had even been possible to listen to Corder just now without feeling any hurt.

Within, however, there was still somewhere the vulnerable young girl
who had been laughed at that day long ago on the moor; but now there
was no David Stroyan to bring her comfort. That she had scorned such
other comfort as he might have brought her over the years was still clear
to Norah now, when she was alone; but no one must guess it, or that she
regretted Stroyan the more now there was leisure to do so. The worst
times were at such public appearances as she must make beyond Curle, especially at church. Norah could not of course cease to attend, and on the
contrary put on her richest gear, as the summer faded; it was as if her
grandeur might dazzle the watching folk and make them deny, if they had
ever presumed to think of it, the possibility that so magnificent a lady
might have a bruised heart. Furs swathed Norah's shoulders, pearls encircled her throat; a wide-brimmed beaver hat framed the handsome
bright-complexioned face which had never needed paint, and wore none
now. The Curle pew was still prosperously full, with Norah and her
household and children, and the new tutor who had come to replace Tina
Pryde and taught Ludovic and Elizabeth and Madge's son Wil Yonge,
who lived at Curle now and only visited his parents occasionally. With all
these to fill the pew, Stroyan's insignificant presence would not be missed.
At the end of the service Norah would sweep out as usual to the bobbing
of the assembled villagers, and back to Curle.

As time went on her son's manner began to trouble her. Ludovic more
than once put in an excuse not to attend church; when asked why, in the
end, he hung his head and replied evasively. "I need your company, lacking your father's," Norah told him, adding that in future he must come.
For the rest of that year Ludovic came and sat or knelt by her side, outwardly docile enough; she had never known him otherwise. But when the
time came for him and Elizabeth to attend instruction for confirmation he
again angered his mother by a refusal to go.

"You cannot refuse such a thing," she told him. Ludovic's sweetly
curved mouth set obstinately.

"I do not wish to be prepared by the vicar here," was all he would say
for a while, as though picking his words carefully. But one day he burst
out as if his mind would no longer contain what beset it.

"It is not a true sacrament," he cried, "and I'll have naught to do with't.
It is no one's concern but my own, mother, if I say I will not."

"Why, what evil speech is this?" For moments she was amazed; then a
suspicion of the truth came to her. Norah was herself aware, as she could
hardly have failed to be, of the occasional visits of the packman to old
Maud, and even who he was; Maud's leanings to the ancient faith were

known, and the disguise connived at. But for an old half-mad, rambling woman to have an influence on her son had never occurred to Norah; now, it horrified her. She blamed herself for not having taken more time to spend on Ludovic: a cold awareness of danger beset her. At the same time, she knew she must not arouse the boy's native obstinacy; he was after all a Curle. "You cannot," she said, deliberately keeping her voice low, level and amused, "take the law into your own hands as others may. You will be squire of Curle. That means moderation in all things, and by nature following the King in matters of religion. They say he would as soon go to the block as grant the Papists toleration." Now she had said the word, tactfully as she hoped; he would know she had understood. How many mothers would not have made a scene! They must resolve it in a quiet, adult fashion between them; Ludovic after all was on the way to manhood.

"There have been other kings. I must obey my conscience."

"My son, you can hardly know the meaning of conscience yet; you have not seen the world. Until you have, do not choose to fly in the face of tradition; it has been well laid down."

"What you mean is, mother, what will folk think? I care nothing for that, any more than you do, in your heart." And he smiled at her; how handsome he was, thought Norah with a sudden glow of pride. Such a fine man as he would become must not be thrown away on priests' wheedlings. She debated whether or not to forbid him to see the packman; he was truthful and she knew would not deceive her in the matter. But it might lead to estrangement between them, and at this time, with Stroyan's defection still raw, she could not bear to have her son removed from her, in mind or body.

But for a squire of Curle to turn renegade! It must not happen. She would not let it.

She strove thereafter to make a companion of Ludovic, to have him with her always. But there were endless calls on her time, and the boy himself must learn by day from his tutor, and sometimes ride out on the moors with Wil. Wil was a dark silent boy with a big head set on his mother's tiny body; he attended Ludovic constantly, like a visitant elf. Norah would question him as to where they had been.

"Up to Churl's Leap, and back again, madam." He was always respectful; he adored Ludovic. Norah felt her heart turn over at mention of the spot she never now visited. "You did not climb the Leap? 'Tis a place of great danger."

"Ay, and gives a grand view of the fells." Wil grinned at her from behind his fringe of shaggy hair. Norah felt comforted. There had been no hazard in allowing the two boys out alone, and she could not forever keep Ludovic tied to her apron-strings. She could trust Wil, she felt, and the tutor, a young man from Wakefield whose knowledge seemed sound; now and again Norah would go into the schoolroom and listen to the lesson in progress, taking no heed of the young man's evident nervousness at her presence.

Thus time wore on; but the problem of confirmation was not solved. Ludovic refused to consider it.

"Go to the vicar, at any rate, and hear what he says to Elizabeth. That will commit you to nothing." The vicar, a Mr. Wayland, could reason better than she herself, Norah knew; her own knowledge of religious matters was scanty and down-to-earth: one went to church because other folk did. Privately she resolved to have a word with Wayland as to how the land lay. "Will you go, Ludovic?"

He lowered his eyelids, and said colourlessly that he would obey her. She did not like that; such behaviour accorded ill with the fire she knew was in him, matching in colour the copper-leaf hair which by now reached her own shoulder when her son stood by her. "They shall not make a whining priest of my son," she thought fiercely. Best make light of the whole matter, her mind told her; treat it as of no importance; perhaps the notion would leave Ludovic as it had come.

Ludovic and Elizabeth went together to confirmation-classes at the vicarage. Elizabeth, docile and dull, made no difficulty; she gave the correct answers as she was required, and asked no questions. But Ludovic led Mr. Wayland a dance, bright-tipped lashes demure over his grey eyes to hide the laughter in them.

"The King the head of the Church, Mr. Wayland, sir? But Henry VIII accepted the golden rose from the Pope. And Canute in his time, they say, journeyed to Rome to ask the Pope's blessing. Why was that, sir, if he was no greater than any other bishop?" The poor parson babbled that those were ignorant times; and later went to Norah to complain. This was a lax valley, with the penal days long past; but it was still necessary for a man to watch his tongue, despite the fact that it was said there might soon be open tolerance through all the country in defiance of the King.

Norah was perplexed; yet she still would not have Ludovic resemble his sister, who at times seemed almost witless in her obedience. In all Elizabeth's childhood Norah could not recall a single memorable saying of hers, or expressive look: she seemed completely passive. In company she was still shy and awkward, and had taken unkindly to dancing lessons and to embroidery, which lack no doubt befitted a Curle. If Corder's Madeleine was a beautiful nonentity, Norah's daughter would be a plain one; and this fact was beginning to mortify her mother in face of the added difficulty with Ludovic. Assiduous attendance at confirmation classes failed to produce any change or improvement in the boy's mind, and after some months Wayland had to confess that while Elizabeth seemed ready enough to be confirmed, he could not in conscience recommend her brother.

"Should I have him whipped?" asked Ludovic's mother despairingly. The vicar shook his head.

"His mind is not of such temper that pain will change it, any more than reasoning has ever done," he told her. "It is as though a seed has been implanted there and has grown; I have never encountered so young a boy with so sure a certainty."

Norah, in some embarrassment, arranged a private confirmation for Elizabeth only; the valley should not thereby know of the situation in her family. Thereafter Ludovic was made to go up to the altar rails on occasion with the rest, but Wayland only laid a hand in blessing on him, not offering him the consecrated wafer and wine. The rest of the folk present were too intent on their own partaking of communion to watch the young heir of Curle, and so Norah's second grief in those years passed unnoticed. As before she resolved to put it behind her, and let time decide the matter. She plunged into a season of gaiety and entertainment at Curle, keeping Ludovic by her whenever he might stay.

I I

CORDER AND AMY in their separate ways still tried to divert her, between the concerts of visiting celebrities, feasts at Christmas and birthdays and exchanging of gifts with the tenants, and attending their weddings. At such times Norah needed no diversion, but more and more her mind grew low nowadays in solitude; she began to be unwilling to be alone. Corder's constant attention did not flag despite his devotion to his pretty nincompoop of a wife: he had a kind heart, as she knew, although his reasons might be largely self-seeking. One day he said to her, "There is a painter coming to take Madeleine's likeness for the drawing-room at Windyett; they say he takes a good one and has studied abroad. May he not paint you, Queen Ceres, in your velvets and furs?" For he still used such expressions partly to make her laugh, and partly to flatter her. Norah agreed to have her likeness taken by the visiting painter; in all of her life such an event had not happened, and apart from such paintings as she had seen in great houses in the south she knew nothing of the art, or of the men who practised it.

The artist himself, whose name was not famous, she dismissed early as a person of no consequence. His manner was boorish, his jaw badly shaven and his clothes shabby and stained with paint and snuff. The portrait of Madeleine Bellingham, however, Norah had gone to inspect for herself at Windyett; it seemed an adequate enough portrayal of that young woman. "If he can do as well for me, it's a bargain," Norah thought, amusing herself, as the painter had told her she need not sit stock-still, with the antics of a toy spaniel Corder had lately bought her. The creature's fawnings kept her amused, and she had commanded that he be painted into the finished portrait. Afterwards she regretted that she had not, while she was at it, told the man to include her son Ludovic in the sittings. But by then the painting was almost finished, the artist himself displaying a peculiar urgency to be gone.

"Will you pay me, Mrs. Stroyan?" he demanded at the close of a sitting Norah had not yet thought was final. She hesitated, turning to look back to where he stood cleaning his brushes, hearing the hushing noise made by the skirts of her own full velvet gown. It was of the colour of rubies, and he had not allowed her yet to see the portrait in its unfinished stage. She had pandered to him, amused at such a person's expressing an opinion of what she, Norah Stroyan, might or might not do. But truth to tell she relished the grain of excitement the prospect of seeing the completed portrait gave her. From the days when, as a girl, she had looked in a mirror and decided that she was not beautiful, she had been reticent about herself to her own mind. Now it would be revealed, to herself and all the world, no doubt, what she really looked like. Was she in fact afraid of facing herself as others saw her?

But now this unimportant person was already asking for his gold. "Why should I pay you," she asked coldly, "before you have finished your task? You would leave it half-done, and be off to the nearest tavern."

"No artist acts so; when we undertake a commission, we complete it. But I am pressed for money." He went on, making a poor mouth over everything, saying that even his paints and canvas were not yet paid for. Norah agreed to have the money ready for him in a canvas bag on the following day, when he assured her the portrait would be completed and she could see it for herself. "And I believe, madam, that you will be pleased to hang it in your hall, beside that other of the man in the old-time garb. You resemble him."

Flattered by this reference to her own likeness to Sir Ludovic, Norah asked no more questions of the painter; and next day, when he put the finishing touches to her portrait, came round with pleased expectation to see what in fact she saw, by the end; a workmanlike rendering of a handsome, large-limbed woman, with curling chestnut hair above her blood-red dress. He had portrayed her flesh as though it had the quality of heavy cream, and Norah was pleased. "You have done well," she told him. "Where do you intend journeying after this? If you care to stay, I can obtain commissions for you, when my acquaintances have seen this likeness; it is well done, and they will want theirs also."

But he demurred, muttering something about further foreign travel; and Norah paid him and let him go.

Next day, while she was at dinner with her children, Corder Bellingham was announced and came in with a white face, stammering an incredible tale. "Madeleine has gone—gone with that painter fellow! She left me word in a letter."

He broke off, and stared at Norah as if this were some nightmare of childhood, no more. She endeavoured to be practical, dismissing the children: then she turned to him. "Which way have they gone? Have you sent out horsemen after them? I'll tell my men," but Corder, dazed as he was, restrained her.

"Could I prevent her—if she *would* go? For her, who was always so fastidious, to choose . . . such a one! Smelling of paint, of dirt, and his beard showing, and she—" Corder suddenly bowed his head in his hands and wept, like a child: Norah realised that he had truly cared for his upstart fool of a wife. She endeavoured to comfort him. "Take heart, man; is she worth a tear, or an hour of your thought, if she'd act so?" And Stroyan, she was thinking, and his governess, are worth less; not that I ever loved Stroyan. "Come, Corder," she said in the end, "let us broach a flagon together, and drown our sorrows; there's naught to equal it, I've found." She lied a little; and she had never yet taken to heavy drinking, though she knew others in her situation did. Corder's wan face eased into a ghost of a smile.

"There's no equal to *you*, Norah; to no other woman would I have come and found—comfort." He drank the wine with her, and lurched home to Windyett later in the night, three parts drunk. She had a man follow him to ensure that he reached his house safely, and his bed: the thought came to her that she must keep a watchful eye on Corder, alone up there without his flighty milliner. Madeleine had never been worth a day's striving . . . the portrait her lover had painted had been wooden, showing the lack of mind within the white flesh he portrayed, with its vacant eyes and jet-black hair. "He made a better thing of myself, over thirty as I am, and stoutening," Norah told herself with honesty. Beauty had never been hers to lose; it behoved her now to count her compensations, which were many and which would not be lost with time. She would foster them.

12

LUDOVIC FELT THE presence of God increasingly near.
He had always been aware of this presence in everything, not only in those he loved but, also, in the separate shapes of the fells above the valley. Inanimate things held God. Also, each sparse tree, growing from root to leaf in a symmetry surely planned, surely created, trembled in worship and communion with God's very storm. He himself was, he knew, a part of the fellowship of hill and tree and hurricane, foaming beck and deep still tarn. He felt this certainty so intensely that it transcended the need to speak of it to anyone. Wil, his shadow, would not have understood; nor would his unresponsive sister Elizabeth nor his mother, at once powerful and helpless as she seemed. With Norah he could only be silent. As for the spiritual pastor to whom she had bequeathed him, the Reverend Mr. Wayland—Ludovic laughed—he would be the least helpful of all: although in his own early years Ludovic, less critical then, had been deeply stirred by the words of the liturgy in church, keeping them in his mind long after he had followed his tall mother out by the aisle and had received the bows and bobs of the valley folk on the way. That churchgoing to his mother was no more than a social occasion, as her dinners and concerts were, early struck Ludovic as wrong; but at least she made no pretence otherwise. Mr. Wayland himself thought of little except his dinner between one sermon and the next.

Ludovic, at eleven, had waylaid him and asked if that were not so; the good divine grew plum-red, cleared his throat a trifle, and answered that Ludovic was only a boy, and boys should be out with a fishing-rod, or attending to their tutors. Yet only a year later he had been sufficiently disturbed by Ludovic's conduct at confirmation-classes to pay heed to him. Much had happened in that year, because of the packman.

The packman was the only person living to whom Ludovic could at last reveal his soul; from the first, there had been this recognition between them. Later they were to speak of many matters, by a beck-side or in a hillside cleft while Wil kept watch for strangers or a Curle servant following. Otherwise it was safe for the priest to assume his real identity for the time, and talk. They discussed the Atonement, the Resurrection, and original sin. They spoke of the changing of bread into flesh and wine into blood. "You must be wary, and not cause comment in the way you act day by day, lest suspicion be roused," the priest warned the boy, and it was at that time Ludovic began to obey his mother passively in external things. He knew that it was needful to be circumspect; for some years now the lessening of persecution had let Father Talbot, who had trained in France, go about almost openly in his known disguise. There were many at Curle besides old Maud who professed the ancient faith. Ludovic expressed his doubts of his mother.

"You must pray for her," said Roland Talbot, and the boy thereafter regularly did so, expressing in such ways the pity he felt, had perhaps done from the beginning, for that self-elevated goddess on her pedestal. It was of no avail to expect Norah Stroyan to become as other mothers, Ludovic knew; nor would he want it of her. He was aware that she had pride in him as the heir, but doubted if she loved him in the way Wil's small mother Madge loved her boy fiercely, protectively, tenderly, and would forgive him anything. If he himself committed what she felt to be the ultimate sin of rejection of Curle, his mother would never forgive him. He knew this, and had already weighed it in his mind.

Father Talbot had a fondness for him which reminded him of that he had known from Stroyan. He spoke to the priest of his father, and that he had gone away. "Be satisfied with the love of God; that will atone a thousandfold for lack of any other." But Stroyan, Ludovic knew well, had not stopped loving him although he was elsewhere. It was a marvellous thing, he found, that with the love of God in his heart all other loves widened and deepened, so that he felt himself rich with outgoing love. His mother, his sister, Stroyan and the woman he had chosen, the folk in the valley, the others beyond; even the gipsy tribes that sometimes trailed across the moor; all were to be loved with a feeling as spontaneous as that of the birds that sang, for it needed no requital. As far as earthly love was concerned Ludovic wanted none of it and never had; as time went on it became evident to him that he must never marry.

It was too soon yet to break this news to his mother. But Ludovic was sure of it, and sure also what was to become of him.

13

THE UPPER CORRIDORS at Curle were untenanted: for some days now old Maud had been bedridden. She lay still for the most part, at times still clutching at her middle and moaning with pain. She had lost flesh and the fine, high-bred bones showed beneath the wasted face. A physician had been fetched to her but as was his wont, did nothing except to give her laudanum. This made her drowsy except when the pain bit sharply, when she would cry out and writhe beneath the covers. It was hard to tell, in other ways, how it was with her; no one except her great-grandson Ludovic could elicit any answer.

He spent much time with her, as much as his tutor and his mother would permit. The former feared her madness and the latter, though Norah would never admit it, Maud's Papistry. Since that time, years ago now, when she had taken the boy to task about his confirmation-classes Norah had refused to allow herself to believe that her only son favoured the old faith. Such things were not for the squire of Curle, and the squire of Curle he should be. She continued to try to mould the boy into the image of his great-grandfather; due to Ludovic's gentle, tactful nature it was not made brutally clear to Norah that she had failed, and that he would never resemble the elder Ludovic in aught save the colour of his hair. Such was her blindfolding of herself that she did not even realise how close Ludovic had become to the dying woman upstairs, close enough to break down the barriers between sanity and madness. They had always, he and Maud, comprehended one another within the framework of the faith.

On the day Maud took an attack of bleeding from the mouth it was certain that the end was near; Norah looked for her son, having been certain that he would be at the bedside. He was nowhere to be found. On enquiry she was told that he had been down to the stables early, and had saddled his horse; now that he had grown tall, almost to young manhood, he was able to mount a beast nearly as heavy as the Cleveland bay which Norah herself had ridden in her girlhood. But Ludovic had not the full weight of bone of the Curles; he was tall yet slender, and Norah had had him mounted on a half-Arabian which she had had brought up, at great price, from the south. It gave her intense pride to see her handsome son straddle it, and ride the graceful beast as part of himself. But now, the groom reported, horse and rider had gone off towards the fells.

There was nothing to be done, Norah knew, save wait for Ludovic's return; no doubt he had not fully realised his great-grandmother's serious condition. She herself sat awhile, a thing she had seldom done in all her life, by Maud at the bedside; and tried to watch the tortured face with equanimity, but could not. She had never cared for sickness or deformity, either of mind or body; before she had been an hour with Maud she had to turn away. Presently the servant came, and Norah gladly relinquished her post to the woman. Rarely, imagination accosted her as to what lay behind the façade of grim-lipped silence in such servants; what did this one, who had attended Maud in madness half her life, think now? That the world was well rid of a madwoman? That all of her mistress's life had been no more than a piteous tale?

One would never ask, that was certain; and where was Ludovic? Darkness was beginning to fall; they brought fresh candles and lit them. Soon, at this rate, there would be candles again about the hearse of the dead. "She will be in her Papist purgatory then, and happy, maybe," thought Norah wryly; she herself knew little of the beliefs concerning the soul's journey after death. A Curle died, and was buried in the family vault, that was all, and in her own case, as in the old squire's, there would be a portrait on the walls of Curle to remind those who came after what she had been like in the flesh, when the same flesh had long crumbled from the bones. That thought brought comfort; how glad she was that she had acceded to poor Corder's request that she help his villainous painter, in the event! Corder now was drinking heavily, alone up at Windyett. She visited him when she could spare the leisure, but the pursuit was no longer pleasant; Corder's breath stank, and his eyes had acquired the staring quality of a drunkard's, while his trembling hands poured more, and ever more brandy. There had been word, from whence Norah could not recall, about the eloping couple; they had parted company after her own gold for the portrait was all spent, and Madeleine was now no one knew where, possibly pursuing an occupation far older than that of painter's model. "She'll fare well enough," Norah thought venomously, "that kind of wordless fool always will, till age comes and there's an end of custom." She reminded herself again that at least she herself had not this fear of losing what she had never had; age, when it came, she could greet decorously and without rancour unless . . . unless it brought in its train pain and madness, like poor Maud's. "Were I a physician I'd give her a quelling dose of some drug, and free her swiftly." But that was not, evidently, to be; perhaps Maud herself would have forbidden it.

Norah went to the window, and stared out at the darkened fells for a sound, or sign, of Ludovic's returning home. One by one, as she had seen them do a hundred times, the glow of lamp or candle shone out from farm-cottage or bothy; Madge Beck, widowed now, was among the first to light her rush-lamp. Madge had stayed on at the cottage where her husband had in the end died of his phthisis, and herself continued to tend the chickens and pigs. Her son was still about Ludovic, and would have ridden with him tonight. "At least he is not alone on the fells," thought Norah, trying to down her anxiety. Why had the boy gone off so?

He returned at dawn, and there were now not two riders but three; Wil riding pillion with Ludovic on the Arab, and the third on Wil's pony. The hunched shape of the latter's figure became apparent to Norah from where she watched in the dawn's light; the packman! "So my boy knew, and rode to fetch a priest to her," thought Norah without anger. The dying woman's breaths were stertorous now, and if she desired a priest to speed her soul, why deny her? But only Ludovic would have thought of it in time, or have known where to go. Norah experienced a twinge of discomfort. "I must ask him how he knew where to find the man," she told herself, moving out to the head of the staircase, a taper in her hand. They had left the mounts with Wil and were, the pair of them, ascending the stairs together. Norah held her taper higher; Ludovic raised his young head, and she saw the pallor of his face, as if he were weary, and took no leisure to look at that other.

"I've been anxious for you, boy," she said harshly; emotion always made her harsh. He did not answer directly, but said clearly, not explaining himself or where he had been, or why, "Mother, will you spread a clean linen cloth on the dower-chest, and have them bring water?"

She could talk with him later, alone, she decided. Without expression she turned and ordered the servants, who were still awake, to bring Ludovic what he asked. Then she waited while he and the packman went together into the dying woman's room, and later Ludovic came out alone.

Still later the priest came out, still clad in his vestment. He said "Lady Curle has died at peace with God; may her soul rest in peace."

Afterwards they went together to look at Maud's dead face. She had died soon after receiving extreme unction; her features now were calm and smooth, almost those of the fair young would-be nun whom Sir Ludovic Curle had carried off long years ago and by force married, so that her high blood and her full coffers would be his and not those of the Papist Church. Norah remembered all of this while she looked down at the smoothed, fine-drawn face, its white hair seemly and combed now, its thin hands folded. She knew that Ludovic was thinking of it also, but could not find the words to ally herself with her son. In the end she turned away and left him alone again with the corpse, as it was what he seemed to wish. She made her way, weary now, down to the kitchens to give orders that the packman be served with a good breakfast. No one, whomsoever he might be, should have cause to complain of Curle hospitality.

Ludovic knelt in prayer by his great-grandmother's body. He was consoled in that she had received the last sacraments and had died peacefully; comforted also by the fact that, an hour since, he himself had partaken in private of the same consecrated bread. He knelt on now partly to recite his formal prayers, partly to withdraw in peace, as he liked to do, from the constant bustle at Curle, the comings and goings, the pervasive influence of his mother whom he both pitied and feared to hurt. That she was vulnerable despite her stern exterior he knew, had known from a boy. His mind withdrew to the scene he had come upon earlier that same day, when after following such way-signs as they both knew of he had found the priest, sheltering as he was again on this occasion among the gipsies high up on the fells. Ludovic had been taken to a caravan which housed the strange dark, silent woman, whose name he already knew was Abigail; by her this time was her son, a tall man with a black patch over one eye. The other eye had been bright, and had surveyed Ludovic curiously, as if the stranger knew him for who he was. "Is your mother well?" the stranger had asked presently, in accents which were not rough, like those of the fell-folk, but those of a gently bred person. Ludovic had replied with the courtesy he always used to strangers; yes, he told the one-eyed man, his mother was well. "Give her my salutation, and say that it will not be long before she sees me again," had said the man then, but Ludovic had taken scant leisure to ponder on the strangeness of this message, as he had his own to give the packman-priest, that his great-grandmother was at death's door, and needed such as he could bring. And the packman had come, and had brought it; and Maud Curle's piteous life had ended in great comfort and peace, and Ludovic did not regret the necessity of his ride, or its outcome.

Later he recalled that he had forgotten to give his mother the one-eyed man's message, and pondered on how this might best be done. He did not want to involve himself in explanations of how he came to know of where the packman was, or of the existence of way-signs. In the end he went to Norah and said, "I met a man, mother, who had but one eye, and a black patch over the place for the other, and his clothes were those of a gentleman, as was the way he spoke. He asked if you were well, and when I said you were, asked me to tell you he would be having speech with you soon."

He faltered into silence, aware of his mother's intent gaze fixed on his face. She might, he knew, say anything, or else box his ears, or burst out in anger; it depended on who the one-eyed man might be, and Ludovic did not know. But Norah Stroyan on this occasion said nothing, lifting her hand an instant and staring at it, then letting it fall again to her lap. "He said that, eh?" she answered her son. "He said he would have speech with me? Not so; I'd not let them open the gate to such as he, a thieving gipsy as he is." And then she fell silent.

They buried Maud Curle two days later, at noon. Norah attended the burial. Standing in the forefront of the mourners she was able to feel, from the newly opened vault, a chill draught strike through her cloak; and to see, in the light of the mourning-tapers, the mildewed handles of Sir Ludovic's coffin, laid nearby in the confined half-dark. That those two should lie side by side till all eternity seemed a grim necessity, a concession to propriety hardly called for in the separate histories of the husband and wife. "Yet what odds will it make to a heap of grinning bones?" thought Norah. In a few years her own would join them, and thereafter Ludovic's when his turn came.

She watched her son, seeing his slim body shoulder the burden of the new coffin with the rest of the pall-bearers, among whom were Jonathan Wraye and Corder. Of them all here today, it was probable that only Ludovic Stroyan felt any personal grief; no one else had known or seen old Maud for years, only recalling her, if they ever did so, as a demented legend, a face at a high window or a voice sobbing sometimes in the night. Yet now she was at peace, "more so," Norah told herself, "than am I." She studied Ludovic's profile again and was alarmed at its pallor, and at the hollows which seemed to have appeared beneath the cheekbones since she had last studied him closely; his whole body was too thin. She must see that he ate his food with appetite, or else get a physician to him. If only there were less to oversee regarding the estate she might devote more time to her children.

The words consigning Maud Curle's dust to other dust were spoken; the coffin was set in its place and the vault again sealed fast. Norah turned away with the others to walk back to the collation which waited at Curle, aware despite herself of a sensation of bathos, of not having had to preside over some grand scene or improper intrusion; for there had not, despite Ludovic's message from the one-eyed man, been any sign today of Jody. She had had all the servants armed with staves and guns, pretending that it was necessary in case the coffin was rifled on the journey and its silver handles stolen. But she knew that within herself she had been waiting, waiting by the cold vault for Jody to appear; now that he failed to do so should not her feeling be one of relief? It would after all have been an opportunity for him to present himself to her, at their own grandmother's burial; and he had not taken it. What chance then would he take? Must she be always on guard, as she had been for half her life, against the gipsy's bastard Jody had proved himself to be?

"I waited, and he did not come," she told herself again later, gazing down into the cup of red wine at the funeral-feast. Her own face, pallid today and seeming heavy as a slab of granite rock, met her in reflection. It was true that she had never been beautiful, she reminded herself; not like the woman who was lately dead.

So she, and all of them, toasted the memory of Maud; and having done so and eaten their fill, the company prepared to depart. Norah watched them ride away with a sense of unreality. This day had not in truth existed for her, she knew, as it might have done; as it should have done, if Jody had after all come and confronted her.

PART III

I

THE TOWN HOUSE in which Sir Ludovic Curle had died had begun, of late years, to cause Nora more expense than it was worth to her; she seldom used it. She kept it in reasonable repair, and let it when she could. This was not always easy, as Border-bound travellers seldom wanted a dwelling-place and citizens already had one. She had decided to insert a notice in the gazettes to the effect that it was for sale, but had only spoken of this plan to close friends such as the Wrayes and Corder Bellingham. To her surprise, having put the matter to the back of her mind meantime as other business pressed, she received a letter from her lawyer.

"This seems good news," she said to Thwaite the bailiff. He bowed obsequiously: but already at sight of his bald and greying pate Norah nursed suspicions. The offer was favourable; why should a Mrs. Manifold, who came from Lancashire, interest herself in an unknown house in Carlisle? "If it had happened after the advertisement, well and good," Norah told herself. Presumably Mrs. Manifold was well endowed. What reason could she have for wanting to move north?

She temporised, and wrote to the solicitor, asking him to set enquiries on foot regarding the lady. His reply was terse. It would be better, he suggested, to accept a good offer when it came. They were hardly as thick as pebbles in this part of the country.

Norah ordered her coach, and set out for the city. Leaning back in the cushioned interior, savouring the well-sprung comfort which made less hardship of the rutted roads than heretofore, she scanned herself and her motives. Why was she a shade unwilling for this sale to take place? It was, she well knew, because she could bear to part with no jot of the inheritance the squire had left. This admitted, his face rose before her; and she reminded herself of another, earlier journey in which a younger woman than she was now had ridden through the storm and the night, in no well-sprung coach but in the bare saddle, to rid the house of her grandfather's harlot. Much had changed since then.

She alighted at the lawyer's, and was ushered in. The man himself was another such as Thwaite the factor, like too many about her nowadays; bowing and scraping, but he performed his tasks. "I'd ha' rid myself of him long since if he had not," Norah's mind told her. Aloud she said "Have you met this Mrs. Manifold? Know you aught of her?"

"Madam, I understand from her son that she is an invalid, and seldom receives or ventures forth."

"Ha! You have met the son, then?"

The lawyer assured her that Mrs. Manifold's son had already visited his office personally, and had offered to put down a substantial deposit pending completion of the sale.

Norah shrugged her shoulders. It had, she knew been no more than that lingering sentiment regarding Curle property that had brought her here today: within herself, she recognised the folly of refusing the offer. What did it matter if the house became one of ill fame, as she half suspected? No worse could happen: and it was possible that the invalid Mrs. Manifold would in all truth retire there and derive benefit from the sharp northern airs about the city. "If she keeps a carriage she can drive beyond the walls," thought Norah. It might be possible to cultivate the lady. If not—and an amused memory of Sir Ludovic himself, and his habits when in the house, came—had its uses been so pure in his day? "I wonder," she thought, "what befell that young whore."

She accepted the offer in writing, thankful in a way; her coffers were not as full as they had been. Over the years she had entertained lavishly, and had grudged nothing in the way of repairs to tenants' dwellings. Windyett brought in an uneconomic rent from Corder, but she would never turn him out. The Moat continued unoccupied. Perhaps she should exert herself more to find a new tenant for the Moat, but under one's very walls it mattered greatly who passed their days there. The Carlisle house might have been a place of refuge; she could have used it more than she had done.

Once her letter had gone she regretted sending it, and had half a mind to write again and cancel the new sale. But it had never been her way to make a fool of herself before her men of business. Let the lawyer have done with it, and trouble her no further "and I'll see," thought Norah grimly, "that no gold sticks to his fingers other than what's his due." It was probable enough that Mrs. Manifold, or her son, had greased the man's palm prior to a speedy conclusion of the arrangement. That was his affair and theirs: on such things small men thrived.

The purchase price was paid, and before letting the new owners move in Norah went again to the city, looked over the house, and removed such objects as might still be of value or interest. There were not many, for she had cleared the house before admitting tenants in former years. There was a fire-dog which might suit one of the smaller rooms at Curle: some old letters which Norah took no time to read, a worm-eaten desk which she would not remove—Mrs. Manifold could do as she might with it—and, in one of its drawers, a faded blue silk garter. Norah took the garter and later wondered why she had done so; she cast it into the fire at Curle and watched it burn.

That was in spring, and affairs in the valley occupied her for the subsequent weeks. Soon the cattle were put out to grass again and Norah went to supervise the grazing-places and matings of the bulls. She took young Ludovic with her, to encourage him to take an interest in the estate and farms. He was nearly of age, and it was not long since Norah had realised, with a shock, that when he became so she should, by tradition, hand over the squiredom. In fact, she would do no such thing. But the young man must be made to take an interest in the inheritance such as she herself had always taken; by God, at his age she'd never missed helping with a lambing-season! Master Ludovic was too fine in his ways, and his frequent silences irritated her.

She rode out with her son to watch the lean bull put to the cows, themselves still showing their ribs beneath their hide after the hard winter. A chill wind blew down from the fells, and Norah was suddenly aware of weariness. Why should she resent the unchanging way in which year followed year, in a pattern which had hitherto been her joy? Now, it seemed pointless: year after year cattle were slaughtered off for salting and the best stock kept over the winter, and there was breeding time once more, and the young calves soon at grass: the short summer, and then the early dark, and killing again. One was born, after all, only to die . . .

She spoke aloud and harshly, to down her thoughts. "In the south, I hear, they've begun to winter all their cattle on dried hay; here the rain prevents our even harvesting the grass ere it's rotted." Yet would she sooner live in the south? She knew that she would not.

Ludovic said nothing. The wind plucked fitfully at the plume in his hat. Beneath, his hair curled brightly as always, and he seemed, with the cold bringing colour to his cheeks, to have lost the pallor Norah had noted, and feared, at the time of Maud Curle's death. Soon he would be a man. "I would he'd take a lesson from the bull, and start to show an interest in wenches," Norah thought. Plans for the coming-of-age, a year ahead as it still was, were already in her mind. Certain pretty, high-born girls should be invited with their county-families, and Ludovic could look about him for a wife. There would be plenty of choice; eligible bridegrooms were scarce, and one of Ludovic's ancient name would be desirable even if he had no fortune garnered by herself, over the years. She'd given fewer concerts and entertainments lately, and the rent-silver had begun to flow again this year since the sale. There would be enough to make the coming-of-age memorable for a generation to come.

Norah opened her mouth to tell her boy some of all this, then decided against it and fell silent as himself. Such maidenly ways he had for a near-man and a Curle! She, his mother, did not know what to make of him; despite the colouring he could not be more different from the squire she had bidden him to strive to copy.

She laid a hand on his sleeve, and felt the young muscles tauten. "Come out of your dreams, boy," she said, making her tone jocular. "It grows cold, and we lack what keeps the bull's blood warm, there in the field."

Lack it? For myself, ay, she thought; it is many a year now since Stroyan left, and almost as long since she had thought of Walter Shillingthorne. The memory of the latter now made her feel faintly foolish: there had been no further news of where he had gone, nor had he passed again through the valley. "In old times he'd have been a monk, and been happy enough turning pegs in his monastery," she thought. But her own body, her woman's body, had not abated its needs. Sometimes in the night she would wake, longing for a man beside her. It was not Stroyan she wanted, God knew, and backward beyond that one must not think. She turned to this son, who might after all be Stroyan's, feeling renewed impatience at his grave face. Could not a little lewdness be let free in the Curle blood again, with jesting and wenching? "Put off your priest's visage, and let us get home," she said, well knowing she stabbed at a tender spot, and caring little. There had been no sign of the packman at Curle since Maud's death, but Norah could no longer be certain that her son never met with him. He would be travelling as was his wont, that man, to and fro among the hills, perhaps back and forth across seas. Priests' ways were devious.

"How fares the priest?" she asked Ludovic suddenly aloud, watching to see him blench at her certainty. But he neither flushed nor paled, nor evaded her, only answering gently.

"He is in France. He will return in the autumn, I believe."

"Damn your beliefs; what the devil are you at, Ludovic? You no longer tell me what you do or where you are."

He smiled. "Do you not constantly exhort me to be as my great-grandfather was, and beholden to no one?"

"I'll not tolerate impertinence. And I'll have no Papists at Curle." She heard herself blustering, and knew it was because she was afraid: afraid both for his sake and for all he stood for. She had never been afraid for herself. "I always gave such matters short shrift," she thought, "best way to treat 'em."

He answered, when she had not expected it. "That shall not be asked of you, mother."

"At least acquaint me of what will. Am I a stranger to my own son?"

This time he did not reply directly. "Come back to the house, madam: as you say, it grows cold."

How quietly he spoke! Now at last there was fear in her. She spurred her own mount ahead of him, as if determined to rid herself and him of the notion that it was he who led, and she who followed. Follow her own son, a Pope's boy, a he-virgin? As well be damned.

2

IN THE COURSE of the next few weeks Norah had occasion to visit the city again, and the notion took her to make a courtesy-call on Mrs. Manifold, who should by now have had leisure to settle into her house. Norah knew that she herself was activated by a mixture of suspicion and curiosity. She had not met a single soul who had encountered, or even heard of, the widow either in the county itself or farther south. Even Corder, still the purveyor of gossip in all directions, said he knew nobody of the name; it was so unusual he would have remembered it.

Curious, therefore, and taking Elizabeth with her in the carriage, Norah bade her coachman set out towards the discreet, narrow street near the Abbey, where the tall old house stood beside others of its kind. The sight of the familiar chimneys brought her discomfort; why had she ever agreed to part with it? "It is like losing a part of myself," she thought, "almost as if I had sold Curle." But that she would never do.

The purchase money, at any rate, had been welcome enough, and today, in a fit of some extravagance, she had purchased new gloves and a bonnet for Elizabeth. The girl sat as usual listless in her place, watching the streets bowl past; she had taken little say in choosing her headgear, and showed less interest in it now it was bought. Norah downed the impatience her daughter always roused in her; there was nothing to be done about Elizabeth's nature, and her looks were still discouraging. Norah wound down the glass as the house approached, and bade the footman alight and try the knocker. It was well enough polished, and the steps were clean; Mrs. Manifold evidently commanded her servants. One of them, in a linen apron, answered the door, and briefly spoke to the footman, who turned back to the coach.

"Madam, Mrs. Manifold does not receive," he stammered. Such a message could never, he knew, have been sent to Mrs. Stroyan before; he had difficulty in pronouncing the words, so fearful was he. What would his mistress say to such a message? No need to ask; she was out of the coach already, leaving Miss behind. Full skirts bunched in her gloved hand, eyes like hot coals, she ordered the waiting-woman in her lazy voice that seldom showed her anger. "Tell your mistress that Mrs. Stroyan of Curle has called, and desires speech with her," Norah stated imperiously. The other returned gaze for gaze, out of bright eyes beneath a forehead now wrinkled as leather, and graying hair wound in a plait about her head. It was still seen that she could once have been handsome, although she had lost her teeth.

"There's small need to tell her, for here she is." The eyes surveyed Norah unreadably, with a gaze as level as her own. The latter felt the blood mounting to her face, and for once was taken at a disadvantage.

"*You* are Mrs. Manifold? Then I am disturbing you at your duties, and will say good-day." The woman did servants' work, that was evident, and the nails on the roughened fingers were not clean. She was not a gently bred person and one need not trouble with her. Yet a lingering half of curiosity, half of regret stayed with Norah, and when Mrs. Manifold somewhat ungraciously bade her enter the house she did not refuse as she had intended to do. Abovestairs was the sound of hammering.

"You have workmen in? You are making alterations?" She turned to Mrs. Manifold condescendingly. "I should like to know what is being done," she said. "This house belonged to my family, and still interests me. It may be that some day I shall want to buy it back." She smiled; no doubt the woman would find her tongue with encouragement. But Mrs. Manifold remained curt.

"'Tis my son's business: he brought them here. I knaw naught o't."

"But the house is yours."

"Houses were never for me. His it is, and by rights he should ha' had it without silver. But he goes his own gait, and follows his will, and I do as I'm bid." The woman had not smiled as she spoke; it was as though all pleasure and laughter had left her while she was still young. Norah began to give way to a feeling that she had met with this woman before. Could they have encountered one another? she asked. The other's expression did not change.

"Never that I knaw on. But I've heard tell on ye, Norah Stroyan."

Norah frowned; the woman was becoming familiar. It would be wiser not to linger, curious as she still was regarding what was to become of the house. The purchase-money for the property was not, evidently, Mrs. Manifold's own, unless she had perhaps hoarded wages over the years, or been left a legacy. It did not matter. Norah excused herself, and without delay returned to the coach to join Elizabeth. Almost as soon as they had started the girl expressed a sudden wish to go out into the air.

"Mother, I feel sick."

"It is the swaying of the carriage, no doubt. We will walk for a while about the West Walls, while they wait the horses." She frowned; Elizabeth since a child had suffered from carriage-sickness, which made journeys with her an ordeal. Norah, beset nowadays with the knowledge of her duty towards the unattractive girl if she were ever to find a husband, had decided that the best thing to do was to take Elizabeth on frequent short journeys such as today's had been, in the hope that with maturity and custom she might outgrow the habit. But today she was as bad as ever, white about the mouth and queasy. Norah sighed; what had she done to give birth to such a creature? Even Stroyan had had more wit.

They alighted presently, and strolled to the ancient parapet's edge to look out over the far-flung, boggy green of the river flats. Presently Elizabeth said she felt better; the fresh breeze blowing had brought relief. It had also fluttered ribbons and dishevelled hair beneath bonnets; Norah was aware that she herself looked blowsy, and Elizabeth bedraggled.

"Mother, who is that man watching us?" said Elizabeth suddenly. Norah frowned, bringing herself back to their present situation; she had been focussing her eyes on the vague skyline, trying to see the coast of Scotland. She turned, unwillingly, to survey the man Elizabeth had noted.

He was tall, and stood with his cloak wrapped about him against the wind. The light was behind him so that she could not at first see his features: certainly he seemed to be regarding them both with a close attention that must surely be impertinent if he were a stranger. Then he moved, and Norah was made aware of the difference between this man and all others. A black patch covered one eye. Jody removed his hat, and made a small ironical bow.

It was in that instant that Norah knew also that he must be Mrs. Manifold's son.

"Mother, he knows you, I think, and is coming to speak—"

Elizabeth's thin mouth fell open on the words. Her mother had gone. She had turned in her tracks, and was walking swiftly back to where the carriage waited, so that there was nothing for Elizabeth to do but follow. How strange and sudden mother often was in the moods she took, and the things she did! Perhaps the one-eyed man was someone who had offended her.

On the journey home Norah was silent, her mind filled with rage at the way she had been tricked. "Mrs. Manifold", indeed! A dirty gipsy! The leman—it was no more—of her dead uncle, the old squire's so-called heir! How dared she lend herself to this?

It was questionable whether there could now be any way of revoking the sale: and she had in any case used the money in various ways in the time that had gone by. The price . . . the house itself had not been cheap. Jody must have made a great deal of money in his trafficking with souls. Jody. "By rights he should ha' had it without silver." By no means, madam Manifold; nor Curle, nor yet myself.

But he had had herself. Sometimes, even nowadays, Norah faced the truth.

She leaned forward to tap on the window and urge the coachman to drive faster. How ridiculous not to be able to rid oneself of the feeling that Jody, like the devil, had the power to follow her carriage, stop it if he would, and re-enter her life!

He should not. He must not. She would prevent it by every means. Of the two of them, had she not already proved beyond all doubt that her will was the stronger?

3

NORAH WAS ABLE to show the strength of her purpose in the splendour of the coming-of-age celebrations for her son Ludovic Stroyan; they were to surpass anything ever seen in the time of Sir Ludovic Curle. She had spent almost a year planning each detail, allotting this field and that for the various sports. There was to be football played beyond the Moat House, the prize to be of money given by herself, a gold piece to each member of the winning side. More prizes were to be won for balancing on the greasy pole, for caber-throwing, as the Scots did it, and bagpipe-playing on the small Northumbrian pipes. She herself would scrutinise each player; let Jody try to make his entry that way again! "I'll have the men take him by the elbows this time, and show him off the field," she thought. There was to be feasting afterwards, and a whole ox roasted over an open fire as had been done in days of yore, and ale for all, and leaping over a bonfire and dancing for all the tenantry while a pipe and fiddle band should play. Those of gentler birth would meantime feast within Curle, and drink wine: but all, whether gentle or lowly, should hear the young squire toasted by the whole assembly, and his reply. Norah had decided to make this speech of Ludovic's the focal point of the day; long after it, there would be dancing beyond and within the hall, and she herself had, personally and after careful thought, sent invitations to certain well-born mothers of marriageable daughters, stating that they might bring these hopeful young ladies in the expectation that Ludovic, now he was a man, might fancy one of them: a rich and personable squire of Curle might, she again assured herself and him, take his pick. She had ceased to feel irritation at Ludovic's silences on the subject; he was, she told herself, shy, as Stroyan himself in many ways had been. Marriage would cure it. She had asked Amy Wraye's pretty god-daughter from the south, and another heiress with dark-gold curls and a complexion which would surely wreak havoc in young men's hearts; and a third girl from Yorkshire, plain it was true, but a graceful dancer and performer on the lute and harpsichord, and with a small portion of her own, and a high-born name. There were others. Altogether the heir of Curle should find no lack of promised diversion at, and after, his coming-of-age and his entry into the inheritance. She herself, it went without saying, would, however, continue to guide the young man's government of his acres and, God knew, his fortune; so many squandered the latter in gaming that it was perhaps a blessing that Ludovic showed no aptitude for such pleasures as yet.

Norah moved her shoulders restlessly beneath her lace fichu, which had been Maud's and had deepened richly with age. An urge for gaming was within herself, she knew; she had been used to enjoy a card-game in her grandfather's day and they had played for stakes when the old man was in the humour. But she had suppressed the urge for her boy's sake. It was long enough since she had held a hand at whist, or loo; someday, perhaps, when Ludovic's children were grown, she'd take to it again. She smiled a little, feeling satisfaction with her lot for the first time since the defection of Stroyan. So much to do, and oversee, and the prosperity of the valley farms at last beginning to repay the anxious years when she'd begun to spend more than they earned, but all that had been worth it now that the roof-tiles of each house let in no rain, and the tenants were contented and stayed in their place, tilling the fields and seeing to the cattle. At the coming-of-age there was to be a judging, in which Jonathan Wraye would help her, between Thwaite's bullocks and Madge's son Wil's. Norah had divided the care of the herd between them, and Wil had done well enough to win against the older man, deserting Ludovic's side often nowadays to see to his stirks where they grazed in the boggy lowland. Sheep on the high ground, cattle on the low; so it had always been, but as she already knew there was talk everywhere in the south now of wintering on all cattle and feeding them stored grain.

"Well, it will be my son's affair when that reaches us here; such changes take long in the north," Norah told herself placidly, bidding the women set out the gear she had chosen to wear for Ludovic's birthday. Mercifully there had been mild weather early, and promise of a fine day; rain would ruin everything, and the hall be overrun with folk and the barns packed, spoiling the stored apples and what remained of the hay from last summer. "They will trample it with their heedless feet, dancing," Norah thought, and hoped for a fair day.

She was not disappointed; the day dawned fine and clear. The stacking of tonight's bonfire could be done with dry wood; a blessing, for trees were none too plentiful and Norah had had to order the felling of three oaks. Jon Wraye had sent a stag for roasting in addition to the fat ox ready killed; they would all have venison till they were full, and still dance. Norah watched from her window to see the figures of the men stacking the fire and clearing the field-space of rubble and stones, for there must be a smooth place for dancing, and no turned ankles, or over-turned old folk. She went over all such matters in her mind as she dressed; then at the end looked at herself in her glass. She was not ill-pleased with what she saw; her dress was rich, of the ruby velvet she preferred and which flattered her skin, and she wore a wide hat of Canadian beaver, with a white plume curling down to one shoulder, and gloves of white kid. She descended the staircase to greet Ludovic with a certainty that he, as well as herself, should look the part; she had selected an olive-green satin for him, and his grandfather's sword-belt which was chased with silver and had been polished with white sand till it shone, then buffed with leather. Norah expected to find Ludovic waiting, and to see him look as she had planned; for once it was so, and she extended her hand with a smile, and scarcely heeded Elizabeth, behind her brother in blue silk, or even yet remembered —she always did forget—that it was the girl's birthday also. She kissed Ludovic, pleased at the shaven grating of his cheek; here was man indeed! His hair, she thought, was like copper against the green; how well the colour became him!

"A very happy birthday to you, my son; see, the sun is shining." She had a gift for him, and had brought it down with her; it was a pair of matched pistols, made in London to her order. The chasing on the barrel matched that of the sword-belt, a pretty fancy Norah had devised. She watched his face, expecting a boy's eager pleasure at sight of the pistols; but all he said was "It is Elizabeth's birthday too," and a memory assailed Norah of how he had said that to her long ago, how long now? She could not recall; but the awareness displeased her, and she handed Elizabeth her lesser gift, an embroidered tucker, with ill grace. The girl took it with a brief curtsy and said nothing.

"Let us go out now, and meet them all," said Norah when they had breakfasted. "They are waiting to be first to see the new squire." She took her son's arm, and they made their way together out of Curle; the sun was bright enough to dazzle the eyes, and Norah put up a hand to her broad hat, pulling at the brim. "It might be summer," she said, greeting first one, then the other; a polite murmur of assent went up from the farm-folk. If the lady of Curle said it was a fine day, it was; and raining, then it was that also, even if the sun still shone in the sky. But she was generous enough with her feastings, and her prizes; those who remembered the old squire saluted his granddaughter with respect, even warmth. She'd contrived well enough, had Mrs. Norah, and her with no man to aid her. To be sure, no man could endure the life they said she'd led the one she had. Well, he was out of it now; rumour had it that his fancy-woman had had a bairn to him in Australia. No doubt they would stay there, away from decent folk. At least he'd given Mrs. Norah a fine son before he left her; ay, a fine upstanding son.

The day passed quickly with games and merrymaking, the tug-of-war with two competing sides manned by strong farmers, hill against vale. There was the greasy pole, a sheep-judging, and a performance by working dogs; everyone drank ale and wine. Norah knew that she should feel weary, for the work of the preceding weeks, making ready for events, had fallen to her; Ludovic took small part in it. Now it was she, not he, who went about among her folk, distributing prize-money, welcoming such guests as she had bidden to come from beyond Curle. There was a collation for these in one of the lesser rooms of the house, pending the great feast to be enjoyed by all at nightfall. If anything could make Norah feel downcast, besides Ludovic's absences and silences, it was the lack of Corder Bellingham nearby today. He had been increasingly erratic of late, and might well arrive last of all in no fitting state, having drunk overmuch wine already at some tavern. Norah frowned; it saddened her to have Amy's brother demean himself before the assembled guests. "It is not my concern; why should I feel it?" she asked herself, wondering why she had always, in a way, felt for Corder as if he were a second son. She reminded herself that he was of her own generation, and the knowledge came as always with a slight sense of shock. Corder had the quality of eternal youth. How long a time seemed to have passed since she herself had first seen him, entering debonair and handsome into Curle as Stroyan's groomsman! "I kept the man, and mislaid the groom," Norah quipped to herself wryly.

Corder came late, as she had anticipated. Twilight had fallen, there was the sound of fiddling and piping, and the bonfire, already lit, cast flickering shadows over the faces of everyone present, so that Norah did not at first see on whose arm Corder was leaning, lurching uncertainly in the way he had when he was drunk. Anger took Norah: what right had anyone to come in such a state to her son's feasting? "If it had been any other, I'd have had him shown the gate," she thought, then came to full awareness of his supporter. The flames leapt between her and the tall thin figure, blotting out the eye-patch he wore. He stood erect and still. He knew that she had seen him.

"Damn him," thought Norah. Once she had promised herself that if he came today, she would have him thrown out. But now? A trembling took her, and she seized a moment to still herself, calm the tumult in her own mind, which should not, after all, be in such disarray over one interloper at the feast; even should that man be Jody.

She had not gone towards them. She waited, her body still and cold despite the turmoil of her thoughts, the heat of the fire, the stir of folk all about her. She watched the pair make their way towards her where she stood, noting that, as might be expected, it was Jody who thrust, and Corder who followed his head like a tame dog. Norah's brows drew together ominously. This thing should not be. She'd not permit it. They might keep company at some tavern as and when they chose—how could she stop them?—but on Curle land Corder Bellingham should no longer walk at Jody's heel.

Yet it was Corder who spoke first, as if to appease her.

"You will know of this bold fellow, madam." His bloodshot eyes flicked up an instant to her face, then down again; he was unsure of himself, like a late cur lurching home. Presently again he tried the personal charm which he still had, and which had never yet failed him with Norah Stroyan. "Forgive my bringing him without your leave: but he saved m'life, I assure you, in a place where 'twas touch and go with it."

"Not that, only your purse," put in Jody idly. His single eye had never left Norah; she felt less than herself, both angry and uncertain, under his gaze. "I was set upon by rascals at an inn," hiccuped Corder, "and your kinsman, as he says he is, beat 'em off with the flat of his sword. A marvellous thing, that; wish you had seen it done. Then he returned my purse to me which they'd taken: returned it to me, not a coin missing. Grateful, I assure you . . . brought him, pro-protect me on the way here; certain no objection to 's presence on such a . . . such an auspicious . . . auspicious . . ." He tailed off. Norah looked at Jody, her eyes opaque with contempt.

"Rascals of your own, no doubt," she said in a low voice, while Corder reeled aside towards the ale-barrel. "Did you think I'd be fool enough to give you credit for any action you had not planned? Any you can beat off with the flat of your sword's your own man, Jody Curle: there are others who'd put up a fair fight."

"You have a heart as hard as the fell rocks, Norah. Would it not have been kindly in you to bid me to the feast-day of our son, as he may well be?" His voice was lowered and he had come close, so that none could hear him except herself; yet she was fully aware of the implied threat in the words. Refuse Jody Curle a welcome, have the servants convey him out of the house and grounds, now or at any other time, and a rumour would soon start up that Norah Stroyan was not the pillar of propriety she had striven all these years to portray; that Ludovic Stroyan was none of Stroyan's get, but a bastard "and God knows it may well be true," thought Norah, "and who is better aware of't than he and I?"

So she said nothing, but let Corder bring his rescuer a cup brimming over with ale, and watched the two men toast one another and her. She turned her back on the toasting, and set off as swiftly as she might up a slight rise on the grass, where beyond the crowd she had espied the figure of her son, engaged deeply in talk with a second man. The packman! "Another uninvited guest," thought Norah, oddly without resentment; it was as if all of that had been expended on Jody and his trick. After tonight . . .

But tonight the inheritance should be made safe. The pretty young girls were already assembled in their muslins and silks, with their mamas; they should sit where Ludovic might scan them at his leisure from the high table, and choose the prettiest to lead out later in the dance. After tonight, no outlawed Popish priest should alter the set road of her son, Curle's heir.

She greeted the two of them, smiling, her face smoothly gracious under the broad hat. "It is nearly time for toasts to be drunk, and for you to make your speech to the tenantry," she told Ludovic. He glanced from her to the packman; the latter's hunched dark shape melted into the shadows. They would never stand up to fight, such folk as that. "Come," said Norah, and set her hand on her son's arm, and led him back towards the great stepped entrance of Curle, where he would presently address his folk as Curle squires had done when they became men by law, from the time of the Saxon himself.

Afterwards Norah knew that her uneasiness had been with her before Ludovic's speech, before Jody came, in fact all day. The speech was short —she had groomed him in a longer one—and, in her opinion, mealy-mouthed; a womanish mumble of trite words, no fit oration for a Curle squire. What Norah had gone over with him briefly, outlining what she thought he ought to say, showed in fact no more than she had all his life been doing for Ludovic, she now thought; that the welfare of the valley must come first. He should have said that, and how he would see to it that the pattern of things, as they had always been, would be unchanged; the care of the tenants, the interest in the farms, the patriarchal nature of the squire's position. She had not thought of, or indeed hoped for, any allusion to herself, and when he mentioned her her first thought was one of anger, not gratitude that he had remembered her in such a way.

"May God bless my mother and all who dwell with her in this valley. I shall remember you in my prayers always. I can say no more."

And he turned and went back to Curle, so that the light of the torches in the doorway, and the dying light of the bonfire in the field, reflected themselves one last time on the brightness of his copper hair and the clear-cut features so newly a man's. They cheered; but it was, she knew, the warmth of the good ale in them, and they would have cheered as loudly whoever he had been, whatever he had said. Norah followed him into the house in great uneasiness, looking for him; but he had already gone from her into some place of his own, and her guests thronged about her and she could not follow.

4

NORAH JUDGED it impolitic to rally Ludovic on the matter of his speech during supper, which passed without incident. She contented herself with surveying the stacked tables; down the opposing wings of the three-sided trestles guests thronged, eagerly talking and eating, their cheeks flushed already with the heat, the ale and good wine. The pale colours of the women's satin gowns were thrown into relief by the darker velvets of the men, puce, olive and deepest blue; everyone wore powder, and the attendants the women had brought to dress their hair and lace them into their tightly boned bodices sat at the lower tables, feasting with the servants of Curle. It was a gala occasion, perhaps the greatest Norah had surveyed in all her own time here: she glanced again with affection at Ludovic, who sat quietly eating his supper to her right, with the Wrayes between them. Amy talked with animation, the rouge she wore outlining little hollows and wrinkles in her face; it was seldom one noticed her age, but with Ludovic's pale youth by her it prevailed, sadly. How they were all growing old, Norah thought, herself no less; there had not after all been any need to dread Jody's intrusion today; her reputation was secure with a generation's tending of her due concerns; even Jody could no longer harm her.

They went out after supper into the hall's centre, where after the trestles were cleared the dancing could begin. Norah could hear the fiddlers, by now up in the minstrel-loft, tuning their strings. She smiled, summing up her own satisfaction at this ending, which was a beginning, to the day; for surely Ludovic would fancy as his partner one of the pretty, eager faces that surrounded them here, Miss Withacott in pink, Miss Castle-Courtney in lilac satin, which became her sallow skin; Miss Cora Abbott, who was the daughter of the detested Amelia of yore, and might redeem herself, if only she caught the glance of the young squire, in apple-green with velvet ribbons, and her hair *a la grècque*, very modish. "I myself would welcome anyone he chose for himself, be she well-born, as otherwise she would not be here tonight," Norah told herself, and searched about for her son, as the fiddles struck up the opening reel. How much it ought to, yet did not, remind her of Stroyan, and the macabre dance they had made together while Jody, with his lost eye newly covered by a black shade, played to her ill fortune! Jody . . . the everlasting shadow, the threat that overlay all!

"But he is not here now," she thought; nobody had been permitted to enter Curle who was not of the county, or by invitation from the neighbouring shires, or like young Cora from the south. She could rest content; if only Ludovic would choose his partner! The fiddles lagged, waiting for the partners to be set.

He had chosen; it was his sister Elizabeth, insignificant in pale blue; Norah downed her anger. The pair went out to the centre, stood in their places, bowed to one another, and the other couples followed, man and maid. The fiddlers struck up in earnest; Amy's sweet voice was speaking in Norah's ear, praising the arrangements tonight. Norah smiled on, disciplining her rage at the way matters had gone; next time, next dance, Ludovic could not refuse to take some young lady guest as partner, for that would be churlish. He shall be forced to wed, the mother thought; then wondered at herself and her own morbid fancies; was it so great a matter if the boy did not lose his heart at the moment she dictated it?

"Many men do not marry early," she told herself, and watched the dancing while sipping ratafia with the others against the wall, nearby the fire which leaped higher as the night grew cold. Many men do not marry, do not marry . . . what ailed Ludovic, and where had he gone? She could no longer see him amongst the dancers; the throng was too thick.

Dawn came. By the end she dragged herself upstairs from the tattered and strewn remnants of the feast, torn ribbons lying about the floor, a favour here, a posy there, dropped from some perfumed bosom. The day had been long, the longest in her life; she was glad it was over; she would get to bed. To bed . . . to her lonely pillow. The wine she had drunk made her wish again for a mate, a man, anyone, lying by her, lying with her. But she was Mrs. Stroyan of Curle who must be above reproach, beyond tongues' chattering.

A timid knock came at her door; she called out to whoever it was to enter, and not waiting for them to open took a lit candle in her grasp in its sconce, and strode over. Elizabeth stood there, uncertainly, one hand to her childish breast; the other held a letter. She tried to speak, but words would not come in presence of her terrible mother; instead she broke down into tears.

"Give it me, you fool; what is this? Is it—" She knew at once, and paled at the knowledge, that the writing was Ludovic's. What could this be? "Where is your brother?" she said to the weeping girl. She did not wait for a reply, but opened the letter. "Go," she said, "go, and do not let me look on you any more, snivelling there." Heaven knew what ungrateful children she had borne! First the great occasion, the feasting, the minstrels and well-born young women scorned; and now this.

What it must be she knew in her heart, and feared to read it, there on the paper. He must have written it ready for her to read, not in the heat of dancing, not at the speechmaking, but earlier. He and his packman-priest had concocted it between them, for her to read where they could no longer make mock of her, here as she sat alone in her room.

"I'd take no priest to bed." Why did she tell herself that? Had any said that she must do so? Priests, women . . . and a tall figure with a black eyeshade, all passed through her mind in a procession, like dancers: dancing priests, dancing whores.

"My dearest mother [it read],

"This will grieve you, but there was no choice. For long now I have waited, and the word has come tonight—" tonight, her feast for him, the handing over of the inheritance—*"that there is a place for me at the college of Saint-Sulpice, near Paris. By this I will be on the way to where a ship waits, and will sail to France. I beg you not to try to deter me, for I will only make shift to go on another occasion, less favourable than this. I ask your forgiveness that I could not be what you wanted, but I hope I am what God wanted, and will strive to do His will. Less can no man do, for the blessed sake of Our Saviour Who died for us.*

I will write often, my mother, and I pray God to bless and prosper all at Curle, and in especial yourself. Do not be angry with Elizabeth for delivering this letter; she knows nothing of its content, only of late that I have gone.

Your loving son, Ludovic."

They said Norah Stroyan ran mad the night her son went off, no man knew whither. She had run to the stable and called for a horse, an escort, any man to ride by her side to the port, to stop a ship sailing. But all the grooms were drunk after the feasting, and in the end it was Madge's son Wil who came to her, and found her demented among the stable-straw, cursing the walls: she made him come out with her, and together they went up on the moors, she all the time urging Wil to hurry, hurry, they would be late, too late ever to stop the ship's sailing. Then up on the moor a stone turned her pony's fetlock, and it stumbled and even she could ride it no more. She asked Wil for his mount, saying they would sit on it together, then, as she was heavy, that she would ride it alone; but Wil knew it would never bear her weight, which was near that of the old squire, and the pony knew it too, and would not move with her. She kicked the beast, and tried to hasten it on; then suddenly abandoned the reins and herself got down from the saddle, running, running always in the direction of the port, though she had no hope of gaining it. They found her the following day, lying half-conscious on the boggy ground, and weeping, her face smeared with mud and moss: and so brought her home.

5

SHE WAS UNCERTAIN when it had become clear to her that wine, and the forgetfulness it brought, were comforts to her. For some months after her son's loss she drank, heavily and silently, always alone, with a flagon in her rooms. Afterwards, perhaps after having slept for a while, she would go out, and taking neither dog nor servant would stride about the moors in solitude. It seemed now as though she needed less than other women in the way of companionship, and more in the way of wine; the old squire, she knew, could have borne her company in her cups, but none other. Stroyan, even Corder would be shocked if they knew her wine-bill now, and the amounts she drank of a night, after returning; yet none of the farm-business was left undone, nor did she flag in her care of the estate of Curle. It was as though after all desires of the flesh or the spirit had left her, this would still be hers; the inheritance, which Ludovic had despised and forsaken for his God.

None dared even condole with her. Those who loved her best, such as Amy Wraye, gently let the subject slide into oblivion, talking only about everyday things, flower-growing, how to prune roses, the like. Wraye himself would accompany Amy, his silence as ever attuned to her talk; he still watched over her devotedly. Often after the pair had ridden off Norah would think of them, hardly pitying the fact that they had no children, that Amy was barren and the title would die out. "Wraye is a new lordship, made only in my grandsire's time; we Curles are the older by far, and now there is no one." It occurred to her at last with a faint sensation of surprise that there was after all someone; Elizabeth must now marry, lacking her brother's heirs. "But I cannot make plans again yet," Norah told herself, never thinking of Elizabeth as other than a pawn, who must do as she was bidden. There would be time; there must be fortune, for no one would wed the girl for her looks or wit. Best let the year elapse, and meantime garner the rent-money; no more gatherings, no more feasting, only the daily tasks of book-keeping and riding about the land and farms.

One day soon after Ludovic's departure Madge Yonge, now long a widow, had come down with Wil by her, her small shrunken mouth mutinous, her black eyes snapping. "We'll be off and away now we're no longer needed, Wil and I." She downed Norah's protests, showing a will as strong as the other's own. They would go to the city, Madge said, where she had kin; Wil should be apprenticed to a butcher there, with all he knew of meat to aid him. "I'm for the easy life, like yon Jody Curle." Her eyes sparkled with malice. "They say he's maken a fortune from his whore-house, that was your grandfer's. Black women and white he has in't, and every man comes, and pays well for what he gets, they tell me."

No one but Madge would have dared bring such news to Norah; the other schooled her features to let nothing or any sensation she felt escape. A brothel in the house Sir Ludovic had owned in the city! It was as she had feared. "Yet what else did *he* keep it for except his own whores?" she asked herself again. However the news increased her disgust with Jody, her deliberate estrangement from him. When Corder Bellingham suggested that they play a card-game together at nights, she repelled the suggestion.

"Bring that half-gipsy whoremaster into Curle? Not while I live," and she brushed aside his descriptions of the convivial evenings they all had at Windyett now, over the cards and wine. It took some time, so great was her withdrawal, for Norah to realise that Jody virtually lived at Windyett, dividing his time between there and the house in Carlisle where he made his money. "It used to be slaves, now it's harlots," thought Norah bitterly. She could not prevent Corder, while he paid rent, from having whom he would as a guest. He seemed more content and less solitary now Jody had come, though he drank as much as ever. Perhaps it did a man good to be no longer alone.

And a woman? Corder himself might have asked her. But it took many months, and the bitterness of lonely winter nights, before Norah sickened of her own company enough to bid Corder and Jody down to Curle to play cards.

6

THEY PLAYED for stakes; Norah could not recall whether it were the second evening or the third. She herself was aware of several things; the wine she had drunk, making her view hazy enough not to see Jody's features, only his tall lean form which sat hunched over the cards; the fire's glow, reflecting itself in a dazzled beam in the wine, which they still drank, in glasses which showed its ruby colour clearly. She still thought of how these had come to Curle with her mother, being little enough thought of for many years there after the familiar leathern flagons, but now for some reason Norah had elected to use them. The third awareness was her constant losing to Jody, the losing of points and, inexorably, of money; the pile of silver coins mounted by his side as they played on, and the night deepened outside the windows.

It had happened so often; why, at cards as in life, must she always be the loser to Jody? She had steeled herself not to think of him as he was, to be no longer aware, in the set game, of any power he might have over her. "He has none, he has none," she would tell herself repeatedly, her inward voice resounding in the caverns of her own mind. He had nothing and was nobody, and she need fear nothing from him . . . except losing constantly, and making herself ridiculous. It was so, no less, to lose each night while she sat in her own hall of Curle.

"If I grow angry I will lose again to him," she thought, and tried to keep calm; Corder dealt the cards, and Norah arranged her hand clumsily, knowing her fingers lacked deftness because she was drunk. It must not show in her playing. The hand was good enough; an ace, two queens and a knave.

Jody raised his head, and Norah became aware of someone at her elbow; Elizabeth, waiting silently till she was bidden to speak. A spurt of irritation raised itself in Norah; they were always at her, the servants, her daughter, about some matter that could have been dealt with among themselves, but she had after all given orders that everything should be referred to her. Well, let it wait till the game was over! Norah played; and watched the others' hands come out, and in the end lie flat on the table; she had won. She smiled, and received the rendering of coins across the table's breadth. Jody gave his wolf's smile. "The luck has turned, kinswoman," he told her.

The luck had turned; perceiving Elizabeth, standing almost witless behind her chair, she muttered, "They say a fool can bring fortune," and heard what the girl had come to say; some unimportant matter which could have waited till the morning. She bade her go and attend to it, then come back again "for sure enough I have won, child, while you stood by me." While waiting for Elizabeth she refilled the wine-glasses, and herself again drank deep. She heard the laughter sound in the hall, among it her own, too loud. What if Elizabeth indeed brought luck with her? She should stand behind the chair each night.

She won; and while Elizabeth continued to stand behind her chair went on winning, until the pile of coins by her was as high as Jody's had been. He did not appear discomfited; would anything take away that devil's self-possession? He even smiled arrogantly, as he leant back to count his lean spoils. "You have a talisman, it seems," he said, and Corder, drunk as at any other time, thumped the table.

"Let us play again, and see to't!" The fourth man, a worker from the estate, dealt the cards, and Norah won again. After that she would have played till dawn; Elizabeth, half asleep on her feet for weariness, did not concern her, except that the girl must stay. In the end the men broke up the party, protesting. "Tomorrow again, good madam; tomorrow!"

Norah won steadily all through that winter. Her daughter, standing behind her as bidden, kept any thoughts she had concealed as always; no one watching Elizabeth would have seen her features alter, and she showed no interest in the cards. By whatever means, she brought luck to her mother; it was almost the only positive attribute about her, and she might have been a bone-thin, undistinguished statuette, apparently without movement or desires of her own. Yet in her slow mind notions wavered. Where she stood, she could see her mother's creamy shoulders and magnificent hair, a trifle unkempt nowadays, and her broad capable hands as she held the cards. Elizabeth would not have had the cleverness to make out the hand and its meaning, nor could she have made any signal to the tall one-eyed man who lounged opposite, even had he suggested it by signs; he had never exchanged speech with her. Yet his appearance was as bizarre as anything Elizabeth had ever seen; during the long hours while they all played, she let her gaze dwell on Jody's figure and face, the thick black hair which was as untidy as her mother's, the thin features and half smiling, half cruel mouth. When he laughed, as he did sometimes when Norah reaped her harvest of coins, his teeth showed white and pointed, like an animal's. Elizabeth felt pity for him in that he was one-eyed. Once, greatly daring, when they were alone, she addressed her mother.

"Mother, how did Mr. Curle come to lose an eye?"

Norah turned on her, causing her to cower. "Mind your affairs, and never ask me such things!" And she bade her be off, in the way she generally did if it were not for the cards, which brought in winning-money. A strange obstinacy persisted in Elizabeth, and she went to ask one of the older servants, Betty Thwaite, who might know of it.

"How did Mr. Curle, who comes here to play cards, lose his eye?" But Betty scowled, and spat on the flat-iron she was holding, to assess its heat.

"Never ask aught concerning that devil's get; the less ye knaw on't the better." And Elizabeth, her curiosity unduly roused, continued to brood on the thing; if only she could ask Mr. Curle himself, except that she would never dare to!

Elizabeth was lonely; she missed the company of her brother Ludovic, who had always been kind to her. She knew that, on two occasions now, letters had come for her mother from him, out of France. Her mother had torn them across without reading them, and had thrown them on the fire. All Elizabeth's weak nature rose in protest; perhaps they had contained a message for herself, and in any event there would be news of Ludovic, how he fared, how his health was; it had been bad sometimes in a cold winter, like this last had been; he'd often taken colds and coughs. But mother cared nothing; and if a letter had come separately addressed to Elizabeth herself, she hadn't been allowed to receive it. Tears rose in the pale eyes.

Now this strange one-eyed man, Jody Curle, diverted her attention from worrying over Ludovic and longing for his news. The wish to find out more about him became an obsession with Elizabeth; she thought of the black eyeshade, with an empty socket beneath, night and day in a kind of confusion of pity, enquiry and terror. So dreadful a thing to lose an eye! "One would almost rather lose an arm or leg, or be deaf perhaps," thought Elizabeth, and again wished she had someone in whom to confide; but there was nobody, although Corder Bellingham had used to be a friend to her and Ludovic before he became so constantly drunk. His changed face roused almost as much fear in Elizabeth as her mother did, or Jody's missing eye. She was a prey to fear, and loneliness; all the dark days she spent brooding, and the nights behind her mother's chair, waiting till Norah won. Afterwards she would sleep for weariness, but sometimes dreamed before waking; the dreams concerned nothing she could remember or recognise, but echoed her fear, of whom she could speak to nobody. If only Ludovic were at home!

Spring came, tardily; the young tight-curled bracken began to show above the remaining snow-heaps. One day Elizabeth got on her pony, and went out riding; she was not an adept at this, and dared do no more than let the gentle beast amble. On her way she saw Windyett, and realised that all along she had had it in her mind to go to visit Corder. He would, if he were sober enough, perhaps give her news of her brother; he had once, long ago now, told Elizabeth of Stroyan himself, living when last heard of above Port Jackson, and doing well with a strip of farming land he had somehow bought up-river. People grew rich in Australia; Corder had told Elizabeth her father was spoken of now as a well-to-do man, though he did not entertain much in his new house because word had long ago come that he and the woman whom everyone had at first thought to be his wife were unmarried. Elizabeth's mother had smiled when the girl told her, and Elizabeth had a sudden gleam of enlightenment; had mother sent word out to Australia somehow about Tina Pryde, the governess, and her father? It would be like mother to do this, in a manner both efficient and cruel. "Why could they not be left alone?" Elizabeth asked herself, for she remembered both the kindness of Stroyan and the gifts and gentle instruction of the plain little governess in her childhood, which by now seemed a long way away; so much had happened since! Yet she was still young, as her mirror told her; a mirror that held a slight flaw in its glass, so that Elizabeth's unremarkable features and thin angry complexion were reflected in a twisted fashion back to her. She had no notion of her looks, but Norah's training had instilled a slight air of consequence, pitiful in conjunction with the plain face and flat dull body. Miss Stroyan of Curle rode out today, on her pony.

She alighted at Windyett, and to her abashed surprise it was not Corder or a servant who opened to her, but the man Jody Curle. She remembered —had she indeed forgotten, or had she never heard that he often stayed there, with Corder, acting sometimes as nurse, sometimes as boon companion? No one—Elizabeth assumed that as she herself did not know, nobody else knew it—no one knew where Jody Curle went at other times or how he made his money. That he was rich was not evident from his clothes today, which were shabby and rubbed at the elbows, and his linen was badly soiled. But mother had told her he had a great deal of money "and so," Elizabeth reminded herself, "it does not hurt him when mother wins it from him at cards." She let Jody take her pony's reins, which he tied to the gate-post; and suffered his bow as he showed her in, though some mockery in its fashion should have warned her.

Jody was disguising triumph. He had thought, had been thinking all this long winter while Norah won his guineas, of a means to obtain speech with the plain, mousy girl who might or might not be his own daughter; for himself, Jody thought both she and her spiritless brother must be Stroyan's; no Curle could have fathered them. He flattered Elizabeth's vanity now, pouring her wine; he knew exactly what to say to fix her interest, for interest with Norah herself would not serve him meantime; Stroyan, living with the governess in Australia, was still her lawful husband. To obtain Curle for himself had never in all these years, while he amassed money by one means or another, been forgotten by him, its lawful inheritor; had Stroyan been nearer, he thought, he would have had him killed. To obtain Norah would have been his chief desire, and with her Curle; but if he could not have her lawfully he had best have the daughter. He went softly, carefully with Elizabeth; he made himself talk of her brother, which banished her fear.

Each night the following week, as usual, they played cards. Norah noticed nothing, except that she still won although hazed with wine. The presence of Elizabeth behind her chair disturbed her not at all, nor by now did that of Jody. So many had come and gone, and the only thing left was to win, and win; she kept the hoard of winnings in a carved chest, and counted them at times by day. Occasionally she would glance at Corder, drowsing over his cards, paying small attention to the game and either winning or losing as his luck dictated; or at the Curle workman, whose playing was adequate enough to make him fill in as a fourth at their table. He was an almost wordless Cumbrian shepherd who had come to her from farther south, and now occupied the cottage where Madge had lived while her miller slowly died of his phthisis. "Word never comes of Madge," thought Norah slowly. She tried to picture the life in the city that Madge now must have with her son, and failed; failed likewise to imagine Jody's brothel, which at any rate kept him in enough silver to lose at cards. Other lives, other ways than her own were still alien; she recognised it.

"Why, Corder lad, I believe you have had enough wine." She saw the other's squat hand reach out, uselessly, to grasp the flagon. Corder grinned weakly. "'S all fair and right," he said, "Jody will see me to th'door, maybe see me into bed; eh, Jody?"

"Maybe," said the other, his single eye dropping to his cards again. What had he been surveying before that, if not herself? The bright intent gaze had not focussed itself on her face as it often did, for she was aware of it; and behind her there was only Elizabeth, and beyond that the fire.

Elizabeth Stroyan was thinking of the thing Jody had told her of the packman. The latter was a priest, she had long known; it had been through his offices that Ludovic had gone off, and was now lost to them; "but he will have news of Ludovic," Jody Curle had assured her. He had told her that, if she would get herself beyond Windyett on a certain night, after the game, he himself would ensure that she met the packman, and heard news of Ludovic, now in France. "He will be in my mother's caravan, which she goes back to in the spring, for she cannot bear a roof over her head in the fine weather; it was all I could do to persuade her to use one in the cold," Jody had told Elizabeth. She was intrigued, trying to think what sort of woman it could be who preferred a caravan to a roof, and said "Where does she stay in winter?" for she knew it was not at Windyett; they would have seen so curious a woman coming and going; the servants, if not her own mother, would have spoken of it. "Where is the house?" she said, wondering if she sounded impertinent; but Jody Curle was not after all of one's own class of person, more like a servant in his dress, though not his manner; so she asked him, and saw the single bright eye fasten on her with an expression which might have been coldness, had he dared; but of course he would not.

"The city."

So he had a house in Carlisle, that place where, perhaps once a year, Elizabeth herself was taken to buy shoes and gloves, and to survey the bonnet-shop. She did not ask further; a house belonging to Jody Curle would not be in the best quarter, where the Abbey bells tolled, but down near the low-lying part where small houses huddled together. She did not ask further concerning that, for what interested her was news of Ludovic, and meeting the packman. "You are sure he will have news?" she said. "I have had none for so long; my mother burns all his letters." Then a sense of disloyalty took her at betraying her mother's doings to such as Jody Curle, and she fell silent. But she knew she would go, on the night arranged, to see the packman, and that she would not tell her mother.

Norah began to be aware of a curious sensation as the days passed: she was losing her aversion to Jody, even, if it were admitted, desiring his physical presence again. He had an attraction his loss of an eye had never diminished; this she knew, but knew also that such things could increase a man's capacity to please, perhaps by way of adding pity to curiosity. She as much as any other was open to such an appeal, and at times, as she fingered the cards, was glad enough of the excuse of having her full and fortunate hand to look down on, veiling her gaze with her lids to hide feelings she was still unsure of. What did she feel, she would ask herself afterwards? Nostalgia for lost youth, for that youth's very promise which should have had another flowering? "Yet I'd been reared to despise him, and still do so for his gipsy's birth," Norah told herself with lessening emphasis. There was, she knew well, the question of her own bereaved body ever with her; her desires were as strong, had always been, as any true Curle's. Many another would have taken lovers since Stroyan's going. But she, Norah Stroyan, had always guarded her reputation jealously. None should point a finger at the guardian of Curle valley, nor question the legitimacy of its heirs.

She would take herself to bed by habit, after the game, tired with victory, and once there fall asleep to troubled, formless dreams. Of Elizabeth she thought no more than she ever had, night or day, except as a talisman. Once or twice she noticed the girl going off on her pony, and torn between pleasure that she seemed to be recovering from the loss of Ludovic's company and irritation because Elizabeth in any case rode like a filled sack, Norah took no leisure to ask where these rides led, in the end. The pressure of daily business, the sessions with the factor, continued; sometimes she would ride about the farms alone, but never took her daughter. Often, as she came in out of the fresh air, the child's cheeks seemed flushed, as though she were almost pretty. "I must give some thought to her season, and to the prospect of a marriage for her," Norah would tell

herself, between Thwaite's office and the staircase. But there was scant leisure, with drinking and gaming in the evenings and her tasks during the
day. At some time she would see to the matter of Elizabeth.

The night which was to become memorable to Norah started as most other
evenings did now, with steady rain pattering down on the pitched roof
and the stones of Curle, due to turn to storm later, and meantime presaging age in all one's bones. Norah moved the cards in her hands stiffly. A
fire roared in the hall; they were, all four of them at the table, shining-
faced with sweat from the heat of it, while about one's back and ankles
came always the swirl of cold from the door, which even the heavy hang-
ings could not keep out. Jody played opposite Norah tonight; behind her
mother's chair, Elizabeth stood, making no sound or movement. Norah
herself might have forgotten, as she often did, that the girl was there, except that the luck was not running as by custom tonight; Jody laid down
his hand of cards, at last, showing two queens, a king and an ace. He
smiled, stowing away the money in deep pockets; Norah swore at her
daughter.

"Curse you, you bring me no luck tonight with your whey-face; get to
your room, child, till I turn the odds alone." It was curious, she thought,
watching Jody's deft fingers deal a new hand, that the luck Elizabeth
brought her had been less constant of late; it was as though the child
let her mind wander, or had her attention diverted elsewhere. Norah
frowned, sorting her lately dealt cards. She did not turn her head till it
grew evident that Jody, his own hand at the ready as usual, had lifted his
head to gaze at the staircase, spiralling upwards to the minstrel-gallery in
the shadows. Norah turned then idly, to behold Elizabeth, still lagging on
the third or fourth stair, her pale face expressionless. "Get to bed, I said,"
she called, "and let my luck turn, lacking you. Go, and do as you're bid,"
and she turned back to the cards; already, a knave, an ace, a queen, no
more. The other pair, the footman and groom—Corder was not here tonight—stared down expressionlessly. They were able players, otherwise
she'd not have tolerated servants at her card-table; as it was, few of the
gentry found time to ride over to play, or if they did must stay the night,
and made poor partners. Norah yawned behind her hand. "Well, then?
Your turn, man; don't be laggard." She disliked having to listen, in the
waiting silence, to the sound of the everlasting rain; it had begun to spit
in the chimney, and Elizabeth had gone.

They played till eleven. By that time the storm had risen, and the rest
went out, with the storm-lanthorn they held tossed sideways in their

hands by a sudden spurt of wind. Such cantrips could mean thunder, and after Norah lay drowsy in her wide bed she thought of it, awoke fully and presently heard the peal in the distance. She flung back the covers; Elizabeth was afraid of thunder, and it might be wise to go and fetch the child into her own bed. A lightning-flash met Norah as she flung on her shawl; that did not trouble her, any more than other natural things. Purposefully, with her way lit by the flashes, she covered the distance between her room and the place where her daughter slept, along a short stone corridor and up a half-flight of stairs. No answer came to her knock. Norah opened the door gently; Elizabeth might after all sleep through the storm, in which event she would leave her be. In the instant's creaking of the door, there was time to reflect on how little she herself understood of cowardice. "All one can do is show compassion," she heard her mind say. Then her eyes focused on the narrow white bed, its virginal quality outlined in this moment by a further flash, lighting up the whole room. It was empty. The bed had not been slept in. Elizabeth's hooded cloak was not on the door-hook. Such things were strange enough to bring Norah's mind for instants to a standstill. Then she shouted for the servants; let them wake from their own slumbers, let them search everywhere till they found her daughter!

They came, and searched all of Curle, from attics to cellars. Then they thought of the stable, and as dawn was breaking found the roan horse gone. There was no other missing; Elizabeth did not, as everyone knew, if she could help it, ride. But pillion on a man's saddle . . . "They'll be over the shire border together now, with the start they've had," the servants murmured to one another behind the noise of the storm. Not one of them dared say the words aloud to Norah Stroyan.

It was about then however that the truth came to her, while dawn streaked the torn sky like yellow banners. They'd be down the Lancashire passes by now, having braved the near defiles by night when none followed, or would dare do for the storm; in any event, of what use to follow now? If she'd had the sense to see, long since, that Jody held Elizabeth captive, snared beneath his single gaze as night followed night, like a rabbit sitting before a snake . . . "Get out the bay, and your mounts, and follow me; you, there, take the west way, and the grooms the north, and I and a few will ride south the way they've gone, I doubt not." Ay, the whole damned pack, Manifold and her son and their kinsmen, carrying off the heiress of Curle like loot, to be marked and kept! "If I ever catch up with them, it's the worse for *him*," Norah swore, when after three hours' headlong ride they had nothing in sight but the soaked moorland marshes, scored by the becks running high and brown with rain. The rain swept down still and caught Norah's wild thick hair and whipped it across her face, and she straightened in the saddle and raised her two clenched fists to the unheeding sky, and cursed Jody. She cursed him with words that had not been heard even at Curle since the old squire's day, and seldom except when Sir Ludovic himself was in direst rage; she cursed him in his going out and his coming in, his fasting and his breaking a fast; she swore that he should never again cross the threshold of Curle, that she would burn the house down sooner than admit him. She sat there with the bitter words flooding from her in the cold aftermath of dawn, with the storm by now subsiding so that most of the weary following—Norah herself was not yet so—were aghast at what they heard said; some of the harder men however swore also, in admiration again, that the old squire himself could not have bettered madam Norah with her tongue, and that in all such ways she was as good a man as he. Then one of the older of them, who remembered the night ride to Carlisle, caused his mount to sidle up to Norah and himself took her bridle which hung loose, and told her gently,

"No sense in lookin' farther this night, madam; best come home. They'll be over the county-border, gone to places where you've less power than they. Come back to Curle and a cup o' warmed wine, madam, lest ye catch cold. Come home, good madam; best come away home."

Nothing was heard of Elizabeth Stroyan for five days, when a rider came to Curle with a letter on soiled paper.

"Jody and I are man and wife," it read. "Later he says we shall come to reside with Corder at Windyett." That was all, with the signature. Norah crumpled it between her hands and flung it into the flames. She sat watching it burn, as the fire leaped high. The rain had stopped and there was calm now over the fells, as if the weather itself had aided Jody.

E LIZABETH COWERED against the dingy curtain of Windyett, staring out behind the grimed glass to where, below the slope, one could see the eastern wall of Curle.

She had been watching now through the long hours of every day, since their return. No one here ate regular meals, and food was snatched as and when it suited the eater. This included Corder Bellingham, whose white toper's face haunted the upper corridors of Windyett like a ghost: he seldom came downstairs. Yet it was Corder who was mother's tenant and paid the rent, not—not that other. Elizabeth's mind shrank now from contemplation of her husband's name. Because Corder had the house, and mother wouldn't turn him out, it suited all of them to live here, herself, *him,* and that grim silent gipsy woman who was his mother and cooked meals of stew that tasted of woodsmoke. The jumble of new facts churned beneath the level of the bride's mind, thrust down less by misery than by the necessity of keeping one thing uppermost in her awareness. She must watch the road for her mother's emerging coach. It had not stirred beyond Curle since their return, nor had mother written.

"Mother, mother," thought Elizabeth, lacking the imagination to ask herself why she should so strangely yearn for Norah, who had been nothing to her all her life and to whom, she knew, she had been nothing. But mother had been, Elizabeth saw now, a pillar of unyielding strength against change; she would have seen no harm happen to oneself.

And it had happened. How naïve she had been, and what a fool, to believe *his* tale of bringing the packman to a rendezvous to tell her how her brother fared!

She had gone, riding alone through the gathering early dusk, hoping there would be time, with hearing the tale and riding back, to reach Curle again before the card-game. That her direction was right according to Jody Curle's instructions she knew; there were the caravans, as he had promised, looming up out of the surrounding scrub and rock, strange hooded shapes like monsters, only there was some homely washing spread out, and smoke rising from a fire that had been lit, with men seated sprawling about it. They had eyed her, idly; for the first time Elizabeth had felt shy of having come here alone. But presently a figure, which turned out to be

Jody, had left the fire and come across the space to her, leisurely as if there were all the time in the world: and with the grand manner he could so well assume, had bowed her into his mother's caravan. Elizabeth could remember the dark interior, where a rush-light burned; and the mingled smells of smoke, grime and herbs. A woman had risen as she entered, setting a brass kettle back on its shelf; Elizabeth had not noted then that it was the woman who had once opened the door to herself and her mother in Carlisle.

There had been no sign of the packman, and as time passed Elizabeth made herself ask when he would come. Soon, soon now, she had been told; and had been given a posset of herbs and wine to drink. It had tasted bitter and strange, but it was warm, and Elizabeth drank it gratefully after the journey. Then . . . then she remembered nothing, except feeling drowsy and, through it, panic-stricken, then no more . . . She had wakened to find the caravan moving and herself naked, lying on a bed of straw, and by the light of the rush which still burned on the wall could see Jody come in past a curtain beyond which it was dark. He was unfastening his breeches.

The pale eyes closed. When she opened them again Elizabeth determinedly focussed on the curtain of Windyett drawing-room, its once elegant pattern almost obscured by dirt. Dirt was everywhere. Once Corder had had a fine house, when his wife lived here, but now . . . Yet they should live here themselves, Jody swore; and sooner or later mother must be made to acknowledge him as the husband of her only daughter, the heiress of Curle. Husband . . . they had been married, of course, next day, as there was no help for it, and by then the caravans had rolled swiftly away from that place down to the south, and stayed awhile, but Elizabeth was kept in the caravan with the old woman, Abigail. Abigail Manifold. It was a strange name, and how she came by it Elizabeth had neither asked nor cared. It had been necessary to Jody that his mother help him in the plot to abduct herself, and it had succeeded; the girl's sick mind refused further memory.

He hadn't touched her again.

"He says now he doesn't like me," she told herself, saying over the words like a child might tell itself a tale. The sight of his cold single eye recurred, and chilled her. What was it he'd said? "As well bed with a newt or a fish," and had left her, and she was glad, but somehow it would have been less humiliating if he'd wanted her, even briefly. To be taken for one's fortune, that only . . . and to take his name. He'd always called himself Curle.

Her eyes opened, and widened a little; up the rise came a coach. It wasn't mother's; smaller, with brighter gilding, and only one footman. Presently it stopped and a slight figure in satins got out: Her Grace of Wraye. Elizabeth felt her knees tremble. The Duchess had been her god-mother, and always kind to her; what would she say now? "I must go and welcome her," thought Elizabeth. But her limbs were dull and heavy, and kept her where she was, clinging to the curtain.

There were voices at the door; would they let the Duchess enter? Surely, there was no need to keep her, Elizabeth, prisoner now the mar-riage was made public. Her hand scrabbled at her bosom; was she tidy? There was only a cracked Spanish mirror upstairs, and she had had to do her own hair these last days and it was out of curl, and her linen wasn't fresh. How different it all was from Curle, where everything of that kind had been seen to! "And now I don't know what to do, or say," Elizabeth thought, "and if she is angry—" But no one had ever seen Amy Wraye angry.

The woman Manifold appeared in the door, in a drugget apron with her black greying hair in its twin plaits, coiled across her head. The bright impersonal eyes regarded her son's dull bride as if she were a stone, a chair, nothing. "Lady to see ye," the voice said flatly. She hadn't asked if Elizabeth was ready. The latter stood still, hearing the rustle of skirts as the Duchess entered. Then she was in Amy's arms; the sensation was strange; in all of her life till now, she realised, few persons had ever touched her.

Amy kissed the bride, then stood back to regard her gravely. "I hope that you are happy, my dear," she said, "but it has grieved your mother."

"Where is mother?" The question itself sounded stupid, asked despite herself while she stared at Amy's exquisite hat; it had, she remembered af-terwards, little rosebuds and forget-me-nots made of silk and velvet, and a shepherdess brim. "Why hasn't she—" But one couldn't say it; everyone must know why mother hadn't called. Perhaps she never would call at Windyett, to see her disgraced, degraded daughter. "To marry a gipsy's bastard!" Elizabeth could hear her voice. But she'd been the one to play cards with Jody, and make Elizabeth herself stand night after night, with nothing to do or divert herself with but looking at that face, that single compelling eye.

"Your mother has been unwell. She is with us at Wraye, and in a little while I hope she will come with us into Italy, for a holiday. After that she will return to Curle."

To Italy! Her mother, who never in all her life stirred abroad even so far as the south parts since her marriage, to cross seas! "Perhaps she will visit Ludovic," thought Elizabeth dolefully. She longed to ask the Duchess if there was news of him—yes, it had been true she wished to hear of that, it was her one desire now, the only thing that could make her feel again, whereas—

"Shall I give her your love, and say that you are happy?" said Amy gently, and Elizabeth heard her as though from behind glass; everything, for Her Grace, had to appear happy and beautiful, and it wouldn't be possible to explain how a marriage could be forced and made ugly, made alien and unmentionable and wrong . . .

But one could never, of course, tell that tale of the caravan and Jody coming in, and taking her, and the squalid struggle and terror and brutal pain. She was Norah Curle's daughter, and Curles didn't whine: the realisation came to Elizabeth in words that might have belonged to someone else.

So she said that she was happy, and to send her mother her love and wish her well on her voyage to Italy, and the Duchess made her farewells and went back to her coach, and drove away, leaving Elizabeth again standing by the curtain.

8

NORAH AND THE WRAYES had left for Italy in November, before winter should descend upon the fells. After their departure the snow came, settled, then melted, leaving wreaths again in the high cold places. Spring made its way with difficulty, as though the young green shoots could not make headway for the cold. Nevertheless, one afternoon a party of pack-ponies could be seen journeying through the slush of ice lately melted in the road-ruts. Among the riders was a young woman who, at first sight, looked like Norah Stroyan. A closer glance showed differences; her hair was smoothly dark, and the eyes that gleamed beneath long sleepy lids had a gentle expression in them, and there was gentleness also in her soft mouth. Her skin had the creamy quality of

Norah's, but was darker, and her body and limbs were thick. Her name was Kate Scarsgill and she came from Yorkshire. She was travelling under the name of Mrs. Vulliamy, and she had come to take up the tenancy of the Moat.

She raised her eyes now from the road, over which she had guided her pony knowledgeably enough; she was a countrywoman and came from the dales. A grey pile of stones had arisen in the near distance which could only be Curle, and Kate turned her head to ask the guide, who had come with her from Carlisle. Behind them were the luggage-packs.

"Ay, yon's Curle ahead," said the guide in his Cumbrian burr. The great house rose like a forbidding rampart, with the smaller bulk of the Moat below and, beyond both, presaging rain with their clear grey-green, the slopes below the fells. These last rose farther off, dark and threatening. Kate shivered a little; how different it all seemed from the gentle bracken-clad slopes of home, which she had left for ever to try to follow Walter Shillingthorne's way! But she must not think of home now, or of Walter.

"I have heard tell of Curle, and Mrs. Stroyan. They tell me she is away." The long north-country vowels, overlaid with a veneer of gentility, almost told Kate's history to anyone who cared to unravel it; a Yorkshire lass born and bred, then sent for a while to a school for young ladies to better herself, as her Dad had told her, instead of ending her life as a dalesman's daughter. She had been happier, though, running wild about the dales among the sheep, and watching Walter turn his pegs and do odd jobs for her father. Then . . .

Kate closed her dark eyes for a moment, as if the memory still brought enough pain to banish this instant of discovery of Curle, and the little house by it where she knew Walter had once lived. That was why she'd come; an improper thing to do, but there was no one now, since Dad died, to ensure that she behaved properly.

"Ye'd lease the house by way of the factor, then?" asked the guide, evidently curious enough to emerge from his native silences. "Mrs. Stroyan they say likes to view all the tenants for herself; like enough she'll send for ye, when she comes back from foreign parts."

"When will that be?" asked Kate idly. She did not greatly care for being viewed by this Mrs. Stroyan. Arrangements had been made in writing with the Carlisle lawyer and the factor, and she had boldly put her signature as Mrs. Vulliamy for the first time. No one had doubted her; as long as the money was paid, why should they? And Dad had left enough to see her comfortably settled, although it wouldn't last for ever. Fear of the future faced Kate for instants, then she banished it. One could live from day to day. At worst, she could obtain a situation as lady's maid in the end, or governess. They'd taught enough at the school to give her ladylike ways, and she could paint on velvet. One thing at a time, as Dad had used to say, was to be the way of matters now. If only Dad hadn't put that clause in his will about Walter's legacy if he married her, and when Walter refused it had set the neighbourhood laughing . . . no, she wouldn't think of that, it was what she had come away to forget.

"It'll be when Mrs. Stroyan chooses," said the guide, "and she suits herself."

He helped Kate down at the Moat door, and unloaded the pack-ponies while she went inside. What she saw made her heart fail, at first; it was so empty, this place where Walter had lived, with the thin sun making pencilled beams of light through the small dusty windows. But the house itself had been swept, and someone—possibly a servant of Mrs. Stroyan—had laid a fire ready in the grate.

"Have you a tinder?" she asked the guide timidly, as she paid him. He inclined his head to one side, and regarded her.

"Ay." He reached into his coat and brought the tinder out, and bending down set a light to the firewood, and saw it blaze up. Kate was grateful to him. He set the tinder down on the mantel, which was of stone. "Keep it," he said slowly. "There'll be none such to be got here, not unless ye were in the town again."

His eyes beneath their grizzled brows surveyed this feckless young lady, who seemed to have no one of her own to deal for her, and was too daft to have brought a tinder to light her own fire. "Ye have no man?" he said to her, compassion suddenly overcoming his habit of minding his own business. Kate replied haughtily, "My husband is dead. If you have unloaded the baggage, you may go now. Thank you for the tinder."

"I'll be off, then. If ye were needing aught—"

"I have everything I require."

She stood and watched him go, torn between the wish for continued company—she was still unaccustomed to being quite alone—and the thought she had that he was becoming too familiar. That was always a danger with lone women, she knew; it had been one reason why she had pretended to be a widow. A young unmarried girl would have had no chance at all of leasing the Moat, or doing any other business for herself. Yet whom could she have brought with her, or confided in? No one at school had been friendly; they laughed at her countrywoman's accent and broad hands, and called her Brown Kate behind her back. She had been sick for home, for the dale cottage and Dad and Walter, who lived there together as they had done for years, ever since Kate's mother had died and Walter came walking out of nowhere, from the north, and asked for a night's lodging and stayed on and on. Dad had been lonely then, lacking Kate's mother, and glad of Walter's company. And she herself, a child then, had run about all day after Walter like a little dog, and in those days he would tell her things.

Walter. Walter Shillingthorne. Kate knelt down beside the newly kindled blaze and warmed her hands, and thought of that strange creature whom she had loved, as though he had been a god. It had been a cruel blow when on first hearing news of the legacy, after Dad died, Walter had packed up his things without a word and gone on his way again, no one knew where. Walter wasn't like other folk. Nothing would ever hold or bind him, certainly no woman. He was as cold as a stone, as magical and implacable as the Fairy King. It had been tolerable to him, no doubt, to have small Kate running forever behind him to do his bidding, mend his torn coat, darn his hose, listen to his stories, perform any errand or task. But marry her when she was grown? Never. The reply he had made to Dad's lawyer stung Kate again now, making her flush hotly in the light of the fire. "I have no wish to marry. Kate herself does not attract me in such a way. I have no wish for the money. I will decline the legacy and go on my way." And go he had, and the cottage where they had all lived had reverted to the farmer who owned it, for with everyone in the place laughing at her once it was known she had been jilted, how could Kate have stayed on there by herself?

If only Dad hadn't sent her away to school in that last year, she might have altered things. But Dad had noticed, as everyone did, how her young breasts were growing big and she was almost a woman, and he had remembered how her mother had used to have a lady's ways and had sent Kate, crying her eyes out, to be a pupil at the grand school in York. Dad had been kind, but once a notion entered his head nothing would get it out. She remembered his beetling grizzled brows drawn together over his face and his saying that she must go, for it was what he'd planned and saved for; he'd have wanted her mother to be proud of her, for she came of fine blood.

"I don't want ye to grow up into a farm-lass, Kate, for the blood that's in ye. I'd have ye a lady, able to do more than cipher and cook; learn fine manners, maybe the French language. It's what y'mam would ha' wanted, and I'd not fail her."

He must have known, she thought, even then, of the cancer which would in the end destroy him, laying him to rest at last, when Kate was seventeen, in the churchyard beside the grave of that mother who had died so long ago that Kate could remember little of her except that she had always been ailing, had had golden hair, and used Dad like a servant to do her bidding. Dad had wept when she died; it had been the first time Kate had ever seen a grown man weeping. "I carried her in from the moor long ago," he kept saying, "cold she was, and wet wi' the rain, but she's colder now where she lies," and then he would start to cry again. Kate had asked nothing of it all and after a while he had stopped speaking of it, but now, when it was too late, she began to wonder what it had all meant.

The blood that's in ye. What blood could that be? Dad hadn't told her any more of it, and it couldn't be anything that was widely known, for the young ladies at school, and the mistresses too, had looked down on her as a dalesman's daughter, and so Kate felt herself to be, despite everything.

Did she still love Walter Shillingthorne? Perhaps, a little. It wasn't possible to be at a man's side all those years and then cut him out of life and out of mind. She would have been happy as Walter's wife living on at the dale cottage rearing their children and cooking Walter's food and looking after him. She was a good cook, and she could keep a house clean. This one, now, that she'd come to . . .

She had seen it in one of the gazettes. This Mrs. Stroyan must have told her factor to advertise for a tenant while she was abroad. Kate herself, as Mrs. Vulliamy, had answered, and had presently got on the coach to Carlisle and had bought a ring there and had stayed at an inn, and later gone to see the lawyer. It had been a great, a daring adventure, but by now she was getting used to being a widow-woman. If the notions of propriety they'd tried to instil at school had stayed with her, she should have felt shame at coming to a house Walter had spoken of once, merely to come and live where he had lived, to touch the stones he had touched, see the fells and the places that he said he knew. But it brought him back to her, and perhaps one day he would come walking by, and then . . . Then what? He would never marry her; he had already said so.

Kate turned her head, cheeks scarlet from her thoughts and the heat of the fire. There was the same scrubbed table Walter had used. He wouldn't—dear Walter—have kept it very clean. She'd scrub it again tomorrow.

The flames leaped high in the stone hearth; there were logs piled by it and Kate cast one on. He must often have sat here watching these same dancing shadows the flames cast on the stones; have caught sight, with his cold blue eyes that missed no detail of what they chose to see, of a stone with a shape like a cat's face, and another that was darker than the rest and speckled like a bird's egg. Walter had used to show her stones he had found near here that had tiny dark-red garnets embedded in them, like pearls in an oyster's shell. Walter . . .

"I shall go mad if I sit here and think of him," her mind said. The quality of the silence, now that the pack-guide had gone, closed in. Perhaps she would meet some people in the village. Perhaps when Mrs. Stroyan came home she would invite Kate up to the big house to be viewed, and having viewed her would like her and ask her back to drink tea. Perhaps . . . but people, other than a few certain people, didn't really matter; it was only that everyone and everything she had ever known had been swept away at once. She would never again, she knew, be as hurt and deceived as she had been over the affair of Walter. No man should ever hurt her so again.

9

KATE SOON DISCOVERED a challenge in the state of the small garden at the Moat, which was unweeded, as it would doubtless not have been had Mrs. Stroyan been at home. The bailiff did not concern himself with such things, or with anything except gathering his rents. Kate went out one day, therefore, and got down on her knees to grapple with the nettles and bishopweed, which were gaining ground. In this exercise she found satisfaction. She had not much experience of gardening; at the croft in the Yorkshire dales they had grown cabbages, which her father had dug and freed from caterpillars twice yearly, and, later, made into broth. The school for young ladies, of course, had not catered for so ungenteel a pastime as plant-growing. But Kate was to learn that the highest in the land loved this for its own sake, and that the habit of growing flowers for their beauty had already spread north from the pleasure-gardens about the Thames, which Dutch William and his wife had planted two generations ago, causing others to follow suit.

On the day when she was grasping, with increased intention, the creeping stinging weeds, she heard a woman's voice; and, still on her knees as she was, looked up. An exquisite little lady sat beyond the wall, perched high up on a four-wheeled gig, with a pony drawing it. She wore a shepherdess hat a trifle the worse for wear; one could tell, nevertheless, that she was not a common person. Kate got up, conscious of her own grimy hands and dress.

"You must be my kinswoman's tenant," said the lady very sweetly. "We have lately returned from Italy, where we left her: she has asked me to enquire if you have all you need. I am the Duchess of Wraye," and she cast the pony's reins over a post and climbed down, seating herself on the low wall and surveying the state of the little garden.

"My two loves, as I have no children, are meeting people and gaining a knowledge of plants," the Duchess observed. "I think that that is a milk-thistle over there; for a time there was a man here who tended them. You are Mrs. Vulliamy, I hear. Is your husband with you?" The blue eyes, innocent of any guile, surveyed Kate with kindly curiosity. The girl shook her head.

"He is dead, your—" She remembered that at school, they had taught her that only lowly persons said "your Grace" and amended it to the Duchess's title. That personage looked very sorrowful, and extended her small gloved hand.

"You are so young to be widowed! But now that you are here we must make you welcome. I am having a small gathering of my friends at Wraye on Thursday week, to play cards and drink ratafia; will you come, Mrs. Vulliamy?"

Kate's mind was in a whirl; here, evidently, was the great world at her door. That she was neither prepared for it, nor very well dressed for it, occurred to her. "Madam, your—Duchess, I have only the one gown," she stammered, and Amy laughed. "Have no fear as to that, half the county live in one gown, and the other half furbish up a second one with made-down lace," she said. "I have a fichu I can lend you, if you are not in full mourning. Do not, I pray you, think that you must come if you would not; it may be that your husband's death is very recent?"

"Last year," said Kate, dropping her lashes. She did not like telling lies to this charming little person, but the harm was done; now and for ever, she must be the widow of Vulliamy. "I shall have to think of an occupation which he could have filled," she heard her mind saying. Perhaps he could have been an attorney; but to have left a widow so badly off argued poorly for his achievement. A poet, maybe, or a clergyman? She would think of something, after the Duchess had gone.

Meantime she made it clear, very prettily, that nothing would induce her to forgo Her Grace's invitation for Thursday week. It would be diverting to meet the great world; more of a challenge, in its way, than the nettles and bishopweed. If she minded all that school had told her she would fare well enough; with, it was to be hoped, the minimum of lying. Even now her cheeks flushed hotly at the thought of the latter's recent necessity.

The Duchess of Wraye's card-party was, for Kate, a success; she had been trained to hold a steady hand at the lighter games of chance, as every young lady must; and here they did not play for money. She met, in turn, three formidable dowagers, a general and his wife, and various county-squires and theirs. She met also, and was surprised at his colourless appearance, the husband of the Duchess, who scarcely resembled one's notion of a Duke. Kate curtseyed bravely to Wraye, and thereafter endeavoured to win him by pleasing manners, as she would have done to any other person. At the end the Duke said to her, "Madam, it is good for my wife to see a cheerful countenance; come often to Wraye, I beseech you." And on leaving, it was made evident to Kate that she had secured a mild triumph among the tea-cups and the ratafia-glasses. One of the dowagers, whom she had hitherto regarded as intimidating, said to her, with what appeared to be a wistful smile, "My dear, if you have made headway with Wraye it is a notable thing; he is exceedingly hard to please, and I hear he is delighted with you. Will you not visit me also, at Marryatt Priory?"

The Moat House was dark when Kate found her way back, but her heart was singing. It was apparent to her that never before in the whole of her life had she been among persons who lived life as it should be done. How sweet the Duchess was, and how hard she would strive to please such a patroness! She entered the house humming a tune, and soon had candles lit, dispelling the night.

10

ON HER WALKS Kate had seen certain tiny bright-blue flowers, with fringed bells of petals, growing in the peat-moss above the grey-stone house called Windyett, which sat high above the valley and Curle itself. She took the Duchess's borrowed trug and a basket, and carrying these clambered up the hill path one day in late afternoon, for she was slow if thorough at household tasks and it had taken her till noon to get through these. Leaving the newly made bed and airless house, she sniffed the clear air of the moors with enjoyment: she was able now, without bitterness—it seemed far off and in another life—to think of the time when she had followed Walter Shillingthorne along such ways and about such ploys, like an obedient dog.

But Walter was far away, wherever he had gone on his own business; Kate discovered that she no longer cared, and humming a little tune for happiness knelt down, when she came to the place where the flowers grew thinly, and dug deep into the moss to fill her basket. One must, the Duchess had told her, leave plenty of the native soil about the roots, otherwise the plants would die. She had already filled a part of the rough plot of garden at the Moat with seed-marigolds, cornflowers, and mignonette which the Duchess had given her, although the latter did not seem as if it would do very well. The newness of enjoyment in all such things made Kate draw deep, full breaths of satisfaction; even if one were only as yet an indifferent gardener, how wonderful to have discovered that there were people who grew flowers for their beauty, and did not only think in terms of cabbages and roots!

"They will not grow anywhere but here; you had better leave them be, Kate Scarsgill."

Her hand flew to her breast, causing her to drop the trug; the place where she had been digging stared up rough and broken, gaping to show damp peat beneath. A man was standing between her and the grey house; his back was to the sun, and at first she could not make out his features; then she saw that he had only one eye. The other was covered with a black patch, and he was tall. Kate made herself act as the Duchess of Wraye, or other of her acquaintance, would surely have done in the circumstances, and gave a cool returning stare; but at the same time fear clutched at her heart. Was it possible that she had, at some time, seen this man before? He was not a gentleman; he was like—yes, the gipsies who sometimes rode on pony-back or in carts across the moor. That might have been when he had seen her, and knew her for Kate Scarsgill. Panic beset her; should she pretend now to have been such a person before having become Mrs. Vulliamy?

But Kate's wits were not equal to the occasion. "I do not know who you are, but you have mistaken my name," she said coldly. She rose, brushing the earth from her skirts, and bent swiftly and picked up the Duchess's trug. How appalling to have left it up here! She made to go, with her basket on her arm; but the tall one-eyed man stepped in her way. He was smiling.

"You may not know me, Brown Kate, but I know you well enough; and your father, as he was known, and Shillingthorne, and what they said of you before you left the dales. What would your fine acquaintance say now, were I to tell them you're no widow, perhaps even no maid?" His smile widened and he began to laugh softly; Kate's face was suffused with blushes.

"I am indeed a—" she was beginning, then knew her tongue had trapped her; no matter what affair of his it might be, what harm he could do! The thought of it, even now, made her tremble; the whole valley would know her for a liar, and worse; an impostor, only the daughter of a herdsman at that, unfit to ask to their tea-parties. And what had he meant about her father? Kate's lower lip quivered and her eyes filled with tears.

"What indeed?" said Jody. "Indeed a maid, or none? I confess it would suit me well enough to find out, Kate; no, do not run from me," for she had taken her skirts in one hand, and the basket tilted dangerously. "If you spill those poor plants by their own place, it's as well, for they may grow on. One does not find this tiny lady-in-waiting anywhere but on these moors, and in one other place I know of, in Scotland." He spoke as if to himself, gazing down on the already wilting plants, their bizarre blue unexpected as a piece of fallen sky among the grass. "I learned the names of flowers from my mother," he said. "Do you remember yours, Kate? She must have died when you were a child, but you may recall her golden hair; I saw her once, when my reprobate grandfather drove me with him into Carlisle." His one eye narrowed, assessing her. "But I'll not tell you more, though I could. When may I wait on you, Kate? I know, you see, that the door at the Moat House latches on the inward side, and if you were to leave it unlatched—"

"I will not do so. You—you think to take advantage of my state, and that I have no protector." These, again, were the brave words that Kate was sure a great lady would have uttered; but they came out quavering pitifully, and she herself was filled with terror and more; what was to stop this gipsy doing as he would with her, using the threat, as he had already done, to tell everyone here of her origins? Would it not be better to brave it out, and let him do so? But to have to inform the Duchess of Wraye that all she had already told her was a tissue of lies, and watch the beautiful eyes grow shocked and distrustful, was more than Kate could bear even in thought.

Jody had drawn closer. "May I not come tonight, Kate?" he murmured. "Leave the latch off, and go to bed; I will come late, not to compromise you with your grand friends; that would never do."

"Then why do you trouble me?" she said piteously.

"Because," he said slowly, "you recall to me someone I knew well when I was young. In certain ways you might be her very self. But you have not her pride."

She had flushed. "How do you know all this of me?"

"Because I travel between here and the dales, and in former times from here across seas. There is nothing I may not know about any person if I choose; if I cannot find out for myself there are others who will do so for me. I have known of you ever since you were a wild brown girl trotting, unpaid, behind Walter Shillingthorne. I know of your . . . father's offer, and how Walter denied it to your shame. There is little I do not know of you, Kate, and that little I would seek to repair."

He did not take Kate at once. The sensation that she was Norah, that he might soon have Norah beneath him again and in his power, and in some way also the dead Sir Ludovic, was too sweet not to prolong; he would do this at his discretion. That night, he knew, showing the same fearful hesitancy, like a small bird or animal in a trap from which there is no escape, Kate would leave her latch off the hook and go, trembling and obedient, to bed. After some time she might manage even to sleep a little; she was young and healthy.

It was so, and when she awoke it was quite dark, and he was already in her bed. She tried to cry out but his mouth came down over hers, silencing her; and against her opened lips she could hear him say "Quiet, lest we wake your grand friends' servants at the house." He drew himself over then till he lay upon her, and presently began tumbling and teasing her, caressing her body in a way Kate had never known or imagined. After the first shock of terror and distress she found that it pleased her, and the fact that this could so soon be, in its turn, brought shame. How could she, Kate Scarsgill, take pleasure in the lascivious hands of a stranger in her bed, a one-eyed man she had only met that day? How could it happen? But it was happening; she heard her breaths come in small short, pleasurable gasps. She no longer cried out or tried to struggle against him. How could a man's hands accomplish so much? For his hands and mouth were all that he used. He had loosened her night-shift by the end, without protest from her for she was by then aflame with open desire; he fondled her naked breasts and thighs, leaving no part of her body unexplored, even as he had said he knew her mind and history. Then he slipped out of her bed before daybreak, leaving Kate bereft, indignant, curious, unsatisfied, eager for more. That she would have wanted more she knew; that he had not given it angered her; yet now that he had gone she was again filled with shame for herself, that in this strange dawn she had wanted the gipsy at last to lie with her as though she were a whore, and he had not.

The next night Jody did not come; and Kate, who had spent the day in trepidation and the night with an unhooked latch, lay wakeful and disappointed, then angry again. How wicked she had been to hope that he would come! How doubly grievous when he did not! What would everyone say if they knew? She could never hold up her head again. Then she remembered those wanton, cunning hands and the places they had touched that they should not, and . . . oh, why had he not come back this evening?

Kate cried herself to sleep, partly by reason of bewilderment at herself and the way she had changed. She had not once thought of Walter all day. If Walter would have done such things to her . . . but he would not, perhaps could not. There were after all other men than Walter. This man with one eye, whose name he had told her was Jody Curle; ah, if she dared ask someone about him! Whom could she ask? The Duchess? That might be dangerous; best say nothing, nothing at all about Jody, until they met again, and then . . .

He did not come the following night either. He must have used her, she thought, for his diversion and then forgotten her. During the day when buying milk she had found that he was in fact married to Mrs. Stroyan's daughter and lived in the house on the hill. How dared a married man use her as a doxy? How dared he, and then . . . and then abandon her?

By noon she was still angry, and now resolved to go up the hill and have it out with Jody. He must never again use her so; she cared nothing of what he might tell anyone, he had no power over her. The Duchess's image—she had not visited Kate for several days and had visitors at Wraye —had meantime faded somewhat and grown less important. Kate's mind was confused, chiefly excited concerning it knew not what, and almost certain it ought to know less than it did. She would be miserable until she had climbed the hill. As she approached its rise, however, she trembled. Supposing he sent a servant to ask what she wanted? Supposing he were not there at all?

But he was there; and came upon her laughing, and without delay thrust her down into the bracken. After that it was no longer ignorance that filled Kate's mind: she lost her maidenhead three yards from where she had found the blue flowers that former day, and had left a half-basketful lying, invisible as they now were for such things do not survive half-death. Her fingers scrabbled now, with perhaps some dim remembrance of trugs and gardens, at the turf and moss, while Jody took his pleasure on her. At the end he kissed her, and promised to come again to the Moat House that night. By now, Kate was no longer sure of anything except that she must continue to let him in, for was it not in any case too late to leave the latch on the door? And she had liked it; she knew she had liked it very much, despite the moment's pain at first, which would not come again.

From her window, Elizabeth had been watching. She knew that Jody would not care whether she saw or not, and for herself she was indifferent that he had found a woman. She went out little and although she knew that the young person herself was a tenant at the Moat, she was not aware that Kate was to be seen very frequently in Amy Wraye's drawing-room. Elizabeth herself received few invitations, and did not care, for shyness, to accept any that came. It might not have been possible to go without Jody, and she did not like that he should accompany her. All she cared about, and prayed for it almost with passion, was that her mother should return soon from Italy. The Duchess had sent on letters which had come to Wraye, saying that mother was in Venice, making journeys by water on the canals, and was staying in a waterside palace with a Marchesa whose name evaded Elizabeth, although Amy had told it her. Elizabeth could not picture the gondolas, the palaces, nor any landscape that was not Curle enclosing her mother. If only she would come home, everything would be different. The days were growing longer now and it was not so cold; there was no reason to stay on in Venice, that anyone could see.

PART IV

I

A COACH LUMBERED north along the dusty August roads, lurching now and again over pot-holes and dried rutted mud from the late summer rains. Inside, Norah Stroyan, clad in Italian brocade, lifted her heavy eyebrows and said to the young man by her, "This is an unusually dry season. At any other time you will see nothing but rain."

She was glad to be home. He sensed it, and bowed, returning her smile with full red lips like a woman's. His curly hair was grape-black and his build slender, and most of his speech was made by means of his expressive eyes. These were dark and full, with the whites visible all round the iris. His name was Giuseppe Manzoni and he was a professional *cavaliere servente*. His age was twenty-seven. Norah had made his acquaintance in Venice, by the piazzas where his kind would congregate daily, in search of custom. She recalled the first time she had noticed Beppo, idly as if it by now mattered nothing by comparison with the surge of thankfulness she felt on again beholding the fells, their shapes fantastic against a sky it had seemed as if she might never behold again. How long since she had been away!

At first—she could remember events clearly enough—she had been like an invalid, nursed by Amy and her husband back to health after the ruinous affair of Elizabeth's marriage. They had been assiduous in pointing out to her this colonnade, that roofless temple, and in planning excursions from which Norah might view Italian lakes and hills and drink the harsh red wine of the country, and let her mind heal. It had taken a long time; she could not, in the nature of things, confide in Amy that the most terrible aspect of all was that Elizabeth might in fact be married to her own father. She could say this to no one.

By and by she had accepted it; the thing was done. When Amy and Wraye had asked, gently, if she would return home with them Norah had declined. She was recovered now, she assured them; she would stay on in

Venice awhile, and see the sights and enjoy the time of carnival. Amy had, with her usual thoughtfulness, provided a mutual friend who might banish solitude for Norah; the Marchesa di Bellogiorno, an Englishwoman who had long ago married a Papal Count as his second wife. She herself was widowed now and no longer young, and knew everyone. Amy had left Norah in the Marchesa's care.

Norah smiled. It had been in company with the old Marchesa, who was less virtuous than Amy supposed, that she herself had first set eyes on Beppo Manzoni. Before that she had been a source of irritation to the Marchesa. "You are rich, you are free, you are not yet too old, and yet you do not disport yourself! Of what use to remain a near-widow, a woman without a man!" The Marchesa herself took lovers as she would, and gloried in it; Norah had found herself, at the first, a trifle shy of such a prospect. She was not, she had decided, naturally promiscuous: but it was a long time since she had had a man, as the Marchesa would have put it, and the blood of Sir Ludovic ran redly in her. Had she not been a woman, no doubt, she would have amused herself ere this with the pretty *contadine* beneath the arcades; as it was, she toyed with the notion of a lover. But nothing came of it until she and the Marchesa had taken a stroll one day past the Piazza San Marco, watching the sun on the canal. Beppo had been nearby among his fellows, and the old Marchesa, who looked like a withered yellow rose, had remarked that there was one who seemed a young god; and Norah had, innocently, turned her eyes in the direction of Beppo's supple comeliness. "Never look," commanded the Marchesa, "look away, and he will come. Such things are not arranged by staring directly as the English do." She had bared her discoloured teeth, which she rarely forgot to conceal, at the revelation of Norah's gaucherie. Later in the evening the young man had appeared at the palazzo. How he had known that he was summoned was a matter beyond Norah's reckoning; the main thing was that he had come, and she had had to make up her mind, as it were, quickly. No one in the company she now kept abroad would have understood the lingering of prudery, a certain unwillingness to surrender. But what had she to lose? Norah asked herself. She'd known nothing, nothing of what other women were able to assume as a part of their lives, ravished first as she'd been by Jody and then, over the dull years, mated with flavourless Stroyan till he found a woman as dull as himself. Why should she not take a lover?

So it had ended, all of it, in the arrangement with Beppo, who Norah at first decided satisfied her well enough. After a further few nights she admitted to herself that he did not, but knew that, at that rate, she herself must perhaps be cold, unworthy of such a professionally practised lover. That Beppo possessed all the tricks of the trade she recognised; he had even, he told her, had the operation recommended to those of his kind, which would prevent his inconveniencing lady clients while, at the same time, permitting them to savour the utmost delight in his services. Norah tried to appreciate these, and blamed herself, not Beppo, that delight was lacking. She developed a maternal affection for the young man, as if he had been her son. It was the same feeling as she had had for Corder Bellingham, although Corder had never been her lover. Perhaps she was intended only to feel motherly to men; she surveyed the possibility, unemotionally. They dealt well enough together, she and Beppo; in the end she had persuaded the Italian to come home with her, and had made him an allowance.

"You are my secretary, if any should have the impertinence to ask concerning it when we reach Curle," she had instructed him; and Beppo made no objection, though he could not himself see the likelihood of anyone's misunderstanding his status with the signora. The English were unusual. In the meantime he minded his manners, knowing very well when he was fortunate. The Wrayes, Norah knew, would need some explanation of the kind outlined; once they were satisfied, others would suspect nothing, or if they did would keep silent. Whose concern was it in any case except her own?

"You are weary, child, with the journey?" she asked Beppo now gently. The young man replied with courtesy that the journey had been a long one, but that the countryside was of great interest. "The roads, however," he said, "are terrible. How can the signora endure to travel so? Already I long for the sunsets of Venice, and smooth water on which to make one's way pleasantly."

"Your canals stink," said Norah. "Wait till you see our mountain tarns, and the fresh becks feeding them. The men will take you fishing, if you would like that. Soon now you will be at Curle, before a good fire although it is summer."

Beppo did not know what becks might be, but assumed them to be one more perquisite of this rich Englishwoman who had, as it were, swept him away, by force both of money and persuasion, from easier clients and familiar scenes. He had allowed himself to be persuaded partly because the signora's demands were not great—Beppo had not, despite his boasting, again achieved the physical gusto he once possessed before the vasectomy, and regretted that operation but it was too late now—and also because the price was handsome. The settlement the signora Stroyan had made on him had enabled Beppo to secure for his invalid sister, who was dying of tuberculosis, a drier room in the canal-side convent she occupied, and better food. It was worth servitude in a foreign country for some time to ensure that the little one would die in comfort and peace. Beppo fixed his eyes on his benefactress now, sensing beyond the rich brocade her opulent, creamy flesh. She was like a painting of Titian, one of Juno perhaps, with a fine bosom and hips. "I do not know if Tiziano ever painted that goddess," the young man told himself critically. He himself was interested in painting and if he had not had to make a living, would have taken up the brush. One could reflect on such things at the same time as pretending to listen to whatever it was the signora might be saying, as she seldom required an answer. She would be talking about this Curle, no doubt, where he was to stay and be taken to catch fish. That would be a chilly pastime, like most others here; but, if he played his part skilfully, the signora might procure him a box of paints. The frowning colours of the sky and hills here already half froze, half fascinated Beppo with their strangeness. They were unlike anything he had ever encountered before, in the same way as the signora Stroyan was herself unlike the customary arch, desperate and ageing ladies who solicited Beppo's attentions on the Piazza San Marco.

The coach wheeled round the turn before Curle, and, as always happened, lurched wheel-deep into water from a beck which ran high at all seasons. Beppo rolled up his eyes, and Norah laughed.

"This is nothing. You will grow used to conditions here."

"As the signora says." Beppo's English, picked up from tourists on the canals and the occasional *padrona*, was fairly free from accent. The fact that he could neither read nor write would not deter him from describing himself as the signora's secretary. If one used one's wits, one would learn. When he returned home again it would be as a person of fortune. He might even buy his own gondola, or an inn. After Maria had had Christian burial—

"Here is Curle now," said his benefactress, and at the same time Beppo saw the grey stones and Norah's raised profile, suddenly eager and innocent as a girl's. She had, as he already knew instinctively, this kind of untouchable innocence; some things would never be evident to her that other women know by instinct. Beppo had developed what was almost an affection for her; he respected her as his mother. He would make it his business to pay attention to each least wish of hers, even to the extent of catching fish.

But he was impervious to the magic of this Curle, which she so loved.

As they descended from the coach at last, Beppo felt his limbs turn cold in spite of the August day. How sharp these northern airs were! Perhaps his servitude here would not last too long. He would pray to the Mother of God that it might be so, and that he might soon return to Venice.

2

NORAH SET ABOUT making good her long absence, seeing her bailiff, examining his receipts, investigating the housekeeping expenses and the servants' pay. It was not for a full week after returning to Curle that she took leisure to visit Amy. The day was fine, and it should be possible to ride over rather than take the carriage; besides— this Norah did not admit except to herself—she was unwilling to present the Venetian to Amy, except by accident. His official post, as they had arranged, was that of secretary; nothing more need be guessed at or gossiped about, certainly not at Curle. But when venturing farther afield, Norah would leave her *cavaliere* at home. He made no demur, agreeing, as it was his place to do, with everything she ordered. As he had given no trouble in the matter, Norah rewarded him by asking how he would pass his time till she returned. She had not previously left him to his own devices for long, and some compassion came to her; he was after all a stranger in a strange country, and how real was the relief at returning to one's native land! She could hardly tear herself away from the sight of the fells, and Windyett and Curle beneath.

To her amusement, Beppo spoke of the fells. "If the signora permits, I will make a drawing of the small mountain." His long lashes drooped on his cheeks; he looked very young. Norah smiled at the statement.

"Do you draw, Beppo? I did not know." He was a creature of diverse interests; on the rare occasions when she had bidden him talk at length to her, his converse had never been dull.

"I have made many portraits of *signore* upon the canals. They would ask that I do so. One day may I draw the signora herself? Upon a horse?"

She warned him in a low voice not to speak of the canals. "Where you have come from is no one's business, you understand me? If they desire to know anything, they must ask me concerning it." Beppo smiled a little, and held his peace.

Norah left him, armed with paper and pencils, and herself set out for Wraye after all in the carriage, as it had turned cold. Exhilaration returned to her as she beheld the familiar road and at last the driveway, and the pillars of the Palladian house of Wraye: how long it was since she had seen Amy, or heard from her! They had exchanged a letter or two while Norah was still in Italy. "But that told nothing," she thought with truth. She realised now how much she had missed the sight of Amy's worn, pretty face, and the knowledge of her affection. Friends were, when all was said, of as much worth as any other thing in life; she must cultivate friendships now that she was growing older, and other things had failed her. Other things . . .

"Her Grace is in the yellow drawing-room," the footman told her. Norah dismissed the man and made her own way to the place she knew well, intent on surprising Amy. Perhaps she would be watering her indoor garden, whose varied plants grew and bloomed under Amy's touch as they did for no other. Or, again, she might be at her harpsichord, which she played indifferently, but with such grace that one still thought of her as a fair performer. Norah smiled; with grace, with charm, a woman might go much further in a shorter time than she herself had ever done. Yet, with the prospect of Amy herself so near, the realisation no longer hurt Norah. Hurt could never ally itself with Amy, the gentle and loyal. Amy turned all things to good; would listen to nothing against oneself, had any attempted to smear, to ridicule Norah. Since her own youth the danger had not been so great, till Elizabeth . . .

She went in. For instants the scene before her eyes remained unchanged, conditioned by the filtered light from the window with its pale-flowered plants and their climbing spiralled leaves. Amy sat with her back to the light, so that her fading blonde hair seemed as if it were under water, and her features were hidden. She was bent close beside another person, a young woman, of somewhat stocky build, in a dark dress. Their heads were close together, and as Norah stood there she heard, as it had not been heard for years, Amy's clear laughter. It was as though she were a young girl again, like that other.

"But how delicious . . . how amusing, Kate!"

Kate. There was a tenant at her own Moat House named Kate Vulliamy, whom she had not taken time yet to visit. Was this the same? "It is strange that I have not yet chanced upon her," Norah thought, at the same time downing a savage urge of envy which gripped her at sight of that close devotion, that shared laughter. In all her own years of friendship with Amy Wraye there had never been spontaneous joy of such a kind expressed, perhaps not felt. Kindness there had been, and faithfulness; perhaps admiration of Amy for herself. "You are so strong, Norah . . ."

Strong. Like a man. This creature Kate was not pretty, too stocky and swarthy, like a Curle. Was it possible that she was a by-blow of the old man's? From Yorkshire, Norah remembered the lawyer had said. A widow.

She moved forward into the room, gloved hand extended. At the sound of her skirts' hushing both women started back from their talk, and Amy clapped her hands together; Kate Vulliamy, if it was she, rose silently to her feet.

"My dearest Norah! To see you again after so long! Pray, did you have a good journey, without storms in crossing? This—" and the Duchess led Kate forward, smiling proudly, an arm about her waist—"this is Mrs. Vulliamy, whom you must call Kate."

"Indeed, I thought she lived at the Moat House," said Norah drily, while the young woman bobbed, a trifle clumsily. She has not been reared in the first circles, Norah was thinking. Who was the late Vulliamy? One must enquire, later.

"Oh, she has been staying with me at Wraye this past week, while my husband is in the south," said Amy gaily. "We have not had a dull minute, I believe. Will you take tea, Norah? Mrs. Stroyan will take your company from me, Kate, as she is so much nearer; promise that you will not forget to come to Wraye."

"How could I forget, when you have been so kind?" replied the young woman in what was, Norah was almost certain, a north-country accent with an overlay of gentility; perhaps she had attended a school to correct her provincial ways. Well, it remained to be seen; in the meantime, after tea was over, Norah offered Kate a seat in her carriage on the return journey, if she should be thinking of going back home.

3

WITH THE discovery of Kate, and the constant presence of Beppo in the house, it took Norah some time to persuade herself that she must visit her daughter at Windyett. There was after all no point in doing otherwise. She could alter nothing. She would choose a time when Jody would not be at home.

She found Elizabeth sitting alone in the room doing nothing, her thin bluish hands lying separate in her lap. The place had its usual air of dust and neglect; in the grate a low fire smoked, sending out thin draughts by way of the casement which stood open to the summer day. Beyond, a few marigolds straggled.

"Why are you not outside?" enquired Norah, seating herself. She heard her own voice talking to bridge the silence. "When I was your age, I remember, I was forever out striding on the moors, or across a pony, rain or shine; they couldn't keep me in, so I hadn't your pallor." Perhaps, a shocked inner place in her mind warned her, Elizabeth might be pregnant. At the same time she was aware of her own lack of feeling such as a mother should have for a daughter, were that so. So colourless a thing was made to be hidden. The sharp, constant knowledge that Jody himself was hereabouts to bid and mind her daughter, and perhaps his own, stayed with Norah bitterly. She heard Elizabeth's answer without surprise or interest. It was what one would expect of so unnatural a creature.

"There is nowhere to go, mother. I did not like to come to Curle in case you would be displeased."

"Then bid some company wait on you."

"There is none. Corder is visiting in Scotland." She did not mention her husband. Norah got up and strode over and kicked at the unwilling fire.

"There are crows in your chimney, I doubt not. This smokes fearfully." She swung about, and heard the hush and sweep of her own skirts, raising dust from the unswept carpet. "Can you not order your servants, girl?" she said irritably. "This room has not been cleaned, I swear, since before you returned. The serving-women are yours to command as long as Corder lets you stay." She had not mentioned the fashion in which Elizabeth had come to Curle. "Bid them be tidy and diligent, and beat 'em if they ain't. Otherwise you will never begin to maintain a proper household. This place is like a sty."

Elizabeth's fingers gripped convulsively together. If only mother knew of the terror and impossibility of such a thought! Mrs. Manifold gave the orders here; few of Corder's own servants would stay with a gipsy-woman. The notion of ordering and beating Mrs. Manifold herself aroused hysterical laughter in Elizabeth; if only mother had a notion of how things were! But she would never understand; anything of that nature would be dismissed with a downward sweep of the large, capable hands whose backs, with summer riding, were already brown with the sun. For mother, the whole world was there to obey or be beaten; she could never imagine events achieving any other order, or oneself a virtual prisoner in this house. In any case there was nothing at all one dared do; if Jody were about, and had heard mother come in just now, and listened to what was said . . .

Her mind shied away from thinking of Jody. His very memory brought fear. Three strong minds, Jody's, Mrs. Manifold's and now mother's, were ordering her separately; in the end, there would be nothing to do but obey and keep silent, hidden away in an empty room.

Meantime she essayed courtesy. "Will you take tea, madam?" she ventured timidly. She remembered that mother had been in Italy; one ought to enquire about that. Meantime Norah had given a sound between a snort and a laugh.

"What, in cracked cups with filth in 'em? No, I get better fare at home, where you would still be had you not been so wilful. What ailed you, Elizabeth? Surely you could see that he—that he—"

She broke off; no point in being harsh with her daughter now. She began to make amends. "Ride over whenever you will, child, and remind yourself of the way of living in which you were brought up. I'll tell you all I know of housekeeping, for if a woman does not know what to ask of her domestics they make a fool of her and live at her expense. D'you keep books? Does Jody made you an allowance?" God help me, she thought, she was speaking like a broody hen of a woman with her new-wedded chick. But one should ascertain such matters.

Elizabeth stared down at her fingers. Suspicion and anger suddenly flared in Norah, born of the innate resentment she had that this fool, this pale shadow who was surely Stroyan's get, should stand between herself and the only man who had ever mastered her. Ay, it was the truth. She heard her own voice, hoarse as if she thirsted, say, "Is Jody a husband to you? Is he?"

And beyond her the girl who was married to Jody seemed to shrink further into herself, like a mollusc into its shell. Elizabeth did not reply for some seconds, and then spoke with head bent, shaping only the appearance of the sounds with pale lips. "Please . . . please do not ask. I . . . I do not wish to speak of it."

Then she buried her face in her hands. Norah, knowing a thing had been said which should have remained unsaid, turned on her heel and left as abruptly as she had come. In moments she was on her mount's back, cantering home across the moor towards Curle.

.   .   .   .   .   .

That night Norah sent for Beppo. For the first time she forced him to try to use her fiercely, as though willing him to do her hurt, but he could not. After he had gone she realised bitterly that she had been passing the hours so in order to avoid the necessity of thinking of what might be taking place at Windyett, or again might not; Elizabeth had hardly satisfied her with an answer. Nor, as she now knew, would Beppo ever satisfy her as a lover. Was it some impossibility in herself that denied consummation? Having so much that other women lacked, did she lack what they had? Yet once, once long ago, it had been different.

She lay awake after the Italian had gone, still aware of the scent of musk he used about him, like a woman. It clung to a bed-gown of silk she herself had bought him from a *bottega* by the canals; he always wore it when he came to her. Beppo . . . a half-man. Norah turned her head past the undrawn curtains towards the window; it was a night bright with stars. She flung back the covers, went restlessly to the window and stood there a long time, idly recalling that other night when, by moonlight, she had seen Stroyan at last creep out of the governess's room. Of such things were her life made. She stood for a long time, watching the great belt of Orion and Sirius the dog-star close by. Close . . . yet a million million miles, maybe, from each other and from here. The awareness came to Norah, as it sometimes did when she was alone, that any knowledge she possessed was banal and superficial; within herself, she was ignorant. What did she know, or care, of those who had named the lights of heaven? What were the stars? Someone, perhaps a despised governess in her childhood, had told her that in old times men had thought the sky was like a blanket with holes in it, and through them shone the glory of God. It was pleasanter to believe that than, as they put it later, that the earth was surrounded by spheres of glass and in each sphere revolved separate stars which at times were conjoint. "Queer stars must have presided at my birth," thought Norah, not moving from the window.

She let her thoughts rove where they would, and found herself for the first time in years thinking again of her mother, Mrs. Emma, and of how greatly that genteel lady would have resented the state of things as they now were at Curle. Despite her melancholy Norah found herself grinning at the thought of such possible effects on her mother; then her smile failed. Against the black crest of the nearby hill, lit by the stars, was silhouetted a rider on a tall horse. She knew him to be Jody. How she knew, as though there were some wordless communication tied like a thread between him and her, she did not ask herself; but knew it was none other. For instants he stayed, then the shape of horse and rider vanished as they descended the slope of the hill; Norah waited, to see which way his strange ploys would lead him. At the same time a kind of madness, goaded by the night's unsuccessful love-making, grew in her; she knew and faced the truth that the feeling Jody roused in her was one of such desire that were he to come in tonight, and open her door, she would admit him, her daughter's husband, to her bed. An incestuous marriage, and double incest with herself! "It would all of it have brought you down to your grave, mother," she murmured; as well perhaps that Emma lay there already.

What was Jody's errand tonight? That became clear to Norah in this bitter hour of truth, as he reappeared on the path below Curle. The stars now showed his tied hair, gleaming like a raven's wing, and the linen beneath, and his hands on the rein. She could hear no hoofbeats; it was as though the mount were shod in velvet. "Gipsies can bid a dog be strange, and a horse quiet, when they choose," she told herself. But why the purposeful silence tonight, and why did he ride by Curle so late? "Had I not been here by the window I'd have had no knowledge that he rode near," she thought. Had it happened on other nights than this? Where did he go on this path that led only to the Moat House and Curle?

He had not come to Curle. It could only be that he went to that other.

Norah found a shawl and wrapped it round her. She was suddenly cold. Then she went downstairs and out into the yard; stealthily, though it was nobody's concern where she, the lady of Curle, went on her own land at whatever hour. Nor did she need a lanthorn for the brightness of the stars, any more than, that other night long ago, she'd needed any candle against the moon. The stars shone into the Moat stable, where Norah made out the mare, the long-legged brown beast Jody rode, tugging at hay in the rack. Of Jody there was already no sign. He had gone . . . to keep a rendezvous. Amy's dear Kate was a whore.

Afterwards, Norah could not remember her subsequent actions with any clarity. She must have walked round to the farther side of the Moat House, where the bedchamber was; inside it was dark, for being summer there was no fire. But Norah had waited and listened instead of watching, and soon, softer than the sound of the running beck in the distance, came the laughter and close murmuring of lovers. They were content and coupling in bed together, her Jody and Amy's Kate.

Now she knew what she had to do. As always, the prospect of action stimulated her. She took no time to feel envy, which might have been expected after her own late admission to herself. All that was done with. It had never been. She made her way quickly back to the great house, deter-

mined now that nothing should occur to interrupt the coupled lovers in tonight's safe embrace. Jody in such ways would be sharp as a fox. She'd
outwit him. The mare had still been munching hay when she passed it.
Norah remembered thinking that the hay was last year's, and had been
left in the Moat rack because there was scant room elsewhere. There was
room in her mind now for such things.

Kate Vulliamy, self-styled widow, *protégée* of Amy Wraye, taken up by
the county . . . by God, wait till she, Norah Stroyan, carried out her
plans! First, of course, it would be prudent—one must always be prudent—
to ensure that the Carlisle lawyer, who had sent the minx here, should
pursue her backward trail to her origins as far as might be. Word of her
parentage, her past life, her husband . . . it might prove that there had
never been a husband. Such a young woman would bed with any man
and never be short of customers. Norah allowed the earlier notion she had
had to raise its head again, namely that Sir Ludovic himself had had a
hand in the young woman's fashioning. If that were so, Jody might have
his aunt for mistress, and his daughter for wife.

Such thoughts must be gone with the day, lest she run mad, she knew.
But she would find out about Kate Vulliamy.

4

EVENTS MOVED SLOWLY, but at last the lawyer wrote to Norah to
say that all enquiries had failed to discover anyone of the name of
Vulliamy at the address from which her tenant had initially written.
It was possible that there had briefly been such a person or persons residing in the city of York itself. Would Mrs. Stroyan prefer enquiries to be
pursued there, or might he himself recommend that enquiries as to other
persons residing at the known address should be pursued as an alternative?

Mrs. Stroyan was highly desirous of the latter course. She smiled over
the quill she held to write a speedy answer, giving instructions. Soon now,
without a doubt, Amy's simple innocent would be proved to be no such
thing, possibly even with a false name; but in the meantime she herself intended to settle the matter of proof regarding the young woman's character
while at the Moat. She had already tried to work out a plan whereby Jon

Wraye himself might be induced to come and see, with his own eyes and ears, what went on there of a night. Unfortunately there was no certainty that, if the Duke rode over at her request as he would surely do, Jody would select that particular night to visit his mistress. Norah had endeavoured to predict his visits without success; they followed no particular pattern, and he rode over when he chose.

In the end she had enlisted Beppo, anxious as always to serve her in any way. She trusted the Italian to a limited extent, in that he would do as he was told; and Norah told him to keep silent on this subject to anyone he might meet. She then, after reflection, asked her son-in-law—how unnatural to think of Jody so!—down to Curle for a day's shooting over the moors. "It is time the breach was healed," she said to him. She had bidden Elizabeth also to come and sit with her, while the men went out with the guns; on this occasion Norah did not herself go out.

Beppo returned with Jody in due course with a fair bag; the two sat down together, at Norah's invitation, to drink wine. "Come with me to my room," Norah told her daughter, and Elizabeth followed her upstairs without a word. Norah detained her there with trivialities, the showing of treasures once the property of Mrs. Emma, lace and the like. All the time her ears were straining to catch the sounds of laughter and talk below-stairs: she was anxious that the two men should become friends, and thereafter it might be possible for the Italian to predict Jody's movements somewhat.

The visit paid, and Beppo was bidden for a return one to Windyett, to shoot over the high slopes with Jody and Corder. After that scarcely a week passed without Beppo seeking Jody's company, though the reverse seldom happened. They were becoming intimate, Beppo told Norah; one day, in his cups, Jody has toasted his mistress, but without naming her. Beppo understood such things. He had listened discreetly.

"When he is drunk, does he go to her?" asked Norah; it was as if she could not leave the thing alone. The Italian shook his head decisively. He had, he said, seen Jody drunk as a lord at Windyett, and he had gone to his own bed. Other times he had ridden down to the Moat drunk or sober.

Norah cursed silently under her breath. Did Jody know of her interest in him and his doings? It was as though he did, and had decided, out of perversity, to lead her a dance, at the same time continuing in enjoyment of Kate. "Has it not been the same through all our lives, and I always the fool, following?" she asked herself. But none must guess. Her resolution hardened, as the time went by; whatever befell, she would ruin Kate

Vulliamy in the eyes of all the county. That young woman should never be received anywhere here again.

In the end Norah secured a readier witness in Corder Bellingham, whose tattling tongue would pass the news to every tavern, as well as the houses of the great. Pure chance, as it turned out, aided Norah; there had been a rout at Duchess Amy's, to which she herself, Corder, and Kate were bidden. Much against her inclinations, Norah offered a seat in her own carriage to the young woman, and to Corder, who was sober for the occasion. During the journey he showed great courtesy and friendliness to Kate, as always; though he had not told her so, Norah often wondered if he saw a fleeting resemblance to his lost Madeleine, who had also had dark hair and said little. However that might be, the afternoon passed, with Norah from time to time looking up over her hand of cards to see the fond glances Amy sent to her *protégée*. "Soon there'll be an end to that," Norah promised herself, assuring her conscience that it was Amy's welfare she thought of rather than her own revenge, if that were the word. It was not apt; even had Kate not been at the Moat House, no doubt Jody would have found some other mistress; Norah had not been slow, knowing her daughter, to guess at the wreck of his unnatural marriage. But to rid the county of Kate, so-called Vulliamy, would be a blessing that would compensate for what she, Norah, had endured in other ways.

On the return journey Norah bade Corder accompany her into Curle for a cup of wine. She pointedly excluded Kate from the invitation; and when the young woman had gone home, evaded Corder's reproaches in some way. She could not, truth to tell, swallow wine herself in her own house beside Kate without retching; or so she felt. In the end Corder, always obedient, sat opposite her at the fire, downing one draught after another; the night closed in, and it had begun to rain. "There's a bed here, as you know," said Norah; it would not be the first time Corder had slept at Curle.

She had had, oddly, no other thought than for his comfort, and to save his plodding uphill by night in the rain. But later, after he had yawned himself off to his room, Norah espied a light, and Jody, riding as was his silent custom into the Moat stable, and leaving his mare. Triumph rose in her; this was what she had asked for and by accident!

She woke the Italian first. "Get your clothes on, and be at the outer door within minutes," she ordered, adding that he must be silent. Then she herself went to wake Corder. He blinked reddened eyes open to the dazzle of a candle, and Norah's hand shaking his shoulder.

"Get up, and dress quickly and come down with me. No, say not a word now; I have a thing I must show you, and it shall be in silence." Somehow she got him downstairs to the door, where Beppo already waited in his cloak; then outdoors into the drizzling rain, taking the hands of both men to lead them across the dark yard, as though she could not bear that they stumble, and accidentally reveal their presence to the two in the Moat House.

They were well seen tonight; Kate had lit a fire against the drizzle, and its flames spurted up now, lighting the room and the couple on the bed. From here, beyond the window, it could not be seen who the man was; only Kate's naked, sturdily vibrating thigh was outlined by the firelight, and her bare arm, laid tightly about the man's neck. "Here am I, God help me, with two half-men to witness it," thought Norah. Corder stared in for instants, then turned away, his mouth set tightly. Norah put a finger to her lips, and led both men away. When they were back in Curle hall, she bent and cast a log on her own fire. Then she turned to the two.

"I have long known of it, but I desired witnesses, that I might not be thought to speak lightly, or out of envy," she said. "But is it right that such a trollop should sit by Amy Wraye, and drink tea with her, and enjoy her protection?"

"No, by God, it is not," said Amy's brother, the patches of colour returning unevenly to his face; it had, as Norah had known it would have, an effect on Corder which outvied that of most men, seeing such a thing. It was as though he saw Madeleine, the lost unfaithful wife: she might safely leave the matter to Corder, she knew. She smiled, bade both men a goodnight and made her way upstairs. This night's work had been well done, better even than Jody reckoned.

Kate was waiting for word from Marryatt Priory, where she had heard they were to have a tea-drinking next Thursday. The Duchess had told her of the beauties of the house, and that she must see more of it. Therefore when no word came, Kate was at first impatient with the posts; then, as the days passed realising that she had not been invited, blamed Amy Wraye a little. It was unfair to have raised her hopes so, and then all to come to nothing. Perhaps it was a smaller party than had at first been planned.

Days passed, and she saw neither the Duchess, who unaccountably did not ride over, nor Mrs. Stroyan, though the latter she felt was no loss.

Jody came, and their now almost nightly coupling became the more delicious as he taught her more; Kate had not known, for she could not have done so, how ignorant she had formerly been of the full delights of love. Once, after ecstasy, she had begged him to be careful. "Supposing I were to have a child?" she said. "That would cause a parlous scandal, and I should have to go away; take care, I pray you." But he had laughed in the way he had. "Have no fear, I shall see to it that you do not," he told her. She had always the awareness that he was in control of himself, even in their most exquisite moments; in a way it made her afraid, and in another way it was strange, for Jody was not a person she would care to be seen with in broad daylight, at, for instance, Wraye; she could not picture him kissing her hand as Corder Bellingham had done among the company the other day, and bringing her ratafia in a tiny glass.

Corder had passed by the other day, but hadn't seen her or returned her greeting. Perhaps he was drunk again; it was a pity that so fine a gentleman as Corder, and one who must have been very handsome in his youth, should have given way to weakness as he had done. His wife must have been a shallow, selfish woman. Perhaps she had married Corder for social advancement. "It cannot have been for money, for he has none," Kate thought. How little scruple some women had, to make such fools of men!

The truth was made known to her in the following week, when no word had yet come from Wraye, so Kate borrowed the short-legged fell pony she sometimes rode and set out that way, to see if there was anything amiss. On her way Norah Stroyan's carriage passed at a great pace, raising the dust, and soiling Kate's hands and hair. She bit back annoyance; that arrogant woman! "Certainly she did it to spite me," she told herself, eyes filling with easy tears. It would not be the thing to call at Wraye covered with dust, and she would have liked to clean herself: but while thinking how to do it another carriage passed, also driving towards Wraye. It looked as though Her Grace entertained company, "but she would never do so without bidding me," Kate told herself. But there was less complacency in the thought than there would have been the week previous; it was a long time, a very long time indeed, not since the rout in fact, since she had seen the Duchess of Wraye. If there was company, and she not bidden, she had perhaps best not go in. But why . . . why, when the Duchess had vowed that they were friends, and that Kate's company gave her pleasure?

"If it is true, then she will be pleased to see me at any time," thought Kate, and pressed her pony forward. In due course she came to the familiar gate of Wraye, and rode past the lodge and up to the great house. Company was indeed arriving; a great many carriages were there, and elegantly attired ladies and gentlemen were descending from them or else going up the steps; none saluted Kate, who stood uncertainly not knowing what to do with her pony or, indeed, herself. Suddenly anger came to her; why should she be treated so? She went round to the stables, which she knew well, and left the pony in one of the stalls; then, brushing her skirts, hurried back to the house again, to be met by a footman at the door; the company had gone in, though Kate was certain someone watched behind the window-curtains. Her heart had begun to hammer. "Is the Duchess at home?" she said to the footman. He was a man she had seen before; despite herself, as one did not acknowledge servants, Kate essayed a trembling smile. With everyone so unfriendly, it would be pleasant to glimpse a return of the smile, even a slight unbending of the footman's manners. But he was stiff as his own hair-powder.

"Her Grace is not at home, madam," he told her.

"But—" The Duchess *must* be at home; there were all the guests; what did it mean? "Will you please tell her that I have called, and bid her good-day?" she said desperately. Something was wrong, very wrong; what it might be tore at Kate's mind, too late; had anyone seen—had anyone guessed, perhaps, and repeated—

"Her Grace is not at home."

So she turned away.

5

HAD KATE KNOWN IT, Amy Wraye had not listened to the first rumour or the second, dismissing them as beneath her attention and unworthy of Kate. It had taken a fiat from her husband, who after a conversation with Corder Bellingham had judged it better that Kate did not return to Wraye, to dissuade the Duchess, who went about thereafter in a tumult of grief, with tears in her eyes and a return of her old melancholy. If Kate was untrue, who could be believed? But she could not persuade Wraye to tell her more of it.

"She shall not enter this house again," was all he would say. "Take heed to it, my dear; there must be no more invitations."

"But she is in the habit of coming over, poor girl, of making free—"

"Then she must be turned back at the door. I have already given orders to the footman."

Amy knew nothing would move him, and went away, wringing her slender hands. She was anticipating a visit from one of Wraye's distant kinswomen, who was to stay for a fortnight, and had planned card-parties and such things to pass the time, for the guest was one of those who must be constantly entertained. It hurt Amy deeply not to be able to send word to Kate that she must come, and play cards, and meet the visitor. But Amy, as always, obeyed her husband, and sent no word; and in the meantime Norah Stroyan came, bowling up the driveway in her coach. Her Italian secretary was with her, but did not alight. Norah did so, sweeping into the long light room with velvet skirts held aside purposefully in the way she had, as if they must not impede her long resolute stride towards Amy. The two women kissed, and Norah seated herself at her hostess's invitation.

"No, my dear, I'll not take wine. I but stopped by to tell you the news; this must come to your ears also, Wraye." And she beckoned Jonathan imperiously. At that moment she was like a puppet-master, manipulating the two slight, gentle people as if on strings. "The widow Vulliamy is no widow," she said, "and it's certain she's no maid. She was never married, and her father was a herdsman in the Yorkshire dales. Her mother, they say, lived once in Carlisle and was of doubtful virtue, but is dead these many years. However the daughter seems to have drunk in, with her mother's milk, no doubt, certain things she should not. To have made her whole life here a lie, after your being so good to her!"

But the Duchess cried out, "Oh, no, no, no! It cannot all of it be as you say! Poor soul, perhaps with no mother—"

"Do not waste your pity on her, my dear," said Wraye curtly, while his wife covered her eyes and wept. "You are certain of all this, madam? But of course I need not ask; you'd not spread any tale that had no foundation."

"My lawyer ascertained it," said Norah. "I had my private doubts about the young woman. I propose now to return her her quarter's rent, and let her go."

"She need not come here," said Wraye grimly. "To think that my wife was at some trouble to introduce her to persons whom she should never have met is—abominable. If she returns here—"

"She must never come here again," said Amy desolately at last. "Oh, never, never, never!"

She had forgotten her tears, which had run down to smear the rouge on her thin cheeks; as if to collect herself she began to wander about among her indoor plants, taking a small spouted vessel which was kept near by and watering one or two. "These do not speak or misbehave," she said softly. "They are safe companions."

"Tush, m'dear, you will have enough company next week, with Cousin Tolland and—"

"I loved her so," said Amy suddenly. "What can have induced her to lie to me? It is that, more than—more than whatever your complaint may have been, Jonathan." It was unusual for her to use Wraye's baptismal name in company. She swung about abruptly and turned to Norah.

"Dear Norah, you are so strong and true, such a refuge . . . when one does not know where to turn . . ." The thin hands made small fluttering motions; suddenly and by the changed expression in her blue eyes, Amy looked distraught. A warning glance passed between Norah and the Duke; she must be put to bed, the glance said, and a physician sent for: all must be smoothed over in time for the Tolland visit.

And cursing the cause of it all, Kate Scarsgill, Wraye set about the care of his invalid wife, and Norah took her leave, promising to call again soon: and returned to where Beppo waited obediently in the carriage. The analogy between her own state and Kate's had naturally not occurred to her. It should be nothing to anyone if Mrs. Stroyan of Curle chose to bring home a young foreign secretary, with pleasing manners; different in every essential from entertaining, by night and with enjoyment, a married man alone in one's bedroom, whether or not one were a widow.

Kate answered a tap on her door to behold Mrs. Stroyan's bailiff, who handed her a sum of money in a cloth bag and told her madam said she was to leave immediately. Kate's mouth dropped agape; what worse could befall? What had happened to everyone?

"I cannot leave at once," she said. "What's to become of my gear?" Suddenly, while anticipating the man's reply, she had the answer, stunning as a blow on the head: this was Jody's doing. Now that he must be tiring of her—men did such things, no doubt, when they had had what they wanted—he had chosen this way of getting her out of the county. Well, she had no wish to stay, if so. "I must go," she thought, "and quickly, then it's done and there is no way back." No way back, and no way forward. Where in all the world was she to go to? With the buying of lace for gowns, and the like, there was hardly any money left, and she—

Well, here was the back rent. Madam would see to her gear, the man was saying. Devil take madam. In some way, Kate was sure, Norah Stroyan had had a hand in cozening Jody.

"It will be sent by pack-carrier to your next address," said the man without undue respect. While this randy creature had been Her Grace of Wraye's intimate friend, and madam's tenant, it had behoved him to treat her with abrupt courtesy; now things were different. "I'd not make any bones about going, if I was you," he said plainly. "Madam's had tenants bundled out before. There's the mail-coach, down valley, you can catch at three."

Kate had caught the mail-coach and sat, clutching a small valise with hastily grabbed belongings and a clean shift, swaying as the coach-body swayed, a passive burden carried along the rough pot-holed roads. They were going south. She couldn't afford to go far. What she would do—what she must do, it seemed—was to take lodging in an inn for a while, till something—anything at all—transpired. She couldn't go back to the dales, where they would laugh at her again: better to alight somewhere beforehand, as soon as some likely place offered itself. She stared from the window, through eyes that were still dry with shock: there had been no time to weep, even to feel yet as though she must. From now on she was—what? Still Mrs. Vulliamy? Kate had a notion that that had severed its turn.

However, when a comfortable whitewashed inn with thatched gables showed itself, beyond a dip in the road and nearby an old bridge and a village, Kate left the coach. Standing with her valise, she concocted a story; her gear was on the way, and had been delayed; she was going to London.

The landlord believed her, though she seemed absent rather than confused; the coin she offered for carrying the valise up to her room was genuine enough, and there weren't so many travellers staying that he could afford to choose. Even so, he'd keep watch that she paid her bills; you could never tell with young women who travelled alone.

6

THAT WEEK two letters came for Norah. One was from France bearing Ludovic's superscription; as always, she cast it into the fire unread. The second came from Wraye. It was from Jonathan.

My wife is very low in her spirits, tho' recovered from the worst of the melancholy [it read]. *Would you or your daughter visit us for a few days to bear her company? You need not write; your presence is what we desire, as you know.*

He had signed his name neatly, as usual; but Norah could guess at the perturbation of his mind. She had her horse saddled and rode up to Windyett. Why had it not oftener occurred to her to take Elizabeth to Wraye?

Jody was at home, as she had prayed he would not be. Norah had heard nothing from him, though the reverse could hardly have been expected, regarding the empty Moat House, nor had she herself vouchsafed any word as to Kate's going. Nevertheless from the ironic way he greeted her she had the uncomfortable suspicion that he knew she had had a hand in ousting his mistress. She rendered back stare for stare; might she not do as she would with her own property, and why should she house his doxy?

Elizabeth was not present, and when Norah framed her request Jody refused to consider it.

She was astonished; what reason could he have for such effrontery? Did he himself expect to receive invitations from such as the Wrayes because he was Elizabeth's husband? *That* would not alter his initial status; a gipsy half-breed he had been born, and would remain. "Why, every ragged tinker in the hills slinks up to Windyett with word from here and there, either for him or Abigail; I've seen 'em come and go," thought Norah. All of this took shape in her mind, while on the surface polite exchanges passed; only over her query regarding Elizabeth's visit to Wraye Jody gave a curt, brutal answer.

"She may not go because her condition may not warrant it. That is the end of the matter," and he turned away and up-ended the hour-glass which stood on the mantel. Norah felt her heart cold within her. So it *was* a marriage.

"She . . . when?"

He had turned, and was regarding her expressionlessly. "Did I say when? Did I say such a thing was certain? I need say nothing at all to you, Norah, save that I forbid my wife to go."

"Then, damn you, I'll go alone." She turned and went out, leaving him staring after her. Anger made her hasten her arrangements, and by noon she was on the road to Wraye. She would stay for a day or two, and bear Amy company. Some excuse must be made for Elizabeth; but the reality should not be mentioned or thought of, not yet, till it proved irrefutable.

After she had gone Jody remained staring at the closed door. His mouth had hardened till it was thin as a thread, and his eye glittered. He was thinking of Kate, and how that bitch had cast her, friendless and helpless, out on the roads; but he knew where she was, had known since one of the ragged men Norah abhorred had brought him the name of the inn where Kate had been set down. There was nothing they would not bring him word of now, those kin of his; he had established mastery over them, and Abigail gave him aid, even as she had taken the name of Manifold to please him.

But Kate . . . It disturbed Jody, interrupted his set plans, that she should remain so much in his thoughts. At the outset she had been no more than an echo of the young Norah, one whom he could, moreover, blackmail, with his knowledge of her past, into providing him with pleasure for the time. It had given savour to his colourless marriage to go down almost nightly and sport with Kate; she had a warmth and innocence, even gratitude for all he taught her, that would have been lacking in Norah Stroyan who had never cared for any except her grandsire, herself and Curle. But Norah was still the summit of Jody's ambition, and Curle his dream; he had married Elizabeth when it was evident her brother would no longer inherit, with Norah still shackled to Stroyan in Australia, for of course she would not demean herself by asking for a divorce. Curle might yet be his, if Elizabeth were to bear him a child. She was not yet pregnant, despite his words to Norah, and he had given her small cause to be. Now that Kate was elsewhere for a while, he must return—he grimaced—to his conjugal duties. He had not hastened to that matter; he had waited for he knew not what. Now, rather than let Elizabeth run about and visit her grand kin who scorned him, he would give her good reason for staying at home, provided she were not barren.

As for Kate . . . well, she could not yet come to Windyett. He had other plans for her. With madam Norah out of the reckoning for a few days, it might be time, tomorrow, to ride south and rescue poor Kate from the pickle she would undoubtedly be in, now that her money must be running low. The wife tonight, the mistress tomorrow . . . and then?

Jody smiled. He had established a friendly relationship with the half-man from Italy. Beppo Manzoni felt at home now at Windyett, would come here unbidden when he had leisure, and talk in his halting English and drink wine. The fellow was lonely, and his heart ached for his native land. "Well, there will be a way soon of letting him return there, and with money in his pockets," thought Jody, who had perfected his plans over the past weeks.

7

KATE SAT ON HER BED in the room at the inn, near tears. She had eightpence left, and the landlord, at first obsequious, had altered his manners markedly today. Kate had stammered out a promise that money would be forthcoming in a day or two, but where could she get it? She was not even sure if her protestations had been believed; if not, the man's wife, failing the man, would soon put her out of the place, and keep such belongings as she still had.

She had thought desperately of ways to find help, even considering, for a few illicit moments, the Duchess of Wraye. But that that avenue was closed even Kate knew. After what had happened—and her mind was still bruised from the late cruel encounters—it would never, never be possible to ask a favour of her erstwhile patroness and friend again. "I would sooner starve," Kate decided. That it might indeed come to such an issue became clear when the inn-folk would not supply any more meals. "Wait for this money, miss," the man had said, looking her up and down as if—as if she wasn't all she should be.

"But am I?" thought Kate disconsolately, and thought then of writing to Jody Curle. There was no other means of help; but he might refuse to come. She had gone off, after all, without informing him: had indeed intended, as he must know, never seeing him again. Would he aid her, and what price would he ask other than what she had already given? From the position of retrospect, Kate looked back. If she wasn't what she ought to be, it was Jody's fault. She hadn't asked him to seduce her, and . . . and lead to all this trouble she was now in. That was it; she must write to Jody, and remind him that his pursuit of her had left her in these dire straits, abandoned by the world. When her present difficulties were resolved she would find some situation, and repay Jody. That seemed the only answer.

Kate started to cry again, remembering that she was hungry; the landlord that day had grudgingly given her a drink of milk, but that wasn't enough to go on with. Would the whole world use her so now that she had left the valley? Oh, if only she hadn't taken up with Jody Curle! If only she hadn't pretended to be Mrs. Vulliamy! They had found out all of it, she was sure, and that woman Stroyan had been glad to lose a rival in the Duchess's affections. That was what it amounted to.

Hoof-beats sounded on the deserted road. Kate moved to the window. It wouldn't be anybody; few passengers stopped here. It might perhaps be the farrier, or the farmer who lived nearby; would the latter maybe give her a chance of turning his hay for a meal? But a lady didn't do such things, and once it was known she couldn't go on living at the inn, and—

Kate gave a small astonished squeal. The rider was Jody Curle. Jody! He had come to find her! But how did he know where she had gone?

Perhaps he hadn't come for her. Perhaps he had only been passing, and . . . should she let herself be seen? No; better wait on here, with heart thudding. No lady ever behaved impulsively in public. Dreary tenets from her brief schooldays floated up out of the places in Kate's mind where she kept them, for the rare times they were needed to trouble her. She waited on, hand to her breast, knees turning to water half with hope, half fear. Supposing he rode on, and never even saw her!

But the door opened; it was the little inn-maid, bearing a tray with cold meats and a jug of ale. Kate gasped a little. How hungry she was! She could have fallen on the fare, but waited to hear what the girl was saying.

"Gentleman downstairs says you're to have this, and he'll be up when bill's settled."

Kate devoured the food. She licked the last of the cold meat from her fingers, and gulped down the ale. When she had finished she set the tray outside and waited, heart still thudding. Presently the door was flung open. This time it was Jody. He was dusty from his ride; his thin lips smiled as she remembered. Kate, forgetting all the proprieties, flung herself on him, and lay sobbing against his coat.

"Foolish brat," said Jody. He did not sound angry with her.

. . . . . .

Afterwards they lay together on the bed. There did not seem to be any urgency in anything except the use he had for her; she felt, through ignorance, a hard pressing need in him that had not shown itself before. Within her own mind was a drowsy awareness of once more being safe; Jody would never let her go, she knew. "And I do not want to leave him," she thought, denying all her previous convictions; what a fool she had been! Long ago, she'd thought she was in love with Walter Shillingthorne; a pale phantasmal image of that creature floated now through Kate's mind, and made her shudder.

"Why do you do that?" said Jody. He was fondling her breasts, still smiling. After last night, when he had forced his way as duty bade between Elizabeth's narrow unwilling thighs, it was refreshing to be again with Kate, artless little fool; he could always rouse her and himself. Presently, he told her, she would have to ride pillion with him back to Carlisle. Her lips dropped open, showing big white teeth.

"Carlisle? Why back there?"

"Because I have a task for you to perform, my love. You owe me something, do you not, for paying your shot here, and for the mutton-bones and ale?"

"Oh, yes, yes; anything—"

"This is a thing you will be very good at. You have a talent for it, Kate; and you will also serve me. You would like that, eh?"

Kate said she would like that. Gradually, still lying within her, he explained to her what she would have to do. Kate recoiled at first in horror.

"In a whorehouse? Oh, *no!*"

"Take or leave the situation, then: if you leave it, I will abandon you here, and you may make your way henceforth as you can, Brown Kate. I'll not ride twice to your succour . . . and, you know, if I abandon you, what other end is there for you than this, with other men? What can you do else?"

"Oh, *no*—" What was the use of telling him she could paint on velvet? "You can do this," he told her again. "You can do it very well." He handled her knowledgeably.

"But not for money, with strangers—I could never—"

"You will have a pleasant room, with plenty of candles, and two new gowns to wear when you go abroad, and a young woman to serve you—"

"No—"

He had begun to ride her insistently again. It was as though she were some instrument that he chose to play on, till he had extorted the utmost sweetness from its strings; by and by Kate felt her indignant body yield and grow fluid. What if it were like this always, and what he suggested, which had at first filled her with horror, were in fact what she had been intended by nature to do? It was true, she didn't mind it. With Jody . . .

She began to cry, and said in the end, "Do not leave me. Don't ever leave me."

"Then you must do as I bid you," said Jody. He inserted his tongue to find hers, within her opened mouth.

They rode back north at last, Kate riding pillion. When they saw the city wall approaching Jody bade her pull her hood-strings tight. "I do not choose that you should be seen yet," he said. "Nobody here is to know you for who you are."

"But surely—"

"Ah, that," he said, and laughed. "You will wear a mask, and a Venetian veil, and white gloves. All of the girls in the house do so; it lends an element of mystery, which the choicest customers pay for."

"You are a devil," she said, and began to weep again.

"Not I; what I offer you is a comfortable, well-fed position, with a chance to save up something for your old age. Had you thought yet of that, Kate? I'll wager you had not, such a goose as you are."

No, she had not. "Will you come to me sometimes?" she said, like a child.

"I will come often. I will be your first client, as soon as you have seen your room, and met Mrs. Manifold."

"Mrs. Manifold?" This was like home. Mrs. Manifold had been the gipsy who had lived up at Windyett. If she were to be in the house, it might not be so strange. But Kate was still frightened.

Abigail Manifold received them at last in her small ground-floor room. She was no longer clad in a linen apron but had a lawn one, trimmed with lace, and a matching turban on her head; but she still did not look clean. Kate was then put in the charge of a tall stout Negress, the young woman servant of Jody's description: had Kate known it, she was the product of one of his sea-voyages, and had been captured eight years before on the Ivory Coast. She was subdued, deflowered and trained now; she carried out certain tasks upon Kate which the latter did not care for, at the first; later she would grow used to them. When she was shown the silken bed whereon she was to learn a living, and the candles shining in their gilded sconces, Kate dissolved once again in tears behind the Venetian mask. But, to her relief, and as he had also promised, her first customer was Jody.

Jody and his mother had faced one another briefly in the small room after Kate had gone upstairs.

"I see you've brought her back," said Abigail sourly. "Was it needful? She'll cause trouble."

"Not when I've done. I could not let her starve, mother—or go on the streets."

" 'Tis the first time in all your life I have known you show any heart. It is not like you, my son, and that disturbs me; you have not forgotten what we swore together, when you were a child?"

"To avenge my father, and gain Curle? No, I have not forgotten; though he himself, you know well, was a stranger to me and I cannot recall his face."

"My kinsmen gave you small chance to. How fares Corder Bellingham?" Abigail tended, when it was possible, the rapidly worsening Corder when she was at Windyett; it was as though his weakness gave her a feeling for him.

"No better, and never will be. I doubt he'll last the year out with the drink that goes down him."

"A pity you had not snared Madeleine to be one of your women here."

"Madeleine will be faring well enough on her own."

"It is a charity-place, this, then, for sad cases?" She gave her rare smile; it gave her a weird infantile quality, lacking the teeth, while her sallow high-boned face broke up into a thousand wrinkles.

"Just so, and Kate's the saddest. I must go to her, mother, and—comfort her. It's the room with the alcove?"

"As you ordered. Will it comfort her to have you sitting at such times in that?"

"She will not know I'm there." He laughed, and was gone. Abigail turned her back on the window which gave out on the narrow street. It presented a view of house-doors, and she hated them and longed for the open spaces. Soon, if Jody permitted it, she'd be at Windyett again. At least that gave a view of the fells.

8

BEPPO THE VENETIAN was unhappy at Curle. It was not the fault of the signora, who was less demanding than many of his customers had been, and who moreover treated him like a spoilt child and had bought him the box of water-colours he craved. No, it was not that; or not altogether, though the effort of taking oneself out on a cold day—and when in this inhospitable northern country were the days not cold?—to paint grey skies and brown moors was unwelcome; he could have painted so much better at home among the bright-dark canals and damp green shadows and glorious sunsets of Venice. No, altogether his misery was due to this being in a state of servitude, of having to depend on the signora not only for paints, but spending-money, of which she was somewhat grudging. Beppo longed for home; and in addition there had been no word from the little sister in her convent room, and he feared she must be worse, perhaps already dying. To be unable to visit Maria, and know for himself, was bad enough; worse that he must ask permission of Mrs. Stroyan before he even set foot out of doors, and she must always be given some notion of where he might be going; if it was to paint, he must show her, on return, what he had achieved in the day's work. If it was to Windyett, he must tell her what talk had passed there. "Otherwise," he thought, his shrewd peasant's mind summing up a situation it could understand well enough; a bargain was a bargain; "otherwise, she feels that I do not give value for money." It was, in short, as though Mrs. Stroyan had bought him, body and soul; and Beppo's soul longed for freedom.

He could not remember the first day Jody Curle, the signora's son-in-law, had come upon him painting in the heather, and had sat by him for a while. Beppo knew enough English, from his associations with travellers on the Piazza San Marco and elsewhere, both to understand and to make himself understood. It was only now he realised how little he and Norah Stroyan talked to one another. Jody essayed some remark, about the weather or the colours Beppo was mixing; and gradually the two disparate creatures commenced an acquaintance, wary at first. Later, after several shooting-parties, they were on easy terms, and when Jody at last made a proposition to the Venetian it was not as surprising as it might have been if mentioned earlier. Beppo narrowed his dark long-lashed eyes and continued to fill in cloud-cumuli with ultramarine dulled down with ochre. He rinsed his brush carefully before replying.

"Why do you ask me such a thing? The signora would dismiss me if it were discovered."

"Would that be a bad outcome?" said Jody cruelly. He lay on the tussocks of ling, plucking at and destroying the small hard blossoms. Beppo shrugged, and returned to his metal palette.

"I have no money," he said simply. Jody smiled, and flung a twig of heather away. "And if I were to offer you enough gold to take you back to Venice and set you up there, eh? You'd not be averse to that, I think."

Beppo's eyes started so that the whites encircled them; had it been so evident that he desired to leave here? "The signora—" he began, and Jody broke in impatiently.

"Have no fear of the signora: I will deal with her, and you need see no more of her after—after what I have told you has been accomplished. It is, when all's said—" he gave his smile, which despite his disfigurement could be charming, and eased the other's mind—"only a question of lending me your Venetian bed-gown. You are certain that it will be dark in her room?"

Beppo replied that the signora seldom lit either lamp or candle when he came to her. "It is as though—" he began, then flushed and fell silent. Jody finished for him. "As though she did not wish to acknowledge to herself the reason why you come? As though she preferred, even in her own mind, to think of you as—her secretary?" He smiled again.

"English ladies have strange fancies," said Beppo sadly, and fell to filling in the heather-patches with viridian, umber and a touch of crimson lake. The flowers here were dull in hue, like the inhabitants' minds, even the women; especially the women. The tales he could tell of that old Marchesa, who had first brought the signora to him in Venice! "But *her* blood did not run thinly, though she was old," he murmured. In a manner, the signora's blood was not thin either; it was only that she was more like a man in her ways, in her responses, which in face of her woman's parts discomfited Beppo. He would be glad if the offer Jody Curle made was genuine, and would give him enough gold to make his way back and live in comfort. Fright still showed in his expression as he said, the more slowly for emphasis, "The money must be there before such a night, that I may be certain of escape." The term, he knew, was not gallant, but it was true. Jody laughed.

"I'll not betray you, nor—" he spoke quietly—"you me. If I were to find that she knows of it—"

"Signore, I will say nothing."

"As well: many things can happen between here and the port. You must take all precautions if you wish to make a safe journey; trust me, if so, and do as I've said. The money will be waiting, in a leather bag, to take as soon as I'm in the signora's room in your bed-gown. You may make off then, or at any time before morning."

"I shall go at once," shuddered Beppo, and disfigured the painted heather with a smear of mistaken crimson. Either Mrs. Stroyan or Jody Curle would have his blood, no doubt, were he to stay and be discovered. "You will come tonight, signore?"

"I shall come every night to your room where you sleep, and you'll let me in, till a night when she should send for you. When that will happen you know no more than I; but when it does, you shall have your money."

He would not, he was thinking, give the little foreign rat his gold too soon; he would be off, if so, and the whole plan ruined.

9

IT WAS IN FACT only four nights later that Norah sent for Beppo to come to her bed. She was finding her loneliness intolerable; there was nothing between her and the prospect of thinking of Elizabeth's possible pregnancy, and that she found she could not bear. To send for the young man was no more, with Norah, than an admission that what she had bought she must use, although now, less than ever, could Beppo himself satisfy her physically. As was her custom she extinguished all candles. He must, she knew, be a thing of the dark, felt and experienced but unseen; so might she disguise her own need of a strength Beppo did not and would never possess. For the same reason they talked together seldom at such times; a spoken syllable here and there, sometimes a murmuring between them in the dark when the thing was done, sufficed.

She heard him come; and smelt the heavy, effeminate scent of the musk he used as he took his bed-gown off, laying it nearby. Then he was with her in the bed, extending himself upon her. Norah did not yet feel surprise. It was only as he possessed her that she became aware of a new energy in him, a force that could by the end leave her drained. It surprised and gratified her.

"Child, child," she murmured; and felt him smile against her. What was this tonight, when the very sinews of his thighs seemed filled for once with power? His hands tore at her; in moments, yielded and dependent as she had never in all her life been before to any man save one, she'd—

The eye-shade grated then against her cheek; and she knew.

She would have cried out; yes, even at the risk of having her household come, and with it the loss of all she had deliberately built up over the years, her inviolable name. But his mouth crushed hers and from her there came, unable as she was to prevent or stem it, the deep harsh cry of consummation; she was no one any more, only a thing of jerking abandoned limbs and the source of the sweet flood, which she had once before known to come, of such passion as she had never thought to feel again for any man.

"Jody."

It was said in a whisper, not the loud clamour she would have made. He had mastered her. She heard him laugh in the darkness. "So you knew me," he said, "Norah, Norah." The pressure of his limbs and mouth did not lessen; his hands exploited her. Was this herself, Norah Stroyan of Curle? Was she demented, possessed by a devil who—

"Go out of me." She had begun to struggle; the climax was over. "Lie still," he told her, "lie still, Norah." But she would not; in the end, as they clawed and fought with one another, he took her again, forcibly. In course of it she set her teeth in him, and he slapped her. He was still laughing. "Should you not have left your light burning for your gigolo?" he said. "Should you not?"

"I'll see you driven from the county—hanged—"

"As my sire was? That would be inhospitable, Norah, after such a welcome as you have given me, this night. It did not displease you that I forced your body. You have longed, have you not, for me these many years?"

Presently he rose from the bed and went and lit the candle, turned meantime away from her so that she could watch his lean, naked limbs. He brought the sconce over to where she lay, and scanned her. His smile had widened and she saw the gleam of teeth. With the sight of his nakedness and his eye-patch, she was suddenly afraid. She sat up.

"Lie down, Norah," he told her. "Why do you fight against yourself? Both of us are as we are, and always meant for one another, except that you'd not have it so."

"You are a liar—a thief—"

"Of madam Stroyan's virtue? Was there so much left to steal? That I took your maidenhead I do not deny, my dear. Would you want the county to know of that, even now?" He took her left breast and squeezed it, in hard grasping fingers; despite herself Norah let out a cry of pain.

"Elizabeth—how can you do as you have done with us both? Ah, leave me, for pity—"

"What of her?" he said sharply. He snuffed the candle and came and lay down by Norah again. "I have seen you as you are, a goddess, as Corder says," he told her. "You are pleasing to bed with, Mrs. Stroyan of Curle; too good for Beppo and his kind; too good, by God, for such as Stroyan."

She lay breathing fast, and no longer prevented him in what he would do; presently he began caressing her with eagerness, as if she were a young girl. "What a fool you were, and none knew it except ourselves!" he said. "Between us, we could have forced the squire. It was your own will held out against me."

She jerked away and said suddenly, "Where is Beppo? Did he gain you entry here?"

"As you suppose, my dear; lie still. I bribed him."

"When I catch him I'll have them whip him out of Curle, the charlatan, the—"

"No need; he is already well on his way to Venice, with my gold. It is all of it my fault, Norah; but you do not need him any more. Tomorrow night I will come again."

"I'll see you damned first."

"Maybe, but you'll leave your door unbarred."

He was within her again and using her hard: she had not been able to prevent it. She heard her voice at last, higher than was its wont and softer; a fulfilled woman's.

"If any should see you come—"

He lay there laughing upon her captive flesh. "They shall not see, hear or guess, my love, that I am coming to you; as I should have come years since, Norah, should I not? Should I not, eh?"

And she whispered "Yes" at last, and when in the end he went the dawn was not far off, and she was left lying wondering at herself, and at everything that had happened.

By morning there was the Italian's robe, restored hanging in its place. Norah took it down and bundled it in the fire and burnt it. She knew that she would never set eyes on Beppo again. Her life had entered on a phase that was unlike any she had known before; there was no room for hatred, rancour or revenge. She forgot, or made herself forget, what kin the man she had lain with all through the night, and would tonight again, was to

Elizabeth. She almost forgot who Elizabeth was. Such things did not matter any more.

The next night Jody came as he had promised, and thereafter for some
weeks made constant love with Norah. Her days passed in a dream, awaiting him. He always left her before it was light. Norah nowadays did not
visit Windyett. She knew also, as well as she had once known herself, that
not a soul saw Jody arrive or, later, silently leave Curle by dawn.

10

J ODY SAT, having left his mother downstairs, in the small an-
techamber that gave off from the alcove leading to Kate's room in the
house in Carlisle. Between the spaces of fretted gilding of a panel
carved like those in a Turkish seraglio, making it possible to see without
being seen, he could watch Kate. He had not cast more than a cursory first
glance over her, masked and naked, on the bed, from which a customer
had lately risen. At present, when his nights were spent with Norah
Stroyan—he smiled—he had no need of Kate. In the course of visits to his
mother he spared time to ask how the girl progressed, and was told she
made an adequate income. Presently, if leisure allowed, he would see Kate
and have speech with her before he left. He was pleased with the way
matters had arranged themselves; he was physically satisfied, as Norah was
also, he well knew, on his account. Together they made such a pair as—he
smiled—Pan and Juno might have done in ages long ago. But meantime
there was this poor nymph, whom he must remember at times to succour.
Somewhere within himself was the awareness that also, in this way as
well as the other, he was avenging himself on Sir Ludovic Curle.

Kate lay surrounded by candles guttering in their sockets, for the hour
was late. Her nipples had been painted vermilion by the Negress, making
her skin seem white by contrast, and she wore black lace stockings with
garters of silver and matching high-heeled shoes. Behind the mask's slits,
her eyes glittered anonymously. She might have been any naked whore.
The room itself was a foil for her nakedness, being richly hung, with a
single door through which clients might enter. It would never have occurred to Kate that the alcove contained a spying-place, or that Jody him-

self would be seated there behind the lattice. He knew all this, and it amused him. He had not watched her here before. The man who had just left her was a client whom Jody did not know, and he found that he had no emotions regarding the man or the occasion. This pleased him; he preferred to regard himself as without sentiment other than those involved in the carrying out of his vow. As far as that went, his mother's enquiries had already been satisfied by the answers he gave. He would not reveal everything to her about his relations with Norah.

The Negress had come in, and finished her ministrations: quiet descended upon the room. Kate lay still, her gloved arms by her sides. Jody assessed her body in sharp perspective, wondering if a painter might find it inspiring; the top of her head, carrying the small triangular coquettish hat that held the mask in place, was nearest him. It had been a diverting fancy to dress certain of the girls in this way, and pleased some, whereas others demanded the naked ebony and rosewood of the young Negresses as they were, without adornment. The establishment was paying very well indeed; Jody had already had offers to purchase it, which he would at some future time consider. But as for Kate—

The door opened silently and the next customer entered. It was Jonathan Wraye.

Jody could not himself recall what happened. He found himself on his feet, going swiftly round to one door and the next, and entering Kate's room. "Sir," he said quietly to Wraye, who turned and gaped at him, "you have been given the wrong number of room; my apologies." Wraye made as if to protest; what was this fellow, whom he vaguely recalled at Curle, doing here, ordering him? But it was not seemly to make a scene, or have oneself identified in any way that might reach ears outside. Wraye had always been the soul of discretion, lest rumours arise which could hurt Amy. He went downstairs in offended silence to search for a new girl, and Jody returned to the room to find Kate with her arms stretched out to him, her mask off and her face scarlet with the heat and blubbered with tears.

"You saw—you sent him off—it is not the first time, but he doesn't know me. Ah, Jody . . ."

He had not meant to bed with her again. He was still in doubt, and some anger, as to what had happened to him a moment since. Why resent Wraye? His Duchess would no longer be able to give the man what he needed; he'd have had discreet recourse, no doubt, to whores for years. But at the sight of Wraye's entering to take Kate, something had risen in Jody himself which might have been feeling, had he been any other man. He caressed Kate absently. No need to use force with her, she'd be weary after the day's custom, and he himself was glad enough to lie gently inside her. Kate . . . his foolish misfortunate love . . .

"What is it, Kate?" She was sobbing, and he smiled. "I had thought you would be glad to see me."

"So glad, so glad . . . please, please take me away from here, I don't want anyone except you, only you, please, please . . ."

"So you hate it, do you? But you have made money at it, I hear."

"I loathe it. Take me away with you, somewhere . . . no matter . . . I will scrub floors . . ."

Had some madness entered into him? Afterwards he would never understand how it had happened. By the end of an hour he had her solaced and dressed and her cloak round her, and was riding back with her to Windyett the way they had come. All the time he was cursing himself for a fool. This had not been, had never in any way been, a part of the plan, now that he had Norah.

11

K ATE FOUND THAT, once back at Windyett, Jody's manner to her changed. She had said she would scrub floors, he reminded her; now she could do it. She was given a small attic room at the top of the house, near where the servant slept, and she ate her meals in the kitchen.

She was active and willing enough, and so thankful to be out of the whorehouse that she set to work with a will. The first day she scrubbed the house-hall and stairs, which were filthy. "'Twill show up the better after another scrub, and maybe yet a third," Kate told herself, leaning back on her knees at last and wringing out the cloths. The house had an air of long neglect overlaying its sound, aged timber and stonework; neither Corder Bellingham nor Jody nor Elizabeth, nor the sleazy local servant they employed took heed to it.

Of the other inmates Kate was soon made aware. She caught sight of a pair of red-rimmed eyes in a sallow face, and found Jody's wife coming idly down the staircase; this would be Norah Stroyan's daughter, whom in all her time at the Moat Kate had never seen; one understood Elizabeth Curle never went out. She seemed completely colourless, even to the hue of her gown, which was not modish. She ignored Kate, not knowing her for the woman she had seen Jody take that time on the moor, and went on her way. Kate returned to her scrubbing. No one directed her, and there seemed no housekeeper or other person to fetch the food; as the days passed, Kate found that the men brought in shot rabbits or other game, or fish from the becks that ran nearby. The food was cooked by whoever had lit the fire, and often strange ragged men came, and shared the meal. It was altogether a strange house, running itself as if it were owned by no one. Later Kate discovered that it belonged to Mrs. Stroyan. She folded her soft lips bitterly. Everything in the valley belonged to that lady, doubtless; there was no escaping her. At first Kate expected Norah to come to Windyett to visit her daughter; but the time passed and she did not.

The other hidden inhabitant of the house was Corder. Kate would see him sometimes, always drunk, when he came down to eat and drink with Jody in the hall at the day's end. Elizabeth Curle seldom joined them, or if she did so sat in silence, picking at the food with her fingers and leaving it messed and uneaten. Kate, her own healthy appetite restored after a day's hard work, was shocked by the waste of good food and the idleness of the house's mistress; but it was not her place to say anything, and the sight of Corder Bellingham admittedly would put a finicky young woman off her food. Corder now was grey-faced as a phantom, his clothes hanging soiled and loose on him, his lower jaw trembling as though he had an ague. It was difficult to realise that he had once been a handsome man.

There was no one Kate could ask concerning all of it, and she began to long for talk with Jody, but he avoided her. After a time, with her ministrations, the house began to look cleaner; she washed the curtains and hung them out to dry on the furze-bushes by the door, then polished the windows till they shone in the sun. She did not take time to tell herself that were she idle, she would spend her days longing for Jody; and that was useless. For whatever reason, he did not want her love at Windyett.

Corder however at last spoke, and that when Kate least expected it. She had not yet begun to clean the men's rooms, partly out of shyness and partly because she preferred to do the greater part of the house first. One day however she was scrubbing the corridor outside Corder's bedroom, and knowing him lately to have left it she went in. The room was in a state of chaos and dirt, the bed unmade and with greasy long-used sheets. On the wall a portrait of a dark-haired young woman hung. Kate went over and stared at it.

"If *you'd* stayed and done your duty, maybe he'd not be as he is," she said aloud, for she had long ago in county-circles heard some breath of scandal about Corder's departed wife. There was no doubt Madeleine Bellingham had been very beautiful, if the portrait did not lie. To have such beauty, and misuse it, and abandon one's husband, and—

"So you have come in here; get out, y'slut, and leave me be." Corder had entered; Kate recoiled at the smell of stale spirits on his breath. "Would ye not like clean sheets, sir, if I was to put them on? 'Tis comfortable with clean linen," she said. It was no use, she knew returning the abuse he gave; this was the tenant of the house, and must be deferred to.

"You know well enough what's comfortable, I'll wager; does Jody still visit y' at night? That's an unnatural thing," and Corder leered at her. The expression in his bloodshot eyes made Kate angry. "Indeed there is nothing unnatural," she was beginning, then held her tongue and minded her place; she must remember that she was a servant now, though no one paid her.

"Unnatural, I swear; d'ye know who ye are?"

"I am Kate Scarsgill." It was a relief to be able to say it again, straight out, after all this time of pretending to be the widow Vulliamy; that lady was dead. Kate stood her ground and stared back at Corder; but if he lays a paw on me, she was thinking, I'll run. However he seemed disinclined to do so.

"Scarsgill . . . maybe. Y'father was old Sir Ludovic Curle. That makes Jody y'nephew. Odd thing . . . unnatural, but the old man tossed every wench in the valley, and most in the city as well. He got y'mother breeding the year he died, and he died in her bed; Norah turned her out in the street that same night. Norah's a fine woman."

"You are talking nonsense," said Kate roundly. "My father was a man of the dales." Yet within her a dreadful doubt was growing, remembering her mother, and the way things had been. Could Corder be speaking the truth, and if not, why invent so cruel a lie?

He had blasphemed, and turned away, telling her once more to get out of his room. This time Kate went; she would not enter there again, she told herself. The heart in her breast was hammering wildly, as though to rid some poison in her blood. Was what Corder had said true? And Dad had once said some such thing . . . . . . *the blood that's in ye* . . .

She must ask Jody. There was no one else whom she would believe was telling her the truth. He'd tell it, even if he knew it hurt her. Perhaps, knowing him as she did, that would be the better reason for telling it. Jody liked, at times, to hurt; Kate knew that.

She waited for him that night, after he should have done eating his supper; they elected, he and Corder, to sit together late and play a two-handed game of cards. Elizabeth Curle was nowhere to be seen. Kate sat her weary body down on the stairs, and waited; she dared not go up to her room lest she fall fast asleep.

After a long time she heard the men scrape back their chairs, and come. She flattened herself into a window-space in the wall, behind the newly washed curtains. Their freshness came to her nostrils strangely. What a coil it was, all of it! If it was true what Corder had told her, then . . . then she must surely leave Windyett. It would be as it had been when she had run away that time to stay at the inn, but this time there would be no rescue, no return. Jody her nephew, and she his aunt. It was horrible, unreal: unnatural, as Corder had said. It meant they could never again be lovers.

Corder stumbled past her at last on the stairs, and went to his own place. Jody had not followed. Perhaps she'd have a chance to speak to him in the hall. Kate went down; but it was already empty. He must have gone outside, perhaps to see to his horse; he surely wouldn't ride out this time of night. She slipped out by the door and went round to the stables. As she went, a rider clattered by: Jody. He *was* going out. Kate's cry followed him uselessly, lost in the sound of hooves. She ran to see which way he had gone; it was a night of half-moon, and she could watch the horse and rider go over the slope, towards Curle. Towards Curle . . . the way he'd used to come while she was still at the Moat. There was nobody living at the Moat now. So where could he be going?

Kate found herself running and stumbling across the moor, twisting her ankles in the uneven clumps of ling and furze. Her breath came in short gasps; at length she put a hand to her breast, and could run no farther. Ahead and below lay Curle, where Jody had gone. A light shone in a window, then went out.

Kate lay and wept on the heather, grotesque imaginings in her brain. Jody her nephew . . . Jody perhaps Mrs. Stroyan's lover. That was why he didn't come to her any more, not the other reason. *That* would never deter him. Jody didn't obey laws like other people. He was . . . Jody. Now, lacking him or any means of reaching him, Kate felt more desolate than ever before in her life. She knew she was too weak to go from him, as she had boasted to herself earlier today she would do. At least she had bite and sup here and could stay near him . . . her *nephew*.

Having sobbed her heart out, she went back to the house, and to her room, and to sleep, for she was very weary.

I 2

ABIGAIL CAME to Windyett after a madam had been found to manage the young women in the town-house meantime. She herself was glad to be out of the city. She would stay awhile, and then rejoin her own people as she did yearly. She had never felt, and did not now feel, that she was at home under a roof whether her son's or another's, and her name was not Manifold but Smith. Her rheumatism troubled her; she was growing old, she knew, but she would always go back to the tribe.

Jody brought her brandy, and himself sat by her while she drank. His own glass stayed half-touched; he was a sparing drinker. She surveyed him, thinking how little the years, despite his loss of an eye, had altered or aged her son; there was grey in his hair, it was true, but otherwise he was the same as he had always been. The women liked him, as they had liked his father.

The door opened and her son's wife came in, bearing a letter. It was from her mother. Elizabeth handed it silently to Jody, who read it aloud.

> *My dearest daughter, I am having a house-party from Tuesday, and will not be able to spare time for other visitors until they have gone. If your husband will permit you, will you join us? There will be the Wrayes, and a flautist from Leicester who is much spoken of.*

He tossed the letter back to Elizabeth. "You may write," he told her, "and say that I forbid you to go. But your mother is welcome to visit you here, if she prefers it."

Elizabeth went out. After she had gone Jody's eyes met Abigail's. The old woman was filled with elation.

"She is three months gone," she said. "I could tell as soon as I saw her. You knew?"

"I suspected it. I am glad of it, for now I need not touch her again. She repels me, mother."

"That matters nothing. Your son will inherit Curle."

"And as for myself?" He spoke with irony. As always she had the feeling that there were matters he kept hid from her. She tried to recollect his father's features, but they were overlaid by the years. She had not loved her second husband, and was still glad that she had borne him no children. Jody alone was her joy and delight. That his wife should bear him a child at last was the summit of Abigail's happiness.

"One day I shall hold my son's son on my knees," she said.

"Maybe. How can you tell so soon that a woman is pregnant? There is no sign yet in Elizabeth."

"I can tell."

He left the matter, and fell to brooding over the unstated message to him which had been contained in Norah's letter. So she did not want him knocking at her door while her grand friends visited her? He surveyed his relationship with Norah with sudden coldness. He had had her to satiety. He could have gone on with it had she not written as she had, but now—

Was she also with child by him? he wondered. She should be; and that was a matter he must discuss with his mother. When Norah came to visit her daughter, as she would do, Abigail must survey her. There was however the question of Norah's age; Jody knew that it was uncertain exactly when courses stopped in women. Sarah, Abraham's wife in the Bible, had conceived in extreme old age. If both Norah and her daughter were with child by him, it was a diverting coincidence: which could hardly fail to be turned to profit.

Abigail stayed three weeks, and went, with her stiffened gait, up and down Windyett, looking forever out of the windows towards the fells. Soon enough she came upon Kate, and was incensed that the young woman should be in the house. The old one went to Jody.

"I wonder at you, having that trollop here. I'd give her a sound beating, and send her about her business."

"You shall not lay a finger on Kate, mother."

Her eyes grew dim with anger, but she obeyed him; she would always obey Jody. Kate Scarsgill would stay; but what did Abigail's son want with such? The whore could play no part in his regaining of Curle, which as always had been Abigail's life's ambition for him. But she could not persuade him to speak of it, and so kept silence herself, watching over things as they progressed at Windyett, never noticing Kate's devoted cleanings and scrubbings; she was not concerned with such things. The weather grew warmer, and Abigail grew restless, longing to be away across the fell-tops to follow the tribe in their journeyings which had lasted three centuries. But she would not leave Windyett until her grandchild should be born. Meantime, Corder Bellingham sickened and took to his bed, and it was left to Kate to tend him.

Norah had begun to lose all sense of outward values, even of propriety. It had been for this reason that she had invited the house-party. If she could receive company again, she might return to what she'd once been, still could be again, if, if . . .

Jody was flesh of her flesh. When they were together they were as one, in a union she had never known existed for all her superficial experiences with Beppo and Stroyan and with Sir Ludovic's coarse tongue. In those moments with Jody she fulfilled her very existence; but she was still Mrs. Stroyan of Curle. She remembered this, but knew also that, with Jody coming to her again by night, there need be no great insistence on state by day. Often she received nobody, not even Thwaite, and spent the whole time in an old wrapper with her hair loose, seated by the fire with a wine-flagon nearby and perhaps a bone of mutton or chicken lest she feel hungry. The managing of Curle, which she had always assumed could not go on without her, did so in some manner, while Norah sat in drowsy contentment, waiting for the night to draw on. Often nowadays she would smile into the flames, turning her drinking-cup so that the embossed familiar silver struck reflections from the fire; why should this pastime give her an instant's pain? At such times, it would be borne in upon Norah that she was no longer young, and like her grandfather cared nothing for the loss of youth. Now, at the appointed time, had come the ripeness and full depth of passion; she already marvelled that in her green youth she had resented that first taking of her by Jody at Churl's Leap. It had happened too early, and much wrong had resulted; but now they were at one together, and it made no odds that her monthly seasons, which for over a year had been coming irregularly, had now stopped. It was one trouble the less, Norah told herself. From now on her middle age, her old age, would be enjoyable. No thought any longer disturbed her regarding Curle's future, or who would inherit. The future would take care of itself.

She was seated thus one day, in some disarray and wearing velvet slippers, one of which she balanced on her foot as she sat before her fire. The slippers were old and comfortable, her wrapper stained with wine. "I am growing like the old squire," she thought, and laughed at the notion. Then a sound behind her made her turn irritably: had not she given orders that she was to remain undisturbed, even to the putting of fresh logs on the fire herself? Yet a servant stood there, his hands twisting nervously at his livery coat. "Madam, madam—"

"What is it?" said Norah sharply. Some news of import, no doubt, or the man would not have come up; she roused herself from her lethargy to listen. "Be quick about it, and give over your mumbling," she told him. "Is it news, and if so of whom?" Elizabeth, she knew, would send none, and the Wrayes were away visiting in Scotland. Perhaps there was adverse news from there of Amy.

"Madam, I—I am to say it is a messenger from a far place, and that he must see you."

"Must he indeed? And if I do not choose that he shall?" It might well, she suspected, be some word of Ludovic; over the years letters had sometimes come, but seeing the superscription in his careful narrow hand she had always burned them unread. The remembrance of her son came faintly now, like that of a person known once in a dream. He was nothing to her any more, since he had abandoned Curle. Norah scowled. "Show this messenger in, then, but tell him to be brief." She drew together the wrapper and put up a hand to her hair, fingering its rich untidy masses. No doubt the half-dark—it had already come down—would disguise her looks, and the fact that she had neither laced herself nor combed her hair this day. "Show him in, I said, damn you!" she called to the man, who had not moved. A voice from beyond, in the shadows, answered; Norah did not know at first to whom it belonged.

"He is already here. Do not blame your servant. I followed him, with news which is brief and sad, but which you must certainly hear."

It was the packman, whom Norah had not seen except briefly that night years back, at Ludovic's coming-of-age, when he had as she knew lured her son away. His hair was silver now and he looked like an old man. Norah's mouth grew hard.

"We all give way to age, it seems. You cannot grieve me now, priest; all that is over."

"It is over indeed," he said gravely. "Father Ludovic Stroyan died four hours after saying his first Mass a month since: this is the news I would bring, as you would read no letters."

"Dead, my son? But—but he was young."

There was a sudden rush of bitter fluid to her mouth; the reality of the thing came to her, as if with a blow on the cheek. Not so young now, her mind told her; youth does not outlast a rigorous training among the fathers of Saint-Sulpice, with fasting and study and prayer. That was what Ludovic had wanted; why had he died? She stared at the packman-priest, while her mind assembled small, scattered things; where had the priest been all this time, up and down other valleys than Curle? He hadn't shown his face here since the death of her grandmother, and the taking away of her heir.

"Consumption is a disease of the young, Mrs. Stroyan. For years he hid it from them, fearing that were it discovered they would pronounce him unfit, and he longed to serve. Then a few weeks before the ordination—and he had distinguished himself as a student and in the practices of the Faith, so that one would have thought he might become its brightest star of late years—a few weeks before, he had a haemorrhage from the mouth which stained his linen, and they could not help but see. He had been, as you may know, very sanguine, and with the colour of perfect health; physicians themselves may be deceived in such matters, but by the end he had lost much flesh rapidly, as if it were consumed. Then—"

"Why did he not send word to me?" said Norah harshly. Then her hand clenched on the settle-edge; it was she herself, not once but many times, who had burned Ludovic's letters. Perhaps, had she known, she could have saved him; money, rest, the doctors, might all have wrought a change. "The life he led killed him," she said bitterly.

The priest, who had not answered her earlier question, bowed his head. "His soul is with God, after a life without blame as far as we who are already stained may know it," he said. "He was respected among them all for piety and charity to others; he was also much loved. For this reason, and at his earnest desire, it was decided to ordain him with the rest; and he had the joy of saying his first Mass even if the hopes he had had, to come out and serve again in the world, were not to be fulfilled. The ways of God—"

"Damn your God," said Norah suddenly. "You took my son and turned him into a phthisical monk; he were better dead, and has been dead to me since he left here. Am I to thank God for taking my son from me? No, for I have you, priest, to thank; were I a man I'd run you through. As a woman, though, I can name you, and describe your face; there'll be less proselytising in the valleys after this, no more boys taken from their homes to become—to become—"

The fire had swelled to a red haze before her eyes; she could see nothing else, not the figure of the packman as he took his departure and went back, a shadow into darkness, saying before he went, "May his soul rest in peace; before he died he asked that we might pray for you, his mother, and this I now do. May God forgive you your harshness and blasphemy, and bring you to a realisation of your own calling here; may He be with you always, and bring you peace."

She would have answered, in the end, with more bitter words, for she felt no peace in her soul; but when she looked up to reply the priest had gone, and she was alone again with the flagon and the wine, and the fire whose depleted logs glowed dully again among ashes. She still would not call the servant to replenish them.

13

NORAH FORBADE the ringing of the dead-bell in the valley church for Ludovic. After the initial horror of learning the news of his death her feelings had hardened. He had deserted his people and herself; he should obtain no recognition as squire of the heritage he had abandoned. Also, she was determined that Elizabeth should learn of the death from no one but herself. After giving the counter-order about the bells Norah called her carriage, and set out in it, veiled, for Windyett.

The road was rough, and the carriage lurched upwards through the cold daylight. Norah found herself thinking less of her son than of those who were left. If Elizabeth indeed bore a child to Jody—she must face the possibility—that child should inherit. Elizabeth herself must be protected against too great a shock from the news. A life that was to come was of more value—Norah put it to herself thus coldly—than a life that was gone.

She left the carriage at the point on the road past which it could not travel, and clutching at her veil and cloak against the wind she began the rough final ascent. The effort of climbing made her breaths shorten; how different it was from the days when as a child she had run up here either on foot, or gripping a fell pony between her thighs! She was growing middle-aged, she thought, and stout; lacing herself into her gown again today had been a task, for she had put on flesh of late weeks with lovemaking and idleness. Tomorrow—

What of tomorrow? What would become of Curle? Would Elizabeth and Jody—the notion displeased Norah and she did not dwell on it—live there together after she herself should be dead? Already, standing alone here in the moment's stillness, Norah felt as she had at times done throughout her life; solitary, no part of any ordinary existence that went on for other men and women. Seldom had the solitude been so poignant as now; why now?

Then a tolling sound came on the wind. It was the dead-bell.

Norah drew a breath; under her veil her cheeks had flushed unbecomingly. So her orders had been disobeyed, had they? Someone—she would find out who it might have been—had officiously taken the initiative, gone in below the church-tower and pulled on the rope. In old days there'd have been a dead-bell soon for *them*, for disobeying Curle.

But Windyett stood above the rise, and she must get there quickly before Elizabeth asked whose death might be rung for. Norah hurried over the last few stones, keeping her anger for when she should descend again to the valley. She tried to down it and feel tenderness for her daughter. Elizabeth had lost an only brother and protector; had he stayed, Norah knew very well, this marriage to Jody would not have been.

The door opened and a figure barred her way; the gipsy woman who was Jody's mother. Norah knew her well enough now; Mrs. Manifold, indeed!

"I desire speech with my daughter," she said coldly. She put back her veil, and stepped into the house.

Upstairs, Elizabeth had been lying on her bed, recovering from a bout of queasy sickness. The young woman they called Kate had come and taken the basin and rinsed it clean, and removed the contents in a slop-pail. She smoothed the covers over Elizabeth. "Lie still, madam," she said gently. "It will be better now."

She was halfway downstairs with the pail when Abigail spoke from the hall. "That's young Master Ludovic they're tollin' for. Who's to tell *her?*" For once, the withered face no longer looked self-sufficient. Abigail had learned of the young squire's death from a man of the tribe, who had come with the news as soon as Mrs. Norah herself would hear it, down at Curle. It had travelled across the fells by word of mouth.

"I will tell her," said Kate, setting down the pail. She knew that it was best that she do so. *He* didn't love his wife. No one here loved her, and if that gipsy were to go up herself with the tidings, poor Mrs. Elizabeth might miscarry. Kate did not know whence she had acquired knowledge of such things. Wisdom had seemed to come to her with charity since the discovery of her relationship to Jody. She looked and felt like a young nun nowadays, with her linen kerchief folded high to hide her breasts. She did all manner of menial tasks at Windyett, including the tending of Corder who was ill. Jody himself was elsewhere today, having ridden to the port to sell one of his ships. Now that there was talk of doing away with slavery there would be less money in the trade, unless one went to America. Jody would have thought of all that.

She entered Elizabeth's room quietly. The sick girl on the bed turned her head. "You need not have come back," she said coldly. She had never treated Kate in any manner save as that of a servant in the house. Kate bore no rancour.

"Madam, it is ill news," she said gently, "and you must bear it bravely."

Elizabeth smiled a little. "There's never aught else," she said. "Is my husband dead?" She spoke idly, as if making no bones of the fact that she would have cared nothing.

"No, madam. Someone you love well." Kate knew she might be rated for impertinence, but this was not a time to heed that. "News from France of your brother, madam. He—"

"Ludovic? He has twice written to me here." The voice was drowsy, as if it had happened a long time ago. "How does he? Is he ill again that word has come?"

"It is more, madam. He is dead. He has been ill for very long. He made a peaceful end."

Elizabeth turned her head away into the pillows. "Leave me," she said at last. "Go away and leave me alone."

And as Kate made her way sadly out through the door, she heard Ludovic's sister speak again, as if to herself.

"He was the only person who has ever been kind to me, in all my life, save my father."

Then she heard the sound of weeping; but it continued quiet, and Kate hoped that the child would be safe. She was halfway downstairs when she found herself staring down into the face of Norah Stroyan, who stood below in the hall. Beyond the open door, borne on the wind, was the dead-bell. They could all of them hear it now.

Norah surveyed Kate as one might do an apparition; it was the first she had known of her presence at Windyett.

"You—here?"

All grief for Ludovic, all resentment at the way they had rung the church-bell despite her orders, paled beside the realisation that Jody kept on his mistress at Windyett. His mistress, all these months waiting up here for him by day, while she—

She endeavoured to keep her voice calm. "How long have you been here? I had thought you on the roads by this."

"No, madam." Kate held her head high, and gave back look for look. She wasn't beholden to Mrs. Stroyan for anything. If it had been anyone else, she would have said she was sorry about young Master Ludovic, whom she had never seen. But with this woman one didn't act so; she must be made of granite. Remembrance of the way Jody must have been Norah's lover at nights came to Kate for instants, making the hot colour flood into her face. They stared in mutual hostility, the old mistress and the young.

Abigail stepped from behind Norah. "You cannot see Elizabeth," she said flatly, and Norah rounded on her.

"Not see my own daughter, at such a time? Have you no heart?"

"I may have, but you've none. And she's in the family way. And," Abigail lowered her voice, "you are in like state. When ye need aid, come to me."

Norah turned and went out of the house. Presently they heard the sound of her carriage-wheels driving away on the lower road. Beyond that, the dead-bell gave a last deep note, and then stopped. The valley had remembered Ludovic Stroyan.

Norah made herself go down to the valley at once; it was the only anti- dote to thinking. A small crowd of men and women met her coach. Foremost among them was a short-legged creature with shaggy hair; Madge's son Wil, returned for today to the valley.

"Do not blame them, madam," he said, " 'twas I rang the peal for him. I remember him, boy and man. Not a living soul in the valley but re- members. 'Twould not have been seemly, madam, had we let him go in si- lence."

She looked at them, clustered about where she was, some of the women with red eyes, old and young men with their faces grave. They had loved Ludovic. He would have made a good squire, if only—

Norah bowed her head. "I am glad that you have shown respect to my family and to myself," she said. "You share my grief with me."

She told the coachman to turn, and her equipage drove her back again to Curle.

Now she was alone. She gave orders that no one was to disturb her in her rooms, and locked the door. She bolted also the side-door by which Jody had been used to come to her at nights, up a twisting stair. He should never come to her any more.

She was alone; and yet there was life in her womb. The gipsy woman had sensed it. She herself should have known it, when—

When? When would the child be born?

When you need aid, come to me. She'd not dare be as near Curle as that. She would go abroad, somewhere, alone and wait for the birth.

Abroad . . . all Curles must be born at Curle. It had been so since Saxon times. But this child couldn't be acknowledged; he must be hidden. He . . . how was she so sure that it would be a son? To recompense her for Ludovic, who was dead?

His name, again, would be Ludovic.

Norah reached for the wine-flagon. Almost, now that it was inevitable that she see the truth, she could smile at her own folly. The stopped courses, that she'd put down to old age; and the putting on of flesh. And up there, at Windyett, Elizabeth also was to bear Jody's child. Generation admixed with generation, would they run mad? What relation did they bear one to the other? Father and daughter, mother and child, and his aunt his doxy . . . best not remember *that*. And that inexorable gipsy seated in the midst, having maybe seen all things from the beginning.

She had a grudge of some sort. Hadn't they hanged her lover, Jody's father? Well, she had her revenge.

Jody. Norah was glad he hadn't been at Windyett today. She never wanted to see him again.

Best forget him, forget everything, for the moment in wine, and then . . . and then the house-party. She wouldn't cancel that. It would divert her to see people, to hear the flautist play, and thrust back the darkness till after they'd gone. There needn't be any official mourning for young Ludovic, who'd deserted his heritage to become a Papist priest.

The dead-bell had tolled. He could be content with that.

That Jody had done with her, as she with him, Norah knew after a night or two had passed. Whether Abigail or Kate had a hand in it Norah was never certain, nor would she ever ask. But no hand touched the bolted door, nor was he ever again to come to her as her lover.

14

CORDER BELLINGHAM died at last. Kate, who had been in his room at the end, ran trembling downstairs to say that his breathing had changed and he lay still. It was the first time she had seen death; her father had died while she was away at school and the coffin had been closed before she had taken the long journey home across Yorkshire. Now she saw the reality; helped Abigail to lay out the almost fleshless corpse and saw it put in its coffin; and those few who still remembered Corder as he had been, and the many who recalled him in the taverns in later years, travelled up to Windyett to look down on the altered face. Some wept; many even in the taverns had experienced flashes of the old, fabled charm amid the drunken maunderings.

The funeral took place on a day of rain, and was well attended. Most folk came on foot, out of the valley. The sole carriage was occupied by the few women present who accompanied poor Corder to his grave despite tradition: Norah herself, her daughter Elizabeth, Corder's sister the Duchess, and fourthly a surprising presence; Abigail Manifold, clad in a black hat with beads and feathers, a silk shawl, a black apron, and wearing her two gold wedding-rings. Norah, who had strangely been thinking of Stroyan today, and the time he had come to Curle with handsome young Corder as groomsman, came to herself, in the jolting carriage, to find the gipsy's bright gaze fixed on her, clear as a cat's. Norah felt discomfort; already today she had felt Jody's child move in her, and it was as though Abigail knew even that, and perhaps also the date when it should be delivered. Norah dropped her own gaze to the woman's ungloved hands, averting her thoughts from that other pregnant woman in the carriage, her own daughter, distended now as small-boned women tend to be, with the unborn child swelling her body by contrast with the thin, gawky arms in their black sleeves, and the thin neck above the collar. Amy Wraye was talking softly, almost to herself, remembering young Corder her brother with his fine witty manners and fair curling hair. "And to die so!" she kept reiterating, "to have in the end to die so!" Kate Scarsgill, the one who had nursed Corder and seen to his needs since he became ill, was not present. Jody rode ahead with the Duke and the rest of the men who were on horseback; behind the carriage, with its lurching motion, came the steady patient shuffle of the folk on foot. Norah stared at the two rings on Abigail's finger. She endeavoured, while not interrupting Amy, to make her own voice light.

"I do not think I have seen two marriage-rings before," she remarked to the woman. Abigail's stare narrowed, and her toothless mouth hardened for instants as she surveyed the woman who had deprived her son of his inheritance, and now was being forced to make amends.

"My son had his father's, which he gave back to me. All his life he had kept it about him."

Norah's lips curved in a smile. "Then why part with it?" Any talk of Jody was, by now, again, talk of a stranger; she carried his child in her body, but none should ever know that she had borne it. When the time came, she was still resolved, she would go alone to some foreign place. This creature's eyes, look as they might, could see nothing amiss with her, nothing. She was a fine-fleshed woman, had always been; her furs aided her. The gipsy and her low-born son had no part or lot with her, neither body or soul with Norah Stroyan of Curle.

"Part with it? He had no more need of it; he's proved his right to what's his. He gave me my gold back again, that my own folk made the Curle heir put on my finger, to make me an honest woman before they hanged him. After that they married me to another, but I bore no son to him. He's dead; died in our own caravan eleven year back, when Jody was riding back and forth from Liverpool. Jody always knew where to find me, for all I left him at Curle when he was a boy. He has but the one eye, but that's keen."

Amy stared, uncertain where the talk led. Norah turned her fur-clad shoulder and addressed her, at the same time seeing that her rouged lips had fallen open to reveal discoloured teeth. Heavens, how we are all growing old! thought Norah. Corder dead, and Ludovic gone his own way, and her own hair for the first time showing threads of grey in it; and now Amy, who had been most beautiful, turning, like the gipsy, into a maundering old woman. For of course the gipsy's wits wandered; it was merely her appearance that gave an impression of unchanged, unassailable strength. Such persons must keep their place, and all would be well. So Norah talked to Amy, in a low voice, till they came with Corder's body to the church, and the pall-bearers carried the light weight of the coffin inside. As they stepped out of the carriage together Amy said aloud, with the air of being elsewhere in her own mind that she always had nowadays, "To have changed as he did over the years, and all for a worthless woman! But she was so very beautiful; do you remember Madeleine?"

She could not have taken great heed to the gipsy woman in her grief, Norah knew. They buried Corder, and came home.

15

"KATE! WHAT AILS my aunt Kate? Turn your cheek, lass, that I may kiss you and—good aunt, you are sullen today and I shall beat you unless you smile."

She had turned her face into the pillow, sobbing. She'd always known this was how it would end, with him in her bed again; she hadn't meant it to happen, and when he first rode home from Liverpool with a pair of hooped silver earrings for her, had refused to put them on. Then, standing there, she had told him that she knew who her father was. Jody had thrown back his head, laughing.

"You are fortunate; that's more than many of us can say. Put 'em on, girl, and let me see—" He had jerked her linen kerchief apart, that she'd worn high and seemly in the past weeks, and exposed the cleft between her big sturdy breasts so that she looked again like a whore; and had taken the pins out of her hair so that it tumbled down her back. Then he had taken her. Kate could not prevent it; she could neither prevail over his strength of purpose nor the elation that was in him. So it was between them again as it had always been, from the first; oh, she was lost, doomed! She knew it now; it stared back at her from her mirror. She was Jody's aunt, and he had her body whenever he chose. She must be the most sinful young woman in the world.

He was on a bed with her again now, only it was not her attic room they lay in but his own, to which he frequently sent nowadays for Kate to come. It was the afternoon, and she still had household tasks to perform; but he'd made her put them aside. Nothing mattered but himself and his pleasure, and that last seemed to overflow from him, so that he laughed both as he loved her and after it was done. In contrast to his laughter, Kate's wretchedness grew; to be so brought down!

Jody's thoughts as he lay, still rigid, within Kate were pleasurable. Two women were with child by him, and one way or the other his seed should inherit Curle. He had heard lately that David Stroyan was dead in Australia, a tree-trunk having fallen on him while he saw to matters on his farm; that meant that, but for Elizabeth, Jody was free to marry Norah, if he would. Perhaps he would not; he preferred Kate's young flesh, and he had already done his will upon Norah with the desired result. Had she been less set in her autocrat's ways a marriage might have become possible in the end, "but a man could never call his soul his own," thought Jody. He called it so now, as much as Kate's body let him. He still could not understand what the feeling was that Kate aroused in him. She was foolish, feckless, weak, and had no great intelligence to match his own; but he would not willingly part with her. Nor—he withdrew from her, as so often, in timely fashion, leaving her climax to finish itself without him—would he give her a child. Kate was a toy, not to be more roughly handled by nature than by himself. She desired children, doubtless. But with Elizabeth's time coming on, and Norah down the hill, he himself was not yet certain enough of his intentions till all should be revealed. Norah's son, Elizabeth's; which should inherit Curle?

Elizabeth passed by and through the open door saw them together, sidling as she was along the passages in the fearful, almost oblique way she had, as though her body had grown too gross for straightforwardness. Elizabeth did not care one way or the other that Jody had again taken to his woman. Kate Scarsgill had been kind at the time of Ludovic's death, but that mattered nothing now; nothing in any case mattered except the deadly fear Elizabeth had of the coming confinement. A child was within her and would grow till it was big enough to force its way out; there was no way of preventing this: she hadn't wanted it, or its father. Giving birth was full of mysterious horror and fear. Who would look after her? She was afraid of mother, and afraid also of Jody's who hadn't rejoined her own folk as she usually did until, as she said, she could see her grandchild born. Elizabeth's thin limbs quailed and she clung to the door-lintel. She herself didn't want to see the child, ever. Perhaps she would die.

Jody rose from Kate and presently went downstairs and out to the stables, where he had his horse saddled. He was going down—he smiled—to Curle to pay madam Norah his due rent. There had been no correspondence between them on the matter after Corder died; it was assumed she accepted him as her tenant, as an alternative to casting her own daughter out on the moor. They hadn't encountered one another, he and madam Norah, since Corder's funeral, and then had not exchanged speech. The time before that they had been making love. "Now, her own time is near," Jody told himself, jesting at the pun. Curiosity was within him to see what Norah looked like, how she bore herself. It was certain that no one in the valley had guessed her secret state. A brave woman, Norah Stroyan! She'd carry the matter through if need be alone, he knew, even if it meant bearing the child under a bush. But he himself had no intention of seeing his heir squandered. "My mother will know what should be done," he thought, and cantered towards Curle.

Norah was seated at a table in the accounts-office; there was no sign of Thwaite the factor, and it was probable that she had dismissed him about his tasks in one of her scornful rages. A handful of tenants stood near by, hats doffed in presence of Curle's lady. Norah took the sum each held and counted it, then put it into a leather bag and handed each man his written receipt, thereafter scraping with her quill in a large long day-book. Her middle finger was stained with ink. Presently she raised her eyes and saw Jody.

"I have brought you the Windyett rent, madam." She had greeted him, and heard his speech, without expression; even her eyes did not change. She inclined her head, on which a lace cap sat. "It is time that the rent for Windyett was raised," he heard her say. "Corder Bellingham had it of me for a pittance."

"Why, madam, you'd not squeeze gold from a poor man whose wife is about to lie in? Suppose I cannot pay?"

"You are impertinent," she said coldly. Jody grew suddenly weary of the talk and cast a handful of gold coins down on the table.

"There, Mrs. Stroyan; that's the next quarter's rent. I was grieved to learn of the death of Mr. Stroyan." He made his voice clearly audible, so that the other waiting tenants might hear it. Norah inclined her head. "It was—sad," she said. "But I am told that he did not suffer, which is merciful."

"How did you come by the information, madam? Have you friends out there?"

"Not friends, but acquaintances. There are others waiting, Mr. Curle; will you give place?" But Jody stayed; it diverted him to torment Norah. Her bosom, he saw, was full, but well concealed under a kerchief arranged somewhat like Kate's had been when he twitched it, but made in this instance of heavy lace. Norah wore a blue cloak over her shoulders, which she would gather about her when she rose from her chair. No one would guess, doubtless, that the lady of Curle was other than grown somewhat portly with the years. "How are his dependants faring, madam?" said Jody.

"They are to come home."

"Is their fare paid?" He was deliberately flouting her. He was aware of the dazed tenantry behind him, marvelling at his familiar exchanges with so great a lady.

"I have made them an annuity. Will you go now, Mr. Curle? Time passes, and I have company at dinner."

A strange woman, Norah! In her way, admirable. Jody admitted it on his ride back again to Windyett.

What he had not foreseen was the grief of Elizabeth at news of Stroyan's death. It had not occurred to anyone that she, who so seldom displayed feeling, would have any left for the man she had not seen since she was a child. But it was as if all the pent-up sorrow for Ludovic mingled to produce a state which was alarming in Elizabeth's condition. She lay on her bed and wept through the long hours, and neither Kate nor anyone else could comfort her. Nor would she eat. In the end, the thing happened that Abigail had feared, and Elizabeth went into premature labour. No preparations had been made yet; in the confusion and wreck of many of her plans, the gipsy remembered one aspect. She set Kate by Elizabeth to minister at the birth, regardless of the young woman's terrified pleas that she knew nothing of such things. "Ye will learn," said Abigail, and remembered the other thing she must do, to guard against mishap. She sent a servant down to Curle with all speed, to summon Norah Stroyan.

16

WRAYE HAD stayed on for a short while after the departure of the house-party, some of whom had gone back with his Duchess in her coach. He seemed thoughtful and silent, and Norah surveyed his small meagre face and figure opposite her across the hearth. Wraye had aged, she was thinking; more than ever his features and hair seemed a uniform grey. There was no single remarkable part about him; he was as he had always been, underestimated until one knew him well; shy, an upholder of the conventions, and given to deep loyal affection to only a few. That his wife was one of these, and herself another, Norah knew without question. He spoke now of Amy.

"She is increasingly *distraite*," he said. "Nothing diverts her any more, not even her garden." Amy had, Norah knew, made in her time a glory of the gardens at Wraye, which in summer were at their best with green lawns surrounded by half-hardy shrubs which grew well for her, if for none other. But at this season there would be little for even Amy to do in the garden.

"She cannot forgive herself," said Wraye, "for her neglect of Corder. He was her only brother and she—"

"She did not neglect him. He was one of those persons who must be everywhere, and gossip with everyone, until—until he had passed beyond gossip." Norah turned the stem of her glass, picturing Corder's altered face in the wine. Latterly she herself, no doubt, could be accused of neglecting him. She raised her head and regarded Wraye. He was frowning into the fire.

"She says now that she sees him still," he said, "and that he comes to her when—when she plays upon her harpsichord. For that reason I do not encourage her to play it." The slight stammer in his voice spoke of his anguish. Norah burst in. "Do not prevent her! It may be that she finds the diversion welcome."

"Diversion!" said Wraye bitterly. "It is the Bellingham taint; the family were unstable, as I knew when we married, but Amy seemed, at that time —you remember."

She remembered a creature all white and gold sweetness. "The Bellingham taint is in my blood also, Wraye."

He said hastily, "I had forgot. No one could accuse *you* of instability, Norah, my dear! You are the sanest personage in the county and beyond." Maud Bellingham's ghost receded: but how greatly had that heritage been the cause of Ludovic's rejection of Curle, Elizabeth's folly also?

She wondered idly how Elizabeth fared. The child was due at any time now. Surely they would send for her when the labour began; it was a mother's due to be beside her daughter, yet Elizabeth herself might not welcome her at Windyett.

Norah let her thoughts drift back to Wraye, lest she start to reckon and count her own days as best she could. She had been eating and drinking well and heartily; her physical health was good, as ever. Recently she had made discreet arrangements with a connection of Mrs. Emma's, who lived in Ireland, to arrange for admission to a convent there of an unfortunate woman who was about to have an unwanted child. No names had been exchanged, and after the birth the nuns would rear the child and later foster it, so that it could be visited on occasion. Norah dared not think of a time when she herself might venture to bring home an adopted infant. Tongues would wag. It would all of it have to be seen to later, later, when she—"I pray that the crossing will not be stormy," she thought. She was to leave in the following week, after Elizabeth's child should be born. A close run, as Sir Ludovic would have said. Often Norah wondered what the old squire would have made of the situation at Curle. He'd have cursed Jody up and down the countryside, never a doubt of that. Well, she herself had put Jody back in his place, where he might remain.

She was about to invite Wraye to pour himself another flagon of wine when a commotion sounded at the hall-door. Norah turned, and saw a man stand there, wet with the rain; the groom from Windyett.

"Madam, I am to say that Mrs. Curle is started in her labour, and would be glad were you to come."

Norah rose. Foremost in her mind now was the gentle sound of the rain. "I will have the carriage put to," she said. She could see Wraye getting up on his feet, laying down the glass he had not yet refilled. He came to her and kissed her hands.

"How can I detain you from such an errand? I'll on my way. You are fortunate, Norah; children—and grandchildren—are a blessing. I pray for a safe delivery for mother and child."

He was gone, and she did not take time to reflect on the unconscious irony of his message. Blessing or cursing, it was all one, and time to enter her carriage, not thinking more than she need do of the rough and jolting journey to Windyett.

When she arrived at the house, it was filled with light. A lamp burned by the doorway, and beyond it she saw the gipsy woman, Abigail. At least she is not with my daughter, Norah thought. Aloud she said, entering, with her cloak still wrapped about her, "Has the midwife been fetched, and the physician? If not, I'll send my coachman ere he return."

"There are none such needed here," said Abigail, "and you may send your coach away."

"But she must have assistance at the birth; who is with her?"

"She's well attended. Seat yourself, Mrs. Stroyan, and take a warm drink against the cold night. It may be many hours yet; sit here by the fire."

Norah sat down, still anxious to go to Elizabeth; who could be attending her? "Take me to my daughter," she said, aware that she had uttered the same words here before. Abigail's dark eyes watched her, making her feel uneasy. What did they see? *When ye need aid, come to me.* Norah rejoiced fiercely that she had rendered such aid needless. Within the week, she would be on the way to Ireland.

"Ye shall go to her; bide still a while. When she calls, ye shall go."

Already the voice that spoke sounded farther off; could it be the ale? It had tasted bitter, as if there were herbs in it.

She thought she heard a cry and tried to rise, to go to Elizabeth; and found her own weight too heavy to lift, as though there were hands holding her down, and this made her angry . . . She'd laced herself tightly, she knew, to appear before Wraye; this and nothing else must be making her breaths quicken, for it could not yet be time . . .

Still at the back of her mind was Elizabeth, and the need she must surely have for her mother now. No physician or midwife, they'd said. She herself must go at once to her daughter's side, to succour and guide her; tell her, from the extent of her own knowledge, that nothing natural came amiss.

Natural! A child by her own father!

The truth came to Norah in that moment, as truth will; staring at her as the gipsy's figure had lately done, beyond the light. "She must never know," she heard her own voice telling her. Had she been repeating that to herself since before Elizabeth was born? Whether or not that was so, she must bear it alone; that knowledge, all things, even this other birth which was to take place.

It would take place soon. She was drowsy with the ale, but she knew.

It was now that Norah saw herself, her own mistake from the beginning; the error of pride. If she had even had more heed to Elizabeth earlier, other than as a talisman to stand behind her at cards, all things might have happened differently. If, if . . . but of what avail to own it now?

She heard the gipsy's voice again; perhaps she had spoken aloud. "Drink down all your ale, now; be at peace."

At peace. A stirring, a disturbance of her blood was starting; it was that damned ale, they'd doctored it. Norah knew almost as she drank it, and yet she finished it obediently as though there were nothing else to do but obey.

Obey! She, Norah Stroyan!

She felt her head swim. She was aware of the deadly, rhythmical pains and their swift commencement; she knew little else, except that the woman Manifold had come forward and, beckoning, led her to a room. A room with a bed; and a fire, another fire, glowing redly in the shadows. The servant must have lit it ready. Everything had been made ready here, for her child that was about to be born: even the untimely birth.

. . . . . .

Elizabeth lay on her bed upstairs and strained and screamed. She had been doing this now for many hours; in the end they had left Kate Scarsgill with her and sent for Elizabeth's mother. It would be a difficult birth, they said. Kate did not know what to do. "Tell her to pull at the sheets, and bear down when the pains come," Abigail had told her, before she went away. So Kate held Elizabeth's flaccid hand and said every so often, "Bear down, and pull the sheet," but Elizabeth no longer heard her. Fear claimed Kate, as if it had come to her through the damp hand's touch; what was she to do? The child wouldn't come, and she was afraid that if Elizabeth went on straining many more hours she would die. A dead mother and a dead child; and her fault, hers, Kate Scarsgill's.

If only the screaming would stop! But Mrs. Elizabeth hadn't any regard for herself or the child, let alone anyone else in the room. She had thrashed about the bed with wild flailing limbs for a time, and now was still. "At least she'll save her strength," Kate told herself. She leaned over and wet Elizabeth's lips with a napkin soaked in water. The young woman moaned, and presently began screaming again. "Stop, stop," Kate heard herself saying. But how could the poor thing do that? It were almost as if Kate herself were having Jody's baby, the pains hurt her so; she clutched her own breasts and felt as if they ached full of milk, for the baby Jody wouldn't let her have. She'd have borne it gladly, not like this, like this . . . the sounds, the everlasting uncontrollable sounds of hoarse screaming . . .

Outside, a carriage came and went. It had grown darker and Kate lit more candles. They made the room too hot, and the smell of sweat and wax and agony became unbearable. Were all births like this? Surely soon . . .

"They want me to die," said Elizabeth suddenly, and screamed again. The scream had a final, agonised quality and Kate hurried to the bed and saw a displaced limb, a child's limp arm dangling. The screaming stopped and Elizabeth began to pant with short harsh breaths, as though she were dying indeed; nothing more happened, and Kate grew very frightened. But she was still more in fear of Mrs. Manifold and Jody, who had said she was to stay with Elizabeth and not leave her alone for an instant. The head would come, Mrs. Manifold had said, and one pressed hard on it and then the child would be born. But they hadn't said what to do about an arm. There was something wrong.

Kate did her best. Afterwards she could not have described to anyone what she had done, or how nearly half-fainting she found herself at the end of it. And there was a mangled dead baby. There was no question but that it was dead, and had been a girl. Perhaps Jody wouldn't mind so much that it was a girl that had died.

Elizabeth lay quite still now in the bed. She was so white that she might have been dead also, and Kate did not take time even to wrap the child's body in a cloth before carrying it, in her two hands, down to the room where she knew Jody and Mrs. Manifold must be. Someone else must come now, and see to Elizabeth, if it were not already too late.

Norah was dreaming. Often afterwards she was to dream again of that night, and what had befallen; or in a state between sleep and waking, or drunkenness and sleep, tell herself that half was as she must have imagined it, through her pain. For this birth tonight had not been painless; her body had aged since the twins' coming, and she no longer had the bounding strength and full health she had assured herself she possessed, when . . . When had she ever said so? It had been an ordeal, tonight, made doubly so by anxiety for Elizabeth, but that receded as the night wore on and her own pains came the more strongly. A secret hurried way, they'd used to bring on this birth . . . that accursed ale. She would never drink ale again.

She would not demean herself by crying out in presence of the gipsy. The latter's presence was assiduous by the bed, the knowledgeable hands doing everything, by morning, that was needed. But Norah would not cry aloud; yet in the midst of labour, when the tide of pain engulfed her like a river of dark blood, it seemed to be not Abigail Manifold who was with her, but Jody. Jody, holding her in his arms, telling her that she was his own brave girl, his good Norah, and all would come right and to have patience, and bear the pain.

Something was wrong; Jody should not be here. He should be . . . where else? "Your wife . . ."

"You are my true wife, Norah. It was intended from the beginning. Our son will inherit Curle."

Strange words; and Elizabeth?

Then she remembered; and at the same time Kate Scarsgill came in at the door, bearing a dead thing in her hands. She was red-faced and dishevelled; her eyes stared blankly.

"It's dead," she said clearly, "and it is a girl. I think that *she—*"

Abigail strode forward and took the child's mangled body and laid it aside. "Shut your fool's mouth," she said to Kate, and slapped her across the face. Kate burst out crying and fled from the room.

They had forgotten Norah for moments, and during them she gave
birth to a son. She remembered it afterwards and hearing him cry.

Later a kind of deadly laughter beset her. It was evident that all their care
of her had been for the child, not herself; once it was safely born their
chief anxiety must have been that she need not stay. She had let them do
as they would with her, knowing she could not help herself; she and
Elizabeth, whom she could not be let see, labouring together under the
same roof, to the same man, mother and daughter. *His* daughter. It was a
situation for souls in hell, and she could prevent nothing . . .

But she would refuse to die. From that moment her pride was renewed
in her and she knew that she would mend. With speed and care, in the
end, when she was fit they bundled her into her own coach which must
have been sent for from Curle; Mrs. Stroyan, fatigued with the long
night's watch by her daughter, was ailing, and must take to her bed.
Carried down to the coach, through the chill morning air; tossed, ill and
feverish, down the path where every rough place jolted, then staggering
up the steps of Curle, and to her room . . .

But she would not die, she knew.

She was not done with them yet, nor they with her. Next day a letter
came from the Duchess; had she been gone from Curle so long?

> *Dearest, we are so greatly rejoiced to learn that Elizabeth is safely
> delivered, and of a fine son. Give her my love, and that of Wraye also.*

Love? thought Norah. There would be, had been, little of that in the business. She was already plunged back into the maelstrom of dark thought
and planning that must have been ever since the night she herself was
born and a small tight-mouthed boy had leaned out of a window in Curle
stable-loft, and sworn to have her inheritance from her even by marriage.
But he had not, nor should he.

17

THE VALLEY had no lack of matter to talk over by the church-porch that Sunday, and thanksgiving prayers had been said at the service for the safe arrival of a male heir. It was the best news, they told one another, since the death of poor young Master Ludovic over in France. Mrs. Stroyan had been a good steward, but she was no longer young; it was pleasant to have the promise of a young squire of Curle blood, even though his father were a half-gipsy who came and went between here and the ports, and here and the city, on journeys connected with whatever unsavoury trades made him his money.

Mrs. Elizabeth they said was mending fast after the birth, but Mrs. Norah was herself poorly. Not even the oldest among them could recall so long a time when she'd kept her bed; they'd missed the big cloaked figure in her pew today. She was like the fells, Mrs. Norah, unchanging, hard, and always to be relied upon whatever else might alter with the times. Those who remembered her grandfather said it was as though he'd lived on. No finer tribute could be made to a woman; and she'd always seen the farms thrive. No doubt she was pleased and proud that she had a grandson. There hadn't been much coming and going between Windyett and Curle, but surely now there was a grandson that would alter? It was time there was an end to feuds.

They watched, accordingly, with mild interest the day Mrs. Norah's coach was called out to go up to the lesser house to see her grandson. That day there was another cause for gossip. A skeleton, with enough ragged clothing left to see that it had been a man's, had been found lying below Churl's Leap. A death came with a birth, they said. Who had he been? George Thwaite, the factor's nephew, brought down word at last that it must be the man Shillingthorne, who had briefly long ago stayed at the Moat. He might have been making his way back here. He had been known by the fragments of fell-slate he carried in his pack, with garnets in them. A young woman in the valley said that when she was a child, Shillingthorne used to show them to her. "He'd carry all such queer things round with him, and would abide in one place for no one," she said. They must ask Mrs. Norah if they might bury him in the parish churchyard.

For this reason Thwaite himself put his head in at the coach-window as Norah was about to set off. He told her the tale, adding "Madam, it was a fearful thing to find a skeleton below Churl's Leap, so far away."

He saw her face turn to survey him, white as milk in the dim interior of the coach; she wasn't looking well, Mrs. Norah; maybe she shouldn't be about yet, but she would be anxious to see her grandson.

"A pity they did not find one sooner," she said, and signalled for the coachman to pull the horses away. Thwaite waited behind, gaping. What had Mrs. Norah meant by that? And he hadn't had time to ask if they might bury the poor bones in consecrated soil. But you never could be sure Mrs. Norah wouldn't be angered if such a thing were undertaken without her permission. Best wait till she returned.

Norah was concerned less with Shillingthorne's bones than with her own journey to Windyett.

During the time she lay in bed her mind had turned and turned about the matter, and had found no answer. She must wait till she was in the house, and had seen Elizabeth and the child . . . if they would let her in.

They must do so, she reminded herself; she was the owner, and could have them evicted next quarter.

Evicted? Her child, to be reared by gipsies? Who would ever know what they had done with him? She recalled his healthy cry; and she had seen his sex herself, for during the birth of the head when the others' attention was engaged she had somehow half raised herself, and helped her own child to be born. She was strong, she knew; not every woman could have done it. It wasn't the birth that had made her ailing and uncertain, it was being hustled out of Windyett too soon after. Now, they must be doubtful whether or not she'd return. They would know well enough that she would never let the valley guess the truth.

The young squire, Jody's son. She had heard of the prayers of thanksgiving in the valley. Damn Jody; by one means or another, she'd be even with him yet, and as for his mother . . . Perhaps that creature had gone back now to her tribe. It would be dangerous having her at large with such a secret; yet what could one do? What would the old squire himself have done, in such a coil?

"He's ha' gone to their door, as I'm doing now, and knocked aloud to enter, and when he was in would have told them to go to the devil." But she herself, situated as she was; what would she do?

She raised a hand to the knocker at last, and waited. They must have heard the coach come, but had made no sign. She had bidden it wait.

The door opened. The girl Kate stood there, mouth agape and eyes blank. She was tousled, and dressed like a servant. Norah looked her up and down. "Take me to my daughter," she said, and when Kate made no resistance followed her inside. There was no sound of anyone else in the house, but Norah had the sensation that eyes watched and ears listened. By the fire was a cradle, where the baby lay. Kate turned back and bent over him, and rocked the cradle with her foot.

"He's asleep," she said. "They couldn't get a wet-nurse, so I've fed him with sippets of goat's milk through a linen cloth; he sucks the corner." She spoke without curiosity, as though she remembered and cared nothing for the birth-night.

Norah had looked only briefly at the cradle. If the child throve, that was well. "Where is Mrs. Elizabeth?" she asked. She did not know whether or not to name Elizabeth as the child's mother. It would be shown to her in time what she must do.

Elizabeth was in the downstairs room, lying on a day-sofa. She wore a striped wrapper and there was colour in her cheeks. She greeted her mother civilly, and said that she was well.

"Will you not sit down?" she asked Norah. "You will like to see my son. When Kate comes, I will have her bring him. I have no milk, but he—"

No, she would have none, Norah thought bitterly. She herself had bandaged her own breasts tightly with linen to quell the ample flow in them. How many ironies there were in this situation, and not least Elizabeth's smugness! "Does she really credit that she gave birth to the child?" Norah thought.

"You will take a dish of tea, mother? Mrs. Manifold is away, with my husband; but Kate makes a good enough cup. I do not know what we would do without her in many ways; it's hard to obtain intelligent servants from the valley."

I should know something about that, Norah told herself. More than ever the realisation was dawning on her that she had always disliked her daughter. Now, Elizabeth was revealed for what she would have been long since, doubtless, but for her subdued childhood and the nature of the marriage to Jody; a self-righteous snob of a woman, secure in her own insufficiency. A sense of unreality overcame Norah; was her daughter mad, or was she herself so? Had the double births in fact taken place, and did Elizabeth either not remember, or force herself to forget, the dead child that had been taken away? She might not know of that last: but how could she accept the fact that she had given birth to a healthy boy? "It was I," Norah told herself amid the welter of rising emotion which rose in her from a depth she had not known existed. "It was I."

The cruel trick, if she permitted Elizabeth to go on in this easy assumption, would succeed. Elizabeth would preen herself here, or even at Curle, as Jody's lawful wife, with his lawful son, while *she*—

It was a thing not to be borne.

Norah rose. She was unaware of anything at that moment save the issue between them. Either my whole life has been a lie, she was thinking, or else we must face the truth. And they might never again let her be alone with Elizabeth, she knew.

Elizabeth smiled. "You are leaving again very soon, mother, are you not? But you have never had time to spare for me."

"I . . ."

"It was always Ludovic who was first in your thoughts, was it not? I used to take second place even on my birthdays. Now, the order of things is changed; Ludovic is nothing, I am the mother of the heir. Perhaps justice is always done in the end, though to be sure I loved my brother."

She lifted up a thin hand to adjust her lank coil of hair. "Even Jody gives me my due now that I have borne him a son," she said. "Before that you had taught him to despise me, but now the boot's on the other foot. Do you know what he said to me yesterday? 'When the old woman's dead, we'll move together down to Curle. Perhaps she will even want us sooner.' After all as the mother of the heir—"

Red rage seized Norah. "You, after all, would speak to me so?" she cried. "In Saxon times there was a word for such as you; nithing. It meant a creature whose value was less than the stones; a sterile, useless thing, incapable either of action or of words."

"Then the facts contradict themselves, mother. I can answer you now, you see." Two patches of colour had appeared on either side of Elizabeth's face; she seemed birdlike, ready to swoop sideways for prey like a young jessel. She bridled a little. "Oh, I can see that you are envious of the position which will be mine now in the valley. It will be I, you see, who am become of more importance than yourself, though they won't say so to your face; habit is strong. But as time goes on they will realise, as my son grows, that it is I and not you who have given them what they need, here in Curle. You were in charge for some years for my brother; now you shall be so, as long as you can, for my son. But in the nature of things such a situation cannot last for ever, and you are growing old. Oh, do not think that I would be unkind to you, as you all my life were to me; but I know the truth when I see it, and you are no longer the woman I was afraid of when I was a child. Suddenly, as happens with such as you, you will crumble; as my great-grandfather did, from what I hear. When that happens, Jody and I will step in and take the reins: it may not be long."

She smiled, showing narrow teeth; and then said, "Are you certain that you will not after all drink tea before you go, mother? After the carriage-journey you will be tired, doubtless. Forget this enmity if you can do it, and I—"

"I forget nothing," said Norah, "and I will tell you the truth. That child in the cradle—"

"We have decided to name our son Ludovic."

"He is your brother."

"Madam, are you mad?" Elizabeth laughed a little. "Poor mother, sit down and let me call for Kate, and she will bring tea, or perhaps a cordial."

"He is your brother. I bore him to the man who says he is your husband. Your own child died at birth. As for Jody—"

"Jody," said Elizabeth. She sounded a little less certain. Her hands had begun to clench inside one another. "You are mad," she said again. "You must be so."

"Jody is your own father, as he should tell you if you ask. It is true I was married to Stroyan, when you were already conceived. I made him play the father to you because I was ashamed of a gipsy mating. But you, poor fool, have lain with the man who fathered you to bear him in the end a girl which died. I should know; I was in labour in the room when Kate Scarsgill brought it in dead between her hands. Ask Kate, who's your husband's doxy . . . as well as his aunt. Sir Ludovic Curle himself sired Kate."

She had begun to laugh, aware of the power which was in her to enable her to speak clearly at last of the tale. "Kate came here by chance," she said, "and I think *he* worked out his frenzy of envy of my grandfather, and of me, on her body. He still takes her, I'm sure; no matter. They are not my concern . . . except that when Jody had done for a while with Kate, and had leisure, he came to my room as my lover, and got me a second time with child."

"The child . . ." The last sounds of sanity came from Elizabeth; she swung her thin legs in their wrapper to the floor, attempted to rise, and staggered a little. "I will fetch the child," she said, "to . . . to . . ."

"You will not touch or harm my son. If I can I'll take him away with me."

"Jody will not let you," wept Elizabeth. "Jody said that I am its mother and the mother of the heir and that I . . . I and he . . ."

"You and he made nothing between you but a mangled wretch killed before birth, as though the devil himself spurned such twisted get and would not see her live. But Jody's more than a devil. In Holy Writ there was a man who was accursed because he lay with his sister. God knows what Jody's fate will be. Come you away with me, my girl, and bring the child; and leave Jody to his own devices." As she said it, she realised her own anger had departed. She could feel pity for Elizabeth. Henceforth she would cherish her, and . . .

"Go from here," said Elizabeth. Saliva had begun to dribble from a corner of her mouth. "Go . . . and do not come back any more." She flung herself back on to the sofa, writhing. She did not speak again and the spectacle of her silent anguish was impossible to watch. Norah turned and went out of the room and into the kitchen. Kate was still waiting.

"Get your cloak on and come with me," Norah said. "I am going to take the baby to Curle. You may continue to have charge of him."

"But I . . ."

"Forget the rest; the first thing now is the child's safety. He must live, and you have done well with him till now. Come with me."

"Jody . . ."

"Will you also wait for Jody, or come with me?" said Norah impatiently. In the end she seized up the child and wrapped her cloak about it, and almost ran with it back to where her coach was. "Quickly," she told the coachman, "back to Curle, and do not slow down for anyone on the way." They might be waiting, she knew; they surely had watched her come and go. She still felt eyes watching her back at Windyett.

Elizabeth did not stir for some time after her mother had left. Then she left the couch where she had been lying and, moving stealthily, went to the door and looked along the passage to the kitchen. Its outer door yawned; Kate was nowhere in sight. Elizabeth returned to the downstairs sitting-room, for an instant turning and looking out over the fells. A shudder went through her. She went to her clothes-chest and opened it and selected from it a brown belt. It was of leather, and strong. She tested it with her hands to ensure that it was strong enough; and then, taking a stool, set it nearby the back of the door on which there was a hook for hanging clothes. She made a looped knot in the belt and set one end about the hook and the other about her neck, and stood on the stool. Before the knot pulled tight she kicked the stool away. In her mind was nothing at all, except a red mist in which her mother's voice sounded, saying words that meant Jody was her own father. They must both of them have known from the beginning.

The body jerked on the leather cord for some moments, and then hung still. No one was in the house. The outer door moved to and fro on a little draught, and the cradle was empty.

Kate had run aimlessly after the coach and had her skirts splashed with mud from its going. She blamed herself bitterly for letting Mrs. Stroyan take away the baby. Jody, when he came home from escorting his mother back to her people, would be very angry. If only she might bring it back to Windyett before then . . . She found herself running breathlessly, stopping every now and again with a hand to her breast, before it came to her that there was nothing she could do; Mrs. Stroyan's coach would reach Curle before her, and once there the strong grey walls and liveried servants would protect Mrs. Stroyan and anything she desired from oneself, a poor solitary distracted girl. How could she ever have hoped to retrieve the baby from Curle itself? Best let Jody deal with the matter; he would know, surely, that Kate hadn't meant such a thing to happen. Yet his rage could be sudden and cold, and Kate was afraid.

A party of men, walking slowly, were beneath her on the lower path, going towards the valley and the church. They carried some burden between them laid under a white cloth. It was . . . it could only be a dead body. Who had died in Curle valley? Kate's mind ranged swiftly over the few she had known by name there, the miller and the baker and the boy who had brought round milk. It might be any of these. Death must have come suddenly, strangely, for the body to be laid so under a cloth, and borne home. Perhaps whoever it was had fallen in the hills. It was easily done. She herself had never ventured farther than the lower slopes where bracken and heather grew. She said a quick prayer for whoever had died, then turned away. Back to Windyett; that was where she must go, and wait for Jody. It was difficult to come to any decision now without Jody, and he would tell her what must be done about the baby. She would wait for him.

She went into the kitchen, and slowly began making preparations for a meal to be ready when Jody should come home. He would be back this evening. Kate skinned the hare which had been hanging for two days since it was shot, bundled the skin and guts and put them on the fire. She moved about putting stewpans on and off the heat; once she scalded her finger and sucked it, ruefully. The smell of herbs and stewing hare began to permeate the kitchen. Kate glanced towards the closed door of Mrs. Elizabeth's sitting-room. Jody's wife didn't like cooking smells. She had been quiet for a long time, but that was usual; she liked to sit in there all day, doing nothing on her sofa. "If it were me, it'd kill me," thought Kate.

She found a tea-pot and went to the fire where water boiled in a great kettle, and made tea. While it was drawing she laid out a tray with tea-things daintily. Mrs. Elizabeth liked to pour and be hostess to herself; before that Kate would steal a cup. She poured the cup, set it by the fire, and took the tray and walked towards the closed door. She had to balance the tray on her knee while she fidgeted with the latch; it was stiff, and the door was unaccountably heavy. There must be something hanging behind it.

"Your tea, madam," called Kate, and went in. The body's skirts swung at her as she entered by the door. For an instant they stayed poised together, the swinging body, the girl and the tray. Then Kate dropped the latter and started screaming. The tea-pot shed its lid and the tea spilled over the floor, and a cup rolled off and was broken, and the body still swung. Kate was far away now, out of the house, running down the road, hands to her ears, still screaming. The sounds she made grew faint like the crying of a bird. Back at the house there was silence, and at last the swinging of the body ceased and it hung still again, congested face turned askew on the thin neck, with the loosened hair mercifully covering it. Outside, darkness was beginning to come down.

Kate had not run far when there was the sound of hooves; she was aware of them through her frenzy. She clutched at the rider's knee and clung to the stirrup, choking with sobs. Jody looked down. "What is wrong, Kate?" he said.

"Jody—oh, Jody—"

He slipped out of the saddle. "Well, it is myself. What's amiss, lass?" He put an arm round her and held her against him. Whatever tale she was sobbing out against his breast sounded crazed. He made her tell it again, slowly. Then he drew a breath and looked up at the house, and then back at Curle.

"Leave it to me, sweetheart," he said. He lifted her up into the saddle and vaulted behind her. Kate began to cry again. "I can't go back in there —I can't, she's in there dead and—"

"If she is dead she will not harm you. You need not see her again.

Leave it all to me." In such ways, almost absently, he comforted her, until they reached Windyett. Then he looped the reins over a post and, carrying Kate in his arms, entered the house and carried her upstairs. He did not look towards the downstairs room. He laid Kate down on her bed. She felt the fiery taste of liquid from a flask pressed against her lips.

"Lie there till I come," Jody said, and was gone. Kate lay in the dark, sobs still shaking her at less frequent intervals; presently she went into a kind of daze, in which Mrs. Stroyan, Jody, the baby, and Elizabeth's hanged face all came and went in turns, then merged to a still and horrifying dream. Ought she to have done more about it? What could she have done? Nothing: she was the kind to whom things happened. Others, like Mrs. Stroyan and Jody, made them happen and always would. It was all of it too much for Kate, drunk with brandy. She let her head roll sideways on the pillow and fell into a deep sleep.

18

THE NEWS OF Mrs. Elizabeth's death was the only certain part of it, according to the valley folk who watched Curle daily, as if the grey stones could tell them what went on within. No one had seen Mrs. Norah. But it was known that, having as it were ignored Mrs. Elizabeth since her marriage until the late birth of the heir, she had—it was like her, they said—sent for the coffin to be brought to lie in state at Curle, in the great hall, in the manner of all the other high-born dead. It lay there till the day of the funeral, surrounded by lit tapers. The lid had already been closed.

The funeral was quiet. There had been so many more deaths than weddings lately in the valley, almost more deaths than births. There was no one left to follow the coffin except the Wraye family, madam herself, who shared their carriage, and the folk from Windyett. Curiosity reigned as to the manner in which Jody Curle would ride to his wife's burial; he'd never been accepted, as everyone knew, by madam herself or by the Wrayes. Would he join them in the carriage? Would he ride by the side of his doxy instead? But he did neither; only riding by himself alongside the coffin, his single eye expressionless and the other profile half hidden by his black patch. He wore seemly weeds, and the doxy was not present.

Mrs. Norah herself was veiled. No one wept, however, except the Duchess of Wraye and some of the women from the village, who had not known Mrs. Elizabeth well but felt that her end was a sad one. It was always sad to have to bury the young.

When the mourners had returned to Curle—except Jody who went off afterwards by himself—gossip started as to whether madam had had the baby sent to her before or after the death, or if Mrs. Elizabeth had perhaps asked her to take the child to bring him up at Curle: no one knew. No one knew anything, and after a few days the matter lapsed as such matters will, and folk found other things to talk about; there would be a good harvest this year, unless it was spoilt by rain. Perhaps later on they would glimpse the young heir of Curle, riding by his grandmother's side as poor young Mr. Ludovic had used to do. The years would pass quickly. Few now remembered the old squire in his young days; Mrs. Norah's own youth was itself long past. It was good that there was young blood in the valley again, and the prospect of a new squire for Curle. The family had always looked after the valley well enough, taking its pleasure and its due. It would not be the same without them; nothing would be the same.

Norah stood at her upper window looking out at the rain. It fell straight and gently, in the fine manner that comes with mist. She hoped that it would clear soon and that the grain could be cut and the hay stored dry.

The cradle was beside her. She had found a wet-nurse at last in Appleby. The baby thrived on the woman's milk and had grown fat and well since coming to Curle. Having ascertained this Norah had taken little leisure to scan him, although if they came to take him away she would resist it. She had never been a motherly woman, but she would fight for this heir.

A carriage drew up outside and looking down, Norah saw Jody Curle climb out. Her resolution hardened. He had come, then! He hadn't had the grace to attend Elizabeth's lying in state, even to the extent of a few moments spent beside the coffin. Norah scowled. Appearances had to be kept up. Jody should have aided her in that. She'd done her best to gloss things over, letting folk think it had been afterbirth fever that killed Elizabeth.

Kate Scarsgill was inside the coach. Her blank face, daubed with rouge, turned itself towards the house-wall and there her eyes stayed. They seemed glazed, like an imbecile's or a wax doll's, and she was grandly dressed in a travelling-gown of satin. "She looks tawdry," Norah thought. She would not allow her mind to dwell on whatever she felt regarding

Kate. It did not matter, and Jody himself would soon be here. She had been expecting him for weeks, and when he had not come had admitted to a vague sense of disappointment. Jody and she were one in a sense she could not identify with other things. Norah loathed him, and yet she loved him. The word love could split itself into a thousand meanings, none of them like other folk's. When she heard his footsteps on the stairs she would think of what to say.

He had come up; he had come in, and was standing facing her. Norah did not speak at once. What a surge of feeling came to her at close sight of Jody, feeling such as she had never thought to know again! But there it was, and within herself Norah faced it. Jody was the only lover she had ever desired, and she desired him still. Her face gave nothing of this away; it was expressionless; over the years, she had schooled herself.

"I have come at last, you see," he said. His tone was dry. He glanced towards the cradle. "He fares well."

"He is better here," she said coldly. He bowed a little in mock agreement with her. "But of course, my dear Norah. Nothing is as well anywhere as if it were at Curle. I used to agree, but of late have wearied of the comparison."

"That is no matter; the place is not yours." A blaze had sprung up behind her eyes; so he thought to discredit her and Curle, did he? He should not; she had vowed it.

"The place is mine, though you would never have it so: but now my son will inherit and I am content."

He took a step forward. "Do you know how many kinds of a bitch you are?" he said softly. "I could have forgiven you everything but the death of Elizabeth; you killed her, as you well know."

"I put no noose about her neck; she did that for herself, and 'tis best not spoken of. The valley folk have asked nothing, and I have told them all they need to know. It is a matter for me to deal with here; do not meddle in't."

"It has been dealt with, maybe, but in dealing you have dealt your last hand, Norah Stroyan."

She stared at him. His eye glowed with hatred till it seemed like fire on ice. "You may keep up your sad pretences, Norah," he said, "no one will take them away from you now. I was the only man who could ever down you, and I've lost heart for the pastime. You have your punishment." He looked at the child in its cradle again. "How often in the time to come you will want to call him by a name you may never speak! He is, and always will be, your grandson only. Your respectability will kill you in the end. A grandmother to him, no more, you must be; though the milk is hardly dry in your breasts."

"Have a care, for God's sake," she said to him. "There may be ears beyond the door."

"Ay, ears . . . always listening for trouble to you, and your pretensions here. You would have been better off with fewer of 'em, my dear, and married to me; then you would have found happiness from the start. Now, you have—power; and it is an empty thing."

"Who are you to talk of emptiness, with your whore as you are and you her nephew?" she sneered. "Dare you ever tell her of that? I wager not; yet unless she is a bigger fool even than she seems, she must know."

"Kate is a fool, as you say; and therefore I love her."

"*You* to love?" She mocked him, but the word as he had said it roused a deep unease in her. This was unlike Jody, the law to himself. Love to him, as to her, had meant no more than the sustaining of bodily lust. That no doubt Kate could give him, but the rest—

"You know nothing of love, Norah, or of cherishing. Three in your life you have thought you loved, your grandfather, yourself, and me; and of those three the second is by far the greatest. Fear not that that last shall ever be taken from you. You have it for the rest of your days."

"And you?" she asked. This was no time to deny that she had loved him, as she understood love. The thought that he might be going from her brought her strange anguish.

"I shall go to the port, where I've bought a house, and I shall set Kate up there as my mistress. Later I may cause her to bear me a child. You yourself will not see her again, or me: I shall ascertain the child's welfare from time to time, in ways I know of."

"You'll let no gipsy near my child."

"Grandchild, my dear; be careful; are there not ears at the doors? You can never admit to it, Norah; 'twould be the end of you and your pride."

She was suddenly aware of a great burst of rage. "Go, then, to hell with your whore if you will!"

"With my aunt," he said smoothly. "Have you ever thought how many in this valley must have mated so, over the generations, at times unknowing? Aunts with nephews, brothers with half-sisters, fathers with children they did not wot of; yet unless 'tis known, the law has no harsh word for it. Kate and I do not trouble with such. She needs me, and I love her."

He turned away. "I bid you farewell, Norah Stroyan. May your days be filled with pride, as they cannot be with happiness. We will not meet again. I am glad that I can tell my mother that I have avenged her, and fulfilled the vow we made that her blood and mine should inherit Curle. It could have happened with Ludovic, had he not chosen to be a priest—"

"Had you no part in that?" she cried. "I cannot credit it. You were no doubt hand in glove with the packman, among you all as he often was, I doubt not."

"I had no hand in it," said Jody idly, "but I sorrowed when I heard my son was dead."

"You are gracious."

"But as he *had* died, 'twas all to do again. Time pressed, and I was no longer young. I made certain of Elizabeth, then later of yourself. The death of her child was not my doing, any more than her own death. The blame for that lies at your door, and is the reason why I am leaving you alone to live out your life."

"How can you blame me for't? I had to fight for my own."

"Maybe, but you could have used gentler words. It was after you were with her that she made an end to herself. It was what you told her that hastened that end."

"Do not tell me that does not suit your book! You'd not have had Elizabeth, your daughter, about your neck always alongside Kate, your—"

"It has all of it been said already, has it not?" he asked, going to the door. "Farewell, Norah." He bowed, with his gaze on her face. Then he went out; and although she did not go to the window she heard him at last enter the coach and the horses draw away, and the wheels begin to turn under him and Brown Kate Scarsgill, whom he said he loved and was going with now; as he had said, she herself would never see him again.

Her first instinct was to reach for the wine-bottle, and pour herself a flagon full and drink it down. Then she poured another. With the flagon still in her hand, she went over to the cradle.

The child had been asleep. As if he knew of her presence his eyes opened. Now that the birth-blue had cleared away, they were brown, hot and angry like a young bear's. His brows and hair were already a thick, dark chestnut. He scowled and yawned, showing strong red gums.

Outside the wind had increased, bringing gusts of heavier rain about the walls. The coach-journey to the port would be troublesome, Norah was thinking; hazardous and rutted with pot-holes. She was safer close by the fire here, at Curle, till the weather grew clear.

She moved to the window again, looking out on the misted fells, then turned restlessly back into the room. Here within Curle all her life had been lived, and here it should end. And when she was dead there was the young squire, image of the man of Oudenarde year who hung below in the hall, to maintain a tradition nourished by centuries of Curles. Ludovic Curle the squire lived again, and should drink and wench to his heart's desire when he was a man: she'd not gainsay him.

She drank down her draught in silence, while darkness came over the fells.